THE MYRTLEWOOD GROVE

FINAL EPISODE

ROYAL LAPLANTE

Black Forest Press
San Diego, California
July, 2001
First Edition

THE MYRTLEWOOD GROVE

FINAL EPISODE

ROYAL LAPLANTE

PUBLISHED IN THE UNITED STATES OF AMERICA
BY
BLACK FOREST PRESS
P.O.Box 6342
Chula Vista, CA 91909-6342
1-800-451-9404

OTHER NOVELS

BY

ROYAL LAPLANTE

THE MYRTLEWOOD GROVE – 1994

PENALOMAH, The Eagle Soars – 1997

COTTAGE COVE, A Chechako in Alaska – 1998

UNCLE JACK'S CREEK – 1999

THE MYRTLEWOOD GROVE, Revisited – 2000

Printed in the United States of America
Library of Congress
Cataloging-in-Publication

ISBN: 1-58275-063-7

ACKNOWLEDGMENTS

The author acknowledges the advice, support, and editing of his wife and partner, Joanne LaPlante, and the encouragement and positive critique of his mother, Margaret LaPlante. Lynette Splinter is recognized for her preparation of this manuscript, and her mother and my friend, Barbara Splinter, provided editorial assistance.

Converting the manuscript into a published book was a task shared by Dahk Knox, Keith Pearson, Mary Inbody, and Dale and Penni Neely. Promotional work was accomplished by Glenna Jacket.

The contribution of June (Knapp) Angell is gratefully acknowledged. Her family memoirs and research assistance lent historical and anecdotal integrity to the story. Family friend Roy Stevens shared his knowledge of Port Orford geography and history in the final draft of *The Myrtlewood Grove – Final Episode*.

Prologue

A fleeting white cloud cast a momentary shadow across the white escarpment, including the grand lighthouse situated upon its weathered crown. A fresh westerly breeze filled the sails of an old lumber schooner making her way inshore. July sunshine warmed the air caressing the coastal promontory, first called Cape Blanco by early Spanish explorers. A steamship cleared the Port Orford Heads to the south, outbound for Portland after delivering cargo and mail.

The gentle neigh of a browsing horse caused the silent figure of an old man to turn his floppy-hatted head to reassure his trusty mount, "I know, Salem, but there's no rush. You have plenty of forage right where you are."

Returning his troubled gaze to the endless seascape, Scott McClure's weathered countenance relaxed slowly, his eyes staring blankly into the distance. Wisps of gray hair matching the color of his eyebrows extruded beneath his venerable but battered hat. His face was characteristically clean-shaven, his morning ablutions including the use of his father's straight razor, an antique predating his seventy-three years. His son Richard held their family Bible, the two articles being the only remaining possessions of the old man's youthful trip west in 1850.

Scott's face had added a few wrinkles over the years, his mouth was minus of few teeth, and his sight and hearing weren't what they used to be, but his back was straight and his large hands were still powerful. Most significantly, his pioneer spirit still burned, albeit with a more genteel flame of life.

His thoughts today were sad ones, the news from the San Francisco Archdiocese shaking the father of the Myrtlewood Grove to his core. His son George had died in China of cholera while tending the sick of body and spirit in his Canton mission. With the grief settling into his heart came a surge of pride, *Oh, my son, so good and so pure a man of the cloth, your crippled body dedicated to God's work. You've used the twenty-nine years Buzz gave you after the demon forest fire of 1868 with much grace. God bless you.*

Gee, I'm as old as Buzz Smith was during the years we built the ranch which Chief Sixes gave me. Those were the good times for the Old-Timer and me. How I miss him and my Melissa, and now our George is gone.

A clattering sound disrupted the serenity of Scott's moment of grief, a glance over his shoulder showing Patrick Hughes wrestling with a wheelbarrow and a pile of rocks. Evidently Jane was going to get her new house since her husband was clearing the site he'd pointed out to Scott last month.

A flash of motion caught the dreamer's eye, the schooner coming about as it passed the steamer, headed inshore to Girard's Mill on Port Orford's harbor.

Drifting back into his reverie, lips curled in disdain, Scott reflected, *The boys will probably load that ship tomorrow. Who would ever think my namesake would turn away from the Myrtlewood Grove and his ranching heritage. Well I guess not everyone is cut out for this frontier life. At least he's in good company working for Girard with Albert Lee, Bill Tucker, and Jack-Jack Sixes. Those boys are turning into fine young men, calling themselves the "Four Musketeers" and all.*

Hrmph, the world's changing I reckon, and events are passing me by. I must be as old as I feel today, with most of my pioneer friends gone. Mary Hermann and Captain Tichenor passed away in eighty-seven, and then Captain O'Keefe's ship was lost at sea the following winter. Fred and Hazel Madsen were a pair of the ship's unlucky passengers, along with Beth Tucker. And then Rachel Knapp died a year later, four or five years before Louie married Ella Stagg.

Seems like our town lost its spirit with those deaths. Gold Beach is the Curry County seat, and H. R. Reed inveigled that railroad to his new town of Reedsport. Port Orford's distinction of being the westernmost town in our country is one of our few noteworthy facts left on this part of the Oregon coast. Of course, Hughes cheese is well known all over the state.

My favorite granddaughter is as fond of Port Orford as her parents. Mary told me she was going to live here forever and then called her brother Albert a traitor for going to Salem to attend college. Young Scott's brothers and sisters all love the Myrtlewood Grove, so I guess those two cousins, Scott and Albert, are the mavericks in our family – take after Uncle George, I expect.

The pioneer old-timer brushed a tear from his eye as he heard approaching horses along the trail from town. *Enough mourning for George* was his final thought, and he faced his son and grandson with a welcoming gesture of his hand. He was ready to share his solitude with his family.

Chapter One

The myrtlewoods sang with the excited laughter of children amid the background hum of their parents' conversations. Under the verdant canopy lay a grassy picnic area where tables were covered with an assortment of home-cooked dishes, ranging from the Larsons' Boston baked beans, to the Hughes' tray of cheeses and breads, to the Sixes' Indian "stew", to the tub of potato salad Fred and Dolores Madsen had made using the McClure stove earlier in the day, to the Knapp's cinnamon rolls. Bill Tucker and George Hermann had brought a tun of California wine and the Tichenors a hamper of smoked salmon. Grandpa Scott was turning a side of spitted pig over a bed of hot coals, a continuous dribble of grease drops popping into flames as they landed.

The occasion for celebration was the seventeenth birthday of Scott McClure, the thirty-fourth birthday of Fred Madsen and the return of Albert Lee to college in Salem. Well over a hundred friends and neighbors had traveled this sunny day in August 1897 to the Myrtlewood Grove for one of the McClure's famous picnics.

Boisterous shouting erupted from the Sixes River swimming hole as the birthday boy was doused in the chilly waters fully clothed, his buddies stripping to their jeans before diving in after him. Soon girlish shrieks joined the cacophony of playful exuberance as their sisters and younger brothers joined in the fun, only sixteen-year old Jane McClure disdaining such childish behavior. Instead she intercepted a curious and toddling Louis Knapp at the river's edge, and taking his tiny hand in hers, she led a now protesting boy back to his parents in the grove.

At a signal from his father and an approving nod from his wife, Rick McClure banged a pie tin on the nearest table and bellowed, "Come and get it!" Only one such call was needed as the children's jubilance quieted in their haste to dry off and line up for lunch.

Albert stepped into the chow line ahead of Scott, assuming his natural place as leader of the Four Musketeers, a sobriquet from their school days together. Billy Tucker commented, "Today is our last day of fun this summer. I wish I was doing something exciting, like sailing to San Francisco."

Jack-Jack Sixes laughed at his buddy and suggested teasingly, "Why don't you go to college with Albert and be a lawyer?"

Billy smiled in self-deprecation but good-naturedly replied, "You're no better in school than me, Jack-Jack. Only Scott is smart enough to keep up with his cousin. But I would like to see Salem. Maybe we should quit our jobs and escort Albert back to school."

The friends mulled the idea over quietly, filling their plates with food and sitting on a log near the riverbank as they wolfed down their vittles. Scott paused in mid bite, and with his characteristic attention to detail, swallowed, then laid out a plan of action, "The mill won't cut lumber until another ship calls at Port Orford. Shouldn't be any hardship for Mr. Girard if we leave. In fact, he's in San Francisco so we can tell Rod Bishop we quit. He's over there talking to Grandpa. We all have horses except Billy, and I'm sure Dad will lend him one of ours. All we have to do is strap on a money belt, load a saddlebag with a few necessities, and meet here tomorrow at nine o'clock. We'll have our adventure for sure."

Albert offered, "Aunt Angela will put you up in her guest rooms, and maybe Uwe will have a little work for you as a teamster or roustabout. What do you say, Billy? Jack-Jack?"

A chorus of yeses decided the matter, with all eyes shifting back to Scott expectantly. He promptly stood and traipsed over to the spit where his father was talking with Grandpa, Rod, and Uncle John. As they turned their attention to him, Scott spoke right up while his nerve was with him, "Rod, Billy, Jack-Jack, and I are quitting our jobs today. We're going to take Albert to Salem tomorrow."

Rod nodded, unperturbed by Scott's statement, "All right. Come see me when you get back."

Rick smiled indulgently, asking a simple question, "I see. Do the Sixes know Jack-Jack is going? And Billy's dad?" When Scott's jaw set with stubborn determination, Rick continued, "Well, Son, if their parents approve of your plans, I'll give you a hand. Also, there'll be a few letters for you to carry to the Gerbrunns. Oh! Oh! Here comes your mother. You'd better tell her what you're doing."

* * * * *

Scott reined Salem about with impatience, his grandfather's horse mirroring the lad's nervous energy. Close behind him were Albert and Jack-Jack, but Billy was nowhere in sight along their forested backtrail.

"Ha! Ha! Billy will claim he's bringing up the rear," Albert joked of their logger friend, "Or he's a rear guard. You know he isn't much of a horseman, so we might as well call it a day. I told you we should have stopped for the night in Bandon. Jack-Jack, you partner with Billy while Scott and I find a campsite."

As usual Albert gave the orders. He was the eldest, and even Scott admitted that he was the calmest. He didn't get excited like Scott, nor morose like Jack-Jack, nor clumsy like Billy. Scott knew his cousin made good decisions, even if he was a pain in the butt sometimes.

"There's a good spot near the creek, Scott. You start a fire and I'll round up some firewood," Albert ordered casually, his leadership taken for granted. He dismounted and tied his horse Hummer to a tree, Scott doing likewise with Salem, the men working quickly to send up a few puffs of smoke to guide their friends to their camp.

Billy groaned in misery as he rode up to the fire and slid off the rump of Myrtle, staggering around the fire as he rubbed the insides of his thighs. Jack-Jack quietly cared for the mare and his own horse, Ai-Ho, before unpacking food supplies. Everyone agreed he was the only cook among the Four Musketeers and divided trail chores accordingly. Jack-Jack's pan-fried biscuits were a treat everyone could appreciate.

* * * * *

Scott was up before dawn rekindling their campfire and boiling water for coffee, impatient to continue their adventure. Jack-Jack appeared at his elbow to assume the breakfast chores, so Scott roused Albert out of his blankets with only a minor complaint. Billy stubbornly refused to budge from his bedding until Albert joined the call to reveille, dumping a cup of cold creek water down the recalcitrant traveler's neck. Thus was the mounted party able to move on when the cloudy sky lightened.

Albert led the uneventful trek around Coos Bay and through the bustling railroad terminus of Reedsport, the seaport W.R. Reed had built on the south side of Umpqua. Billy fell behind his companions constantly, griping about horses and riding until Albert pushed him to the van of their small caravan and steered him along the railroad grade past Gardiner. As the western sun fell behind the coastal hills, the party camped beneath a trestle where the tracks began climbing the Calapooyas on their route to Drain. Billy once again complained about their rough campsite in the wilderness, "We should have gone up to Scottsburg and slept in a decent bed."

Ignoring his lament, Scott turned to Albert, who was reading a crumpled old newspaper by the dim firelight, and asked, "What's new in the world, Albert? You seem engrossed in that paper's front page."

"An article from the *World*, Cousin, Pulitzer's *World* to be exact. This Portland paper calls it the 'Yellow Press', but I find it interesting. Here, read this report about Theodore Roosevelt, the Secretary of the Navy. His speech at the opening of a new Naval War College back East is intriguing. Roosevelt claims we need a bigger navy and says Spain should be kicked out of Cuba. There's a revolution down there you know, and maybe he's right. Maybe we should help the Cubans free themselves from that colonial government."

Scott took the paper in hand and replied, "I thought Hearst's *Journal* was the rabble-rouser. It's pretty warlike in its editorials."

"Yes, both newspapers talk of national honor and patriotism as they attack McKinley's foreign policy. They call him indecisive and support men like Roosevelt. Well, it sells a lot of newspapers, I guess."

Billy and Jack-Jack had turned away from the fire and sought their blankets, a practice they followed whenever their two friends discussed politics and national issues. At least Scott's "Early to bed, early to rise" motto would let them sleep in tomorrow if the cousins debated the Cuba issue all evening.

* * * * *

Continuing their ride along the railway right-of-way in the morning, the four horsemen sent Billy to the forefront again and walked their mounts as if they were in no hurry. As the sun rose over the forested ridges above them, Scott's patience ended and he trotted past his friend to explore the short railroad tunnel ahead. He entered the mine-like rocky entrance at a calmer pace, studying the straight parallel rails of steel which ran into the dim cavern, reappearing in the sunlight a couple of hundred feet away. He thought quietly, *I don't like caves at all, but this tunnel is short enough to see my way clearly enough. Hmph! Salem sure doesn't share my feelings of eeriness, nor does the darkness bother him.*

The horse gracefully pranced through the dark maw with sure footing, his heightened senses finding the tunnel to be no challenge at all. As they emerged into the bright sunshine, Scott pulled his horse onto a gravelly shoulder perched over a cascading stream, a natural fishing hole five feet below the grade. Suddenly the high-pitched sound of a steam whistle echoed off the surrounding cliffs. Scott recognized the warning issued by the daily train to Reedsport and now heard the rumbling of railroad cars running down the tracks somewhere beyond the bend upstream.

Glancing over his shoulder, he saw that his three friends seemed to be unaware of the oncoming train, perhaps deafened by their enclosure within the tunnel. Scott reined Salem about to signal with his arm as he called out, "Train coming!" Albert comprehended immediately and led Jack-Jack back to the siding beyond the west end of the tunnel, but the nearest rider was a confused Billy, who stopped dead between the train tracks and yelled back, "Huh?" in confused tones.

Salem was skittish as he felt the ground tremble under his hooves, his alarm transmitting their impending peril to his rider, but Scott didn't hesitate as he spurred his mount back into the dark tunnel. Hearing Billy, he shouted, "A train is coming, Billy, follow me!" His friend's eyes widened in shock as the speeding locomotive roared around the bend, its whistle loudly proclaiming its right to passage. Scott rode straight at the smoking "Iron Horse", waving imperatively for Billy to do the same, his progress enhanced by his mount's fright.

Scott emerged from the darkness into a flash of color, eliciting another blast of steam and warning whistle from the steel behemoth, the surprised look on the engineer's face accompanying his hand jerking the overhead cord. He wrestled a frantic Salem onto the gravel shelf, sliding off his mount to hold his muzzle as the locomotive sped by. Gentling the trembling horse, he looked over his shoulder for Billy and saw nothing in the smoky face of the tunnel. Myrtle's terrified scream was muffled by the noisy passage of the train, whose caboose flashed by the shaken musketeer, the figure of the train conductor waving amicably from the car's small platform.

Scott dropped the reins and ran afoot after the flickering caboose light, his eyes blinded by the sudden change from sunlight to darkness as he entered the tunnel. He shuffled forward hastily, stubbing his toes and slipping on creosoted ties before stumbling over a bloody carcass beside the tracks. With a feeling of trepidation he ran his hand over the warm hairy rump of a horse, relief and anguish mixing freely in his voice, "Billy, where are you?"

Sounds of hooves mingled with the shouts of Albert and Jack-Jack, drowning out the faint rumble of the disappearing train. Scott yelled loudly, "Myrtle was killed. I can't find Billy. Get down and help me look."

The three companions raced eastward, and their eyes became accustomed to the dimness, Jack-Jack sputtered in excitement, "There! Against the wall by those rocks. Is it Billy?"

They rushed to the shadowy crevice in the rocky face on the south side of the tunnel to find their friend sitting up, mumbling irrationally, "Dumb horse. She threw me over against this wall. Where is she?"

Scott sighed in relief as he answered, "The cowcatcher hit Myrtle and threw her down the tunnel. I bet that engineer didn't even know he killed a horse. Why didn't you follow me?"

"Myrtle had a mind of her own when she caught sight of that locomotive coming at her. She spooked and jumped straight up into the air, and when I landed here, I made myself awfully small to fit this little crack in the wall. Thanks for coming to warn me Scott. I didn't know a train was coming," Billy explained.

Turning practical as usual, Albert took charge, suggesting, "Scott, you help Billy to fresh air while Jack-Jack and I drag the carcass out of here. I suppose we should butcher the animal and sell the meat. Is that all right with you?"

* * * * *

A strange entourage entered Drain, drawing stares and comments from people along the streets. Three horses plodded into town, a scraped and battered Billy in the saddle astride Salem and bloody quarters of horsemeat strapped across the saddles of the other two horses. Each animal was led by its footsore owner, the tired travelers seeming as weary as their mounts. Scott turned up a side street with his charge toward the doctor's sign while Albert stopped before the butcher shop to haggle with its proprietor over the price of fresh meat.

An hour later the Four Musketeers, looking scrubbed and wearing clean clothes, stood against the bar of a local inn where Albert reported the incident to the town marshal. The muscular ex-logger with a no-nonsense look about him didn't object to the lads drinking beer, although he did give Jack-Jack a funny look before asking Billy, "Did you own that horse, son?"

"No, sir. My friend's grandpa loaned her to me so we could ride with Albert to Salem," and as the lawman raised a critical eyebrow, Billy hastily added, "Isn't that right, Scott?"

With a confirming nod and smile, Scott offered the town official a handshake as he introduced himself, "How do you do, Marshal? My name is Scott McClure and the horse…"

The innkeeper burst out, "Why you must be a Sixes River McClure. I'm a friend of your Daddy's, and I've met old Scott a time or two. You surely look like them, I should have recognized you when you walked in." The friendly man waved aside questions of horse ownership with a casual flick of his hand, and the lawman shrugged in agreement, acceding to their gray-haired host's endorsement of Scott and his friends.

The young man quickly offered the official a drink, "Marshal will you join us in toasting Billy's good health. And you too, sir," he added to the innkeeper.

* * * * *

Albert wandered to the far end of the bar to talk politics with a pair of railroad workers, the marshal left the men to continue his rounds, and Scott visited with his father's avowed friend. The innkeeper produced four fresh beers at Scott's request, his smile disappearing as his eyes fluttered in nervous tension, background conversation quieting.

A surly voice muttered loudly enough to be heard throughout the room, "Damn Siwash doesn't belong here," and as the speaker stood up, his chair scraped across the floor with an ominous threat. "Hic! Only good injun is a dead injun! Can't drink with real men."

The drunken logger staggered forward and swatted Jack-Jack's glass aside, beer slopping over Billy. The innkeeper's protest and the two boys' befuddlement only spurred the besotted bigot on, and he swung a huge fist at the retreating Jack-Jack. Scott acted instinctively in driving his shoulder into the burly logger, driving him into a nearby table and eliciting a roar of anger accompanied by a cursing tirade, bloodshot eyes suddenly in focus.

Scott thought the fellow seemed considerably more sober as he squared off to do battle, swiping at his smaller opponent with the back of a scarred hand. Scott shrugged at the inevitability of the fight, and doubling his fists he struck his adversary's nose with a left jab, and boxed his ear with a right hook, then shifting his stance to block several retaliatory blows. The enraged logger lunged forward to pin Scott against the bar and pummel him with slopping punches. When he stepped back to swing a looping haymaker intended to end the fight, Scott ducked under his arm and moved out of harm's way, jabbing his foe's bloody nose again.

Another wild haymaker did land on Scott's shoulder, powerful enough to numb his muscles and sweep him aside on stumbling feet. Grinning at his success in using brute force, the man rushed forward, another poke in his nose erasing the smile but not his moving advance.

"Bernie, Scott, stop fighting before I have to put both of you in a cell," the marshal ordered authoritatively, stepping between the combatants as he imposed his law-and-order will over both men.

"Bernie, sit down and finish your beer." As the logger begrudgingly obeyed, glaring at everyone in the room except the lawman, the marshal said, "McClure, you and your buddies get out of here. I won't abide fighting in my town. You're welcome to stay in Drain, but stay away from this bar."

As the four friends walked out the door, the marshal's lecturing words to Bernie carried outside, Billy's murmur the only comment made, "Do you reckon that logger will hold a grudge?"

* * * * *

Albert led the musketeers out of town before the rising sun had burned the morning mists off the meadows, Billy riding double behind Scott. Beside a log cabin stood the foreboding figure of the combatant logger, grinning good naturedly as they passed. With a casual wave he shouted, "Good fight, McClure. Stop by again and I'll buy you a beer."

"Thanks, Bernie, but you'll have to buy Jack-Jack a beer, too," Scott called over his shoulder in teasing tones.

The would-be roughhouser's riant laughter echoed through the mist as the caravan plodded up the trail.

"Does Bernie mean he wants another fight or another beer?" the puzzled Rogue asked his sense of humor smothered by his concern.

"Ha! Ha! Maybe both, Jack-Jack. Let's find out on our return trip," Scott replied playfully, not put off by his friend's Tututni stoicism.

* * * * *

After roughing it overnight in a quiet Santiam River campsite, the hungry and tired young men rode into Salem with a subdued eagerness. Scott led the familiar way to the Gerbrunn's, Hummer showing the strain of carrying both Albert and Billy as Salem opened a gap between them.

Uwe was helping a teamster hoist a crate aboard his wagon, looking up at the sound of approaching hoofbeats, a welcoming grin lighting his weathered countenance. Gray hair and wrinkles about his eyes bespoke of his fifty-four years, but his step and voice were still youthful as he strode across the freightyard.

"Scott, my boy, did you bring Albert back to law school? How are Dolores and Fred? And my granddaughter? How are your folks? And Grandpa Scott? Why is Albert riding double back there?"

"Hello, Uncle Uwe," Scott replied, pleased with Uwe's warm reception. He dismounted, and the two men embraced in a bearhug, the youngster answering, "Everyone is just fine, and send greetings. Albert's carrying letters from Dolores, Grandpa, Mom, and your father-in-law."

"Why's Albert riding double?" Uwe reiterated, adding, "Isn't that Billy Tucker behind him?"

Scott nodded in response, "Yup, Old Myrtle was killed by a train in the hills the other side of Drain. Can you use some extra help around here?"

"Of course, and I have a horse you boys can earn while you're here."

Scott quickly offered, "And help pay Aunt Angela for board and room, if she'll have us."

Both men turned toward the house as Angela stepped onto the porch and greeted them, "Yes, you'll stay with us, Scott. Hello, Jack-Jack, Billy and you, too, Albert. Uwe, take care of their horses while I feed these young men apple pie and coffee."

Now at the forefront again, Albert followed Angela into her kitchen, chattering with news and handing her four letters when he caught up with her. Scott was content to soak up the cooking aromas and the ambiance of the old house, watching the youthful-looking matron as she served slabs of pie and cheddar cheese to her seated guests. Abruptly remembering a promise, he jumped to his feet, grasped her free elbow, and leaned over to deposit a hearty kiss on her cheek, murmuring, "Grandpa says hello."

Angela blushed with pleasure, curtsying before kissing him back, "That's for both Scotts. You take after your grandfather, young man."

Scott shrugged plaintively and replied, "Except for his obsession with the Myrtlewood Grove. I'm a disappointment to him because I'm not a rancher. Dad seems to understand, but not Grandpa."

Albert shook his head vigorously and disagreed with his cousin, "Grandpa understands, but he doesn't like it. You're his favorite, and Uncle Rick's, too. They want you to carry on the McClure tradition."

"Yes, I know, but I want to see the world. At least more than a bit of Oregon," Scott replied, smiling suddenly at his hostess and asking, "Do you have this kind of conversation in your family, Aunt Angela?"

"Ha! Ha! Oh yes, Scott. When Dolores and Fred were courting we had an argument or two, and later when they married and moved to their Elk River ranch, Uwe was upset. But they're happy, and she and little Angela are a great comfort to Daddy in his old age."

After a brief hesitation, she added, "I was much calmer with my other daughters even though their families aren't living in Salem."

Uwe had stood silently in the doorway for several minutes and now spoke his mind, "I know how Scott and Rick feel, young man. My father was pleased to have me take over the business since Johann's interest was in law, but he was doubly happy when my nephew Kurt came into the business. I feel the same way with my son Donald working alongside me. By the way, Don and Kurt are due back from Portland this evening before supper. They'll be glad to hear we have a few extra hands for our busy fall. We have several contracts with farmers in the valley to haul their harvest to the railroad depot. Can you stay until after those jobs are done?"

* * * * *

Angela left the men around the supper table sipping brandy and arguing politics, a natural conversation for respected attorney, Johann Gerbrunn, and his late partner's son Albert. As usual, Kurt sided with his father, being a dutiful son in Scott's mind, and Uwe supported his young boarder. Scott asked more questions than he stated opinions while the younger Billy, Jack-Jack, and Donald remained politely but inattentively quiet.

"McKinley is a poor excuse for a president. Wishy-washy he is, never making a decision when he can avoid it. Look at Cuba, for instance. Its Spanish masters are brutalizing the people and insulting our nation with its imperialistic behavior, yet McKinley sits in Washington and does nothing. Hearst and Pulitzer both call for action in their newspapers, but the only politicians willing to challenge Spain is that Roosevelt fellow," Albert participated with enthusiasm.

The elderly lawyer smiled sparsely as he replied in a calm tone, "Theodore Roosevelt is only the Under-Secretary of the Navy, Albert. He didn't get elected to run our nation, President McKinley did. The Yellow Press loves to rattle a saber and sell papers, so they lambaste his government loudly if not with much cause."

"He's a good president, and the country's in good shape," Kurt echoed.

Albert retorted, "But he does nothing about Cuba. Why, I read when the Spanish soldiers were searching suspected rebels for weapons and made them strip – even three young women. Dastardly behavior I say, and I bet Teddy Roosevelt would agree with me."

Scott frowned in puzzlement as he asked, "But haven't the rebels bragged that their women are with them and carry weapons for them?"

"I guess so, but that's no excuse for innocent women being humiliated, Scott. Maybe you should attend a history class or two with me this fall and find out about the Cuban Revolution."

Uwe nodded agreeably, offering, "Good idea, Albert. I'll give Scott time off when your college is in session. Now let's talk about a more interesting subject. Have you all read where the steamer *Portland* landed in Seattle with a ton of gold from the Klondike? Donald wants to go north for the riches, but I disagree. It's a long trek over ice and snow to reach Dawson. I think hard work in Salem will produce more wealth than grubbing in the Yukon gravel."

Chapter Two

Scott held the team's lines fisted in his left hand as he perched on the wagon's seat and waved goodbye to Donald. His young friend clasped his father in an emotional bearhug and boarded the Seattle-bound train. The Klondike Gold Rush had claimed another adventurous soul, with Uwe reluctantly accepting his son's determined decision, financing his trip once his fatherly conservatism lost the family argument. Bridled emotions controlled their final words as the cars rolled away from the platform, father saddened to see his son's departure, and Donald apprehensive about leaving this comfortable life in Salem.

Uwe turned away as the train sped around the distant bend in the tracks and trudged morosely toward the loaded wagon, mumbling, "Let's deliver this wheat, Scott. Angela will be waiting our supper and expecting a full report."

A half smile formed on his lips as he hoisted himself onto the seat, his words now nostalgic, "You know, my boy is now a man. Hmm! Maybe I should have jumped on that train with him. Ah, to be young again, eh Scott?"

Releasing the wagon's brake, the young man snapped the reins to spur the horses into action, remaining quiet, no answer necessary to the rhetorical question. Silence was maintained during their delivery of wheat, and only when they were headed home did Uwe feel sociable, asking, "Why doesn't the Klondike interest you and your friends?"

After a moment of thoughtful consideration, Scott responded with a smile, "Actually it does, Uncle Uwe. We've talked about Alaska, what with Don going north and all, but we don't have the money. Besides, Albert's in law school and Billy's too young. Maybe next year."

* * * * *

A few days later Scott joined Albert in his college history class, the subject of Cuba and its revolutionary movement a lively topic of discussion well beyond the normal class period. Albert led a cadre of Roosevelt admirers attacking Spanish imperialism and his professor's conservative viewpoint. To his credit the college teacher took no umbrage at his student's emotional critique, allowing a spirited intellectual discussion.

Scott found himself respecting the man and his skill in eliciting exciting yet philosophical thought in his classroom. The visitor silently observed, *Albert and his professor are having fun, and I'm enjoying myself as well. College isn't so bad.*

Albert cited an article from the *World*, "Pulitzer says our nation should force Spain to stop brutalizing Cubans. Even Americans aren't safe in Cuba, and Theodore Roosevelt is the only member of McKinley's cabinet with the courage to say so. Pulitzer as good as predicts that war is inevitable."

"Ah, but Mr. Lee, don't you think that the Yellow Press overstates any danger to America. Spain hasn't threatened our country, nor its citizens," the professor responded.

"That's right!" Scott blurted out, flushing at his own audacity in speaking before a college class, but determinedly explaining his viewpoint as eyes turned on him. "McKinley's running the country just fine. He's the man we elected as President, not Pulitzer or Hearst, who write to sell newspapers. I do agree with Roosevelt's ideas, and McKinley surely trusts his cabinet – even a junior member like Teddy. However, if we tackle Spain over Cuba, it won't be because Americans are in danger, but because Americans are looking for a fight."

"Well said, young man! Albert, you must bring your cousin back for another visit. I like his thoughtful analysis of the Cuban situation. Class is dismissed!"

* * * * *

Albert rushed out of the house with a hamper of picnic lunch in his hand, Angela's bequest to her departing guests. Scrambling aboard Hummer, the young law student spurred after his friends, his belated call echoing in their stead, "I'll be home for supper, Aunt Angela."

Scott reined his frisky mare Rimpar about and waved another farewell to the Gerbrunns, rubbing the full-sized filly's neck before proceeding down the lane. After buying the horse as a replacement for the ill-fated Myrtle, Billy opted to ride the less rambunctious Salem in their southbound trek. Silence followed the Four Musketeers as their horses trotted along dry roads, the unseasonable sunny weather being a blessing for mid-November. Although the sun's rays brightened the Willamette valley, a morning haze and cool breeze necessitated that each rider wear a hat and coat to ward off nature's elements.

The riders passed through the settlement of Tangent before a word was said, a complaint from Billy in the form of a moan accompanied by an epithet, "Damned saddle!"

"Hang on there, pardner. We'll stop at that river over yonder, and Albert can share Angela's largesse with us before he heads back," Scott called over his shoulder.

Albert laughed playfully and teased his companions, "Jack-Jack is homesick, and Billy's got a sore bottom. How are you going to manage this journey home, Cousin?"

He spurred Hummer past Ai-ho toward a hospitable lea beside the stream and stopped his horse near a gnarled old fir stump. Knotting his reins about a protuberant burl of the decrepit tree's bole as he dismounted, Albert gathered twigs and moss to start a fire, his efforts resulting in a bright flame for coffee by the time Billy slid off his saddle.

"Still think you can reach Drain tonight, Scott?" Albert queried with a meaningful glance toward the saddle-worn Billy.

"No, I suppose we'd better save some of the food Aunt Angela fixed for us. There's enough vittles in this basket to last us two or three meals. Maybe we'll stop at that campsite we used two months ago on our trip north. You coming home for Christmas, Cousin?" Scott concluded.

"There's not enough time to visit the folks and my friends in Port Orford, what with a short college recess and work in Uncle Johann's office. Beside, winter is poor traveling weather by horse or by ship. I figure to stay in Salem until early June," Albert declared, turning his attention to Billy and Jack-Jack before asking in a teasing voice, "Why don't you ride back to Salem in May?"

Chuckles echoed around the campfire, highlighted by Billy's sheepish grin and a gentle but firm shake of his head. Small talk was plentiful as the friends relaxed, enjoying each other's company before Albert headed back to Salem and his studies.

* * * * *

Denmark's scattering of houses didn't slow the three drenched comrades, nor did the muted greeting and wave of a farmer standing in his barn door deter the impatient Scott. Now that he was close to home, his eagerness to see his family overcame the stormy weather as well as roadside distractions.

Billy was right behind him, Salem sensing his Sixes home as well, and he teased, "What's up, Old Buddy? Passing by the Korber place without a 'howdy' when Giselle might be home and figure you'd want to see her. Doesn't she have a crush on you?"

"Now Billy Boy, you know she is my sister's friend. Besides, Jane tells me she's engaged to one of Langlois' hired hands, even though she's only a year older than the twins."

"Fifteen? I thought she was your age or older. She looks twenty and some," Billy remarked.

Scott smiled insouciantly, "Yeah, well some women mature early. One day she looks like Melissa or Anne, and the next day older than any of my sisters. Giselle is a nice person, and I wish her well. What about that Clarke girl you were sparking?"

Billy flushed self-consciously but replied openly, "Ah, she was just visiting her aunt for the summer. She went back to San Francisco bay. Maybe I can look her up if we go down there next summer."

Jack-Jack growled quizzically, "To San Francisco? Nobody said anything to me about going to San Francisco."

"Billy and I talked about saving our wages for a summer trip while you were being buddies with Bernie back in Drain, but your idea of striking out for the Klondike seemed more adventuresome to me," Scott explained.

"Ah, that was Bernie's idea after a few beers. You know, he's a nice guy for an Indian-hater," Jack-Jack concluded with a mischievous grin.

Soon the three wet and weary companions reined their horses in, the Sixes River ford before them. Billy eyed its rain filled banks with apprehension, breath whistling between his teeth as his jaws tightened.

Scott offered, "You can stay with my family until the river drops, Billy. The letters you're carrying can wait, and my father would be glad to have you visit."

"No, as long as it's storming along the coast, the Sixes will be near flood stage. I've seen it worse. Besides, didn't you tell me Salem is a good swimmer?" Billy replied with casual bravado and quickly turned the faithful beast into the roiling currents.

The horse was a veteran of crossing their ford and managed to walk and swim its width without mishap. Billy didn't even leave his saddle, although he was just as soaked as if he had swum across the waters himself. He waved goodbye over his shoulder as horse and rider struggled up the far bank.

"Come on, Jack-Jack, let's go home. We could stand a good drying out. This damned rain hasn't let up since we passed through Reedsport."

With an assenting grunt, the Tututni lad spurred Ai-ho into a tired trot, leading Rimpar along the upriver trail toward the Myrtlewood Grove.

Forging ahead after the duo crossed Cascade Creek, Scott coaxed a lethargic trot out of his weary horse. Descending the familiar knoll, Rimpar sensed his rider's exuberance and proved to be a bit of a prima donna as he pranced through the yard.

The elder Scott appeared before them from the direction of the corral, grinning a broad welcome as he called, "Hello, Scott my boy, and you, too, Jack-Jack. Did you have a good visit in Salem with the Gerbrunns? And where did you get that fine animal you're riding?"

Scott slid form the saddle stiffly to hug the old-timer affectionately, answering, "Of course, Grandpa, and everyone sends..."

He broke off his reply as Julie emerged through the opening door, mother and son embracing in filial warmth, kissing before finally separating, happy tears in both pairs of eyes.

"Your mother has missed you, Scott. Hrmph! Well, so have your dad and me. He's in town picking up supplies.

Should be home soon. Now tell us about your trip," the elder Scott chattered delightedly.

As mothers are wont to be, Julie took charge by offering food to the hungry-looking young men, "Son, you and Jack-Jack come into the house. You boys need some fresh apple pie and a glass of hot cider before Jack-Jack goes home. Dad, you tend the horses while I feed our travelers come home."

"All right, Julie, but at least save a slab of pie for me. I want to hear all the news, too."

* * * * *

Days faded into weeks as the McClure family tended the farm, Scott helping his father with haystacks while Grandpa hunted for game along Cougar Ridge. Mother and daughters made apple butter and harvested the last of the potatoes and carrots. Shortly before Christmas, Scott and Jack-Jack drove a mixed herd of cows to Coquille, receiving a cash payment destined to last both the McClures and the Sixes all winter.

Little brother George was a great help before and after school, and when he begged to accompany his brother on the delivery of cows, his parents had a hard time refusing. His mother was adamant about school attendance, and the lad settled for a half-promise from her, "Maybe you can go next year when you're twelve years old, George."

On New Year's Day 1898, Jack Sixes slipped on his frosty stoop and suffered a severely sprained ankle. Jack-Jack enlisted Scott's help with a half-completed barn repair and hunting expedition to fill the family larder. His visit with the Sixes family broke the winter monotony and gave him an opportunity to study the Tututni culture from inside a tribal home preparing for a wedding.

Sixteen-year old Julie had blossomed into a pretty young woman during the past year and had caught the eye of a distant cousin at a tribal gathering along the Pistol River. The two young people had decided to marry when her beau, Henry Smith, had accepted a job as a reservation police officer with the Umatillas on the Columbia River. When Scott wondered how Henry had found such a good job far away from Tututni lands, Jack-Jack explained that Henry's uncle had a cousin who was a Umatilla sub-chief.

The McClures were present for the wedding in mid-February, and Scott stayed on as caretaker so the entire family could escort the newlyweds to Port Orford to await a ship bound for Portland. The Smiths would sail to that port and travel up the Columbia in a series of steamships and railroad rides to their destination – a small government house on the Umatilla Reservation.

Stormy weather delayed ships scheduled into port but didn't deter Rick from delivering fresh bread and eggs to his lonely son during a brief visit. A couple of days later Grandpa arrived with more of Julie's baked treats and a checkerboard, staying overnight and keeping his namesake company.

Scott was forking hay into the corral filled with hungry cows when he heard horses approaching and caught a glimpse of Jack-Jack riding Ai-ho up the trail. He assumed the Sixes family was coming home and quickly finished his drudgery before straightening his tired back. He was pleasantly surprised to hear his cousin's resonant voice teasingly greet him, "Hello, Scott! Enjoying the life of a farmer, eh? Is the manure pile next?"

Momentarily wordless, the young farmer merely nodded as he spotted Albert and Billy riding in beside Jack-Jack. With a broad grin showing his welcome, he exclaimed, "Golly, it's good to see you fellas. The Four Musketeers are together again. Hmm! Albert Lee, why aren't you in class?"

"Those damn Spaniards blew up our battleship in Havana harbor two weeks ago, even though the Maine was there in a peaceful visit. Hearst claimed an enemy mine was the dastardly weapon used and wrote in his journal that 'dishonor is more dreadful than war.' Now our do-nothing President has to take action, and I'm going to do something too," Albert's voice cracked emotionally and his face flushed self-consciously.

"Something? What can we do, Albert? Join the rebels in Cuba?" Scott queried in confusion. As Albert nodded hesitantly, resolution firmed the lines of his cousin's face. Contemplating the challenge before him, Scott turned to Billy and Jack-Jack with serious question, "Are you two with Albert and me?"

As they nodded with infectious excitement, Albert counseled calmly, "We'd better talk to our fathers about how we feel, and we need to watch the news reports from

Washington. McKinley will have to do something according to all the newspapers."

After a moment's silence, Billy asked the practical question, "Have we got enough money to go to Cuba?"

* * * * *

Rod Bishop waved acknowledgment to the mate on the lumber schooner anchored offshore, darkness ending the loading of cut cedar for the day. Turning to the dozen men working the stacks along the beach, he called out, "That's it for today, men. See you at first light to finish this job."

The Four Musketeers drifted together as they left the yard, tired enough from an eleven-hour day to forego conversation. They plodded up the broad stretch of road toward Port Orford, puffing a bit as they clambered up the rugged bluff east of town.

Heads bowed as they tromped through the brush atop the hillock, they almost missed seeing George Hermann and James Girard waving excitedly at them from the elderly merchant's home. James thin voice carried well enough in the damp, salty air, "Come here, lads. George has the latest news from back East."

Suddenly awakened from their lethargy by a spark of anticipation, the four comrades ran down the street toward the waiting men. Albert led the way, asking as they neared the house, "Are we at war?"

George chuckled before he replied, "Not quite, but McKinley and Congress are talking about it. And your hero, Teddy Roosevelt, is rattling his saber, sending naval ships to the Orient, and volunteering to raise a regiment to fight for Cuban liberty. I do believe you're right, Albert, war is coming."

Girard asked a direct question, "How do your fathers feel about your going to war? Albert's old enough to decide for himself, but what about my friends, the McClures, the Sixes, and Bill Tucker?"

Scott and Jack-Jack shrugged non-committingly while Billy hung his head, blurting out his concern as he raised eyes sparkling with defiance, "I will go whether father says yes or not. He thinks I'm too young, but he was on his own at my age."

Girard smiled sympathetically, "Well, you'd better talk to him again, Billy. I expect you all have minds of your own. Anyway, that schooner captain out there has a four-berth cabin available if you men want to sail to San Francisco tomorrow. I can pay him out of the wages I owe you. What shall I tell him?"

"Go ahead and book passage, James, and we thank both of you for relaying the latest news," Albert said gratefully.

George spoke teasingly, "I don't know if your families are going to appreciate either effort on your behalf, lads, but I was young once. Good luck in your adventures."

With a round of handshakes and best wishes, the group disbanded, the four companions agreeing to meet at Girard's mill in the morning.

*   *   *   *   *

Seated around the supper table, the McClure family was uncommonly quiet following Scott's announcement, even little George silently looking on. In an equally rare manner, Julie cleared her throat preemptively, and when there was no objection, spoke for the family, "Scott, you're just like your father and grandfather. Once you make up your mind, there's not much room for argument. We love you and will worry about you, but go with our blessing. Just come home after your adventure is over."

Rick grinned suddenly, offering his support by proffering a leather money belt and a bit of advice, "Here's a hundred dollars in gold coin, Son. You lads watch yourselves in San Francisco; it can be a tough town. Stick together and hang onto your money."

"Ha! Ha! Your dad's right, Scott. It hasn't changed much since the Gold Rush days. Respectable folks live on the hill, and the waterfront at night is no-man's territory. You might look up Captain Tichenor's daughter, Ellen McGraw, and say hello for me," Grandpa concluded.

*   *   *   *   *

Scott was finishing breakfast and saying goodbye to Jane, Melissa, Anne, and George, while their mother was collecting her morning basket of eggs in the hencoop. George was still confused that his big brother was leaving home because of a revolution in Cuba, a country far away from Oregon. Even their sisters couldn't help explain foreign relations to the lad, although they kept trying. As always, Jane was her older brother's best supporter in the family.

Julie slipped through the door to place her wicker basket on a chair, announcing tearfully, "Jack-Jack is here, dear. You'd better gather your gear. Your dad's saddling the horses."

Her younger children followed her outside as Scott hustled about the room, donning hat and coat before grabbing a pair of baking powder biscuits in one hand and his bulging canvas bag in the other. As he stepped into the yard, he tossed one biscuit to his mounted comrade, who adroitly caught it with his free hand, a well-practiced move between two friends. Jack-Jack was always hungry for Julie's treats.

Scott listened as his Tututni partner responded to Julie's question of what his parents had said. Jack-Jack stated simply, "Father told me to be a brave warrior, and to fight with honor."

Rick nodded in approval, and as he handed Rimpar's reins to his son, parroted that counsel, "Good words! Your family offers the same advice to you, Scott, with all our love. Hurry home, Son."

Grandpa had mounted Salem and now suggested in gruff tones, "Come on! I'll keep you company to your ship and bring the horses home. So say your goodbyes, Grandson."

Unabashedly displaying tears, Scott hugged each of his loved ones briefly, and was quickly in the saddle. With a choked-up "Bye!" and a farewell wave he spurred up the knoll after Grandpa and Jack-Jack. His adventure was about to begin.

Chapter Three

Scott stumbled a step or two off the gangplank before his landlegs recognized the solid footing of the dock's timbered surface, clucking to himself at being less than a true sailor. It felt good to be ashore after the long voyage from Port Orford. His curious glance showed San Francisco's waterfront was bustling with activity, men and cargo everywhere and several ships berthed along the Embarcadero. He looked over his shoulder, dropping his bag when there was no sign of his comrades.

He watched the steamship across the pier as men suddenly surged aboard its two gangways until not a soul stood on the dock. There were three empty and untended horse-drawn wagons beside the vessel, evidently abandoned, since the ship's lines were being cast off. When the steamship moved into the bay, he heard a feeble chuckle from a dark-bearded and well-dressed older man walking toward him. Scott noted the man's expression of consternation at the departing ship and smiled at his half-spoken murmur, "There go my three teamsters on their way to the Klondike. Ah well, I guess I might go myself if I didn't own this business."

Having caught the young man's attention, the stranger's bushy-browed countenance turned calculating, brown eyes glinting with a bit of hope as he asked, "Say, young fella, would you be willing to help me load those wagons for an honest day's wages?"

As Billy strode with thundering footsteps down the gangplank behind Scott, the businessman expanded on his offer, "Both of you can earn two dollars to load my wagons with lumber and deliver it to the train depot. You aren't bound for the Gold Rush, are you?"

"Ha! Ha! No, but we are in a hurry to reach Tampa Bay in Florida. I hear that's where our troops are gathering to go to

Cuba," Scott replied in friendly conversation, his glance taking in the approaching Albert and Jack-Jack in his comment. He added with curiosity, "What is the latest news about our nation's trouble with Spain?"

"Well now, gentlemen, we've been at war with the Spaniards for a couple of days according to the *Chronicle*. I hear Teddy Roosevelt and an Army colonel named Wood are forming an outfit in Texas to take Cuba away from the Spanish army. Some have named it 'Teddy's Texans,' but the cowboys are calling themselves the 'Rough Riders'. If you work for me today, I'll put you aboard a train that will get you to Arizona Territory in time to enlist. Same train will probably carry the Arizona Company to San Antonio."

Albert's tone was doubtful as he queried, "How do we get to the depot, sir? I don't see how we have time to help you."

"I'm Jacob Freeland, young man, and I'll guarantee you will be on the next train to Los Angeles. Everyone knows me and will tell you Jake's word is his bond. Tickets cost a bit, lads, but I'll give you each two dollars toward the train fare and a basket of beer to quench your thirst when the job's done. Shall we get to work?"

Albert continued to hesitate, so Scott made the decision for his comrades, striding over to the nearest wagon to rub the horse's ear and mane. Grasping her bridle in his fist, he led horse and wagon to the gangplank, the smiling businessman hurrying to the schooner's captain with papers in hand. The four new teamsters were soon handling lumber, a film of sweat on their faces as the morning mist surrounding Nob Hill gave way to Golden Gate sunshine.

Before noon Jake led his cavalcade of top-heavy wagons along the Embarcadero, skirting San Francisco's famous hills, but encountering plenty of foot traffic and drayage wagons on its busy streets. Scott thought, *I see why Jake has us leading the horses through the city. All this bustle spooks me, too.*

Jack-Jack's interest was expressed in bewilderment as he wondered aloud, "Where do all these people come from, Jake? And who lives on all these hills to starboard?"

Everyone chuckled at Jack-Jack's sailor language, Albert chirping teasingly, "Ah, Jack-Jack, starboard is a word for the sea, and right is what we landlubbers use. Or maybe west is even better, what say you, Jake?"

"Why I believe you lads are having the adventure of a lifetime, and you haven't even reached Cuba yet. Ah, to be young again. To answer your question Jack-Jack, San Francisco is the biggest and richest city out West. And the hills on your right are filling with both rich and poor. Why, that area is where all the coolies live," Jake informed them as he pointed west, concluding his roll as guide with a final fact, "Everyone calls it Chinatown."

"Golly, look at that carriage climbing the hill without a horse. People are even hanging onto the outside. How do they make it go, Jake?" Billy puzzled in muted voice.

"That's a streetcar, Billy, only we call it a cablecar here in San Francisco. It's pulled by a cable under the tracks. Sure makes life easier on folks up there," Jake concluded with a grin.

* * * * *

Scott glanced over his shoulders as he climbed the steel treads of the passenger car behind Billy and paused briefly to watch a red-faced and cursing Jake maneuver his last wagon load of lumber into the warehouse. The Four Musketeers had stowed two loads aboard a railway flatbed on the near siding, and despite the teamster's pleas to wait for storage space for his other wagon's cargo, they had hurried to board this Los Angeles train.

The din of a crowded aisle was punctuated with gruff cursing accompanied by a convulsion of bustling men. Scott heard Albert's reasonable lawyer's voice answer the angry stranger, and when a "Damned Siwash" echoed from the ceiling, his cousin's tones became strident in confrontation. A bushy-headed, full-bearded, and mean-looking bruiser broke free of the packed men, his fingers twisted through a tangle of black hair. Jack-Jack's pained face followed as the bully pulled the Tututni down the aisle, roaring a snarling vindictive, "Damned Siwash! Indians don't belong in a car with real men."

Blinded by a sudden flare of temper, Scott lunged past Billy, driving his shoulder into the roughhouser's ribs and twisting him onto the floor. He was struck by a probing knee on his hip as he spun away, his own elbow cracking solidly into the culprit's sternum. A body fell atop him and was buried under a heaving pile of passengers.

Scott felt fingers grazing his cheeks, evidently seeking his eyes. With his arms pinned helplessly under his own body, he stretched his neck toward the invading fingers, opening his jaws to seize a protruding thumb between his incisors and clamped his mouth and eyes shut. He thought he heard a muffled scream amid the moans and groans of the surrounding bodies, but he refused to release the writhing digit until the weight over him was removed. Spitting out the offending hand and more than a little blood, Scott reared back, Billy holding him erect as several men struggled to their feet.

The enraged bruiser was the last to attain a staggering posture before Scott, Jack-Jack now surrounded by his three comrades and the husky logger from Drain, Bernie Heisel. Grinning widely and flexing his powerful shoulders, Bernie took the offensive against Jack-Jack's cursing assailant.

He roared angrily, "You keep your hands off Jack-Jack, Matey, or I'll teach you proper manners. This lad is all right I say, he's my friend." After glancing at Scott's ruffled appearance, he added, "And be careful of this young tiger, I've gone a couple of rounds with him – he's tough."

The bruiser backed away to the doorway, his friend wrapping the crimped thumb with a soiled bandanna, and soon both exited the car under the steady glare of the five comrades. Bernie cleared out facing bench seats with an impervious frown and a casual gesture of his hand, and brought the scene to order as a whistle sounded and the floor jerked under their feet.

"Here Jack-Jack, sit by the window so we'll have no more arguments about Indians. Albert, you and Billy sit across from him, Scott and I will be on the aisle to deal with any bigmouths. Now, are we all going to Los Angeles and join Teddy Roosevelt's Rough Riders?" Bernie concluded with a questioning glance around the Curry County contingent.

Scott grinned and offered belated thanks, finally answering, "It's good to see you, too, Bernie. Yes, we're going to join a company of Rough Riders, but it's forming in Arizona from what we hear."

"Ha! Ha! I heard that, too. Well, I guess this logger will have to go hungry for awhile if I have to buy another train ticket," Bernie bemoaned in a good-natured reply.

Albert held up a burlap bag and offered, "You're welcome to share out bread and cheese. I suppose we'll all be hungry by morning, but we'll make do until we find our company in Arizona."

* * * * *

Clickety-clackety, clickety-clackety resounded through the metal fabric of the passenger carriage as the train rolled southward, following parallel steel rails toward Los Angeles. Scott stared at the green hills of spring, spotted here and there with the dark silhouette of a gnarled oak tree, and smiled at the nodding heads of Jack-Jack and Billy before his window view. As the sun's rays turned into a magenta glow, individual features of the landscape blurred into muffled shadows, Bernie's rumbling snore joining a minor chorus of somnolent travelers aboard the train.

Albert's soft voice echoed McClure's aesthetic appreciation of the deep purple nightfall, "Isn't it beautiful out there, Scott? Seems a shame to sleep while California passes by our window. What time did the conductor tell you that we will arrive in Los Angeles?"

"Eight o'clock in the morning is the railroad's scheduled time, but he said the train stops at several stations along the way. He'll wake everyone before we pull into the depot," Scott replied in like tones, adding a wistful breath, "Would there be a bite left in your knapsack?"

Albert grinned as he dug out a chunk of stale sourdough bread and a small piece of cheddar cheese, offering his own snack, "I didn't eat all of my share – too excited, I guess. You take it, I'm going to catch a wink of sleep now."

With a barely audible reply, Scott mouthed, "Thanks, Cousin. Enjoy your nap." Surreptitiously he broke apart the dry and crunchy bread and chewed its pieces quietly, savoring the last bite of cheddar as he thought about his next meal – some time tomorrow. His eyes fixed on the night shadows outside the window until the rhythmic clickety-clackety sounds lulled him to sleep.

* * * * *

"Los Angeles! Los Angeles! We'll be in Union Station in twenty minutes, gents," the conductor announced in stentorian tones as he strolled down the aisle and the jostling rumble of men awakening.

Albert had the presence of mind to ask, "Conductor, how do we find the eastbound train to Arizona? We're going to join up with Roosevelt's Rough Riders."

"Hmm! I heard there's a company forming in Cactus Junction, barely a siding some thirty miles this side of Phoenix. I think that train left Union Station at eight o'clock," the uniformed official volunteered.

Albert blurted out a perceptive response, "But it's quarter of eight, sir. Might the train still be at the depot?"

Grinning at his fare's quick thinking, the conductor offered, "You're right, let me check with the mail clerk. Sometimes he has a bag or two to transfer to the eastbound train."

By now the five comrades were wide awake and sitting on the edge of their seats, eager to be moving on. The train was slowing to a crawl amidst the network of tracks in the vast railyard when the man returned to beckon them.

Scott noted they were passing a departing train some four or five tracks over, just as Albert queried, "It's five past eight, sir. Are we too late?"

The conductor ignored the question, leading his charges into the mail car and hurriedly explaining, "Harvey has six sacks of mail for the eastbound express. If you can tote them to that moving train across the way, you'll be in Cactus Junction late tonight."

Harvey was a gnome of a man but with bulging muscles. As he looked out the half-open doors, he promptly began throwing bags onto the neighboring tracks. Scott immediately jumped from the slowing train to catch the sixth bag and staggered to maintain his balance. Harvey followed on his heels and ran back to pick up the nearest mail pouch, calling over his shoulder, "Grab a sack and follow me to that open mail car over yonder."

Harvey and Scott ran side by side across three pairs of tracks and then raced after the accelerating train leaving the depot. As they ran between parallel steel rails, they came abreast the gaping doors, another mailman laughing at their challenge, "Run, Harvey, the mail must go on."

Harvey threw his bag into the railway car, still running alongside as he motioned Scott to follow suit, calling out, "These fellows are headed for Cactus Junction, Zeke. Give this lad a hand up."

Scott cast his bag after Harvey's and accepted Zeke's proffered hand as he leaped belly first into the mailcar. A bag bounced off his back as he squirmed about and grasped Jack-Jack's hand to pull him onto the floor beside him. Billy and Zeke rolled over them in exaggerated parody of Scott and Jack-Jack, both breaking into cheerful laughter at their exhilarating adventure.

The train was gaining speed as Albert lunged forward, bag and all, relying on his friends to catch him and lug him aboard. However, the heavy-set Bernie was a half dozen steps behind Albert and wheezing badly, Harvey seizing his bag and casting it into the mailcar before staggering between two tracks. Scott pushed the sliding door to its rear stopper, and grabbing a steel brace in his left hand, leaned outboard, Jack-Jack's arms circling his waist adding a degree of confidence to his call, "Come on, Bernie, six more feet and I can reach you."

The logger leaned forward, driving his legs desperately into the ties and gravel as he lunged ahead with right hand extended. The two hands met and grazed lightly, Zeke's fingers encircling Heisel's wrist just as his feet flew out from under him. Albert grabbed a piece of jacket and Billy fisted a handful of hair, a team effort needed to hoist their flailing friend aboard.

They all sighed with relief, nervous chuckles resounding as Bernie complained, "Thanks, but you didn't need to pull my hair out."

Zeke banged the steel doors closed, locking them as he suggested, "Why don't you rest while I round up the conductor? You all have money for your fares, don't you?"

* * * * *

The five friends lay astraddle piles of cargo in the baggage car, eating the last bite of the conductor's warmed-over stew from a common kettle. Scott had dug deep into his moneybelt to pay for Bernie's fare as well as his own and to satisfy the railroad official's greed in filling their stomachs.

Scott thought to himself, *At least we all have a ride to Cactus Junction, a bellyful of food, and a warm spot to sleep. I wonder if our stop is really unscheduled – and at midnight.*

Bernie was properly appreciative and waxed philosophical as he spoke, "Thanks, Scott. I guess I could have ridden the rails to Arizona, but I don't know where such a tasty meal would have come from – and my bed among these sacks of potatoes. You sure are a better friend than enemy."

"I expect we won't have much use for money after we reach that company of Rough Riders," Scott mused with a rueful grin, adding a comradely, "In fact, I might as well divide the rest of Dad's money with you. We'll each have a couple of dollars for food until the army feeds us."

"Did that conductor really sell us a bag of potatoes, Scott? Are they his to sell?" Billy asked in naïve tones.

"Ha! Ha!" Bernie chortled, punctuated by vigorous nods, "Yes, as long as we only take a couple from each bag in this car. Don't worry, Billy, Scott paid up, and I'll be the one to fill this empty gunnysack we got from the conductor."

Scott glanced surreptitiously at his cousin who raised a quizzical eyebrow, winked and then pulled his hat over his face before resting his head on a pile of canvas. *Well, I guess I shouldn't worry about my conscience when I've paid hard cash for food. If Albert the lawyer can sleep, well so can I.*

* * * * *

The clickety-clack of wheels on the tracks changed tempo, a squeal of steel upon steel signaling that the mechanical behemoth was slowing. All five voices in the pitch-black enclosure mixed together, Bernie's dominating the medley, "Where the hell are we, friends?"

A subtle yellow glow permeated the darkness, shadows cast by the rising figures approaching on the walls as the conductor shouted, "Up and at 'em! Cactus Junction is dead ahead. Leave by the far door, lads, and head for the campfires along the siding over yonder. Good luck in Cuba."

Billy reached the door first, swinging it outward as the lantern light disappeared. A moment later the train came to a jerky halt, seven campfires visible nearby. Billy plunged into the darkness, landing with a thud and calling back softly, "Careful of the broken rocks, or you'll turn an ankle."

Bernie followed with a gunnysack over his shoulder, Albert, Jack-Jack, and Scott leaving the car in turn. The starlight gave him more light than the interior of the baggage car, and Scott had no trouble slamming the door shut and trailing his friends across the siding tracks. He heard voices on his right, and his glance fell on the passengers advancing toward the fires.

Albert spoke softly of their fellow debarkees, "So much for our conductor's special stop." Before he could elaborate further the engine's driving wheels spun on the tracks, taking hold and moving the cars on toward Phoenix.

Shadowy figures were outlined by the flickering light of the campfires as Scott hurried after his friends. Several cries of "potatoes" rang out as Bernie came into the thin luminosity, and the muscular logger roared, "Back off!"

A couple of startled men jumped back a step, but a third man stood his guard, authority lacing his voice as he stated, "I'm Tom Case, and we are all here to join Teddy Roosevelt's Rough Riders. Some of us have been waiting all week, and as more men arrived, our food was eaten. We haven't had a meal since yesterday. Can I buy that sack of potatoes from you?"

Bernie shook his head no and Albert remained quiet, so Scott stepped forward, extending his right hand and asking, "I'm Scott McClure from Port Orford, Oregon. Are you the Arizona sheriff in charge of this camp?"

Case shook hands and grinned affably, replying, "I was a deputy sheriff last month, but no one's in charge yet. A U. S. Army train is due to pick us up any day now. But I can speak for these men, we're hungry."

Scott motioned Bernie forward, declaring, "Give the sack to the sheriff, Bernie. Of course, we'll share our food, Tom, but only if everything in camp goes in a common pot, and you're our captain until the army says differently."

One of the newcomers from the train walked over to Case and handed him a bundle wrapped in greasy newspapers, mimicking Scott's offer, "I'm Carl Yeager. Here's the remains of a ham my friends brought on the train. Sorry the bread's all gone. I feel like Mr. McClure here, Sheriff Case. You're our captain, and every bit of food in camp comes to you right now."

Tom Case nodded as his glance circled the camps, words unnecessary as his command presence dominated the gathering. Scott's eyes followed their leader's steely gaze beyond the third campfire, and after a moment, a tall scrawny cowboy with belted pistol around his waist moved into the firelight, proffering a gutted jack-rabbit with a single affirmation, "You're boss, Tom Case."

Their leader smiled briefly, commenting and directing in single words, "All right! It's all for one and one for all while I'm camp boss. Slim, you and Durango are camp cooks. Scott, you and Carl give them a hand making a kettle of stew out of these makings. The rest of you get busy and clean up this campsite and make room for our new members. We'll sleep after we eat."

* * * * *

Scott tossed and turned on the hard sand, a coyote chorus, a westbound train, and a trio of mounted cowboys punctuating his sleep. He finally gave up trying to rest and observed dawn activities in camp from his bedroll. Tom Case moved about camp with the gun-toting Slim and a note-taking Albert on either elbow. The former was to keep the peace and the latter was to gather a list of men in camp. Scott had informed the ex-lawman that his cousin was a law student, and Captain Case immediately appointed him as company clerk.

The night horsemen were arguing with Albert about his list of names, and when Tom joined in the conversation, Scott quickly rolled out of his blankets and strode across camp to stand beside his cousin. From the glances of the three cowboys, Scott assumed Bernie was close behind him.

"Sheriff Case, our names and where we're from are personal business. This clerk is too nosy for his own good," a clean-shaven, handsome young man asserted, his bewhiskered older compadre nodding agreement. Scott noted that their shifty eyes wandered in all directions, nervousness expressed in their manner.

Tom replied in querulous tones, unmoved by the six-shooters strapped to their waists, "Sheriff, you say. Have we met before, gents?"

All three newcomers paled at the query, hands hovering near their sheathed pistols. Tom brushed back his jacket to reveal a Colt .45 tucked in his belt, and Slim suddenly shifted a couple of steps to his right. The silence was poignant as everyone waited for an answer.

With a deep breath, the youngster carefully tucked his thumb in his belt as a sign of peaceful intent and admitted, "We met, Sheriff. You ran me out of town last year for calling on the mayor's daughter. I'm Jess Killbride from down Tucson way."

"Ah yes, I remember now. The mayor claimed you stole some penny candy from his store and wanted you arrested. The girl's story matched yours, but I didn't want the mayor to dream up another excuse to jail you. Any of you men wanted by the law?" Tom asked abruptly.

All three men sputtered a no, Jess hemming and hawing until he finally muttered ruefully, "Nothing worth mentioning, Captain Case."

"Then give Albert your names, and Tucson can be your home of record. We're headed through New Mexico and Texas to San Antonio as soon as the army gets our train here."

The three cowboys breathed an audible sigh of relief and volunteered their names to Albert, the camp noises once again filling the Arizona desert, almost masking the distant shriek of a locomotive's whistle.

Within minutes a string of open boxcars headed by a caboose appeared along the rails from Phoenix, a single steam engine puffing along behind them. As the rickety, well-worn caboose neared the siding, a man leaped from the steps and ran forward to wrestle the switch, bringing the siding tracks in line. The cars proceeded slowly, squeaking and creaking as their wheels rolled over the rusty rails beside the camp.

An officer and two sergeants stepped out of the narrow door onto the steel platform, a three-stringer leading the way onto the sandy campgrounds. Tom Case stood patiently before the congregated recruits-to-be, waiting for the army officer to speak.

"Good morning, men! I'm Lieutenant Sam Scholl from Colonel Wood's staff. Are all of you prepared to join the army today?"

"Yes, sir! I'm Tom Case, speaking for every man present. We are ready and able to serve with the Rough Riders. When will the passenger cars arrive, Lieutenant?"

The officer smiled dryly as he responded, "What you see before you is our train, Mr. Case. We're going all the way to San Antonio in these cars after we enlist these men and have noon mess."

"Sir, there isn't room for our horses, and as I recall, it gets mighty cold in the New Mexico mountains after sunset," Tom pointed out in respectful tones.

Nodding his agreement, Scholl explained, "That's correct, Mr. Case. I've been authorized to buy your horses for the army, and the Sergeant Major will take them to the post. I'd appreciate your assigning two recruits to accompany him. If they leave soon, they can catch the train in Phoenix, where we will pick up food, blankets, and a half-dozen more volunteers. I didn't choose these cars, but they are our ride to Texas. Now let's prepare our enlistment rolls before the army cuts our size again."

"Cuts our size? What do you mean, sir?" Case asked.

"Our regiment has been cut back to 350 men, and Bucky O'Neill in Prescott has turned volunteers away from A Company. Ha! Ha! Except his troop has enlisted a regimental mascot – a mountain lion cub."

"Good, sir!" Tom replied as he barked orders, "Albert, assist the Lieutenant. Slim and Durango, swear in first and help the Sergeant Major with our horses – you're his detail. Scott and Carl are next as cooks for the day. Jess, swear in with them and stand watch on the caboose's platform. The rest of you men line up as Albert calls your name."

"Well done, Mr. Case. Carry on, Sergeant-Major," Scholl ordered, turning to his clerk, "Albert, is it? You and Tom Case raise your right hand and repeat after me your oath of enlistment."

The Cactus Junction Troop of the Arizona Regiment formed proudly along the desert railroad siding ready and eager for action.

Chapter Four

This shuffling column of Arizona cowboys and western volunteers is far from an impressive army company, Scott reflected to himself as he glanced over his shoulder. Several of the recruits still wore cowboy boots which made this march from the railroad a footsore activity, and several others were not in good physical shape. *But we should reach camp before those rails are repaired and the pile-up of trains can move again, and we'll get into better shape after some real military training,* he concluded hopefully in his innermost thoughts.

Lieutenant Scholl raised his right hand palm up and shouted, "Column, halt! At rest men – for ten minutes. Carl, Slim, see everyone gets a drink of water."

The two recruits gathered several canteens and passed down the column, doling out a swallow of water to each man. Tom Case was in conversation with the officer and his sergeant when his eyes met Scott's. He beckoned him forward with a jerk of his head, the younger man hearing the Lieutenant's voice as he stepped forward, "... and remember we want a good company site. Don't let anyone foist that creek bottomland off on us. See Colonel Wood himself if need be. Lee and McClure will be your clerk and your runner. We'll be in camp within the hour."

"Yes, sir! Come along, men, we'll have to double-time it to Camp Wood if our comrades are to eat a hot meal in an hour," the Sergeant commanded.

Following the veteran at a steady trot was easy enough for the two cousins, but no conversation was attempted until they sighted the helter-skelter cluster of clapboard and canvas in the distance.

Slowing their pace to a fast walk, the Sergeant explained, "Not much of a camp, men, but it's home for a few weeks. The wooden buildings are warehouses, with the far one over yonder the armory. That large tent is the mess hall, where we'll go first, and that tent with the flag is regimental headquarters."

As they neared their goal, Scott's curiosity focused on the makeshift camp, its partially uniformed troops attempting to create order out of seeming chaos. Used to living in a forest, he was disappointed at the lack of trees, only a few cottonwoods scattered about the encampment. He thought, *I bet wood for campfires is at a premium. Probably that's what happened to most of the trees. Hmm! Wonder why that fellow is waving at me.*

"Scott! Hey Scott! Quit daydreaming and come with me. Albert will arrange a meal with my waving friend at the mess tent. Let's get a bivouac assignment at headquarters," the Sergeant announced.

"Sergeant Hokey, which outfit are you with?" queried a smartly dressed captain standing beside the flagpost.

"Lieutenant Scholl's Arizona Troop, sir. I'm here to arrange bivouacs for our men. That site over..."

"No! No! Sergeant," the Captain interrupted, pointing in the opposite direction, "You can take that meadow down by the creek. There's plenty of water and firewood down there for your outfit."

Sergeant Hokey frowned, remembering the Lieutenant's orders, but stymied by the domineering officer before him. Scott slipped aside, recognizing his superior's dilemma, and approached the regimental headquarters tent just as a commanding figure emerged through its flaps, the officer eyeing the Captain and the Sergeant.

"Sir, I'm Scott McClure of the Lieutenant Scholl's Arizona Company. May we bivouac on that site near that big field?"

"Good day, son, I'm Colonel Wood," and pausing to shake the naïve recruit's outstretched hand, asked, "Where is your company?"

The Captain hustled forward, saluting smartly as he gave Scott a nasty look and stated authoritatively, "Sir, I've told Sergeant Hokey that he can occupy the creek meadow. My company will occupy the parade ground site."

Playing his naïve role to the hilt in the Sergeant's silence, Scott ignored the Captain and answered Colonel Wood's question, "Lieutenant Scholl and our company are on a forced march cross-country. He's breaking the men into training early, sir, and they'll need a good night's sleep over there."

"Thank you, Recruit McClure. And where is your company, Captain?" the Colonel asked with a tongue-in-cheek jibe, sandy mustache quivering in humor.

"Sir, they are waiting on the inbound train from Chicago. The track is jammed with traffic some six or seven miles out."

"Well then, Captain, it appears that the old first-come, first-served slogan applies. First company in camp takes the parade ground, and the other gets the creek meadow. Fair enough, gentlemen?" the Colonel directed with a twinkle in his eye.

Scott saluted awkwardly as his sergeant did, Wood's return gesture clearly a dismissal. Hurrying after the fast-paced sergeant, he almost bumped into him when he came to an abrupt halt. The sound of horse's hooves faded as it left camp.

"McClure, that horseman is headed for the train. Quick, run to the Lieutenant and tell him our deal, and avoid that captain. He'll try to sidetrack you. Go through the cottonwoods and across the creek, lad. Hurry!" the Sergeant encouraged.

Scott nonchalantly wandered around the corner of the mess tent, spotting the Captain striding down the road to the creek crossing. Out of the officer's view, he broke into a run behind the screen of tents and entered the cottonwoods, ploughing through muddy soil and into hip-deep creek waters. Following the course of a shallow arroyo, he ran doubled over to avoid detection, puffing heavily as he breasted a ridge some hundred yards ahead of the Captain's position at the crossing. *Playing deaf as well as dumb is easy,* Scott chuckled quietly as he ignored the officer's shouts and ran out of earshot.

A few minutes later he came upon Tom Case and Sam Scholl, leading the Arizona column along the dirt road. Quickly shouting his story in gasping breaths, both of his superiors caught on immediately, the Lieutenant raising his closed fist twice and shouting, "Double-time, march!"

Scott retraced his route with renewed vigor, serving as company guidon. Everyone ignored the fuming Captain who was forced off the road by the now inspired cowboys, morale rising high as word of the contest passed to the rear. The Arizona Company formed into passable ranks as Scott led the men to their prized bivouacs even as a train whistle sounded – first on site and looking like a real army to boot.

* * * * *

The Captain hied into the regimental tent, soon appearing en route with Colonel Wood to confront Lieutenant Scholl, his voice of complaint carrying through the camp, "I want that young whippersnapper court-martialed for insubordination and disrespect. And I outrank this company's commander, so this site should be mine."

The Colonel listened respectfully to his subordinate officer as they strode up to Lieutenant Scholl, returning his salute with an eye on his captain, who belatedly did likewise. Wood cut off any further complaints with a distinct palm-up gesture to everyone, addressing the company and its officer, "Well done, men! This spot is yours until we leave for Tampa Bay. Lieutenant Samuel Scholl is hereby promoted to captain and assigned as Commander of D Company."

Smiling at the low groan of disappointment from the ranks, Wood continued, "Sheriff Tom Case, Teddy Roosevelt and I concur on your leadership and fighting ability. You are issued a brevet commission as Captain of this Arizona Troop. Sergeant Hokey will serve as your First Sergeant. Lieutenant Reynolds will be your second in command, Captain Case. He should arrive with Lieutenant Colonel Roosevelt tomorrow."

The frustrated captain burst in, "But, sir, what about this insubordinate soldier?"

"Ah yes, Private McClure must be punished, Captain Case. I suggest he runs five miles a day for ten days. Dismissed, gentlemen! Captain Scholl, will you accompany me to my tent. I believe I have a spare set of shoulder boards for your uniform," Colonel Wood directed as he left the irate captain to himself.

"Cheers! Three cheers for Colonel Wood," Albert shouted, and a clear, "Rah, rah, rah," pealed through the tented encampment, all the Arizona recruits conspicuously turning their backs on the retreating captain.

* * * * *

Dewey's stunning victory in Manila Bay was old news when Scott heard it, and his approbation of it to Albert was muted by his many miles of running. Besides, Albert was a corporal and had met Teddy Roosevelt while Scott was doing his company punishment. He felt a bit sorry for himself as his friends relaxed, and he waved a desultory goodbye to his cousin, trotting southward to his personal hideaway where his visits of the Texas sunset was awaiting him.

Sprinting up a gentle slope in a burst of reserve energy, Scott topped the familiar ridge with rasping breath, only to find someone was occupying his favorite stump. It seemed as if someone else enjoyed meditation as the sun slid behind the broad horizon. Bending over at the waist and grasping knobby knees in his palms, he rested as the twilight colors deepened, his breathing quickly returning to normal.

"Soldier, you're in pretty good shape for a recruit. I wish I had your youth and stamina. Would you be Private McClure by chance? On your punishment route?" the high and somehow tense voice of the compact figure asked without turning his gaze from the colorful panorama.

Scott was savvy enough to know any man older than thirty was likely an officer, and consequently replied with proper military courtesy, "Yes, sir! Running is good training, voluntary or not. But you must be in good shape yourself, sir, since we're about three miles south of the flagpole."

The man rose abruptly, nervous energy now apparent within his short, stocky body, and he turned to study Scott's face. Even in the fading light, Teddy Roosevelt's distinctive countenance was easily discernable, and the young man snapped to attention with a brisk acknowledgment, "Colonel Roosevelt, sir!"

Continuing his study of the young private, Teddy beamed his famous trademark smile, teeth flashing under his mustache as he adjusted his pince-nez spectacles on his nose, asking, "So you recognize me? Scott, isn't it? Well, Scott, a certain captain told me you were an insubordinate pup, but Colonel Wood reported you had the makings of a fine soldier. Which is correct, young man?"

"Both, sir! I heard the Captain's order but chose to use my common sense. I felt it was unethical for him to cheat in our contest, so I ignored him. I put my company and my comrades ahead of that officer. Colonel Wood understood my dilemma quite clearly. He's a straight thinker, isn't he? His punishment for my offense was fair to me, and I'll be a better soldier for it."

"Well said, Private McClure. Now I am appointing you as my personal trainer, but nary a word to anyone. The men think

I'm as fit as I am stubborn, and I plan to be in top shape before we land in Cuba. I'm going to run with you every evening. Well, at least part of the way. Lead off, man! I have an evening conference with the quartermaster," Teddy ordered as he trotted after Scott down the faint trail.

* * * * *

Camp Wood training was carried on haphazardly, but cowboy marksmanship was high, and a semblance of military order pervaded the Arizona Regiment. Scott slowly saw his punishment as a blessing in disguise, for he was in the peak of physical fitness and well ahead of his friends, except maybe for rank, since Carl, Slim, and Jess were corporals, and Albert was named Company Clerk and a sergeant.

Lieutenant Reynolds was from upstate New York, a West Point graduate, and a friend of the Roosevelt family. Still, he was a well-trained officer with a sense of humor and made an excellent second-in-command for Captain Case. He had displayed good sense in bringing two shavetails and three veteran sergeants into the company with him. A dozen or so cowboys from Montana and the Dakotas were on his train and ended up with Case's company when he inveigled their services from a staff officer.

Teddy Roosevelt had run with Scott on two additional occasions, being forever swamped with evening meetings as he was. Rumors were flying about camp that the regiment was leaving camp soon, and Scott was hopeful his running partner would show up this evening. He enjoyed listening to the officer ramble on, Teddy confident his enlisted "trainer" was close-mouthed.

When Lieutenant Reynolds joined Scott on his daily run without invitation, challenging the enlisted man to a race to Roosevelt's Roost. Scott digested the disturbing revelation that his secret spot was known, ever since Teddy had claimed it in their last sunset rendezvous. Reynold's laughter echoed across the slope as Scott lagged behind, the sound full of humor and camaraderie.

Both men raced vigorously across the rolling plains, putting their last energy into the slope before the vista site. Light

clapping and jovial high-pitched laughter greeted them as
Teddy encouraged their contest. The Lieutenant was two
strides ahead of Scott and he came to an abrupt halt and gave
Roosevelt a snappy salute, Scott following suit.
"Well done, gentlemen. Scott, you're learning, letting your
Lieutenant win the footrace. You're off company punishment
as of now. Will you be good enough to watch our backtrail and
let us talk," Roosevelt ordered good-naturedly. Scott breathed
a sigh of relief that he hadn't been indiscreet, pleased that the
two officers had planned this meeting.

On the return trip Teddy dropped out short of camp with the
Lieutenant chuckling as he warned Scott, "Forget we saw
Colonel Roosevelt, and you'd better run for the next couple of
days – until we leave for Tampa Bay." Scott's reward for
silence was confirmation of the rumor he'd heard today –
another secret to keep.

* * * * *

Although the train's passenger cars were splendid accommodations compared to the Arizona trip with open cars, it was
still crowded. Albert was the only Oregonian assigned a seat
along with Corporals Jess, Carl, and Slim. Privates sat or slept
in the aisle except when friends would loan seats to them.

Scott smiled ruefully as he perched on the caboose's iron
railing and watched the countryside roll by. He thought hu-
morously, *Here I am, out in the open air and wondering why I
ever complained about the trip from Cactus Junction. And
there's another bayou off to the gulf side of the tracks, or
maybe I ought to say a swamp now that we're in Florida. Back
home folks would call it a pond or a creek or something.
Funny how I miss our Sixes ranch when I was so eager to get
away. Is it June already?*

"A penny for your thoughts, Scott," came the familiar voice
of Lieutenant Reynolds standing in the open door behind him.

"Just thinking of home, sir. My family's probably harvesting the first crop of hay, and Grandpa is sure to be fishing
along the river in the evenings. He claims age has its prerog-
atives, but he always lets me tag along – when I'm home, that
is," Scott replied nostalgically.

The officer stepped to the rail beside Scott and reminisced briefly, "It was my uncle who took me bass fishing since my father was not one to hunt or fish. Dad played with me almost every day, particularly card games. I'm a fair hand in a poker game. Dad claims that's how he met Teddy Roosevelt, although Mom insists it was in a proper setting – a Republican Party dinner."

The two men lapsed into a comfortable silence, a casual friendship present between the young Oregon volunteer and the mature career army officer. The Lieutenant sighed as another scenic bayou passed from view, remembering to inform Scott of an assignment, "By the way, Colonel Roosevelt wants you to be his runner when we land in Cuba. Welcome to the signal corps, Private McClure."

Scott grinned broadly as he glanced at his sober commander and remarked hopefully, "Gladly, sir, as long as we see a little action against the Spaniards."

"Never fear that you'll be anywhere but at the front, my daring young friend. Teddy Roosevelt will lead his troops into action just like Colonel Wood. They're officers to follow, believe me."

* * * * *

Bernie tossed his mess tin to the ground in disgust, his disgruntled curse receiving concurring nods from his comrades in their bivouacs, "Damn beans! That's all we've had since we arrived in Florida. Beans last night and beans before daylight."

Scott glanced at an empty tin before teasing his friend, "But I see you ate every bite, Bernie. Besides, everyone has been eating the same food these past two days."

"Yes, but this camp is nine miles from Tampa, and we're stuck here. Army Regulars are going aboard ships today, even those Buffalo Soldiers left this morning," Bernie griped.

Always ready to harp on the hypocrisy of the army command, Jess's laugh sounded like a sneer as he complained, "I bet the brass don't have to eat beans everyday. Particularly that fat General Shafter, who called us 'volunteers' like we are poor cousins or something. Hmph! He reminded me of that lying Arizona mayor with the pretty daughter."

"Enough Corporal Killbride, or you'll be a private again," Sergeant Hokey admonished in a stern voice, his humorous grin spoiling the reprimand as he shook his head with perplexity, "Captain Case says pack up your gear and stand to muster beside the railroad tracks. Colonel Roosevelt is madder than a wet hen and planning to do something about it."

Scott quickly followed orders, trailing on Hokey's heels as they came upon a northbound coal train, slowing as its whistle sounded repetitively. Roosevelt had blocked the line and was even now riding "Little Texas" next to the cab. Teddy swung directly into the cab from his mount, his hand signaling the Rough Riders into action. Tom Case led his troops aboard the last two cars, a clean caboose and a gritty coal car.

The men didn't question how Colonel Roosevelt coerced a ride nine miles back to the docks, but they loved him for taking the bit in his teeth and making a decision. Tom Case was first to debark, his men following eagerly, only one complaint heard about leaving their horses in camp.

That gripe was silenced when Colonel Roosevelt rode up and answered in a gruff voice, "Better to fight as infantry than to be left behind. Captain Case, get your men up to that gangplank and hold the way open for the other companies. The Yucatan will be ours by right of possession. Let the Regulars worry about berths for a change. Navy mess and soft bunks will be our reward for forthright action. Hurry now, the train is getting underway north again."

* * * * *

Scott ignored the curses of the men sandwiched about him, his thoughts turning inward as he watched evening shadows fall over Tampa Bay. *Hrmph! Hurry up and wait! We've been aboard this sardine tin for a week. I hear a different rumor every day about sailing dates. A few days ago our escort ships left the harbor and our ship's engines turned over, but we didn't go anywhere. Below deck is insufferable during the daytime, yet there's not enough room for all of us on deck. Nothing to do but swelter all day and air out the troops' quarters when it cools. No one can leave ship because the generals are scared of desertions. Of course, I'm lucky because Lieutenant*

Reynolds has taken me ashore several times to run with him. He claims my legs need to be in shape when we get to Cuba, but I suspect he's just being a nice guy.

"Case's company to quarters! Hey, Scott, any of our troops up forward with you?" called Albert from amidships.

Scott looked about, seeing only Carl and Bernie, both making their way to his cousin. He pointed to his comrades, responding with, "We're on our way, Albert."

He followed the three troopers down passageways into the bowels of the transport, hearing Captain Case's voice as soon as he entered their wardroom, "...and don't be discouraged by the long wait. Our fleet is prepared to take on any Spanish battlewagons in Cuban waters. We should be leaving port within the week. Remember the slogan we've all been shouting, Sergeant Hokey yelled out, "All together, Arizona Company..."

A chorus erupted in their cramped quarters, "To hell with Spain! Remember the Maine!" The cheer drowned any low spirits left over from the sweltering day. Arizona Company was ready.

* * * * *

Scott awoke to the ship's tremble, signifying the start of her powerful engines. Without pausing to consider other possibilities, he rushed topside to view their departure from Tampa Bay.

Sure enough, naval escort ships were lined up, steaming across the bay, and transports were getting underway. His ship's lines were cast off, and with the help of a tug, she was soon in the midst of the fleet moving into the Gulf of Mexico. The Fifth Corps was headed for Cuba.

Hours stretched into days as the ships sailed southerly, passing the diminutive Key West before changing course to the east. Rumors of landing in Havana died slowly, even after they were well beyond its harbor. Daily gossip was of little concern to many of the men, lying seasick in their bunks, Bernie and Jack-Jack included. Albert, Billy and Scott vied for the first sight of land. Each won a mark for seeing Cuba, only to watch it pass behind the venturing fleet. One night their progress was slowed by cross-seas, and when dawn flared astern, Scott knew they were at the south coast of the island.

Albert was envious as he said, "Being company clerk is a pain, Cousin. I have to return to that stinking wardroom and fill out reports. You're lucky to be a private, and free to watch for our landing place."

Scott chuckled as he retorted, "Yeah, but I didn't even get out to that saloon in San Antonio where Teddy bought everyone a beer, or have a seat on the troop train, or..."

"All right! All right! So my rank has a few privileges. Lieutenant Reynolds has assigned you as Teddy's runner because you're so well trained. Ha! Ha!" Albert chided, getting in an added jibe as he left, "You'll miss all the action, Cousin!"

Scott frowned as he mulled over the last barb, half-believing action might be elsewhere. He wanted to fight beside his friends, not run messages back to the generals. Well maybe Colonel Roosevelt would release him when the fighting started in Cuba. At any rate they should reach their destination very soon, the island's shoreline was becoming more visible as they sailed toward it at an oblique angle.

Chapter Five

Amid the hubbub of Daquiri's small mercado, Scott received only a few curious glances from local shoppers as he ran down the street toward the embarcadero. He veered across an empty lot toward the American flag flying over the customs building where regimental headquarters was situated. His message pouch was slung over his shoulder and flapped against his left side while a non-standard Colt Bisley 38 banged his right hip – a loan from Slim. His uniform was standard and freshly laundered, an armband designating him as a courier.

He slowed to a walk as he approached the Officer of the Day, who happened to be his old nemesis from Camp Wood – the upset Captain. Coming to attention as he halted, he snapped a precise salute, and controlling his gasps of breath, announced, "Private McClure, sir, carrying dispatches for Colonel Roosevelt."

The Captain saluted in a casual manner, eyeing the message pouch held by Scott, and with a smirk on his lips, ordered, "Very well, McClure. Give me the dispatches, and I'll see the Colonel gets them."

"Sir, my orders are to hand these messages to Colonel Roosevelt in person. With all due respect, Captain, my orders are specific," Scott replied solemnly, determination overriding his apprehension. It was clear the Captain was being a martinet once again, probably to embarrass him before the guards standing watch along the portico.

"McClure, I'll have no..." the Captain was interrupted by Roosevelt's jocular voice coming from the doorway, and Scott was saved from the tongue-lashing everyone was expecting.

"There you are, Private McClure. Come ahead, I've been waiting for those dispatches. Was there any sign of the Spanish army across town?"

Scott walked around the Captain and saluted his commander, unslinging his pouch and handing it to Roosevelt after he returned the greeting. He replied, "No sir! I saw some of our Buffalo Soldiers and several Cuban rebels patrolling north of town, but there wasn't a Spanish uniform in sight. The local people seem to be out today, shopping and visiting, and ignoring the war."

"Thank you, Scott. Colonel Wood has an urgent dispatch for that Negro Regiment's commander. Are you up for a return run?" Teddy asked, stepping into his spartan office. Motioning to a mess tray on his desk, he offered, "Grab a bite while I read my messages."

A moment later he slipped a paper into Scott's pouch, adding a caution as he handed it back, "Be careful, my boy, I hear there's a sniper or two hiding up there."

* * * * *

Chest heaving in exertion and sweat staining his clean shirt, Scott slowed to a walk as he approached a squad of Buffalo Soldiers in a street intersection. Accosting their gray-haired and competent-looking leader who was watching him with curiosity, he spoke courteously, "Hello, Sergeant. Can you direct me to your Regimental Commander?"

Nodding deferentially but without timidity, the Negro replied, "Colonel Halsey is in those trees beyond the villa at the end of the road – two of three hundred yards straight ahead. Be careful with the sentry – he's a young lad and a bit nervous."

Scott smiled his appreciation and responded, "Thanks, Sergeant. Have a good day!"

Hesitating a split second, the veteran offered another friendly caution, "There's a sniper in the area, but we can't catch him."

Scott nodded with understanding, waving a casual farewell as he resumed his trot, almost forgetting the Sergeant's words until a buzz sounded near his right ear, the thud of a bullet hitting a palm tree meshing with a rifle shot. Belatedly startled, he jumped up the narrowing lane, smiling grimly at his reaction to being ambushed.

An inane thought crossed his mind, *Well, I reckon Lieutenant Reynolds was right; any bullet I can hear isn't meant for me. Hope the squad finds that sniper before I head back down the hill.*

"Halt, who's there?" came a shaky and southern-accented challenge at the edge of the woods.

"Message for Colonel Halsey from Colonel Roosevelt," Scott announced as he froze in place, suddenly feeling as nervous as the young Negro recruit looked. The rifle waving in Scott's direction was discomfiting.

"Corporal of the Guard!" croaked the jittery sentry, gulping visibly before he remembered to add, "Post Number Two," and stood trembling with his awesome responsibility.

A Negro officer responded first, an oddity to Scott who had never met one before. He saluted properly, receiving a return gesture promptly, a corporal standing to the side, as he ordered, "Return to your post, Number Two."

Nodding to Scott, he said, "I'm Lieutenant Jefferson, Private. Follow the Corporal, and he'll take you to Colonel Halsey."

Scott replied, "Yes, sir," and soon stood before a white officer, exchanging salutes and delivering his dispatch. The officer read the message and dismissed Scott, "No reply necessary, Private. Be careful of snipers on your return to headquarters."

Hustling into the narrow lane beside the white stucco villa, Scott kept his eyes open for danger as he began a zigzag trot to the harbor. He spotted the Negro soldier on the grounds around the prominent casa, with the Sergeant in a heated argument with a beautiful young woman before the front door. Her olive-toned cheeks were flushed and her dark eyes flashed with spirit, her tirade in Spanish vehemently denying him entry to her casa.

Having slowed to a walk to become a spectator, Scott's presence did not go unnoticed. The Sergeant waved him over to the portico, almost pleading for help, "The shot at you came from this villa, but this lady refuses to allow a Negro into her house. Would you enter and search the residence for a sniper?"

The lovely young lady smiled charmingly at Scott, ignoring the Sergeant as she spoke in well-articulated English, "Sí Señor, you are welcome to enter my home, but no one else. This casa is the home of Doctor Ricardo Chavez, a respected citizen of Daquiri and a Cuban patriot."

"Gracias, Señorita Chavez. If you will lead the way, please," Scott accepted with a half-bow in deference to the lady.

Spinning on her heel, the Chavez woman promenaded through the parlor, continuing through the lower floor rooms until she arrived in a large kitchen. Scott was attentive to details as he followed her, finally pointing to a servant's stairwell set in the far wall. A girl bounded down the steps, seating herself near the bottom and studying the intruder with curiosity.

Her coloring and features marked her as another Chavez daughter, albeit more open. *Perhaps even more disarming than her sister*, was his thought.

She rose with youthful exuberance to offer her hand as she chattered in English equal to her sister's, "Hello, I'm Maria, Anita's little sister. Are you an American officer? Where are you from? Can I show you the upper floor bedrooms?"

"No, Señorita Maria, not an officer but just a plain soldier from Oregon. My name is Scott McClure, and I'd be pleased to see the upstairs, even though I must apologize for our intrusion. By the way, you both speak English very well," Scott remarked as Anita led the way up the stairwell.

Scott sensed the Chavez sisters' nervousness until they were in the upper hallway, and then both entertained him with a pleasant three-way conversation. As they descended the broad stairway leading down to the foyer, Maria smiled goodbye and stayed above, a more confident Anita wrapping her arm about his elbow as she maneuvered him to the door and announced, "Thank you for being a gentleman, Señor McClure. Perhaps you will call when my father is home and when you are not acting as a conquering soldier."

Scott nodded agreeably, allowing himself to be led outside as he admired her beauty, finally bidding farewell, "Adios, Señorita Anita. I'm sorry we upset you. I look forward to calling upon your family in more genial conditions."

He walked around the house to find the Sergeant talking to one of his soldiers. The veteran nodded to Scott as he commented, "Eddie reports there are no snipers on the grounds, and I expect you'll tell me the same about the house."

"Don't look so frustrated, Sergeant. Only the two charming Chavez daughters are in residence, but I still believe you're right about that shot coming from here," Scott declared, adding thoughtfully, "There's something fishy going on. The sisters were nervous in the kitchen area, and the scullery maid was missing even as food was cooking on the stove – and the ladies' hands were neat and clean. I believe Anita Chavez stalled you at the door to give the maid time to lead the sniper away."

"How could that be? My men saw no one leave."

"Hmm, what's under the house? Does a fancy villa have a root cellar? I saw no door to such a room, but part of the kitchen floor sounded different to my step. The ladies kept talking when I was in that area and didn't relax until we were in the upstairs hallway. I expect we should watch the family closely. In fact, I can help. Señorita Chavez extended a social invitation for me to visit when her father is in. I suspect her charm was to get me out of the way, but I could come back as a suitor."

"Ha! Ha! Now I suspect your motive. I think that lady made eyes at you, but your offer has possibilities. Call on the Chavez family before dark, and we'll watch the villa until then. Maybe we'll uncover something," the Sergeant connived.

* * * * *

Scott appeared late afternoon at the Chavez portico with the Sergeant's assurance no one had come or gone except for the father who was now at home. He wore a clean uniform and held a bouquet of flowers which he'd purchased outside the quiet mercado. A middle-aged, dumpy woman in maid's clothing answered his knock, raising a questioning brow as she asked, "Qué pasa?"

"Will you tell Señorita Chavez that Private McClure wishes to present his apologies and these flowers?"

A deep bass voice sounded from the darkening interior, "Consuela, escort Mr. McClure into the parlor."

A well-dressed and handsome Cuban met Scott at the room's entrance, his smile framed by a pencil-thin mustache and trimmed goatee, both showing a tinge of gray to match his sideburns. He extended his hand to greet Scott, "Welcome to my home. Consuela, take the flowers to Anita's room. I'm sorry Mr. McClure, but my daughter is resting after the stress of this day, but your apology is not really necessary. Both of my daughters reported that your gentlemanly behavior was exemplary. I'm just glad you Yankees are here rather than those dreadful rebels. I'm proud to be a loyalist, even though I don't expect Americans to approve of my politics."

"You have every right to believe as you like, Doctor Chavez, but your family resides in Daquiri, which is occupied by our troops. Your loyalist sentiments are common knowledge, but when a shot was fired at me in the lane before your villa, you can understand my concern," Scott ventured, pausing when he heard a footfall in the hallway.

Maria entered the parlor, her face mirroring anxiety as she blurted, "Scott, you were the target? Oh, I'm so sorry, we won't let it happen again…I mean…oh…," and dumbfounded by the implication of her outburst, she broke into confused tears.

Scott smiled wistfully, ignoring both her words and her tears as he said, "Sniping by Spanish soldiers is a risk we take in war, but my friends, Cuban citizens are not soldiers and must not harbor snipers."

Doctor Chavez glared at Scott for several seconds, affronted by Scott's lack of tact in the brief speech. Putting a hand on his daughter's arm to keep her silence, he finally spoke, "You are very blunt, Private McClure, but I feel no threat in your words. I will heed both your friendly warning and Maria's wishes. You are welcome in my casa, señor."

"And I will tell the Sergeant that his men may return to their bivouacs in the woods. Thank you for your hospitality, Señor Chavez, Señorita Maria. Please give my regards to Señorita Anita," Scott stated somberly as he rose to his feet to take his leave.

Feeling the gentle touch of Maria's fingers on his arm, he took them in his hand, bowing to brush his lips across them, feeling foolish at trying to be a gentleman until he saw the approval in her eyes. Her smile became teasing as he murmured, "Good evening, Señorita Maria. Perhaps you will give me a tour of the entire house on my next visit."

* * * * *

The next morning Scott was returning from delivering several dispatches, including orders for the Buffalo Soldiers to support the Rough Riders at the crossroads known as Las Guasimas on the road to Santiago. He argued unsuccessfully with Lieutenant Reynolds to rejoin his unit, unable to make the same request of the venerable Teddy Roosevelt. Continuing his courier duties as the Fifth Army Corps advanced toward Santiago, Scott was privy to all the news – both dispatches and gossip. He never read a single message, but everyone assumed he knew their contents and talked before him. Most disturbing was the first casualties report, where Captain Capron and a fellow named Fish were shot dead. Scott remembered both men visiting Lieutenant Reynolds in Florida. As he recalled, their families were friends, and he managed to take the sad news to his officer friend.

Scott had seen the Chavez sisters in the mercado on one occasion, the dour maid Consuela acting as their duenna. He enjoyed talking to the ladies, and though conversation was stilted, their smiles were friendly. It was Maria who remembered that he was from Oregon and told him a ship by that name had arrived offshore. Anita shushed her sister, making Scott think that the Chavez family knew a lot about the war for plain civilians.

Hearing the distant thunder of artillery, Scott raced up the road toward El Pozo, believing the advance against the fortification atop the San Juan Heights had begun. He slipped past the familiar guards without pausing, stopping beside Colonel Roosevelt, belatedly saluting as he handed his pouch to the new Regimental Commander. Colonel Wood had been assigned a general's duties, and Shafter had reluctantly promoted Teddy, or so the rumor mill had it. Regular army generals hated to give volunteers any credit in the campaign, but Roosevelt and the Rough Riders were one and the same. They would be fighting side by side with Regulars tomorrow.

"At ease, Private McClure. Scott, tell me the news you've heard from the troops. I think your gossip is better than official dispatches most of the time. Go ahead, I can read and listen at the same time."

"Sir, the men are eager to fight although yellow fever is around. Lots of soldiers are ill but still want to stay with their outfits. Are soldiers usually so cheerful before a battle?" Scott poses rhetorically, continuing his report when Teddy glanced up, "Division artillery is pounding the Spanish fort near El Caney. Are the Rough Riders going into action?"

"Yes, but the Division is attacking El Caney, and we have another fortification to tackle. I suppose you'd like to rejoin your company. Do you know where they are?"

"Yes, sir, I can find them. By your leave, Colonel Roosevelt," Scott saluted and moved away, Teddy already issuing orders to his adjutant. Running with armband in place, he exchanged friendly waves as men recognized him, no challenge slowing his progress. He finally came upon his troop in bivouacs, Captain Case calmly drinking coffee beside the cook's fire as he talked to a half-dozen obviously sick men, including Jack-Jack and Bernie.

"Ah, McClure, there you are. Any message from our new Commander? Or are you here to fight by our side?" Case queried with a companionable smile.

"No message, sir. The Colonel released me back to my company. Everyone seems to be on the move, Captain," Scott reported as he stripped the messenger's band from his arm.

"Yes, Lawson's troops are attacking El Caney on our right flank, but our regiment hasn't received orders yet. I heard our objective will be Kettle Hill in the San Juan Heights. There's a major fort on top," Case said as he regarded his friends, concluding, "I'm glad you're all with us to fight the coming battle. You'd better rest while you can, you'll need your strength by morning, I bet."

Jack-Jack was pale with the camp illness, and Bernie wasn't much better with his big frame appearing gaunt. The seven volunteers walked down the company street to find their bunkmates, Scott supporting his two shaking friends. He managed to trade the Bisley for his rifle in passing Slim's tent, greeting Billy in the next tent with enthusiasm. *It feels good to be "home"* was his errant thought before he drifted off to sleep.

* * * * *

Awakening abruptly in the pitch-black night, Scott muttered, "Huh!" and felt a hand shaking his shoulder. Albert's whispered voice near his ear ordered, "Wake Billy and join me at the campfire. We're going on patrol at daybreak."

Dragging his groggy and yawning friend along the path toward the campfire was a chore, especially so when Scott was being quiet. Billy whispered, more in secrecy than in courtesy, "I don't know why everyone's so eager to fight. I'm kind of scared, myself. How about you, Scott?"

"Yes, scared and excited both, but still ready to go into battle. I wonder if I'll be a good soldier. The real question is when do we attack?"

Scott quit talking as they neared the Captain, observing Slim and his squad drifting stealthily into the darkness west of camp, while Jess Killbride's squad moved northerly.

Tom Case didn't waste any breath in giving further orders, "Sergeant Lee, you three head east to the division lines and then scout north. McClure can help find our troops, I know, but I need to know where the Spanish positions are when we move out this morning. A quiet reconnaissance is what I want, Lee. No shooting if you can avoid it."

Following Albert's hand signal, Scott led the way along a trail becoming more visible as daylight arrived. Five minutes later a voice challenged them, "Halt, who goes there?"

Scott immediately answered, "McClure of the Arizona Company with two comrades. May we advance?"

An authoritative voice granted permission, "Come ahead to be identified, McClure. I'm Sergeant Halloway of D Company. We met when you were running dispatches."

Halloway nodded as he saw Scott, waving his comrades forward as well. Albert introduced himself, "I'm Sergeant Lee. We're scouting the division's flank for Spanish positions."

"I heard you might be joining the attack today," Sergeant Halloway commented, then pointed to a heavy shadow in the distance before adding, "Our scouts went as far as those woods without spotting a Spaniard, but be careful up there because it's not far to the stone fort we were bombarding yesterday."

As the three men moved ahead, Halloway called in low tones, "I heard Teddy was leading the Rough Riders charge today. Good luck!"

Albert waved in reply and stepped in front of Scott, waving him toward the division's line in case they met another sentry. Light had improved by the time they neared the woods, Scott's eyes searching the scrub brush to their right while Albert scrambled behind a protective tree stump.

Scott's glance picked out movement behind the brush, a white shirt briefly seen sure to be the enemy. He called urgently to his comrades, "Get down! I see a …"

A pair of shots rang out, Billy and Scott returning fire at muzzle flashes in the forest before the thud of a bullet striking flesh was recognized. The moan of a wounded man brought Scott to his cousin's side, Billy continuing to answer Spanish rifle fire. He discovered Albert doubled over behind the stump, blood pulsing from a neck wound. The critical head wound was visible, and his cousin's eyes were open and lifeless. A blind rage stiffened Scott's resolve as he and Billy rose to meet the charge of a dozen Spanish soldiers.

Ignoring the buzzing of bullets, Scott faced the enemy with a measured yet ferocious attack of his own, other American rifles joining the fray. A vicious blow struck Scott's leg, spinning him into a tree, wondering what had happened. He soon realized he had been shot, pain breaking through the numb shock, but he continued to fire his rifle. A second flash of agony stabbed his chest, and he lost consciousness, unaware that Billy was carrying him to safety.

Chapter Six

Awareness came slowly to the comatose soldier lying inert on the hospital bed in Daquiri, the quiet murmur of voices punctuated by a shrill scream coming from a newly arrived amputee. The gentle touch of a cool cloth bathed his brow as he sensed light beyond his closed lids – which refused to budge. In a far corner of the consciousness, a flicker of humor kindled the heretofore dormant soul, *I'm so weak I can't even lift an eyelid. But I remember who I am, Scott McClure, and I was shot helping Albert near El Caney.* This thought soon joined other more momentary flashes of cognition into Scott's dream world.

* * * * *

Lying quietly in the dim room, Scott's eyes found the only source of light in the large room, the lantern's smoked chimney and smoldering wick far from his bed. As his gaze took in the somnolent scene, he studied a dark-haired woman dozing in the chair beside his bed, cloth in hand but face turned away. Scott was feeling pretty good until he tackled the seemingly gargantuan task of turning his head toward his nurse. His strength was nil and his shoulder heavily wrapped in a restraining bandage. His mind pictured the girl beside him as lovely Anita Chavez, and he muttered her name as he slipped into a melancholy dream.

* * * * *

He awoke in daylight to find Consuela feeding him broth, one small spoonful at a time. He watched with hooded lids until she realized he was awake.

She called to her mistress, "Señorita!" and Scott saw the
Chavez features on the girl across the way, falling asleep with a
muttered "Anita."

* * * * *

Bernie's familiar voice was at his side, urging him to wake
up and eat. The burly logger took Scott's hand in a surprisingly
gentle grasp and repeated his plea until his eyes opened, "Come
on, my friend, wake up. The nurse says I can feed you a bowl
of real food. Here, try a bite. I had some earlier. Nothing like
bean soup to get your strength back."

Bernie came around the bed, lifting the patient's head from
the right side, ladling the thick liquid into his mouth. He
chuckled in good humor as Scott took the nourishment with
gusto, optimism riding his assurances, "You'll live, lad.
Although I've seen you look better. You can handle meat tomorrow."

Scott pushed the spoon away finally, and taking a breath, he
answered faintly, "Aye, but how am I? And why are you here?
Is Albert dead?"

A more somber Bernie, replied, "One subject at a time, my
friend. Yes, Albert was killed before you were shot, or so Billy
says. He saved your life, you know – a real hero. He's with
the company up on San Juan Heights, where the big battle was
won by Teddy Roosevelt's Rough Riders."

"Jack-Jack?" Scott sobbed weakly, in distress but obviously needing to know about his friends.

"Sorry, lad, I don't know. He's been missing since Arizona
Company's first fight, and nobody has any idea what happened
to him. Billy's asked around the battlefield and I've checked
out the hospitals, but no luck. We both had the ague in
bivouac, and when I passed out, Billy and Jack-Jack loaded me
into an ambulance. Then the company moved forward to fight
its first skirmish, and Billy never saw Jack-Jack again."

Bernie paused before continuing regretfully, "I don't think
we'll ever know, Scott. And more bad news, Tom Case was
killed storming Kettle Hill. Lieutenant Reynolds assumed
command and was wounded slightly but still led the charge.
Teddy brevetted him to captain and gave him the Purple Heart

and a commendation. The Lieutenant…er Captain will be here tomorrow to see the doctor. I bet he looks you up."

"What about me?"

Bernie grinned now, expressing confidence as he explained, "You have two bullet wounds, with your right leg all but healed. It's this left shoulder that's causing you problems, but Doctor Chavez promised you'd be as good as new in a few weeks. You're scheduled to go home in a couple of days on a hospital ship – if you're strong enough. I expect…you need your rest…"

Bernie was interrupted by Scott's murmur, "Anita?" and silently straightened the sheet over Scott's sleeping form before walking out of the ward and on to rejoin his comrades at the front.

* * * * *

Scott woke with a clear mind and a ravenous hunger, his head actually rising from the pillow before he realized how weak and infirm he was. A hooded Catholic sister hastened to his bedside, rapid-fire Spanish accompanying her ministrations, a damp cloth caressing his brow, a sip of water delivered to his lips, and a fluffing of his pillow. Weakness not to be discounted, Scott lifted his shaking right hand to his mouth and motioned for food, the effort draining what little strength he possessed.

The nun's wrinkled countenance broke into a beatific smile of understanding, her plain face brightening happily as she chattered on. Maria Chavez appeared at her elbow carrying a steaming bowl of food, and thanking the old sister, the girl settled into the chair by his bed.

"Good morning, Señor McClure. You are much better today, I see, and ready to eat some real meat. I expect this stew will be more satisfying than the bean soup I fed you yesterday."

"Good! I'm hungry," Scott croaked agreeably, his vocal chords stiff with disuse. He said no more as Maria fed him spoonfuls of beef stew, plus a running commentary on hospital affairs and the war's progress. *Her English is as good as mine,* he thought, *and getting better with practice. She's pretty too, and maybe not such a little girl at that.*

Doctor Chavez appeared behind his daughter with a handful of fresh bandages, smiling at his alert patient. He exhibited good humor in greeting Scott, "I see you are much better now, visiting with your nurse. Did you eat your food, Mister McClure?"

"Yes, thanks to Maria. How did you come to work in an American army hospital?" Scott asked in curiosity.

The doctor grinned amiably and replied, "A good reason, or maybe two, if we count Maria. When she heard you were here, she appointed herself as your guardian angel. I had no choice but to keep her company. And, of course, I had another reason. I don't get along with the rebels at all. In fact, they threatened us at our villa after Anita ran away with her Spanish lieutenant. You know, they were married in Santiago before he was wounded in the battle for San Juan Heights. Actually he is a good man, but fortunately a poor sniper. I expect they will be evacuated to Spain any day, now that the fighting is almost over. Probably he will be stationed in Morocco if his orders are unchanged when they reach Spain. I regret losing a daughter, but she is happy."

Scott's confusion was clear to both father and daughter as he queried, "But Anita was just here, wasn't she?"

Maria flushed with embarrassment as she explained, "You called for Anita several times, but she was never here. You mistook me for my beautiful sister. I'm only two years younger, but the gentlemen all called on her."

"Bless you, Maria. You are beautiful, too," Scott murmured as he dozed off, missing the brilliant smile his words had elicited.

* * * * *

During the ensuing days Scott ate heartily, and his wounds healed rapidly. Long conversations with Maria cheered his progress, and when she missed consecutive days, he found himself in a foul mood. The old nun explained in her rapid-fire Spanish that Doctor Chavez was not present either, but there were two soldiers in the hospital to see him.

While translating her words in his mind or at least puzzling over their meaning, he spotted Billy and Captain Reynolds entering the wardroom. Billy rushed forward to grasp Scott's outstretched hand, while the officer smiled a greeting, laying his left fingers on the clasped hands of the two Oregonians. The Captain's right wrist was wrapped in a fresh bandage and carried in a cavalry bandanna fashioned into a sling.

"How's everybody, sir? Is your arm going to be all right?" Scott asked his new company commander.

"I'm fine, Scott. This would be free of bandages if Doctor Chavez were here. Say, you look better than the last time I stood by your bedside. Your friends will be glad to hear you're recovering. Our company is in bivouac outside Daquiri, with the Regulars doing all the fighting now. I hear that the division will be in Santiago any day, and we can all go home before the end of July," Captain Reynolds said.

Billy inserted his report during the pause, "No one's seen Jack-Jack, but a medic remembered loading a wounded Indian aboard a hospital ship. The soldier was named Jack though – not Jack-Jack."

Captain Reynolds added his optimistic support, "Our Killed In Action Report didn't list Private Sixes, and the company adjutant says he isn't in any hospital in Cuba, so he may well be in Tampa already. I'll send a letter of inquiry through the military command, but I bet Doctor Chavez could get a message through medical channels faster. Where is Ricardo?"

Scott blurted out his concern forthwith, "Maria isn't here either. There may be trouble with rebels who know they're loyalists. Could you go by their villa? Maybe talk to the rebels?"

Reynolds nodded decisively as he agreed, "Of course we will. Let's go, Billy, and call on the Chavez family."

* * * * *

At breakfast the next morning, Maria appeared with his meal, informing Scott, "Your friends talked to the rebels in the woods near our villa. I believe they will leave us alone, at least while your army is here. Father is talking of leaving Cuba and working for your army – maybe a hospital ship. Times are very uncertain for loyalists with the Spanish army all but beaten."

Scott listened to the girl as he consumed every bite of breakfast, the two friends continuing to visit regularly as he recuperated. Billy brought a couple of dog-eared newspapers for the patient to read, while Bernie sneaked in a half-pint of local rum. The three friends promptly toasted the Rough Riders, much to the disapproval of the elderly Spanish nun, whose harangue soon drove the two friends away.

Teddy Roosevelt chose a bright, sunny day to visit the hospital, stopping by each bed with a word or two for every wounded man. He called Scott by his first name and asked if he was ready to go home, now that the Spaniards had surrendered.

Scott quickly replied, "Sure, Colonel, or back to the regiment if I'm needed."

His attitude earned him one of Teddy's toothy grins and a comradely slap on the leg, fortunately Scott's uninjured limb. Moments after the Colonel and his aides had departed, Billy, Carl, Jess, and Bufe appeared with a stretcher, Billy waving a sheet of paper at the ward nurse and calling out, "Scott, there's a hospital ship bound for Savannah in the harbor. We're going to take you down to the dock and put you aboard it. Are you ready to go home?"

"Sure! If you'll pack my gear in a bag for me. My shoulder's still sore, but my leg is fair. It holds my weight anyway. Where's Bernie?"

Talking as he worked, Billy replied, "With Captain Reynolds in Santiago. He's the muscle in the Captain's escort, and Slim's the pistolera. He said to say goodbye. He'll see you in Drain."

* * * * *

Scott was sitting erect in the bow of a small boat still tied to the dock when the hospital ship weighed anchor and departed. The bo'sun's mate dispatching the wounded signaled with no avail, handing the medical records of all five patients back to Billy with a shrug, and walking away from the problem.

The petty officer in command of the floating ambulance saw the disappointment of his charges and showed more gumption than his boss, declaring, "The hell with it, lads.

We'll just put you aboard that transport offshore. I hear your regiment is going home next week anyway. The ship's doctor will take care of you. Can one of you soldiers help us?"

Billy volunteered immediately, "I'll go with these men's medical records and lend the doctor a hand. Carl, will you tell our company clerk to send our pay records out to the ship? Unless Captain Reynolds objects, I'll stay aboard and assist the doctor."

* * * * *

Scott stumbled onto the platform, grasping a steel railing with his strong right hand, and then shuffled to the waiting ambulance where he sat mulling over his own thoughts. *Golly, three days in Daquiri harbor and four days of sailing to Tampa, plus the train ride north to Montauk make it August already. It was nice of Colonel Roosevelt to invite everyone to a celebration on Long Island. A lot of men are recuperating here in camp before discharge from the army. I wonder if Captain Reynolds is right when he says Teddy is a big enough hero to be elected president. It would be kind of exciting to say I was the President's personal trainer – and dispatch runner in the war.*

Billy ran up to the ambulance, panting as he reported, "Come on, Scott. If you can walk to that headquarters building over there, we'll be mustered out immediately and paid $68.50 each. The train to New York City leaves in an hour, and we'll get a special fare to Seattle if we hurry."

Billy had worked out their schedule on the train journey north, his only concern in Scott's haste to leave the hospital was his friend's shoulder, "Your leg is strong enough to travel according to the doctor, but he's worried about the shoulder healing. Should we stay in Montauk a few days?"

"This sling suits me fine. Makes me look like a war hero. You know as well as I do that our war pay is barely enough to get us home, so let's buy the Captain a beer like I promised," Scott concluded in high humor. He was glad to be back in America and about to be a civilian again.

* * * * *

Beautiful weather graced the Puget Sound as the Northern Pacific train pulled into King Street Station in Seattle. The two travelers had wearied of the long rail journey across country and decided to walk the streets of the bustling metropolis – the gateway to the Klondike gold strike. Scott's leg was almost as good as new, and his left shoulder was healed but weak. He still needed a sling to ease the strain when he did use his left arm. With that colorful sling and their brown uniforms they made a patriotic picture, particularly when Scott limped a little.

Not averse to benefiting from their status as Rough Rider veterans, Scott and Billy accepted first-class treatment at a waterfront restaurant. Sitting with a view of Elliot Bay and its busy docks and paying a ridiculously low price for Olympia oysters, they satisfied the curiosity of fellow diners by answering questions, and when treated to a stein of beer, telling tales of the Cuban War.

They spoke fondly of Teddy Roosevelt, already a genuine American hero to those gathered about them, and didn't bother to correct the fanciful newspaper accounts of the Battle of San Juan Hill. Instead Billy included Kettle Hill into the growing legend and related the July First battle with Scott bravely repelling the Spanish charge at daybreak. Albert Lee and Billy earned a little credit in supporting the hero's deed, but the story was not diluted by including Jess Killbride's sharpshooters nor the division soldiers.

A grizzled old sailor cackled his appreciation for a good yarn, walking to the door as he said, "I hate to miss the rest of your story, young man, but my packet is sailing away any minute. Say, would you fellows like a ride to Tacoma? You can catch the southbound train in the morning at Union Station."

* * * * *

The *Duwamish* left the Seattle dock fully laden with freight destined for stops in the south sound, but without two crewmembers. Scott offered to man the wheel, and Billy went below to stoke the furnace when the Captain bemoaned their desertion and cursed the Klondike. The two volunteers soon discovered their schedule included stops at Alki Point,

Redondo Beach, Dash Point, and Quartermaster Harbor before they'd reach Tacoma.

When Billy came topside for a breath of air and a breathtaking view of a golden-orange sunset over Vashon Island, he suggested, "Maybe we ought to help Captain Milsen tomorrow, too. Those two sailors jumped ship and left him in a lurch."

"Ha! Ha! Billy, the engineer just told me those two guys went north last week. Don't you feel like we've been sort of shanghaied? We're certainly cheap enough labor."

"Well, Pardner, we aren't in any hurry, and we can catch our train in Olympia. Room and board for a couple of days sounds good to me," Billy opined, ignoring Scott's reference to shanghaiing. A single expression of happiness on his face reflected his optimistic outlook on the adventure.

From above came the Captain's amused voice, "Well, have you decided? Will you stay aboard until we dock at Olympia?"

Scott nodded agreeably, and Billy eagerly replied, "Yes, sir! As long as we can spend the evening looking Tacoma over."

* * * * *

Scott and Billy had every intention of sailing with the *Duwamish* to Olympia, but fate intervened at a bar on Pacific Avenue. The packet's engineer had accompanied them up the bluff from Dock Street and had bought them a beer at his favorite tavern. As he left their company, he cautioned them to be aboard for the midnight departure. Several men heard the sailing announcement, but the two friends were blissfully unaware of the covert glances from four ne'er-do-wells slouched around a table in the dim corner.

Billy bought another round with the change in his pocket, Scott's groping left hand conveniently entangled in his sling as he chuckled, "I'll buy the next one, Billy."

Moments later Scott felt a gentle brush of feeling below his sling, not realizing it was a stranger's hand in his pocket until Billy shouted, "Watch it, Scott! This bugger's a pickpocket."

Scott spun violently about, his pants slipping as a ferret-faced small man reared back, Billy seizing the grasping paw to jerk the squeaking thief into Scott's clenched fist. A silver dollar bounced off the sawdust-covered floor, Billy once again quick to scoop it up and return to his friend's side before anyone else moved.

The wretched culprit crawled away, his malevolent-appearing comrades advancing ominously toward the two youngsters in soldiers' uniforms. The entire crowd looked menacing, not a friendly look from anyone, and Scott decided discretion was the better part of valor.

Deciding fortuitously to avoid a conflict, he held out his open palm to Billy, and accepting his silver dollar, slapped it open-handed on the bar, declaring, "Bartender, a round for our friends in the house, as long as that thief is shown the door."

Smiles appeared instantly, more than a few hands aiding the retreating pickpocket to the door and beyond, his three friends following docilely enough. Scott noted looks scurrilous enough to kill and kept the men in sight until the door closed. Within moments the barroom was back to normal, Scott and Billy relieved to be rid of the crooks.

Another stranger bumped against the slinged arm, a hasty explanation voiced by an old salt, "No! No! I'm not a pickpocket, lads, I'm a sailor off that three-master at the dock. I'll give you a bit of friendly advice, you being heroes of the Spanish-American War and all. Watch yourself on the way back to your ship, those cutthroats are likely to waylay you, and they'll want more than your purses. They have a bad reputation along Tacoma's waterfront, and you'll have to pass through their territory along Dock Street to reach your ship."

"Thanks, friend," Scott replied and added to Billy, "I guess we'd better get moving. Let's see if we can reach the Duwamish before those hoodlums are ready for us."

* * * * *

Billy crept down the steep slope with Indian-like stealthiness, scouting ahead of Scott who was favoring his left arm. They worked through the brush, staying clear of the cart path and walkway, believing their fellow sailor's warning. A low curse below them froze both veterans in their tracks.

A warehouse door had banged open, spilling a faint yellow glow across Dock Street and outlining several moving figures. Scott counted four men in the street, and with the curser on the lower hillside, he concluded they were outnumbered. He tapped Billy with his extended fingers, silently tugging back up the hill, giving up any hope of reaching the Duwamish. Union Station and the railroad yards seemed their best bet to avoid a one-sided fight. *Besides*, he thought, *we still have train tickets to Portland, and the railroad police may scare off these would-be thieves.*

As he topped the hill, he was struck by a charging ambusher, darkness saving him from a wild swinging tree branch. Scott reacted automatically, those months of military training proving useful as he dropped to his knees and spun his adversary over the edge of the bluff. Without worrying about that threat again, he called softly, "Run, Billy. Union Station is straight along Pacific Avenue."

A vehement curse sounded from the scrambling ambushers as he struggled back up the hill. Scott's fingers searched the ground for the club-branch, curling around its diameter with vengeance, and he hurled it straight at his assailant's position.

He trotted after Billy in the all-but-dark street, catching him within the block, both runners picking up their pace when voices behind them sounded the alarm. Scott moved ahead racing effortlessly toward the station's lights, only to see a pair of roughnecks cut in front of them a hundred feet ahead. He quickly swerved off Pacific and headed for the railyard itself, where a slow-moving freight train was heading toward Portland.

Eyes and ears attuned to the pursuing footfalls and occasional voices, Scott remembered a similar race in Los Angeles earlier in the year. He called softly, "Come on, Billy. There's an open car ahead, just like that old mail car."

Glancing over his shoulder, Scott recognized a shadowy figure closing in on Billy, and he reacted spontaneously. Bending low to grasp a rock, he slowed without breaking stride and flung his missile at the pursuing thief. As he heard a satisfactory thunk, he raced to the now speeding rail car and leaped after Billy into its dark maw. Fingers grasped one foot, but disappeared as he lashed out with his other, rolling over away from the door. He saw Billy kick a hand from the doorframe with a yell, "Stay out of our way!"

Scott and Billy guarded the entrance for several moments, not sure the gang of thieves was behind them. Finally another locomotive's headlights showed them milling about the yard, and the two friends relaxed, the clickety-clackety sound of wheels welcome. They were headed home for Oregon.

Chapter Seven

The two homeward-bound Rough Riders trudged along Portland's wet streets, heading for a warehouse where the Gerbrunn wagons often visited. The railroad had taken over most of the freighting in the Willamette Valley, but a few old-timers distrusted the new-fangled "Iron Horse." Uwe was only too happy to have their business and carried their drayage to the growing metropolis.

Scott's unerring memory worked like a compass, the two friends following a series of shortcuts from the railyards after they had jumped from the slow-moving freight train. Scott's wounds were declared healed when no pain was felt on the trip south. Their journey had also been without incident, not even at a short stop in Kalama when two chattering railroad police had passed their car.

As they came within view of their destination, they saw three wagons at the warehouse loading dock and renewed a more purposeful stride when they spotted a wagon fronted by two distinctive Gerbrunn horses. Almost trotting the last half block, they all but collided with the teamster coming around the tailgate, a sack of potatoes on his shoulder.

In surprise Scott exclaimed, "Don! I thought you were in the Klondike."

Don Gerbrunn grinned broadly, dropping his burlap sacks to hug his two friends, and then frowned as he replied, "Hah! So I should be, but I was robbed in Seattle by a pair of new 'friends' before I ever got aboard ship. Damned thieves even waved farewell from the deck of my steamer. I had to work a couple of months to earn fare home. Two men working together stand a better chance of getting to the Yukon."

Billy quickly agreed, sounding like a volunteer, "You're right, Don. I wouldn't mind going, but not alone."

Nodding with a calculating look in his eye, Don remembered the sad news from Cuba, "I'm sure sorry about

Albert and Jack-Jack. And I heard you were heroes, too. Tell me about the war."

Scott agreed, "Sure, if you give us the news of your family. Here, let us help you unload."

Don rambled on for several minutes, detailing happenings in the state, Salem and Port Orford at the crux of his report. Billy told the story of Albert's death and Jack-Jack's disappearance, and Scott related life from a hospital bed and their trip home. By the time they were talked out, the wagon was empty and the agent had handed Don a receipt.

As they stood beside the tailgate in repose, Don's voice rose a notch as that scheming glint returned to his eyes. He proposed in quizzical tones, "Dad gave me another purse, grubstake if you like, and I was going to catch today's train to Seattle, but our hired hand beat me to it. He sneaked off early this morning with a fellow we met coming into Portland. I reckon they had plans of their own for the gold rush. Would you be willing to take Dad's empty wagon back to Salem? Will you give me a hand?"

Scott grinned, assenting, "Yes, of course, but are you going alone again?"

Don nodded eagerly, "Yes, unless one of you wants to go along."

"I'd go if I had a stake, but the army didn't pay us much," Billy shrugged regretfully.

"Come anyway, Billy. We'll partner all the way. This time Dad gave me a draft on a Seattle bank. We'll both owe him a grubstake if we get to the Klondike before all the gold is gone," Don stammered with infectious enthusiasm.

"I'll do it, Don! Scott, will you give Dad and everyone my love?" Billy responded.

Scott looked dumbfounded for a moment, finally clapping each friend on a shoulder as he suggested, "Good luck, Billy, Don! You gold-struck prospectors better race for that train. I'll take care of everything on this end."

A round of handshakes seeming insufficient for their comradely parting, the three friends embraced in a circle before Scott pushed them along their way, the new teamster a bit envious of their proposed adventure.

* * * * *

Scott had wheeled into the Gerbrunns' Salem yard, un-hitched the horses, and led them to their stalls before notice was taken of the wagon's return. Uwe entered the dimly-lit cavernous stable, and seeing a figure working in one of the stalls, posed an offhand yet anxious question, "Did Don catch the train on time?"

When the uniformed teamster straightened up, Gerbrunn's expression was startled, changing to a broad grin as he cried, "Scott, what a surprise! But I heard you were wounded in Cuba. How come you're stabling my horses? Did my son put you to work so he could go to Alaska?"

"Ha! Ha! It's good to see you too, Uncle Uwe. Yes, Don and Billy are partners on their way to the Klondike. Your hired hand is, too, I guess. Anyway, I'm here to fill in for a few days."

"What about your wounds?"

Scott quickly described his physical condition, "My leg is ninety-nine percent healed, but my shoulder still aches a bit. I drove the wagon and handled the horses easily, but those sacks of potatoes were a real chore."

"Uh huh, you need Angela's cooking to recuperate fully. She'll be pleased to see you. Maybe she'll quit moping about the house about Donald's giving the Klondike another try. We'll both be more comfortable knowing Billy's with him. They can look out for one another. Come on up to the house, and you can tell everyone about Albert and the Spanish-American War at supper. I'll send Kurt over to invite his dad to join us."

"Uwe, is Donald there? Who are you talking to?" called Angela from the front porch.

Scott stepped into view, trotting across the freight yard to embrace the matron, planting a sound kiss on her cheek before murmuring "Surprise!"

Angela returned his greeting in kind, drawing him indoors to jabber on about the family, Salem, and Port Orford, a piece of apple pie keeping him silent. Scott just smiled and gave monosyllabic grunts when necessary, perfectly happy to listen to her discourse. His turn would come when the Gerbrunns gathered at the supper table.

* * * * *

Scott rode Graf along a country lane, the young stallion occasionally fractious but still a good-natured steed. Albert's shirt and trousers didn't fit him very well, but his uniform was finally packed away for good. His thought drifted as he cantered east, turning to last night's supper and Angela's sorrow as he told of his cousin's death in Cuba.

Golly, I could have told that tale differently, but Albert would still be dead at the end – a true hero, but gone nevertheless. I think Aunt Angela was sad because Don is away, and her house seems a bit empty. I'm glad Kurt remembered to ask about Jack-Jack and Billy when the older folks kind of forgot them. Of course, Johann was preoccupied with the war and my service with Teddy Roosevelt, the next president as any good Republican could tell you. The old lawyer actually believes Teddy will be vice-president after the next election. He is a colorful national figure, a real leader, and a protégé of the Yellow Press.

Graf reared his head, side-stepping until Scott tightened his reins. The young horse was demonstrating his willingness to do more than trot down the road. Scott laughed aloud at his new friend, patted his neck, and promised him they could gallop home.

Well, I have to work off the price of this horse and pay for my room and board while Uncle Uwe finds a couple of teamsters. Riding home to the Myrtlewood Grove sounds more interesting than taking the train to Reedsport. Besides, Grandpa wrote Uwe that Salem had gone down and had to be put away, a touchy chore for poor Grandpa.

I expect he's riding Rimpar regularly, so I'd better have my own mount. Graf is a distant cousin to faithful old Salem. Gee, it'll feel good to help Dad with ranch chores. Maybe Grandpa can get some hunting in.

Aloud he remonstrated his eager horse, "All right, let's see what you can do on the open road. Giddy-up, my friend." Graf responded with a surge of power which jarred Scott in his saddle, the cheerful rider hanging on for dear life until Graf settled into a mile-eating lope.

* * * * *

A week later Scott found himself kissing Aunt Angela goodbye, giving Uwe and Kurt each a manly hug, and mounting Graf with sack lunch in hand. He waved a casual farewell as he left the yard, letting his horse have his lead on the trail south. He had high hopes of reaching Drain in a single ride and looking up Bernie Heisel.

Unfortunately, mind and body had disparate notions, and a farm near Coburg claimed his aching and willing body for a night of rest. Scott exchanged his war stories for a hayloft and a meal, chewing on last night's biscuits as he moved through Eugene at daybreak, the Cascades silhouetted by the rising sun. He arrived in Drain to sleep in Bernie's cabin, only to discover Bernie was in Reedsport courting a young lady named Beth.

As luck would have it, the two friends had less than an hour of conversation in the Reedsport station before Bernie's train left for its run to Drain on the following day. Scott shrugged his shoulders fatalistically as he watched the train puff out of sight, eschewing a comfortable bed for a dry hummock in the sand dunes north of Coos Bay.

The next morning he was up early, well on his way into the Coquille Valley before he was sure today was another bit of Indian summer. Graf showed his youth and his strength as he maintained a brisk pace through Bandon, both horse and rider earning a brief respite at Langlois' store, oats for Graf and homemade cheese and bread for Scott. Nearing the Sixes' River late in the afternoon, the homesick traveler marveled at familiar sights and landmarks, holding Graf to a walk until he spotted the bridge near the cascading creek. Then he spurred Graf forward, trotting across it and down the knoll trail into the McClure yard. He had arrived home in the Myrtlewood Grove.

* * * * *

Reining in near the house and sliding from the saddle in the same motion, Scott reflected to himself in high humor, *Getting here at suppertime has its merits. Everyone should be gathered around the table, and I get to eat some of Mom's cooking. I'm starved.*

George came out the door with an exhilarated "Whoopee!" and gave his brother a wrestling-style bear hug. Scott could feel the boy's beefed-up muscles from a summer's growth.

In a replica of her tomboy days, Jane emulated George's enthusiastic greeting. His eldest sister's figure had filled in some, and she blushed happily under Scott's scrutiny, "Gosh, Sis, you've become a young woman."

"As all the boys around here have discovered, Son. Welcome home! You look fit enough for a wounded veteran," Rick exclaimed as he too clasped the world traveler. Scott's quick take of his father revealed an older man than he remembered from their spring parting, and yet he realized the maturity was in himself. He had come of age in Cuba.

Grandpa stood aside to let Julie greet her son, tears instead of words greeting the warm embrace for a moment, Scott finally uttering an emotional quip, "I see where Jane gets her beauty, Momma. I love you."

"Still a charmer, eh, Grandson? Welcome home to the Myrtlewood Grove," the older Scott said as he wrapped his arms around the pair. Scott squeezed his Grandpa's shoulder companionably, noting the old-timer looking healthy and fit but older than his mental image of him. Finally the twins claimed his attention, one sister under each arm.

He thought, *My, how everyone has changed over the summer,* and then corrected himself with a flash of insight. *How I've changed. It's good to be home.*

* * * * *

During the ensuing weeks, Scott consoled Aunt Anne over Albert's death, puzzled with an aging Jack Sixes about his son's disappearance in Cuba, and then explained to Bill Tucker that his son would return from the Klondike a "rich man." To all friends and relatives, he told his war stories with humor as well as sorrow, each adventure becoming a more distant memory with the recitation. However, his tale of Jack-Jack and their last meeting remained firmly fixed in his mind, neither laughter nor telling diminishing the enigma.

Fall harvesting completed, and feeling very fit and energetic, Scott teamed up with Uncle Fred in driving a half-dozen steers to the Coquille Valley. This time George got to go along and become a cowboy, and the boy beamed with pride when he handed his father a purse of cash sufficient to tide the family over the coming winter months.

One rainy day before Thanksgiving, Scott was searching for a missing steer along the river by the east pasture, Graf enjoying the outing, too, when a disheveled and hirsute man walked down the trail from the Sixes. He had heard that two brothers about his father's age and a son about his age were working an old gold placer claim above Jack Sixes' place. He figured this fellow to be one of the brothers, since his beard showed gray and his step was faltering like an old man's. Scott forced the horse into the frigid waters and lifted his boots clear of the stirrups as they crossed the rising Sixes. Remaining in the saddle as Graf reached dry land, Scott observed a pile of cow dung and obscure hoofprints in the muddy soil. He nudged the horse forward, studying a trail left by the animal, which in his mind was clearly too straight to be wandering.

"Howdy, Mister. I'm Bill Caskins, your neighbor from upriver. You got a moment to talk?" the dirty old man implored in a whiny tone, both his manner and sound grating on Scott's nerves. Not usually judgmental about people at first acquaintance, he nevertheless disliked and distrusted this man on sight.

"Just a moment," Scott echoed the man's greeting as he spurred past him, following the trail into a copse of dense young firs. A flicker of color to his right proved elusive, but his eyes continued scanning the verdant forest as he circled the stand of seedlings. There was his steer; he recognized it immediately, munching in a miniature pasture of tall grass amidst the expanse of trees.

As he heard the old man running past him on the trail, a suspicion crept into his consciousness. Sliding out of the saddle, he stepped forward to stroke the grazing steer. The beast's neck had hair rubbed away and a couple of nasty abrasions showing blood – rope burns. His steer had been led here, and he was sure he'd seen the would-be thief fleeing the scene.

I bet that Caskins fellow was an accomplice, Scott thought, *and those fellows working the gold claim upriver are hungry rustlers. They sure couldn't sell the meat. A fine passel of neighbors Jack Sixes has squatting next to his ranch. I wonder if he's missing any livestock. I'll look him up after I get this steer back to the corral.*

Grandpa insisted on accompanying Scott on his quest, loaded Sharps across Rimpar's saddlehorn, saying with a twinkle in his eyes, "Now when I was a young buck…"

The younger man laughed dutifully, disdaining any weapon for their "neighborly" call, his philosophy of civilized law and order being tested. A simple warning and a report to Saul Langlie, the Port Orford marshal, should make the Caskins bunch behave properly.

Riding up to the Sixes family cabin, he experienced a serious doubt when a battered Jack appeared in the doorway with rifle in hand, his face bruised and swollen. His leg buckled, pants torn and bloody, Sandy slipping under his arm to help support him.

Old Scott spoke without hesitation, stating simply, "Caskins!"

Jack tried to grin, but twitched in pain for the effort, his will unbroken even as his body ached, "Yes, the youngster beat me while his father and uncle laughed and called me a 'damned Injun'. If Jack-Jack were here, we would take care of those bad men and get my cow back."

"Well, Uncle Jack, I'll stand in for Jack-Jack. Grandpa can keep the oldsters at bay, and I'll take care of young Caskins," Scott promised, feeling good about doing something for his dead comrade at arms. *So much for being peaceful and law-abiding*, he added silently in his mind.

* * * * *

As the McClure's neared the prospectors' mining claim, Grandpa explained an old ruse he had used with Buzz on one occasion years ago, and with Rick in more recent times, "You ride straight in, but take your time. I'll meander around their camp and cover you. Say, be sure to locate all three men before you punch Caskins in the nose."

Scott chuckled in consonance with Grandpa as he agreed, "Dad's told me that story often enough. I know what to do. Are you up to sneaking around their camp?"

Ignoring his grandson's teasing jibe, the old man rode into the forest and out of sight, Scott counting to a hundred before letting Graf continue up the trail. When he reached a slight rise, he dismounted and walked to its crest, seeing Bill Caskins first, standing beside a milk cow with basket in hand. Beyond him was a campfire, the younger Caskins standing erect and listening, finally dropping a log on the fire as he said something to the man lying beneath the lean-to shelter.

I wonder if Grandpa is losing his touch, he thought, *or maybe that fellow heard me. Anyway, it's time to move.* "Come on, Graf, let's go!" he murmured aloud as he swung up into the saddle and moved at a leisurely pace toward the camp.

Bill Caskins's eyes grew round as he recognized the horseman bearing down on him, and dropping his basket, he scurried sideways to the campfire while choking out an alarm. The son stood behind his father, a surly and challenging look on his clean-shaven face, mean eyes following the single rider in his approach. Taller than his father but just as unkempt in appearance, his build seemed wiry and tough.

The third Caskins was the spitting image of his brother but maybe slyer in manner. He stayed near the lean-to and within reach of his rifle, his eyes darting to and fro in the search for a second visitor. Seeing none, a furtive smile curled his lips, and he whispered something to the father and son.

Scott calmly dismounted and walked up to the pair, putting his open left hand on Bill's chest and thrusting him aside as his right fist smashed into the son's nose with a "splat," father scrambling on all fours to his brother's side.

When the latter figure reached toward his rifle, a bullet fractured its butt, and a Sharps crack carried to the men. Grandpa stepped into view with his rifle cradled in his arm, but with a finger ready on the trigger, and ordered, "You men sit down and stay quiet, or I'll put the next bullet in your gizzard."

The younger Caskins had ducked under Scott's follow-up left fist, and holding his bleeding nose, bent over to pick up a firebrand as a weapon. Scott didn't hesitate to attack in a swarming army style, lashing out with his boot into Caskins' ribs and clubbing him with a fist to the head as he staggered backward. Scott continued his advance, fists swinging into his foe's face and arms as he cowered before the ferocity of striking blows. A long looping right into the same ribs caused Caskins to grimace and yell for help.

Finally realizing his father and uncle were sitting very still under Grandpa's Sharps barrel, Caskins charged Scott recklessly. Grasping his adversary in a bearhug, he tried to trip him into the fire but found himself airborne, hitting the ground beside the fire and rolling over it. His bottom scorched by hot embers and his courage flagging, Caskins turned to run away, only to be tackled by Scott and pummeled about the head and shoulders.

Squirming free with unexpected strength, Caskins swung wildly in self-defense, both fighters giving and taking several blows before Scott thumped him on his ribs for a third time. Caskins tumbled to the ground, screaming, "Ouch! Enough, I've had enough, I give up."

Scott refused his surrender, fisting his greasy hair with his left hand while punching his exposed face with his right fist. Repeating the punishment until Grandpa called a halt to the beating, "Whoa, Grandson! I reckon he's learned his lesson by now. Drop him."

Scott complied readily, the sobbing figure conscious enough to roll away in a defensive ball, all fight gone from the younger Caskins. Jack Sixes was avenged, even though Scott didn't feel as good about the result as he had anticipated.

* * * * *

Leading a procession onto the Sixes yard, Scott looked relaxed as he turned in the saddle to study his charges. All three Caskins men were laden with heavy backpacks as they trudged reluctantly behind Graf, Bill leading the milk cow, followed by his staggering and bruised son, then his complaining brother. Grandpa rode Rimpar behind them, his Sharps cradled in his arm.

Jack was waiting on his stoop with rifle in hand, his step spry as he moved up to Bill and took the cow's makeshift rope halter. His battered face broke into a grin despite its condition, the old Tututni showing his uplifted spirit as he said, "Thanks, Scott. I see you caught up with my cow, as well as the rustlers. What are you going to do with them?"

"Take them into Port Orford to visit with Marshal Langlie. Say, these fellas cleared out their camp, but there's still a lot of trash up there. Would you clean up the claim site and burn the garbage?" Scott asked, concluding with a menacing statement, "The Caskins won't be coming back to the Sixes."

* * * * *

Screened by blackberry brambles and stunted coastal fir, Scott chuckled quietly at the scene unfolding along the northern trail. The three Caskins were running lickety-split toward Denmark, casting harried glances over their shoulders as they disappeared into the forest.

Daydreaming for the moment, the young man considered Grandpa's plan of deception. *I'm glad we don't have to sign a complaint with Saul Langlie, or go down to the county seat. We've got too much work to do on the ranch. Still, those Caskins deserve to be locked up. Oh well, maybe we've scared them enough to make honest men of them. Ha! Ha! Small chance of those characters changing.*

Letting them escape is easy enough to do, although I feel like a stage actor turning my back on them and hiding in the brush like I am, but I reckon I'm just that. They seem convinced they escaped and expect us to chase them, so we'll do just that until they're past Langlois.

Scott's attention was caught by movement on the ridge where Grandpa was stationed. Waving back, he set the stage for the second scene of the drama. He spurred Graf forward, firing a bullet into the air as the horse's hooves drummed a tattoo on the trail. Grandpa answered with a shot of his own and soon thundered down the Sixes' road to join Scott.

Shouts were improvised as the two men acted out their surprise at the escape, and they noisily pursued the fleeing Caskins at a snail's pace. In Denmark they talked to people for half an hour about the thieves before continuing their pursuit to Langlois where they repeated the story.

It was growing dark as they neared a familiar campsite between Langlois and the Coquille River, playing out a third and final scene of their farce. Having spotted the trio up ahead, Scott was sure they were within earshot as he bellowed, "Where are they, Grandpa? It's getting dark. Gee, they must be in Bandon by now."

"I reckon so, Scott. I expect we'd better go back and tell Marshal Langlie our story. He can follow them north tomorrow. The Coos County sheriff is a friend of his."

The two men reined their horses about and rode back down the trail, their laughter growing louder as they distanced themselves from the culprits. The Sixes Valley was well rid of the thieves was the attitude of both men.

Chapter Eight

Wintry rays of sunshine streamed through the window, brightening the McClures' kitchen and spreading Christmas joy over their feast. Decent weather had graced Julie's party invitation and had allowed guests to relax during their visit. The room was filled with friends and relatives seated around one larger table and two small ones. Rick had extended their regular table with sawhorses and planks while Jane and George had put small tables in their bedrooms for the children.

Scott sat quietly in the far corner, studying faces and sipping a glass of California wine and half-listening to one of Grandpa's oft-requested stories of the good old days. He smiled in response to George Hermann's conspiritual wink, both men catching an inconsistency in the Christmas tale. He decided George's frail appearance belied a still sharp mind as the old man kidded the McClure patriarch about the error. A congenial debate between the two fast friends punctuated the story for only a moment, Grandpa not to be deterred from completing the yarn.

Beside him Aunt Anne sat quietly watching her father with undiluted affection, smiling to humor him, but not really cheerful. She still mourned Albert six months after her son's death. John rewarded her smile with a gentle hug, his own gregariousness put on hold as he attended his wife. Scott thought Johnny looked younger than his aunt and felt great empathy with both of them. He missed Albert, too.

Fred was sitting near Rick, looking fit and prosperous while Delores helped her sister-in-law serve apple pie with whipped cream. Scott accepted his piece with a smile of gratitude, receiving a like expression from Delores. He thought Angela's daughter looked much like a younger version of the Salem matron when she smiled.

Sandy nudged his arm lightly with her elbow, catching his attention for her husband. Jack handed him a single sheet of paper covered with printing, whispering aside, "From Tampa."

Scott read the standard form letter, which basically stated Jack Sixes had contacted the wrong office. A postscript in neat handwriting suggested he contact the U.S. Army Headquarters in Washington for information on Jack-Jack Sixes. When Grandpa concluded his story, Jack and Scott excused themselves from the supper table and stepped outside to talk.

"What should I do, Scott?" Jack muttered in frustration, determined to find what happened to his son but stymied by the null response.

"I'll come over to your place tomorrow, and we'll write a few letters together. You can send an inquiry to the army, and maybe a note to the Red Cross – Clara Barton's nurses treated a lot of our wounded soldiers. I'll write to Doctor Chavez in Daquiri and ask him to check Cuban records, and a letter to Teddy Roosevelt in New York might help."

Jack nodded eagerly, adding, "Could we send a letter to our Congressman in the capital? And Senator Lodge, isn't he a friend of Roosevelt's?"

"Yes, and I'll write a letter to Tampa with more specific questions. Jack, I don't think Jack-Jack is alive, but your family deserves to know his fate. We'll keep asking questions."

* * * * *

With a frown crossing his youthful visage and with eyes downcast, Scott bumped into Louie Knapp as he left the post office. He grinned sheepishly as he stumbled to a halt beside the hotelkeeper, apologizing with a self-censuring tone, "Sorry, Louie, but I guess my thoughts were elsewhere. We McClures have been holed up on the ranch for too long."

Looking at the young man's handful of mail, Knapp laughingly replied, "I saw you coming, Scott, so no harm was done. Your Grandpa picked up mail last week and told me about your letters to government offices in search of information about Jack-Jack. I take it there still isn't any word on the Sixes boy."

"That's right. Neither Jack nor I have received any news," Scott stated.

With a twinkle in his eye, Louie added a jibe, "And no letter from a young lady in Cuba either, eh?"

Blushing and grinning at the same time, Scott shook his head, replying, "No. I suppose Grandpa has told you about my friend Maria. I had hoped for a letter by now."

"Why don't you come over to the hotel with me and tell Ella about your young lady friend. Mail's due in from Coos Bay this afternoon, and Ella will fix us a bite to eat while we wait," Louie offered.

The two men chatted as they walked toward the harbor, Scott motioning with his hands to describe his fight with young Caskins.

Marshal Langlie called out from the store porch, "Your story sounds better each time you tell it, Scott. Surely Louie has heard it before."

"Ha! Ha! Nope, Marshal, this is our first talk since the Caskins left the Sixes Valley," Scott retorted with an impish grin.

"Well, you'll be interested to hear all three Caskins are sitting in the Eugene jail. Got caught stealing horses from a ranch outside Springfield. Country's getting downright civilized, I reckon. That rancher and his crew didn't hang 'em, just turned them over to the sheriff."

Scott shook his head in mock disbelief, commenting, "Those yahoos didn't get any smarter, did they, Saul? When are you coming back to the scene of their crime for a little deer hunting? Grandpa and I have time on our hands these days."

Langlie nodded agreeably, accepting the offer as he concluded, "I'll be out in the morning, Scott, if I can get all my chores done today. See you then."

The marshal was moving as he spoke, Louie's belated "So long!" falling on deaf ears. The two men turned into the doorway in silent consonance, Scott to give Johnny a list of supplies and Louie to collect his daily order.

A clerk was waiting on two ladies Scott didn't recognize while Johnny worked at his lawyer's desk in the corner. Glancing up as they walked down the aisle, he greeted them with a smile, "Hello, Louie! It's been awhile, Scott. Did you bring me any venison to sell?"

Louie nodded as he continued to the counter to collect his bag of groceries, and Scott stopped to visit Johnny, "No, but Saul will bring you a deer in a couple of days if we have any luck. How's your family? Is Aunt Anne feeling better these days?"

"Yes, she's still grieving Albert's death, but time is a good healer. You should stop by the house and see the women while you're in town. Can you stay for supper?" Johnny asked.

"No, thanks, I'm going home after you fill my order here," Scott replied, handing his list to his uncle before continuing, "And the afternoon mail arrives. Say, why isn't George working today?"

"He's sick in bed with a cold. I'd appreciate it if you'd look in on him. Make sure he's eating Anne's chicken soup and is resting."

Overhearing Johnny's last words as he stepped up to the desk, Louie said, "George was outside in his bathrobe gathering firewood an hour ago. He was coughing and looked so pale that I helped him carry it inside. His box by the stove was full, but he didn't seem to notice. Anyway, I helped him into bed after we stoked the fire, and he fell asleep right away. I guess he just wanted something to do."

"Oh he forgot I filled the firewood box early this morning. He is getting absent-minded in his old age, but I suppose that's normal for an eighty-year old man," Johnny remarked in a concerned voice, adding as he waved Scott's list at his idle clerk, "I'm writing Angela a letter about his condition now. She thinks he should move to Salem and live with her."

Scott shrugged and grinned playfully in answering, "Maybe she had better come down here and tell him that. He sure doesn't pay any attention to you or Grandpa when moving is suggested. And I guess I agree with him – he's happy in his own small home. I'll leave you with that thought. Give my regards to Aunt Anne and Mary Anne."

* * * * *

Moving quietly about the kitchen, Scott stoked the fire in the old cast iron range, washed dishes and cleaned the counters and then swept the floor. He was heating a pot of bottled soup taken from the cooler when he heard George's voice asking from his bedroom, "Who's there?"

"Scott McClure, George! I'm warming up some soup for lunch. Do you want me to bring it to you?"

"No, I'll come out and eat with you," George declared with an increasingly clear voice as he shuffled through the parlor into the kitchen.

Sitting in his armchair at the table, he declared, "Well, Scott my boy, it's good to see you, and thanks for tidying up my messy kitchen. I'm not really very hungry, but if you're joining me for soup I'll eat, too. You can tell me about your family. How's Grandpa Scott?"

Scott dutifully sat down to eat a second noonday meal, Ella's stew sitting heavy on his stomach. He figured the only way to ensure his friend ate properly was to share the soup with him. He considered Angela to be right about George's needing a caretaker. He looked old and helpless today, a depressing condition for Scott even if George did seem happy enough at his visit.

* * * * *

Scott rode home in a jovial mood, a sharp contrast to his feelings while talking with George. He had received two replies he'd been waiting for concerning Jack-Jack Sixes, a short and official know-nothing letter from Tampa and a long and friendly letter from Maria Chavez. Somehow her words were expressed with personal interest and warmth he found charming. His spirit was buoyed by her manner as well as her news of Cuba. Her father would make renewed inquiries into Jack-Jack's fate, and she would write again with further news. Would Scott please answer her questions about Oregon and his family? And how were his wounds?

Scott recalled Ella Knapp's predictions about his social life, wondering why he didn't take that Earley girl to a dance. Louie coughed a couple of times to divert his wife's attention away from the meddling match-making, but her noisy two sons were the cause of her eventual silence. Scott bobbed Orris on his knee and gave Louis a bear hug, managing to amuse the boys while Ella finished cooking her stew.

Louie had promptly announced that another baby was due in the summer, a proper subject for their supper conversation.

As Graf pranced up to Elk Creek, Scott's awareness returned, his eyes inspecting the rushing waters at the ford. His young steed charged across the creek with enthusiasm, seeming to frolic in the challenge of strength, allowing the rider to return to his reverie. *Maria is sure pretty*, he thought, *and much nicer than her sister*, worrying about Anita and her husband serving in Morocco. *Good place for them in my opinion.*

I wonder if Momma would help me write a letter tonight. She's so smart about good-manners – sensitivity she calls it. And Jane might help, she's about Maria's age. What should I say in my letter?

* * * * *

A few weeks and three letters later, Julie called her son into the kitchen for lunch. Grandpa Scott was hunting on Cougar Ridge, and the rest of the family was visiting the Hughes' place – swapping venison for cheese and the latest gossip.

Scott settled into his chair at the kitchen table as he studied his mother's sober expression, foreboding a mother-son talk about something that was bothering her. Seating herself next to her son after placing hot venison stew and freshly baked bread before him, Julie ignored the food as she gazed at her son. With an expressive sigh, somewhat between determined and exasperated, she began talking.

"Your father thinks I'm nosy, even meddling, but you did ask for a mother's advice on women, so I'll ask you outright. What's going on with you and Maria Chavez? You're writing each other nice letters. I know, Scott, because you've let me read them, but is this girl the reason you won't call on the Hughes girls or take that Earley girl to a dance? Girls seem to like you, but since you've returned from the war, you don't seem interested in any social life. Your behavior is so changed; it worries me. You were always the life of the party before you were wounded."

Scott listened attentively to his mother's concerned tones, smiling gently as he answered, "Don't fret, Momma, I recovered from my wounds without any problem, but I did grow up some while I was a Rough Rider. Heck! Grandpa and Daddy think it's wonderful that I'm working on the ranch and enjoying it. Being the only musketeer left around here had made me a bit of a loner, but not deliberately unfriendly. I'm just not interested in any girl who has marriage on her mind – old man Earley has a shotgun behind his door."

Julie smiled knowingly at her favorite child, understanding him so well as she stated the obvious, "You are dodging my question, dear."

"Ha! Ha! Momma, you know I care about Maria. She nursed me around the clock in that Daquiri hospital. Why, Maria and her father are the main reason I came home healthy."

Scott paused in deliberation until his mother's hand covered his own, urging him to continue, "I think about her a lot, Momma. She's pretty and so wise, you know, a special person. She makes me feel good about myself, even her letters carry a warmth in her words. She's exciting to be with, but yet I'm always comfortable in her company. Is that love, Momma? I don't know. What do you think I should do?"

Julie smiled broadly, following her son's rambling explanation, answering cheerfully now that her concerns had been addressed, "You'll never know unless you talk to her in person. That means you should go back to Cuba and visit the Chavez family. You're like your father in many ways, Scott, and you'll never be happy until you face this situation and find out how you really feel."

Scott nodded thoughtfully, the idea of returning to Cuba obviously not a stranger to the young man. He smiled ruefully as he essayed, "You know, I've been saving my money. Unconsciously, I think Cuba is the reason for my doing without things. Jack Sixes wants me to go to Washington, D. C. and check on Jack-Jack's status. I could do both, but it takes money to travel that far away."

"Your family will help you, Son, but we'll need time to make plans and gather a purse to pay for them. Talk to your father and grandfather. They'll have some good ideas."

Scott left the table deep in retrospection, somewhat pleased with his clear thoughts about Maria. His mother's advice was sound, and he told her so as he opened the door, "Thanks,

Momma. I'll ride over to the Hughes and help Dad with the cheese – and talk to him."

* * * * *

His mind still awash with thoughts of Maria and his chat with his mother, Scott all but rode Graf past Rick and Patrick standing near the almost completed Hughes mansion. A call from the dairy farmer caught his attention, and with a sheepish grin on his face, he spurred his horse up the hillside to the house.

"Hello, Patrick, are you living in your new home now?"

"And happy Saint Patrick's Day to you, young Scott! Yes, Jane moved us up here first chance she had, but there's still a lot of work to be done. What brings you over?" Patrick queried.

Scott shrugged his shoulder and then answered in good humor, "Why, to greet you on your namesake's day, and to see your new home – even if I daydream along the way."

"Well, son, you can load a pair of cheese sacks over your saddle while George and his sisters stay here to play with their friends," Rick directed as a secretive smile crossed his lips.

Jane Hughes waved from the doorway, her words of greeting drowned out by the noise of the youngsters playing. Rick waved back and concluded his statement, "I won't keep you from your building chores any longer, Patrick. Scott and I will take our cheese and head home."

* * * * *

As father and son followed the well-worn trail upriver, Scott sneaked a look at his father's countenance with its hint of a secret grin and asked rhetorically, "Did you know Momma was going to talk to me today? I suppose that's why you're grinning."

"That's right, Scott. We've worried about you since you got back from the war. Dad sees a grandson who loves the ranch again, but your mother and I see an unhappy veteran. Jack Sixes sees a conspirator to find out what happened to his boy, but I see my boy wrapped up in an obsession. So your mother asked me to take the children for a ride to the Hughes place. You know, if you need any help, you can count on us."

Scott nodded, grinned and quipped, "That's why I'm here now, Dad. Momma convinced me to settle my unfinished business, so I'm going to Washington to ask about Jack-Jack and to Cuba to visit Maria. Momma said you'd have an idea or two on how to pay for my trip. I thought you might be willing to tell me how you fell in love with Momma. What is love anyway?"

* * * * *

"Come on, Slowpoke! Julia's supper will get cold. For a young fellow you sure take your time," Scott gibed his grandson.

"Hah! You gave half your venison to Jack Sixes, and suddenly you want to race home. Grandpa, how about swapping backpacks?"

"Nope, a deal's a deal. I'm carrying my hindquarter for the family, and you're carrying two quarters to sell to Johnny at the store. You know, that trip to Washington and Cuba costs a lot of money," Grandpa teased further.

Young Scott chuckled aloud, answering in good humor, "So you keep telling me. But hunting venison for sale in town is better than working for that black sand mining company. Do they really take gold out of that pit?"

"They certainly do. You know, I worked for one of those outfits once. The owner made good money, and I got paid regularly, but never again," Grandpa paused to wave and pointed ahead, "Say, there's your daddy riding out to meet us. Rimpar can carry our packs home. You still plan on going into Port Orford after the noon meal? I could use a bottle of brandy."

Rick pulled up beside the older Scott and dismounted, helping his father strap his backpack to the horse's saddle. He commented, "Patrick brought out our mail today. No son, there was no letter from Cuba, but Kurt Gerbrunn wrote he's coming to visit George. I believe Angela is worried about her father, and Kurt is her agent to convince George to move to Salem. You did get a letter, son – one from Canada. Mother didn't open it, but I expect it's from Billy or Don or both."

* * * * *

Scott rode into Port Orford atop Graf and leading Rimpar, whose rigging was encumbered by the two quarters of venison and two crates of chickens. The rider gingerly balanced a box of eggs on his saddlehorn, daydreaming off and on about the Klondike and his friends. Billy and Don were still seeking their fortune at Dawson, often working for others to buy supplies to work their own placer claim. They would stay another year, not willing to give up their dreams of striking it rich.

He steadied the bouncing box with both hands as his horse side-stepped a fallen tree limb, shifting his thoughts to consider Jack's proposal to sell Ai-Ho and a milk cow to Sandy's cousins in Pistol River. The Sixes would give the proceeds to Scott to help finance his trip to Washington. He'd agreed to handle the deal after Battle Rock Days next month, having promised Johnny to work in the store during the grand celebration. His dad had agreed to help Saul Langlie keep the peace, and Grandpa was one of Tichenor's guests of honor. *I bet Grandpa tells one of his stories when he gives his speech — maybe the bees tale.*

Passing the post office he heard his name called and waited for Rod Bishop to catch up with him.

"Hello, Rod, isn't the mill cutting lumber today?"

His old boss shook his head as he announced, "No, Girard and Trucker are in Gold Beach looking at a used saw blade for the mill. Bill said he had a letter from his son, and the prospectors are spending another year in the Klondike. Did you get a letter, too?"

"Yes, tell Billy's dad I got the same news, and say hello for me," Scott concluded as he cut behind the store. Both he and Rod waved to several passing acquaintances and then to each other before they went separate ways. Dismounting with his box of eggs with extra care, he slipped past the door Johnny opened and set his box on the counter.

"I'm glad to see you, Scott. I can sell all the eggs, chickens and venison you delivered. Is Rick selling me a steer before Battle Rock Days?"

"Sure thing, Uncle Johnny. Now I think I'll go visit George before I head home," Scott said as he turned toward the doorway.

"Anne will insist you stay for supper. George just went over to our house to chat with my wife, and I know he had one of your Aunt's meals on his mind. Go ahead, I'll be home as soon as my clerk shows up for work."

* * * * *

Scott walked his two horses over to the Larsons, unsaddling the animals as they got reacquainted with Johnny's old mare. A brief rubdown with a tattered burlap sack, plus a few oats, satisfied Graf and Rimpar, and Scott moved across the yard to the kitchen door.

Slipping into the kitchen unannounced amidst a plethora of fragrant cooking odors, he literally bumped into his cousin at the dining room doorway. Mary Anne gave a surprised squeak, followed by a hug and kiss on the cheek.

She called over her shoulder, "Mother, I'll have to set another place at the table – Scott's here."

"And Uncle Johnny should be coming pretty soon. When's supper, Aunt Anne, I'm starved," Scott declared with a laugh, one arm encircling the daughter as the other embraced the mother in a familial hug.

His eyes sought George's, whose wizened form was ensconced in the familiar myrtlewood rocking chair, and he asked the old-timer, "Is your spare bed available for the night?"

"Heh! Heh! Glad to have you, my boy, but only for one night. Kurt Gerbrunn's ship is due tomorrow. I'm looking forward to firsthand news of Angela's family. I expect Delores and Fred will be here to meet the ship. How about you? Got time for a real visit?" George asked in hopeful tones.

"Of course! It'll be fun meeting a ship again, and Kurt's a good friend. I thought I might leave Rimpar here for his use. We want him to come out to the ranch and see us, too," Scott said, and promptly switched his attention to the ladies he was holding, "Now tell me all the news of Port Orford. Are you ready for summer weather again?"

Chapter
Nine

Sunday morning dawned as a sunny and cheerful summer day in the Myrtlewood Grove, Scott checking on stock in the east pasture before setting up the picnic tables and barbeque under the venerable yet verdant stand of trees. When Kurt's ship had failed to make port on time last week, Scott had left Port Orford after inviting everyone to the ranch for a venison feast – Kurt as guest of honor.

Scott eyed the coastal fog bank crowding Slide Ridge to the west, wisps of gray moisture skittering through the firs at the gap. *I hope it isn't too foggy along the trail from Port Orford,* he thought silently, *our guests may be delayed. It's annoying how this clear blue sky can turn to a wall of fog just a mile or two downriver. Maybe I should ride down to the Sixes Crossing and meet our friends.*

With that idea before him, Scott spurred his horse toward the yard where George was cutting kindling for his mother's woodbox. Announcing his intention as Graf cantered past the house and pranced playfully up the knoll, Scott's attitude was as carefree as the horse's. When they rounded the far end of the gravelly trail and entered the gap, flecks of moisture casually brushed his cheeks. With light fading behind him, Scott blinked his eyes rapidly, but his vision was blindfolded by the coastal blanket of dense fog.

Scott's high spirits dwindled to a feeling of melancholy as Graf's hoof beats became a hollow and plodding sound. Recognizing his mood swing with waggerish humor, his brisk chuckle pierced the somewhat omnipresent gray wall.

"Hello! Is that you, Scott? Are you lost, too?" came Johnny's strong voice from the distance.

"Yes! I'm almost to the crossing but I can't see a thing. Are you up to the Sixes yet?" Scott replied, another rueful chuckle echoing in the fog bank.

"Yes, my wife is ready to cross over to you. Can you sing out now and then to guide her?" Johnny requested in concerned tones.

"Be careful, Aunt Anne. Yesterday's rainstorm has swollen the Sixes a bit. Of course, you're an old hand at this chore," Scott droned on as he listened to splashing in the fog before him, keeping his monologue going as a beacon. "Do I hear George in the water now?"

"Yes!" echoed in the damp air, the voices of George, Johnny, and Anne almost in unison. Anne appeared beside him like a wraith in the mist, and she called out, "I'm across, Dear, and I see George behind me. Is Kurt coming?"

"Yes, and I will…," Johnny's words were cut off by Kurt's startled cry.

"Damn! An old log bumped into Rimpar, and he's headed downstream. Oops! We're in deep water now," Kurt's voice seemed anxious as its sound moved away.

"I'm coming, Kurt, keep away from that snag. It may have roots or branches which could entangle your horse's legs," Scott called out as he urged Graf along the riverbank. Paralleling the sounds from the river, his encouraging words were intended to calm man and beast. He spotted the shadowy specter of a horse and rider a few feet away just as he came to the large mass of blackberry bramble.

He shouted a warning, "Swim Rimpar below this berry patch, Kurt. I'll meet you in the shallows a hundred yards downstream." Scott was silent as he spurred Graf forward along a narrow path around the obstacle, relying on the horse's senses to skirt any danger.

They were approaching Girard's old mill pond when he reined the horse toward the river, entering the well-remembered shallows, a gravel bar most of the summer days.

"Where are you, Scott?" Kurt called from but a few feet away, still lost in the smothering mist, his voice near panic.

"Head this way, Kurt. Over here, Rimpar, old buddy. Come to the shallows."

No more words were necessary as a dripping horse and rider lunged up onto the solid footing beside their rescuers, the tumbling old snag rolling its massive roots over the far end of the shallows.

Teeth now chattering from the cool air and perhaps the shock of his un-asked for peril, Kurt muttered, "Some welcome to the Sixes Valley!"

Following Scott onto dry land and around the massive blackberry patch, Kurt rambled on about a calm passage aboard ship, and his pleasant days in Port Orford. When they met the trio waiting at the crossing, Aunt Anne immediately fussed over Kurt's shivering body, soaked and chilled as it was. Their guest bemoaned the dreadful summer weather today, a feeling chorused by the others as they set off for the McClure ranch.

Fumbling their way across the meadow and into the gap through a gray shroud, everyone's spirits were buoyed by the lifting of the mantle as they entered the bright sunlight bathing the other side of Slide Ridge. Anne laughed gaily, expressing the group's changing feelings in a nutshell, "Isn't the Sixes beautiful now?"

* * * * *

The entourage galloped down the knoll into the yard, skirting both Julie's wandering chickens and her fenced garden as they reined their horses before the open doorway. Julie emerged quickly to mother the dripping Kurt, and Scott volunteered as hostler, directing his other guests to the myrtlewood grove where the family was working.

His mother soon joined him in the barn, feeding the animals as he rubbed them down with an old gunnysack. Together they turned the horses into the corral and were headed for the house when they heard Jane's startled shriek and young George's hilarious laughter.

Entering the doorway they discovered Kurt wrapped in a blanket, red-faced and speechless as an equally flushed Jane apologized, words of contrition erased in a giggling silence. George wiped a laugh from his lips and explained, "Kurt and I were talking in my room. When he handed me his wet clothes, Momma, Sis walked in and screamed. Kurt found a blanket real quick."

Mother smiled in genuine amusement, taking her daughter by the hand and exiting with a chuckling comment, "We'll let you finish dressing in private, Kurt. Join us in the picnic area when you're ready."

George ran after them and Kurt resumed donning his trousers. With a hem and a haw and sideways glances at his friend, he remarked, "Your sister has grown up since the last time I saw her, Scott. How old is she now?"

Scott regarded Kurt for several moments, knowing that his casualness was feigned. He smiled knowingly as he replied, "I found a young woman when I came back from the war. She's attractive and nice to boot, as several beaus will testify to. You don't have to mince words with me, Kurt, she's old enough to speak for herself."

Flushing cheeks now split by a charming grin, Kurt nodded in agreement as he observed, "She's very pretty, Scott. I can imagine the boys like her, but I'm much older and I don't want to offend your parents."

"Ha! Ha! Just watch out you don't offend Jane, my friend. She has a mind of her own," Scott stated in teasing tones, adding with a more sober expression, "By the way, she doesn't pay attention to any of those boys. She claims they are immature."

Kurt's grin broadened as he slapped Scott on the back in a comradely manner, no further words passing between the pair as they walked down to the picnic area.

* * * * *

Arriving guests reported the fog had cleared just after noon, making their short journey quite pleasant. Ella Knapp was in a family way and sent her regrets with Louie and their two sons. Louis was voluble about swimming in the old hole, but as it turned out little Orris was the boy who spent the most time playing with George and Angela in the water. Louie had to hold him in his lap to keep him away while the older kids roughhoused.

During the picnic meal Rod Bishop rode into the myrtlewood, excited and breathless as he reported, "Sorry I can't stay, Rick. There's a ship aground near Garrison Lake – a small coaster steamer. The skipper missed the Port Orford Heads in the fog this morning and needs help to get off the beach on this afternoon's tide. I'm notifying everyone as far as Langlois while Bill Tucker covers the town and the mill."

Rick nodded curtly, suggesting, "Get down and grab a quick bite to eat, Rod. Dad can ride up to Langlois with the news while Scott and I ride with you to the ship."

The younger men echoed their host, family men gathering their wives and children and preparing to go home. Kurt dogged Scott's heels as he trotted toward the barn to saddle horses. Kurt's welcome party was breaking up in a flurry of activity.

Ten minutes later Rick led a dozen volunteers toward Port Orford's oceanfront fresh water lake, Kurt riding double with Scott and brother George in the saddle behind his father. In less than half an hour of pushing their horses, the group arrived on a chaotic scene stretching along the sandy beach. Fred Madsen waited for Rick to dismount before doing so himself, striding beside his brother-in-law to the lapping waves of the water's edge.

A tall, skinny, uniformed man stood amid a score of passengers and crew, the ship's dory unloading two elderly ladies.

The officer turned a weather-worn and tired face to Rick, his gray eyes under dark brows worried and a bit confused. His immediate concern was evident in his hopeful query, "Do you have a boat to help tow us out of the sand? Any of you?"

"No, I'm afraid not, but we're ready to lend a hand. How can we help? Have all your passengers been put ashore?" Rick asked.

"Yes, and thanks for volunteering. We'll need manpower when the fishing boats get here from Port Orford. I'm First Mate Bill Heinz of the *S.S. Dondell*. We're bound for Coos Bay after calling in Port Orford. Fortunately we're half-loaded, and there's no damage to our hull. I expect we will be all right if we can float her free on the afternoon tide."

Rick empathized with the distraught sailor, "Too bad you're stuck in the sand, but I expect you'll sail clear if the weather holds. How can we help now?"

"Well sir, five passengers have walked into Port Orford on their own. Could you escort these ladies to Knapp's Hotel on your horses?" Mate Heinz asked in plaintive voice.

Scott reacted immediately, motioning Kurt to grab the reins of two horses as he did the same. He led the animals over to the isolated foursome as Rick agreed, "Yes! As you can see, my son and his friend will care for the women. The rest of us will wait here to do whatever is necessary."

"Ma'am, may I help you mount Graf? I'll take you to the town's hotel," Scott addressed one elderly but sprite grandmother.

The woman smiled in gratitude and grasped the saddle horn, lifting her foot into Scott's cupped hands. Gently raising her atop the horse, Scott asked worriedly, "Are you comfortable in the saddle?"

"Yes, thank you. Will you help my daughter, too?"

The other elderly lady looked every bit as old as her mother, with an unhappy and cross manner which declared she was a casualty of the ship's misfortune. Complaining when she wasn't crying, she called Rimpar a "skittery old nag," a rather disparate description in Scott's opinion. He ignored her whining as much as possible, blocking her shrill voice from his mind as he hurried down the beach and into town.

The quiet grandmother thanked him gently and smiled as he helped her dismount before the hotel where Louie took over responsibility. Her daughter barked orders at him to have her trunk brought to her immediately. He departed aboard Graf, reflecting that the trek had been an ordeal – so much for being a Good Samaritan.

Hurrying out of earshot, he slowed his pace so Kurt could catch up, his friend's amused chuckle the only comment necessary on their return to the Dondell. Both men studied the activity, Kurt concluding with a query, "Isn't the ship clear of the beach now?"

Scott nodded, noting, "Bill Tucker has gathered a small navy. All the Dondell needed was a fair tide and a little push."

He pointed seaward to a half-dozen fishing boats, hawsers stretched taut as they towed the steamer into deeper waters. "There, she's under her own power now that her propeller is clear. Come on, we may as well go home and eat some of Julie's apple pie."

* * * * *

Jack Sixes found Scott stacking hay in the east pasture when he returned from Port Orford. He rode across the mowed field waving letters over his head – a batch of mail from the post office.

"Three letters for me and two for you, Scott. I didn't open them yet. Ha! Ha! Maybe you don't want to read Maria's letter aloud, eh?" Jack teased in good humor.

Scott dropped his rake and stood at Jack's knee, urging his friend on, "Go ahead, open one."

"A letter from the Montauk hospital, the army or my congressman? Which is first?" Without waiting he tore an envelope to shreds and unfolded a single page form letter, muttering sourly, "That damned Montauk hospital sent me the same paper as Tampa's."

Scott accepted his two letters, placing Maria's in his pocket as he opened the flap on the second, stating the obvious, "It's from New York. Must be from Colonel Roosevelt."

A short note with personal greetings and a report that he had no knowledge of the missing Jack-Jack Sixes was found, only the last sentence worth reading aloud, "I have forwarded your letter to Raymond Johnson in the Navy Department. He's a bully man. He will contact you after he reviews this matter."

Jack nodded and ripped open the army envelope, a frown twisting his wrinkled face as he read another form letter. Hurriedly he opened the other letter, his Congressman writing a personal letter of condolence. He reported Jack-Jack Sixes was missing in action in Cuba – hardly the answer to a father's question.

"What about Cuba? And the Chavez's?"

Scott drew the fifth message from his pocket, gingerly opening it to find two pages covered with Maria's neat handwriting. He perused them quickly, finally glancing up to meet Jack's eyes with a shake of his head, "No real news, Jack. Maria says the government is in shambles, Americans and Cuban rebels arguing all the time. Besides, she says her father was a loyalist and not very popular with those in power."

Jack asked, "What about Senator Lodge? And the Red Cross? We haven't heard from them yet."

"And Raymond Johnson's report should come soon. We'll wait for those letters, but I'm not very hopeful," Scott mused in a discouraged voice.

"Can't you go to Washington and find out?" Jack wondered aloud, "This Raymond Johnson fella might help. I'll pay your fare. When can you deliver Ai-Ho and my old steer to my cousin in Pistol River?"

"After Battle Rock Days, my friend, I'll make that trip. In the meantime we'll wait on the mail and plan my investigation."

* * * * *

Kurt had been a frequent visitor to the McClure's home during his June stay in Port Orford, often remaining overnight in Grandpa's cabin. His attention to Jane did not go unnoticed by family members, particularly her sisters and her trips to town with anyone who had an errand to run were dead giveaways to the mutuality of interest. The "non-outdoors" girl even went hunting with Grandpa and Kurt one day. Everyone concluded that romance was in the air.

Scott visited George's home one day to discuss the Battle Rock celebration plans, and soon found himself taking a walk with an anxious Kurt. He was not surprised at his friend's manner nor that the subject of their evening conversation was his sister. Kurt revealed "his secret" as soon as they were out of the house; he was in love with Jane and wanted to marry her. Did Scott approve of his suit? What advice could Scott give him? His real concern emerged in the last question, am I too old for Jane?

Scott maintained a sober demeanor even though his mind chuckled at his friend's expressive eyes, he smiled as he replied, "Of course I approve, Kurt, and age has little to do with your romantic pursuit of my sister. I believe I can judge my parents' reactions as being very favorable, but what does my sister think? It seems to me you should be talking to Jane, not me. Or are you practicing on me because we're buddies?"

Kurt stared at Scott in consternation, silence emphasizing his hangdog expression. Scott finally threw up his hands in exasperation and chastised his friend, "You're too serious, Kurt. You need to loosen up. Where's your sense of humor? Laugh a little at yourself, and you'll gather courage to talk to my sister."

"But I think marriage is serious – even a little scary. Just thinking about asking someone to be with you for the rest of your life is a big decision. I know Jane thinks it's serious, too," Kurt declared righteously, missing Scott's point entirely.

Grinning despite other intentions, Scott conceded, "Very well, be a sobersides, but you still have to talk to Jane yourself. She's riding in with me tomorrow when I pick up the ranch supplies at Johnny's – plus the mail. I'll expect you to meet us at the store. I'm willing to have a big brother talk with Jane if she wants, but not until you propose to her."

* * * * *

Scott bumped into Jack Sixes in the Port Orford Post Office the next afternoon, his neighbor holding a pair of opened letters in his hand and looking dispirited. He repined, "Neither the Red Cross nor Senator Lodge has any news about Jack-Jack. Both tell me that he's missing in action in Cuba – same old answer."

"Wait for me to pick up my mail. Maybe I have some news," Scott suggested as he waved to the clerk.

He returned a moment later reading a letter from Cuba, explaining to his friend, "Nothing in here about Jack-Jack. Maria sends her greetings." A quirk of his lips gave away his feelings as he added, "She enjoys my letters and wishes she could talk to me. Little does she know how much I feel the same."

Untouched by the young man's happy tones, Jack shrugged and shuffled over to his horse, turning as he untied its reins to ask, "You're going to Pistol River right after the celebration, aren't you?"

"Yes, and we still might hear some news from Colonel Roosevelt's friend in the Navy Department. Anyway, I can't leave until Dad and I sell some steers next month. Well, I have to meet Jane over at the store. See you later," Scott concluded and walked across the street to visit with Saul Langlie on his way to Uncle Johnny's.

* * * * *

Scott watched his sister out of the corner of his eye during their ride out of town, Jane's expression of sobriety a surprise to him. It was not until they crossed Elk Creek that she returned a sly glance and chuckled. When he regarded her mischievous look with only a raised eyebrow, she accused, "Kurt talked to you, didn't he, Big Brother?"

Grinning now but still reticent, Scott replied, "Yes he did, Little Sister."

"I mean he told you he was going to propose marriage to me. Quit looking like a cat playing with a mouse and tell me what he said," Jane pleaded.

"Kurt's obviously madly in love, as we all know – besides he told me so. He's worried about the age difference between you, which really isn't a big deal at all. Anyway, I told him you were a mature young woman with good sense, and he should discuss his concerns with you," Scott concluded.

Jane nodded agreeably, and with a rueful smile on her lips she ruminated aloud, "Hmm! Thanks for 'woman' status, but I'm not so sure about my maturity. I do love Kurt and age makes no difference to me, but he's already decided where we'll live in Salem. He just plain assumed I would leave the Sixes Valley without even asking my opinion. Am I selfish to want to live here?"

Scott's demeanor turned serious as he considered his answer – advice actually. Finally he chose a single question as his reply, "Do you want to marry Kurt?"

"Yes I do, and I told him so. He's coming out to the ranch for supper this evening to ask Father for my hand. But I'm having second thoughts."

"About your love or where you'll live?" Scott interjected.

"Oh I love him, Scott, but I don't know about living in Salem. I know! I know! I should have told him how I feel about the Myrtlewood Grove and Port Orford and all my family and friends," Jane lamented, reining her horse about to face her brother.

"Your know, Jane, Kurt's worry about age difference and your fretting about leaving here and setting up a family home in Salem are related. You should talk them out with Kurt before he talks to our father," Scott advised as he added, "There's talk of both a real road up to Coos Bay and a railroad down the coast. Salem and Port Orford will be but a day trip before too many years go by. Family visits will be much easier in the future, and if you lived in the Willamette Valley you'd grow to love it – you're a very adaptable young woman."

Jane chuckled again, "First mature and now adaptable, I love you too, Scott. Come on, race you to the ford."

* * * * *

The McClure family sat about the supper table expectantly waiting for an announcement. Whispered conferences had abounded before and during the meal, and Rick and Kurt had stepped outside briefly as Julie served her blackberry pie dessert.

Everyone strove to be nonchalant when Rick sat down, and Jane stood up beside Kurt, the girl pledging her troth, "Kurt asked me to marry him, and I accepted as soon as Daddy gave us his blessing."

Clapping hands and excited cries of congratulations were spontaneous despite everyone's anticipation, hugs and kisses following. Befitting the eldest family member's position, Grandpa Scott produced a bottle of homemade apple cider and toasted the young couple's happiness, "Prosit! Here's to a long and happy life together, Jane and Kurt, grandchildren of my old friend and me. Now tell us all the details."

Jane gladly replied, "Kurt and I will be married later in the summer, and we plan to honeymoon in San Francisco." With a knowing wink for her brother, she continued, "Kurt will arrange a home for us in Salem. I hate to leave the Myrtlewood Grove and all my family and friends, but Kurt's business is there. I'm sure with the railroads growing and roads being improved, we'll soon be only a day's visit away."

Kurt quickly added, "I love this county, too, and I promise we'll visit our family regularly. Now I must go home and tell my family the good news. I'm sure they will all come to our wedding. Would late August be a good time?"

Julie nodded in approval, offering good sense advice, "Yes, my daughter and I will plan a proper ceremony. Aunt Anne, Angela, and her sisters will help us, and you men can figure out how you'll pay for it."

Scott volunteered, "I think my sister deserves the best wedding of the summer. We McClure men will manage the money, you women go right ahead with your plans."

He felt the grip of his father's hand on one shoulder and his grandfather's on the other, expressing approval for Scott's declared support of Jane's wedding and assurance that his fall journey would be possible. The McClures stood together as a family during this busy summer of 1899.

Chapter Ten

Scott kneed the recalcitrant horse forward, his bareback perch on Jack-Jack's steed a lazy compromise for the drover. Graf remained saddled as the rider gave him a breather. Ai-Ho plunged into Brush Creek, striding for the far bank and Humbug Mountain. On a tight line the saddled horse and two steers followed suit.

Battle Rock Days had been fun for everyone, Scott mused silently. *Saul Langlie paid Dad for his stint as a deputy even though there was no trouble. And Johnny paid me for minding a customer-less store yesterday. Aunt Anne won the cake baking contest, and brother George and a friend came in second in the potato sack race. Of course, I won my for-fun bet with Louie that Grandpa would tell the old-timer's story about Buzz Smith and his bees.*

Coming to a steep climb in the trail behind Humbug, Scott slid off Ai-Ho. Switching mounts before traversing the grade, he returned to his reverie. *Jack Sixes gave me another steer to sell so I could leave for Washington, D. C. early and didn't seem to hear me when I told him I couldn't go until after Jane and Kurt get married. George Hermann heard us talking and offered us fifty dollars for our quest – for old time's sake. With the expense of a fancy wedding I can sure use the help! Hmm! Old George isn't looking very well these days. He has trouble working in the store with that game leg of his.*

The lead line snapped taut, Scott's daydreaming abruptly over as a steer's bleating cry echoed off the mountain. The old brindle backed steer which Jack had dug out of Sixes side canyon had fallen and now thrashed about in loose earth, noisy and unable to stand.

"Must have broken a leg," Scott muttered loud enough to silence the beast. He pulled his Sharps from its saddle sheath, dismounted, and approached the steer carefully. He didn't have to examine the animal very closely to determine its foreleg was shattered. He grimaced as he administered the coup de grace, humanely necessary but, leaving its carcass in a difficult position on the steep slope.

Scott set about making camp on the narrow bench above the precipitous trail, picketing the other animals before tackling the job of skinning and butchering the dead steer. He was still pondering his problem when he heard noises approaching from the south, three Indian lads riding their ponies bareback suddenly appearing at the other end of the bench.

Glancing from the dead steer to the Sharps Scott was cradling across his arm, one lad called out, "Do you need help, mister?"

Scott slipped his rifle into his saddle sheath, waving the boys forward as he replied, "Yes, come on into my camp. Can your family use some fresh beef?"

A deal was struck immediately, the Indians butchering the carcass in exchange for one forequarter and the heart. They wrapped the intestines in the animal's hide, handing the liver to Scott before hanging the other three quarters from a stout branch of an old Madrona. They chattered excitedly in Tututni as they worked, obviously pleased with the deal.

Promising to return in the morning with burlap sacking for his meat, the trio led their ponies down the south trail. Scott now smiled, thinking he could sell the meat in Gold Beach for as much as a steer on the hoof. He was as pleased as the boys were – each benefited in their deal. After a moment he wondered if he'd ever see the burlap cloth they had promised to deliver.

* * * * *

He was frying strips of liver and sipping hot coffee at daybreak when the boys returned, accompanied by an old Tututni – their grandfather, they told him. The trio began wrapping the hanging beef quarters with burlap, loading Ai-Ho as Scott visited with the old man.

Introducing himself to the Tututni grandfather resulted in a chattering, fast-paced monologue which stymied Scott's understanding of the language. Seeing his look of frustration, one of the lads translated, "Grandpa says he knows 'Old Scott' from the Sixes River and is happy to meet his grandson. Thanks for the cow meat. Our people will enjoy it. Can we help any more?"

"No thanks! Tell your grandpa that 'Old Scott' will be glad to hear of his Tututni friend after so many years. Now it's time for me to go to Gold Beach and sell the rest of the meat."

The Indians all waved farewell as they rode away, the lad telling his companion what Scott had said. He never caught up with the group although he saw them in the Cosutt-heutens' village as he passed on the high trail south of Humbug Mountain.

Five minutes after all sounds had quieted from the Indian's village, he heard the drum of a horse's hooves coming down the trail. Turning in his saddle he spotted his Indian translator galloping toward him, soon reining in his pony, a big grin on his face. He handed Scott a piece of singed meat skewered on an alder branch exclaiming, "Grandpa sent a piece to you, Scott."

"Thanks, my friend," Scott replied and bit into the warm flesh, nodding approval as he murmured, "Good!" between bites. The lad happily raced home with a casual wave of goodbye, Scott grateful that he had made a few friends today.

* * * * *

His mild satisfaction pervaded his ride to the Rogue River and Gold Beach. Reining his horse before a general store, he and Graf ignored the yipping mongrel on the wooden sidewalk. Ai-Ho was less tolerant, prancing about to kick at the dog. A thin man in his thirties with a gloomy expression on his mustached face shouted at the cur, "Spot, get out of here! Go home!"

Scott dismounted, smiling but a moment as the crabby fellow kicked the dog and then swatted the yelping pest with a willow stick. Scott didn't like to see any animal abused, but he was standing on someone else's property and held his tongue, if not his disapproving look.

Patting Ai-Ho's load of meat, he offered it for sale to the storekeeper, "Hello, I have three quarters of beef for sale. Steer broke a leg on Humbug, and I had to shoot him. Are you interested in buying?"

The man's morose look turned shifty as he calculated a possible profit, still unsmiling as he offered, "Killed yesterday, I imagine. Not prime meat and dirty from the trail to boot. Hmph! I'll give you five dollars in trade goods. Take it or leave it mister."

Not deigning to reply, Scott remounted and led his animals away from the skinflint, ignoring his call, "All right, eight dollars...ten dollars...in gold coin."

Scott rode past the Curry County Courthouse in a foul mood, thinking as he frowned visibly, *I never liked this town much. First they steal the county seat, and now some yahoo wants to steal Jack's butchered steer. I'd rather give it to the Indians than sell it to that storekeeper. Sometimes Indians are better neighbors than white men.*

Spotting a butcher shop across the street, Scott led his pack train to its door. He dismounted and tied Graf's reins to the hitchrack and then entered the dim and cool shop. Two glass showcases filled with cuts of fresh meat and fish braced the thick butcher block made of Port Orford cedar.

A portly bald man wearing a white apron greeted him jocularly, "Hello, Mr. McClure. How can I help you?"

Scott's puzzled countenance and lack of words for the stranger elicited a sly and self-satisfied grin as the butcher explained, "Your horse gives you away, and you look like a McClure. Let's see, I bet you're Rick's son – Scott's grandson?"

With a friendly smile, Scott admitted the man's deductive reasoning was correct, "Right, Sir! I'm Scott McClure from the Sixes River. And you'd be...?"

"Fritz Mueller at your service, young man. Your dad and I are old friends. In fact, he sold me a steer while you were with Colonel Roosevelt's Rough Riders in Cuba. Rick was mighty proud of you and maybe a little envious that you were seeing the world. Did you charge up San Juan Hill with Teddy?"

"Ha! Ha! Roosevelt certainly is famous, isn't he? No, I was wounded at El Caney and missed the rest of the action. My buddies told me it was tough going – the Spaniards fought well. Several friends were killed in the fight for San Juan

Heights, but we won that battle and the war," Scott reminisced nostalgically.

Fritz commented, "But your wounds must have healed properly. You carry yourself well. What are you doing in Gold Beach?"

"I'm delivering a horse and steer to Pistol River for my neighbor Jack Sixes. A second steer broke his leg on the trail over Humbug. Are you interested in buying three quarters of freshly butchered Sixes beef?" Scott asked and then told the story of his mishap.

* * * * *

Change jingled in Scott's pocket as he rode out of Gold Beach, Jack's butchered steer bringing in a gold eagle coin, a pocket of pennies, nickels, and dimes, and a small slab of bacon. Graf picked up his ears as his rider chuckled, his muttering monologue comforting to the steed, "Well, old friend, Fritz's price was certainly better than eight dollars, which that crusty sourpuss uptown offered. Maybe Gold Beach and its citizens aren't so bad. What do you think, Graf?"

His horse snorted on cue, somehow knowing the questioning tone and name invited a response. The entourage moseyed south, its pace set by the slowest member – the ever hungry steer. Buildings appeared in the distance, marking the settlement of Pistol River. A rider galloped out of a draw, a town boy carrying a fishing pole and a string of trout in his off hand.

The lad kneed his horse alongside Scott with the friendly greeting of a would-be huckster, "Hello mister, want to buy fresh trout? I'll make you a real deal on these beauties I caught this afternoon."

"Howdy! Those fish of yours appear to be a might small. Not worth much, I reckon," Scott's tones psuedo-sober as he bartered with the young man.

"These fish are pan-sized and fresh as can be – worth at least a dime each," the boy retorted in like tones, enjoying the bantering challenge of a prospective sale.

Scott leaned over to inspect the trout, feeling and counting the fish before he countered, "I'll pay you a quarter for all six – that's fair."

Their bargaining lasted until they neared the village's out-buildings, Scott finally paying three dimes for the boy's catch and receiving directions to the house of Sandy's cousins for free. Their home lay east of town, a ways up the Pistol River. He'd present the fish for supper, knowing family news given and taken would require a lengthy visit. And because this deal of Jack's would take most of his cousin's cash, he figured he'd give the children each a penny for candy. He'd use the bacon on the trail with the rest of his coffee since the journey home was a long day's ride.

* * * * *

Scott had been home for only a couple of days when Grandpa returned from town with the news that Ella had de-livered a third son – Lloyd Knapp. He playfully doled out the mail as repeated happenings in Port Orford, first three letters to Scott, then a like number to Jane, leaving a single message to George last. The twins complained in unison that there was no letter for either of them.

Squealing in delight as he tore open the envelope, George announced, "They've accepted me at the Salem Preparatory Academy for the fall term. Gee Mom, do you really think I'm smart enough to be a lawyer?"

Scott gave his elated brother a congratulatory hug before retiring to their bedroom to read his own mail. He half-listened to Jane's excited voice as she recited wedding news and the Gerbrunns' plans to attend, hearing the question she called to him, "Are you sure it's all right for us to be married on your birthday, Scott?"

He dutifully answered as he had a score of other times, "Yes, Sis, I think it's fine to share the date with you and Kurt."

He opened an official U. S. Navy envelope, finding a personal offer of assistance by Raymond Johnson following his disclaimer of information regarding Jack-Jack Sixes' missing in action status. Tucking the letter into his travel bag for use in Washington, he opened a letter from Billy Tucker, a short note saying he and Don had sold their gold claims and were on their way home before freeze-up.

He saved Maria's lengthy letter for last, reading it slowly as he imagined her sitting in her room thinking of him as she wrote. His eyes widened a mite as he read that her father had a lady friend, a widow from the war, and Maria often served as a "duenna" when they kept company. She extended another invitation to visit the Chavez casa when he searched for news of the fate of Jack-Jack Sixes.

Summer work occupied all the family in the weeks preceding the August 19th wedding, Jack helping with their haystacks when he came over to report a cougar sighting near his place.

Grandpa Scott rode over toward the Sixes ranch the next morning to track the beast, George tagging along for adventure's sake.

Rick and Scott had finished stacking hay and were chasing steers out of the brush on foot when a distant shot was heard, both men recognizing the sound of Grandpa Scott's trusty old Sharps. Five minutes later a second shot resounded through the forest, this one closer at hand, followed by three spaced shots signaling for help.

Father and son responded post-haste, running up the valley in the direction of the shots. They spotted the old-timer aboard Graf charging recklessly through scrub brush and young firs, his vigorous wave urging them to the river ahead.

Rick ran directly to his father, but Scott swerved aside when he spotted George's horse floundering in the Sixes River. Grandpa's lamenting voice was tragedy's call as he shouted in frustration, "George is down. His horse rolled over him when the cat backtracked. The boy's in the river somewhere but I can't see him."

Without breaking stride Scott lunged into the knee-deep waters, eyes searching the shallows as he plodded into deeper water toward his Grandpa's voice. A flash of white accompanied by a languorous movement under the tangled root of a dead fir prompted a shout of alarm, and he dove into the pool and swam below the obstacle with fierce determination, his groping fingers entwining themselves in the tendrils of hair spreading under the root. Tightening his fist he pulled George free of the entanglement and heaved him upward into the bright sunlight.

Waiting hands seized the boy, carrying him to shore as Scott struggled to the low bank behind his father. Grandpa rolled George over, attempting to drive water from the lad's lungs, but the despair showing in his father's eyes telegraphed the realization that his brother George was beyond help. No water came from his lungs, a twisted neck testifying to his instant death in the tumble.

Rick put a restraining yet empathetic hand on his father's arm, drawing him away from the body as young Scott checked for an absent pulse, turning his brother over to find his lifeless eyes frozen open in death. When he cradled the familiar form in his arms and rose to his feet, Grandpa stepped forward to take George, shaking with tearless sobs as he started walking down the valley to their ranch.

"Dad, take the horses home and tell our womenfolk what happened. I'll stay with Grandpa and George. We'll be along in a few minutes," Scott suggested, his experiences in the war shielding him from the shocked reaction both of his forebears were showing. He knew he would grieve his beloved brother when he had time to think and feel, but for now he must be strong for his family – for Grandpa especially.

* * * * *

Scott stood solemnly beside his brother's grave in the family cemetery, embracing his mother and Jane in a protective manner. Melissa and Anne tearfully released their father so he could render his heart-tugging eulogy, following Grandpa's sparse words of love. The McClure strength of character shone through their sadness on this day. They had grieved together for a day before laying the youngest member of their clan to rest. Rick's voice choked momentarily, eliciting a responsive sob from his wife, and Scott gently squeezed his mother's shoulder in comfort, an introspective concern touching his subconscience.

In acting grown-up with Grandpa carrying George home, riding to family and friends to announce George's death and funeral, and providing emotional support to his distraught mother and sisters, Scott had been somehow untouched by grief – a pillar of control. *My experience with death in Cuba has served me too well*, he thought. *I've neither cried in grief nor raged at the fates. Am I too cold?*

Dad's nerves are like tempered steel. He was devastated by George's death but recovered enough calmness to help Momma and the girls while I spent time with Grandpa. Scott McClure is an original personality, an old veteran used to death but taken unaware by this tragedy – maybe he blames himself a little. No reason to do so, it was just a rotten accident. I wonder why I feel so little – almost numb.

Rick's words ceased, the babbling of the river currents mixing with a raucous call of a bluejay in the myrtlewood grove. His father turned to him with a low-voiced comment, "I'll stay with our womenfolk, Son. You need to speak to your brother one last time."

Scott answered with a compliant nod and traded places with his father, quick to feel the comfort of Grandpa's hand on his shoulder. Facing the gathering, he found his throat constricted and his eyes blinded by sudden tears. Facing his delayed sorrow he relied on George's favorite bedtime prayer when he was a tot, "Now I lay me down..."

As he finished his brief recitation, a great sob shook Scott and silenced his voice for a moment. He continued after taking a deep breath, "Brother of mine, purest of soul and mind, may you rest in peace knowing that all of us are better for having shared your life with you over these few short years. Amen!"

Unable to say more, yet comfortable in his heart that he had said enough, Scott stood with head bowed as his family tossed soil onto George's homemade casket. Adding a handful of his own, Scott sought Jane's hand with his fingers, escorting her up the path to their home in a forlorn silence.

* * * * *

The Gerbrunns arrived by ship late the following week, Kurt borrowing Uncle Johnny's horse to ride out to the Myrtlewood Grove immediately. He expressed his sympathy to the McClures, Jane leading her fiancé to the cemetery to place more flowers on George's grave. Scott was walking down the path to join them when he heard Jane's excited voice ring out in happiness. He smothered his first big grin since his brother's death as he was spotted, wondering about Jane's sudden recovery from grief – and his own happiness for his lovely sister. But he intuitively realized that both he and Jane had lives of their own to live, and while his family was still grieving, Jane was preparing for her wedding and many happy times.

Scott rode to Port Orford with Kurt and Jane to share a meal with the Gerbrunns in Louie Knapp's dining room. Kurt and his father would sleep at George Hermann's and Uwe and Angela would stay with the Madsens. Saturday Old George was hosting a bachelor party while Aunt Anne was giving Jane a shower, and Sunday would be the wedding – also at the Larson's home. Kurt and Jane would spend the night in the hotel's "presidential suite" before sailing to San Francisco for their honeymoon.

* * * * *

Scott studied old George's slumbering form, wrapped in a blanket and reclining in his motionless rocker. *My, George looked peaked today. Everyone's gathered outside enjoying Kurt's party because it's still hot in here, yet he's all covered up and resting. He looks ten years older than when Kurt was last here, and we both thought he was looking poorly at that time.*

Well, it's a nice party anyway. Grandpa has loosened up some and is telling stories again, and Dad is laughing a bit. Even Momma had a wan smile at Jane's shower, and she's been real busy getting ready for tomorrow's big event. Aunt Anne has been a big help and so has Aunt Angela. She wants her father to live in Salem with her but she can't get him to change his mind about his own home in Port Orford. Looking at George right now makes me think she's right. He's not doing well at all.

"Think I'm sleeping, don't you?" George quipped, his laughing eyes studying Scott in turn.

"Nah, old-timer, you just took a little break in telling me about the price of Port Orford cedar in San Francisco – maybe ten minutes."

"Pshaw! That'll teach you to keep an old man company. Do I hear everyone else outside? Did Uwe and Johann talk to you about their horses?" George queried.

"No!" Scott grunted as he helped his friend out of the rocker, standing at his elbow as George stumbled out the door in shaky legs.

"Uwe, Scott wants to know about your horses. Come talk to him while I eat a little of Louie's grilled salmon."

"Sure, Dad. I was just talking to Rick about hiring his son," Uwe replied, turning to Scott as he added, "Are you up to delivering a herd of Gerbrunn horses to California, Scott?"

Rick nodded affirmatively on Scott's behalf, stating in his don't-argue-with-me voice, "I told Uwe you were just the man for the job, Son. Dad and I can handle ranch chores until you get your wandering done and go see your girl." A small smile and a twinkle in his eye betrayed his tongue-in-cheek directive. Uwe continued in explanation, "Old man Johnson over in Keiser passed away this spring, and his wife is selling the farm. Johann and I brought home all our horses we'd been boarding there since Dad died. We don't have room for all the animals, so we sold eighteen mares and geldings to a rancher named Art Simms in Auburn, California. He bought and paid for them last week with my promise I'd deliver them to Auburn. As a matter of fact, he bought one of our studs, too, and took him away after branding all nineteen horses."

Scott glanced at his father, raising a family concern, "Will Momma and the twins be all right if I leave now? I thought my being around the house might be comforting to them, what with George gone and Jane married."

"She told me you should leave on schedule. Your mother knows what's good for you, and Dad and I will be with them. You'll have to pack tonight and catch that Portland-bound steamer with the Gerbrunns tomorrow," Rick stated.

Uwe added with an encouraging smile, "You can take Kurt's place in my brother's cabin. We'll buy your rail ticket to New York and give you fifty dollars in expense money, Scott. Is that fair?"

"You'll spoil me, Uncle Uwe. No cash is necessary but I would like a pick of your young mares when driving your wagons," Scott counter-offered, figuring he had more cash than he wanted to carry already.

"That's a deal, young man. Knowing your appreciation for fine horses, I'll hold you to working off that difference. Let's find George's bottle of brandy and drink to our agreement. Are you old enough to be drinking?"

"Ha! Ha! A former Rough Rider and taking charge of your herd qualify me as an old man before my time. Seriously though Uncle Uwe, I thank you for the offer and that cross-country ticket."

* * * * *

Scott stood up with Kurt by the altar, watching his lovely sister march down the aisle on their father's arm, following in the path of Melissa, Anne, and Mary Anne – little Angela was flower girl. He squeezed his about-to-be "brother's" elbow lightly to quell its trembling while whispering, "Relax, Kurt. Isn't the bride beautiful? You're a lucky man, old buddy."

Failing to get any response, Scott glanced into Kurt's somber countenance and saw his unfocused stare. Promptly nudging him in his ribs, he gave him a quiet order, "Smile, Kurt. That's all right, just stare at Jane and everything will be fine."

The groom followed orders effortlessly, first from his best man and then from the padre, the marriage ceremony going smoothly, including the newlyweds' kiss. Once free of the pressing formality of the rite, Kurt turned loquacious, and the reception mirrored his happy mood.

Scott reflected on the gaiety of the afternoon, comparing the occasion to the family's sorrow of the past week, and was happy for his sister. Seeing Jane across the room, he winked in an exaggerated fashion at her and was rewarded with a beaming smile and a thrown kiss. She caught Scott by surprise a few moments later, sneaking up behind him to plant a real kiss on his cheek. Not given to emotional demonstration, nevertheless both of them shared an endearing hug and many rather trite expressions of filial love.

Minutes later bride and groom slipped away in a shower of rice, Scott covering their retreat until they disappeared into the Knapp Hotel with nary a glance back.

Scott quickly changed clothes and walked with Johann down to the harbor, bidding fond farewells atop the bluff to family and friends, getting last minute instructions from Jack Sixes, and finding Uncle Johnny beside him on the path to the beach. He slipped a Derringer pistol into Scott's hand with an observation, "Fella traded me this gun for a pack of supplies last month. Figured you might need it in your travels, what with the responsibility for Gerbrunn's horses and then your fat moneybelt for your trip East. Sell it when the Derringer weighs more than your purse," Johnny teased with a grin, giving him a friendly cuff on his shoulder.

Scott was first out to the ship in his eagerness to get started, but found himself blinking back a tear or two as he waved farewell to his loved ones on shore. It would be a long time before he saw them again.

Chapter Eleven

Uwe cajoled a recalcitrant gelding up the runway onto the cattle car, where Scott held the sliding door half open. *Or half closed as a pessimist might say*, the would-be-cowboy thought to himself. He grinned as Uwe struggled with the last horse, Gerbrunn temper flaring as the animal balked again, a slap on the rump necessary to get him aboard.

Scott quickly slammed the slatted door closed and chained it tight, padlock and all. He dropped to the ground and helped Uwe and two railroad workers push the ramp aside.

"Are you sure you want to ride with the herd, Scott? That Pullman car would be more comfortable," Uwe asked again.

"Nope! I'm responsible for your horses until Art Simms meets me in Auburn, and I intend to stick close to them all the way. Aunt Angela fixed me a mighty fine looking picnic basket of food. Thank her for me, will you, Uncle Uwe?"

Uwe reached under the wagon seat and lifted out a bottle of red wine, offering it to Scott as he advised, "Well don't let those horses disturb your sleep, I hope that stall will give you a bit of room to relax. Now you'd better climb aboard, the conductor is signaling the engineer an all clear."

"Thanks, I'll be just fine. See you in a few months to pick up my horse," Scott chuckled at his jibe as he scaled the car wall and swung through the window-like opening, waving goodbye as the train jerked forward.

Answering Uwe's final hand salute with a second wave, Scott closed the shutter and tied it down, dropping to the hay-covered deck with bottle in hand. Several horses crowded up to the stall railing for attention and maybe a treat, but he ignored them as he made a nest of hay in the far corner and sat back on his work saddle.

Daydreaming as he watched the Willamette countryside pass by, he recalled his busy but short stay in Salem. *I enjoyed the fair skies and quiet seas on the voyage north. We were lucky to catch an afternoon train to Salem, and I did find the evening at home with the Gerbrunns quite pleasant and relaxing.*

And then Johann's conductor friend showed up at dawn to tell us a cattle car was available for the trip to Sacramento, but it was leaving at noon. Ha! Ha! Naturally Johann had an important meeting today, and most of Uwe's teamsters were on the road already. Uwe and I decided to take the horses, tethered six at a time, and catch that train. Old Slowpoke, the hired hand, hustled when he heard our plan. Why he moved faster than I've ever seen him do before. It was clever of him to pick six of the gentlest mares and quickly leave for the depot, where he could twiddle his thumbs until I arrived with my six animals. Anyway, we did quite well in herding them aboard although Uwe had to drag the more cantankerous horses across town – and the hired hand left before he got to the depot.

* * * * *

Scott was jerked awake, at least startled out of his drowsy contemplation by the metallic screech of steel on steel as the train ground to a stop. He didn't have a schedule for this "milk run," and wondered which town he was observing through the slats of his cattle car. As the engine whistle sounded to the tracks ahead, the herky-jerky motion of the train's departure was felt. Scott observed a small depot with an Albany sign over its platform which confirmed his guess.

Several horses exhibited nervous and upset behavior, stamping the floor and banging the sides of the car. Scott sighed as he rose to his feet and talked to the herd. He climbed slowly over the stall railing, his familiar voice gentling all but two or three of the ornerier beasts. Circulating through the animals, he patted manes or flanks, his course set for one agitated young gelding.

Avoiding a malicious nip of clashing white teeth, Scott grabbed a handful of mane just behind an ear and pulled the horse toward him, gently stroking the horse for a few moments before releasing his grip. The gelding shook his head and nuzzled the wrangler, all thoughts of antagonism gone.

Repeating his strolling monologue and caressing hands with all eighteen horses, he was soon back in his stall, singing a popular ditty from his Rough Riders days in Cuba. As off-key as his efforts were, they did seem to calm his charges.

Drover and horses soon became accustomed to the unsettling clamor of stopping and starting, Eugene being the only layover of any length, Scott fed the animals from a feedbag of oats, meticulously making sure each horse got a bite. A time or two he felt the heavy crush of hungry horses crowding against him, but they responded obediently to his voice and touch. Guessing with fair certainty that each had eaten his or her share, he proceeded to pour water from a five-gallon can into the trough next to his stall. Both can and trough were dry by the time Scott called it a day.

Dusk was masking the hills above the north Umpqua as the train rumbled through Winchester, and Scott dug into Aunt Angela's picnic lunch for fried chicken and biscuits. He washed the meal down with a tin cup of Uwe's red wine, donning his denim jacket before settling into his nest, head on the old saddle and body sprawled over the hay padding on a hard deck.

The jolting stop and sound of voices awakened him in pitch-black darkness, a pair of swinging lanterns casting shadows as they approached. He rose to his feet and climbed up the wall, unlatching his shutter to call out, "Hello, men! Where are we?"

A chuckle echoed through the still air, mixing with the hiss of their steam engine in the peaceful night. A voice replied, "Medford, mister! You traveling with those horses?"

"Yes, sir. Any chance of getting some water for these beasts?" Scott queried hopefully.

A quick exchange of muted words preceded one lantern moving away as the friendly yardsman affirmed Scott's request, "Yes, Hank will bring a couple of buckets over in a minute. This train won't move until the northbound passes through. Where you headed, mister?"

"Auburn, California! I figure to be there late tomorrow. That sound about right to you?" Scott replied, reaching for a proffered bucket as Hank returned.

"The train is due in Sacramento around five o'clock, but I don't know about Auburn. Your car will have to be switched in the yard there. Two buckets enough? I hear the northbound's whistle across town," the yardsman stated, the headlamp's bright beam visible in the distance.

Scott traded an empty bucket for a full one, rushing in the darkness to slop water into the trough. As the steel behemoth thundered alongside, he picked his half empty bottle of wine and clambered to his window with both hands extended to the pair of railroad workers, "Thanks! You've been a real help. Here's your bucket and a little wine."

* * * * *

The gentle sway of the railway cars provided a lulling effect on the horses as well as their drover, the animals quiet and troubleless while Scott dozed through the Siskiyous. The moonlight was bright in the clear night skies, causing him to toss and turn on his makeshift bed. Awakening with a pain in his side, he discovered he was lying on his Derringer pistol.

Aunt Angela had sewn a pocket holster inside the left fold of his jacket and fashioned an ammunition belt on his right side, sort of a section of a miniature bandoleer, which held eight bullets. She had advised him at the time, "If you feel the need to carry that awful pistol, you'd better keep it handy all the time. And I bet your grandfather told you to use it if you had to point it at someone. Right?"

Scott smiled at the memory, both pieces of advice on his mind as he lay on his back to catch another wink, the weight of his weaponry lying comfortably on his chest.

Real sleep eluded Scott in the minutes to follow, and when a pair of his charges began fussing, he began singing his ditty softly. Climbing fluidly over the stall rail, he walked among the horses and calmed the two geldings with a friendly hand. On the far side of the cattle car he gazed upon a beautiful sight, Mount Shasta illuminated by the moon and standing in silhouette against the not so black eastern sky. Figuring dawn was not too far off, Scott worked his way back to his nook, checking the half-full water trough before lying down.

A few moments later the train began slowing down. Pressing his face against the slots he could see a red light beyond the steam engine's headlight, a single lantern swinging beside it. As the train crunched and clanked to a complete stop, Scott was startled by the sound of low voices in the shadows beside the tracks. His padlocked chain rattled as someone pulled it, an angry curse resounding from near the car door.

Scott responded immediately, moving over the stall rail as he shouted, "You people stay clear of this car. I'm riding herd on these horses, and you're not coming in."

"Shoot him, Harry. He's in the corner stall there. We'll never get those horses with him inside," called a muted voice from the shadows.

Scott dropped to the deck, drawing his Derringer as he crouched behind the slatted walls, two pistol shots sounding close at hand. Hearing the thuds of bullets hitting his saddle resolved any hesitancy in his reply. Aiming below the pistol's flashes, he shot both rounds in rapid fire, rolling to his right as he reloaded both barrels. Hampered by the excited horses stomping around his legs, Scott leaped to his feet before firing back at a second gun's shot. Scampering backwards to the water trough, Scott waited patiently for the railroad workers and their lanterns to light up the area.

"Cowboy! Are you all right? What's the shooting all about?" the conductor called excitedly.

Scott replied calmly, "There's three of four thieves out there, Conductor. Be careful, they're armed and mad to boot. I'm just defending my horses."

One of the railroad men shouted, "Look, here's a Colt .45 on the ground. And some blood next to it. You must have hit one of them, mister."

A second voice added, "But the crooks must have dragged him into the brush. They got away, boss."

The conductor ordered, "Give me the gun. I'll turn it over to the deputy sheriff in Dunsmuir. You men look around for any other evidence while I get this train moving."

* * * * *

Scott was more upset by the shooting than the horses, not able to relax until the train left Dunsmuir station. His conversation with the deputy sheriff was laconic, the officer listening to both Scott and the conductor with a friendly smile and agreeable nod. His two questions were simple, "Would you recognize the horse thieves? Was anything stolen?" and concluded the interview. The deputy took the Colt pistol and left, the conductor laughing outright at Scott's expression.

"Did you think he would mount up and ride after the crooks?" he asked the young man.

"No, but he didn't seem...well...much of a sheriff. I guess I shouldn't complain – he was nice enough," Scott bemoaned.

The conductor waved to the engineer leaning out of the locomotive's window as he concluded, "He knew we have a schedule to follow and didn't waste our time. Why didn't you show him the holes in your saddle?"

"Ha! Ha! I guess I'm in a hurry, too. When will we reach the locomotive switching yard?" Scott asked.

"Maybe five o'clock," the conductor replied as the train jerked into motion, running to his caboose to board.

With decent light in the car, Scott fed the horses again, both oats and water gone by the time the train coasted onto the valley floor. He talked a railroad worker with a hose to the water tower to spray the trough full of water for his thirsty animals and then sat back and enjoyed the ride beside the Sacramento River. The hot sun was still bright in the western sky when the train crossed the river one last time and pulled into the large switching yard outside the state capital.

The massive confusion of switching cars and engines dumbfounded the "country boy" in Scott; a seemingly endless frenzy of movement and activity to the uninitiated mystified him even with his experiences in the Rough Riders. Fortunately his friendly status with the conductor paid off, as the man inveigled the yardmaster to handle his friend first. Scott's car was quickly hooked onto an eastbound freight train on its way up the American River.

By the time Scott was settled into the journey and enjoying the gentle hills with its orange groves, the engine began laboring in a serious climb up the Donner Pass. He circulated about the car gentling his horses as the noise of the locomotive

increased, and was back in his stall when its steam whistle
sounded repeatedly with a distant voice calling out Auburn.

* * * * *

Scott climbed the slats up to his window and swung the
shutter open, head and shoulders thrust outside to view the
Auburn yards. The train was moving along a deserted siding
beside a half-dozen corrals. Four railway workers were
wrestling the stock ramp into position before an open-gated
pen. Perched on the top bar across from the gate was a cat-
tleman wearing working clothes – plaid shirt, tattered Levis,
and scuffed leather cowboots. The only ostentatious article of
apparel marking him as unusual was a clean, white, broad-
rimmed Stetson obscuring his features.

The object of Scott's appraisal waved a calloused hand in
greeting, his deep voice carrying over the metallic screech of
braking wheels on the rails, "Howdy! You'd be Scott McClure,
I expect. Are all my horses healthy? I'm Art Simms."

"Yes sir! Pleased to meet you," Scott replied with a relieved grin.

"And glad to be rid of this herd if you're like me. The
railroad sent a wire from Redding that you had trouble with
would-be rustlers. Any damage in that shoot-out?" Art asked,
then chuckled aloud as he dropped off the bar and walked up
the stock runway.

Scott swung out his window and crabbed sideways along
the slats until he could drop onto the ramp beside the rancher,
shaking hands as he studied his weatherworn face. Art Simms
was fortyish and still handsome, despite a nasty white scar
along his left jawbone, an average build, shaggy brown hair
and mustache visible under the shadowed brim of his Stetson.
With cowboy's garb showing, Art Simms appeared unim-
pressive, except when Scott looked into his steely-blue eyes.
Their commanding gaze reminded him of his hero, the late
Captain Tom Case. Here was a man of confidence and leadership.

Scott shook his head at the rancher's concern, adding, "I
don't know how all three of those rustlers' bullets missed your
horses, Art. In fact, I'm not sure how they missed me. We
were all lucky, I guess."

Simms empathetic smile was accompanied by a nod of approval for the young herder's modesty as he drawled easily, "Just another day on the ranch, eh? Well, let's open that padlock and get those animals into the corral."

"Sure thing but let me lead one of your horses down the ramp. The rest will follow us," Scott replied as he slid the gate open, singing his silly little ditty as he seized the ornery gelding by his mane and walked him into the corral. A slap on the rump sent the beast forward with the other horses following their leader docilely.

Scott retrieved his saddle and traveling bag before the yard workers closed the car and moved the ramp. The waiting engineer tooted the steam whistle just before the string of cars jerked into motion. Within moments the area was relatively quiet, Art's cajoling voice seeming loud as he wended his way through the herd, getting reacquainted with his horses.

* * * * *

Scott settled on the top rail where Simms had waited for the train, watching a natural horseman at work. Art ignored him and the girl rider leading a Gerbrunn stallion across the tracks.

It took a moment for Scott to recognize the frisky horse he'd befriended as a yearling two summers before in Salem. He dropped to the ground and called out, "Hi Jerry!" startling the stallion into a nervous prance over the tracks. The girl and her mount handled the situation with confident authority, leading him up to the grinning cowboy.

Leaning forward to hand Scott a carrot, the girl suggested, "Here, feed him a carrot, and King will remember you immediately. You must be Scott McClure. I'm Louise Simms."

"Thanks, Louise. It's a pleasure," Scott replied as he made up to his old friend Jerry – now King. He studied Louise Simms out of the corner of his eye, appreciative of her poise with horses. The girl's auburn tresses squeezed out of her narrow-brimmed and flat-crowned hat, matching eyebrows suggesting a redhead in the family – perhaps her mother's side. Her blue eyes studied him in return, a mischievous smile springing to her lips as their gazes met.

"Do I pass inspection, Scott?" Louise teased, a flush highlighting her freckles as she laughed.

Art slipped through the corral gate, observing the young man's handling of his stallion and ignoring his daughter's flirtatious manner as he asked half-seriously, "Nice work, Scott. Are you interested in a job wrangling horses?"

"Just for a day, Art. I promised Uncle Uwe that I'd see the herd to pasture. Is there an eastbound passenger out of here tomorrow?"

Louise was quick to respond, "Yes, at eleven o'clock in the morning. My Aunt Ann is taking it to Denver. Where are you headed?"

Scott smiled, and Art frowned at the girl's forward manner, answering easily, "I'm headed for New York and then Washington, D. C. Can you use my help now?"

"Yes!" answered both father and daughter.

Art asked the obvious question, "Think we can loose herd them through the yards and north to the ranch? Louise and I had planned to tether them together and take them home, but with your help we can save time."

Nodding in agreement, Scott answered, "I bet if I saddle up that ornery gelding and ride him out of here, the whole herd will follow. Three of us should be able to handle this bunch."

Toting his saddle and the hackamore hanging from its horn, he stepped into the corral beside Art and dropped the saddle on the ground. Taking the rough halter to the gelding, he had little resistance from "Henry," the name sounded nicer than "Ornery," when he placed it over his head. Talking gently all the while, he led Henry to the gate where Art slipped the saddle smoothly across his withers, sliding it backwards as he tightened the cinch.

Louise handed him his bag after he mounted Henry, and Art pointed to an aisle through the trees north of the tracks, directing, "You lead the way. My daughter and I will drive the horses behind you until we're clear of town, and then Louise will show you the trail to the ranch. It's only ten miles or so and easy riding. My sister Ann will have dinner waiting for us."

Scott nodded and reined Henry through the gate and across the tracks, the horse undecided on fighting the rider or running in the wind. However, he did neither while in the young man's firm grip, and the procession entered the woods without incident even much work by the Simms.

Louise rode past him as he crossed a meadow, and Scott kicked Henry into a faster pace, staying behind the girl as they raced along the trail. When the pair of riders looked back, they saw a string of horses running behind them, Art bringing up the rear with a good-natured grin splitting his face.

* * * * *

Scott looked up from his cleaned plate to find everyone waiting on him. Blushingly he apologized, "I'm sorry, Mrs. McCarty. My table manners suffer badly when a meal is so delicious. No!" he said as she pushed the meat platter towards him.

"It's flattering to hear a hungry man appreciate my cooking, but we all want to hear about those bullets in your saddle. My brother tells me you're a veteran of the Rough Riders. Don't be shy, Scott. Tell us your story," Ann requested.

Scott spoke the better part of an hour, Ann serving apple pie as he talked of his experiences in Cuba. When he paused to eat his pie, Louise brought up tomorrow's train ride, "I want to go with Aunt Ann to Denver. I'm sure Scott will escort us. Won't you, Scott?"

Swallowing painfully to clear his palate, Scott looked to Art for help but saw just raised eyebrows from the head of the table. He glanced at the girl for a cue but was met with a coquettish smile.

Ann explained, humor in her voice, "My brother thinks women should not travel alone, as he pointed out to me when I arrived. My nephew Lester returned to college at Berkeley last week, and Art has a cattle roundup going on right now in his east pasture. Louise would like you to allay her daddy's objections by being our bodyguard. Seriously Scott, I'd love to have your company, and I would feel more comfortable with you along."

"Please, Scott. Daddy will buy your ticket, and Aunt Ann and I will be eternally grateful."

Scott laughed agreeably, "Since your father hasn't said no, I accept, my young friend. Even though I think you ladies are overrating my protection, it will be an honor to be your escort."

Art added ruefully, "You're probably right, Scott. Since I've become a widower, I've found these two women are tougher than most men. I bet they do a good job of protecting you."

* * * * *

Scott slept until the morning sun pierced the drawn curtains, rising to don clothes which were magically cleaned and pressed. When he joined the family at the kitchen table for toast and coffee, Aunt Ann complimented him on his appearance. He promptly turned to Louise and thanked her for washing his clothes, bringing a look of pleasure to her eyes for having done a good deed and a softly spoken, "You're welcome!"

Chuckling, Art inserted his comment, "My daughter's idea was good, but I was the culprit who borrowed your clothes in the night. You were sound asleep. Are you rested enough to load the carriage with the women's luggage? We'd best be going if you're to catch that train at eleven."

Art's team of matched chestnut mares was fussing in their harness as the men loaded the trunks and bags. Scott found time to admire the Simms' horses before Louise appeared on the scene, urging her Aunt Ann to hurry. She snorted in exasperation when her father went back into the kitchen for a picnic basket of food for the trip.

During the lengthy buggy ride to Auburn, Scott realized the old road they were traveling was longer than the horse trail. He began to feel a little anxiety like Louise's as eleven o'clock neared, and to forestall thinking about the time he asked conversationally, "Louise, you told me your brother is studying at the university, but what about you?"

"I finished grammar school here last spring, but father won't let me attend Mills until I'm older. I'm almost fifteen years old. How old are you, Scott?"

"I was nineteen last month," Scott responded, despite Simms' grunt of disapproval for his daughter's forward manner.

"But you said you fought with the Rough Riders in Cuba. I thought you were older. Why, my brother Lester is older than you are. You're closer to my age," Louise stated smugly, seeming pleased with that thought.

Further conversation was limited as the buggy approached civilization, several people greeting the Simms as they hurried down the road. On reaching the depot, Art went inside to buy tickets while Scott engaged an obliging Negro porter to handle the women's trunks. Art returned just as the passenger cars pulled up to the platform, making goodbyes short but emotional, ending with the conductor's gusty shout, "All aboard!"

The three friends quietly admired the view of the Sierras as the train climbed over Donner Pass and followed the Truckee River into Reno. As they stopped at its depot, Aunt Ann asked, "The Truckee meadows are so hot. Can you find us some cool water to drink? Or maybe a bottle of sarsaparilla?"

Scott left the train with several other men in search of drinks, dutifully bypassing a sudsy beer to fill Ann's simple request. Even so he had to run to catch the moving train, the women laughing at his out-of-breath condition. He wondered if the other men had returned in time.

During an early picnic supper, Scott rambled on about his days with the Four Musketeers in the Rough Riders, his service with Teddy Roosevelt, his short fight near El Caney, and his hospital stay with Maria nursing him.

When he mentioned Maria's name a second time, Louise frowned and muttered, "She's your sweetheart, isn't she?" He nodded and the conversation ended, Aunt Ann suggesting everyone take a nap before the train reached Salt Lake City.

* * * * *

The train was well into the Rockies when Scott left the sleeping ladies to join the conductor on the platform between cars. The man was smoking a cigarette and, therefore, standing still long enough to answer Scott's question about connections to Chicago and New York. The car's dim lantern light was lost when he closed the door, but the glowing cigarette provided sufficient light to visit with the man.

Their conversation produced a modified ticket to New York on this very train, his recognition as the Shasta cowboy who fought off rustlers, and a bit of daylight on the eastern horizon. He thanked the friendly railroad officer and reentered his car.

One of the fellows he'd seen get on and off the train in search of drinks – likely liquor, was sitting in his seat badgering Ann for a handout. His voice was slurred and his manner sullen as he demanded money "to protect you fine ladies traveling alone."

Scott grinned at the offer while his anger rose at the man's insulting behavior. *Maybe I'd better earn my keep as escort*, he thought as he walked down the aisle. Louise's relieved smile as she spotted him alerted the hoodlum, who rose to his feet pulling his coat tails clear of a holstered pistol. His manner was threatening enough to elicit squeals from both ladies.

Acting with impetuosity, Scott struck the fellow with the back of his left hand, driving him into the empty seat. Drawing his Derringer with his right hand, he cocked both barrels when the hoodlum grasped the handle of his revolver.

"Don't shoot! Don't shoot! I was just trying to help these ladies. I didn't mean no harm," the fellow whined piteously.

Scott thrust the Derringer's barrels into the man's chest and leaned forward to draw the pistol from his holster. The conductor appeared at their sides, stating, "I'll take that Colt Bisley, Mr. McClure."

Quickly uncocking his own weapon, Scott sheathed it and asked, "Are you ladies all right?"

A nod from them brought on a righteous complaint from the hoodlum and a disavowal of any wrongdoing. Confidence growing in the presence of the conductor, the fellow's language slipped into four-letter words not acceptable in the presence of ladies.

Scott drove a fist into his mouth, and before he could resist, grasped the man's jacket and spun him about. One hand entwined in his long hair and the other gripping his belt firmly, Scott marched the mewling beggar out of the car, the conductor hurrying forward to open the door. The three friends never saw the man again.

Ann planted a motherly kiss of gratitude on his cheek and thanked him for dismissing that horrible bum while Louise just stared at him with hero worship. He thought both were a little frightened by his violence but warmed up to him as they chatted the remainder of the journey into Denver.

John McCarty was waiting on the platform when Scott escorted the ladies out of the car and ordered the porter to bring their trunks. Ann introduced her husband to Scott, and they shook hands, McCarty a little confused as both ladies kissed Scott farewell and thanked him for his company.

Chapter Twelve

Scott stepped down to the gravelly bed of the railroad siding in Montauk, having hitched a ride in the freight's caboose – a silver dollar ample payment to the conductor. He stretched his muscles as he strode across the familiar post grounds, heading for the old headquarters building. His eyes swept to and fro, comparing similarities and differences with each glance, wondering if many soldiers were still recuperating in the hospital to his left. A year had passed since he'd hobbled away on Billy's arm, both with discharges in hand.

"Scott! Scott McClure! Welcome back to Montauk. You're looking fit, lad," called a familiar voice from an open office window dead ahead.

Grinning broadly as he leaned over the casement to shake hands was First Sergeant Hokey, his mentor from the Rough Riders. They greeted one another enthusiastically, Scott laughing joyfully as he returned the friendly greeting "I'm fine, Sergeant. What are you doing in Montauk? I thought you were assigned to Tampa after the fighting."

"And so I was Scott – for six months, and then I became a record keeper. Ugh! I'm bored sitting around an office. Say, did you get the letter I sent to Port Orford? I found your inquiry regarding our buddy Jack-Jack Sixes and did considerable checking in our files and then talked to the few veterans still around Montauk. I'm sure he never came through here. Have you tried Tampa?"

The two men spent the day catching up on each other's past year, then visiting with other men at evening mess. Jack-Jack Sixes was not known by anyone else, nor was there a trace of information about him in camp.

Scott slept in a spare bunk in Hokey's quarters, and the two friends rode the morning train to New York City. The sergeant took a couple of day's leave to sight-see with his buddy and then led him to Fort Hamilton in Brooklyn to visit an old friend in the record center. Their quest was fruitless but highly enjoyable, and that afternoon Scott boarded a train for Washington.

* * * * *

Scott strolled down Pennsylvania Avenue, glancing over his shoulder at the White House now and then, resisting the urge to pinch himself. He was enthralled with the history of the capital and its government buildings. He turned west on I Street, passing George Washington University on his way to the modest inn near the Potomac River which he had called home for three days. Raymond Johnson was returning to town tomorrow, and Scott had an afternoon appointment at his office.

Gray skies and the fall equinox combined to darken the neighborhood earlier than Scott had expected, his inn still visible a block away when he was approached by a pair of seedy characters. Crossing the empty cobblestone street to avoid contact, he found the two men followed suit, setting a course to intercept him midway to his destination. Figuring their intentions were at best begging, and at worst thievery, he flipped his jacket lapel wide open to expose his Derringer. Walking straight at the taller ruffian, he reached his right hand over his chest.

His intended threat made the man's eyes grow round in fright, the would-be badman skittering sideways out of his path with his partner beside him. Approaching the hostelry's old Bavarian façade, he saw the innkeeper standing at the door with cudgel in hand.

His host nodded as he commented, "I was about ready to come to your aid, Mr. McClure, but I see it isn't necessary. Do be careful around here at twilight, sir. Footpads like those two characters are always on the lookout for a lone walker."

"Thanks, Mr. Mayer, I appreciate your advice. It surprises me that the nation's capital would harbor such scoundrels," Scott remarked and then added an obvious conclusion, "But I suppose it's like anywhere else. There are good people and bad people in every community."

* * * * *

Another day of delay resulted when Raymond Johnson spent the next afternoon in a meeting with the Secretary of the Navy. His congenial clerk offered Scott two pieces of advice, suggesting, "Why don't you come into the office early tomorrow morning, and I'll try to arrange a few minutes of Mr. Johnson's schedule for your visit. And you really shouldn't wear a gun in this building – a guard might show you the door."

Scott followed the man's advice to the letter, leaving his Derringer in his room and reporting to the clerk at eight o'clock sharp. Sure enough, minutes later he was ushered into Raymond Johnson's presence, the Navy official greeting him warmly. Any friend of Teddy's was welcome in Washington these days.

Fifteen minutes later the clerk entered to remind Mr. Johnson of another meeting, Scott excusing himself after thanking both men for their time. Once again the young veteran was disappointed by the lack of information on Jack-Jack Sixes. Washington had no knowledge of his friend's fate either.

That evening Scott drank a pint of beer with his host, bidding the friendly innkeeper farewell and asking about his bill. Earlier in the day he had purchased a ticket on the morning train to Florida, heading for Tampa and a visit with one of Sergeant Hokey's army friends.

"Would you be interested in selling your Derringer? And your jacket? I could use the protection of a small pistol in my business. We might be able to do a bit of horse-trading against your week's bill," the innkeeper offered.

"Well, I figured on selling the pistol in Tampa, but I need my jacket. Besides it's too small for you. Maybe your wife could transfer my holster rig to one of your jackets. I'd trade you even up if you'd throw in a couple of beef sandwiches for my trip south," Scott counter-offered in a bantering tone. A deal was consummated when Scott paid the wife a silver dollar for her sewing work.

* * * * *

A week later Scott walked out of the railroad depot shaking his head in disgust at the delays he'd encountered. Two train detours and a bout with influenza in Atlanta had sapped his energy and depleted his finances.

Well, at least it's only a mile or so to the army barracks where Hokey's friend, Sergeant Allen, is stationed, he commiserated with himself in silence, his legs already feeling the weakness from his illness. *Golly, I hardly recognize Tampa. Our train came down that track by the docks, but I never walked around town except when I was following the Lieutenant. I guess I'd better ask that policeman on the corner for directions.*

"Pardon me, Officer. Could you direct me to the army barracks in town?" Scott inquired.

The uniformed older man suggested, "Why don't you walk my beat with me for a bit, and I'll point it out. Are you enlisting?"

"No, I served with the Rough Riders during the war. We came through here last year, but I didn't see much of the city. Spent most of my stay in Florida on a transport in the harbor," Scott related with a self-deprecating chuckle.

"Oh yes, I remember the story of Teddy Roosevelt preempting a transport one morning. How was Teddy as a commander? Do you think he'll run for president next year?"

Scott added another chuckle as he replied, "He's a good man. I was his runner in Cuba until I volunteered for scouting duties. I expect he'll be out in front of the candidates for office. I'd vote for him if I was old enough."

A fatherly smile creased the police officer's face as he pointed up a cross street and said, "Me too, lad! Those buildings yonder are your destination. The headquarters office faces the parade grounds on the south side. Is there anything else you need to know?"

"Yes, sir! Where would I find out about ship sailings to Cuba – Santiago or Daquiri that is?" Scott queried.

"There's a ship in port loading cargo for Santiago today. I heard it sails in the morning. I don't know which berth, but anyone along the waterfront can tell you. Good luck, lad!"

* * * * *

Sergeant Hokey evidently was acquainted with most non-commissioned officers in the United States Army. He described his friend, Sergeant Allen, as a crafty thirty-year veteran who had never seen a day of wartime action. On meeting the man in his Tampa office, Scott could see why. Allen was almost as broad as he was tall, his rotund shape forcing him to wear suspenders to hold his pants up. He could have doubled for General William Shaftner who so uncomfortably commanded the V Corps in Cuba.

His friendly greeting didn't impress Scott half as much as his phenomenal memory for details. Sergeant Allen recounted every letter he and Jack Sixes had written and then described his thorough search for any records which might indicate Jack-Jack's whereabouts – dead or alive. Admittedly showing a greater interest in the case after receiving a letter from his old buddy Hokey, he nevertheless had done a credible research of the records. Within an hour Scott acknowledged that he'd reached another dead end.

Thanking the fat but happy veteran as he bade him farewell, Scott realized when he left the headquarters office that Allen had never left his comfortable oversized chair. *So much for fat and able fighting men leading our army*, was the humorous thought which crossed Scott's mind as he hurried down the Tampa street with bag in hand.

Following the policeman's useful advice, Scott headed for the most likely section of the waterfront, asking an idle group of dockworkers for information on a Santiago-bound ship. In unison they pointed to a drab tramp steamer two piers south of their dock and then went back to doing nothing. Scott figured their boss must be away.

Within twenty minutes Scott was ensconced in a tiny cabin tucked below the wheelhouse of the *Tiburon*, his money belt much depleted by the exorbitant fare. Three gold coins in his belt and a pocket full of silver would not be enough to return home. He'd have to work as he searched for Jack-Jack and courted Maria Chavez.

* * * * *

The Caribbean voyage had proven quite unlike last year's ordeal aboard ship, Scott's private cabin and good mess had been complemented by the captain's granting him the run of the vessel. Freedom of movement and beautiful sailing weather, seemingly a pre-curser of the coming hurricane season, had resulted in a vacation for the traveler. His sighting of Santiago had been almost anticlimactic by the time the *Tiburon* had entered the spacious harbor.

Scott's gaze took in the scenery, signs of war all but gone although he did spot the hull of a sunken ship in the waterway and noticed a few scars along the gunports of the fort. The only other visible remnant of the Spanish-American War was the American flag flying over the local customs house in the city, a reminder of the Continental United States presence in Cuba.

Shrugging aside the lethargy of idleness and the mild apprehension of being a guest, Scott collected his bag and climbed to the bridge wing to thank the captain for the pleasant cruise. Moving with renewed purpose, his hurried departure down the gangplank was stymied at the customs house by a grouchy siesta-interrupted Cuban official clad in rebel-type clothing. To Scott's disappointment the American Sergeant in the room was of no help, insisting on seeing a passport – something Scott didn't possess. Exasperated by his detention with the two officious public servants, Scott pulled out the letter Raymond Johnson had given him, suggesting he look for Jack-Jack Sixes in Cuba. Set on U. S. Navy letterhead paper, the document looked official enough to satisfy the two men. Inadvertently several silver coins spilled from his pocket onto the low customs table, one or two rolling onto the floor.

Catching a glint of avarice in the Cuban's eye at the money before him and sensing the Sergeant's favorable view of the Washington letter with a U. S. Navy stamp, Scott offered a casual suggestion, "I trust this letter will be sufficient identification for me to land in Santiago and visit Daquiri. Sorry I dropped those coins on the table, perhaps you gentlemen can use them for a beer after work."

At their respective nods of assent, Scott retrieved his letter and asked, "Which road do I take to Daquiri?"

He was out the gate as soon as they pointed easterly, disappearing amid the people on the streets before they changed their minds. He'd worry about proper papers again when he returned to Tampa. His smile and his carefree step attracted a few like smiles as he walked through the city along a well-used avenue, a roadside sign indicating the route to Daquiri dead

ahead. Seeing the San Juan Heights from the west side convinced Scott that he was on track.

* * * * *

Munching on a dried old sea biscuit as he perched on a
downed tree, a circle of stones at his feet, Scott mused on his
location. *I'm only a few yards from where I was shot and
Albert was killed, but I can't find the actual spot. So many
trees are gone, and this forest is faceless. I bet local people
have plenty of firewood for their cookstoves. Gee, there are
more villages and people than I remember. I thought El Caney
was the only one. I guess Cubans just stayed out of the way
during the fighting – pretty smart, I reckon.*

Scott slipped off the log and walked to a clear pool in gently
flowing stream nearby, crouching low to drink his fill before
washing sweat and dust from his face and neck. Refreshed he
began retracing his route from the July First battle, finally
giving up as he muttered aloud, "I can't find that stump I
ducked behind when I was shot. I don't suppose I'll ever find
the exact spot."

"Sí, señor. The forest is much changed from the great battle
last year," an elderly man spoke from behind a woodpile only a
few feet away.

Scott hadn't seen either the man or his stack of firewood
and was startled by his voice. He quickly agreed, "Yes, I'm
still a long ways from Daquiri, and the sun is setting behind the
San Juan Heights. Is there a place I can buy supper hereabouts?"

He studied the English-speaking peasant as the man mulled
over his words, noting a wrinkled countenance split by a gap-
toothed smile. His gray hair was topped by a floppy straw hat,
his dark eyes showing intelligence beneath its brim. The old
man looked ancient but moved with agility and strength, his
wiry build younger than his appearance.

"I am Jose Guevera, and you are welcome at my table for
tortillas and beans," the old-timer offered in slow accented
words–rusty English but clear enough for conversation.

"Thank you, Jose. My name is Scott McClure. As you
know I was with the American army last year and was

wounded around here somewhere. I'm on my way to visit my doctor friend, Juan Chavez of Daquiri."

Jose reacted strangely, smile gone as his hat brim flapped over his eyes, saying, "I have heard of the loyalist, Doctor Chavez. The rebels told bad stories about him."

Abruptly the smile returned to the old man's lips and eyes, his hat flung back as he philosophized, "The war was last year. Rebel and loyalist are both men of Cuba this year."

When he picked up an armload of wood, Scott followed suit, trailing his new friend along a path toward El Caney village. Maybe the Guevara's had a shed for his bed that night as well as tortillas and beans.

* * * * *

Scott's ever-quickening pace carried him to the Chavez casa low on breath but high in hopes, the streets quiet during the siesta hours. He had helped Jose move his firewood this morning, earning his bed and board, and had arrived in Daquiri later than planned.

Approaching the portico he straightened his jacket and brushed his hair back, bracing himself psychologically before rapping his knuckles firmly against the door. Moments passed without a sound from within, but as he repeated his knock, the door swung open to reveal the dour Consuela. Her solemn greeting in Spanish matched her look for a split-second, until she recognized him belatedly and with a rare smile and a pleasant monologue ushered him into the study. He understood that no one was home, but he was welcome to wait in the parlor until Doctor Chavez came home.

To her concluding question, he responded, "Gracias, Consuela. Lemon with my tea would be fine."

Scott was drinking his second cup when Maria breezed through the front door, hurrying down the hallway past the parlor. She did a double-take as he rose to his feet, almost tripping as she spun about and ran into his open arms, their warm embrace seeming so very natural. Observing an approving smile from the maid, Scott figured he'd been accepted by the Chavez household as a proper suitor.

"When did you arrive? I'm so glad to see you Scott. Your mother wrote me a nice letter saying you were on the way. I've been waiting for ages. Can you stay…," Maria chattered gaily, her eyes dancing as she studied his face. He silenced her by kissing her full lips with amorous intent, his emotions overcoming his good sense.

Consuela's tongue-clucking warning caused Maria to place an open palm against his chest and step back, her chuckle stilling his ardor as she resumed her monologic conversation, "My duenna disapproves of our embrace I do believe, and besides I need a little air. We can visit for a little while until Father arrives home with Pilar for supper. You're invited, of course, and you can sleep in Anita's room while you're…"

Scott's mesmerized gaze at the lovely young lady before him reflected much of his adoration, stopping Maria in midsentence again, the couple recognizing the spark of love which had been lit. He dropped his arms to his side as he leaned forward to kiss her again, the buss gentle and silencing as he declared, "With all due respect to our chaperone, I just had to do that. I'm so happy to see you. You are a beautiful woman, Maria Chavez."

Seeing surprise and no displeasure in the girl's eyes and noting a nod of approval from the ever-present Consuela, Scott was more discreet this time as he took Maria's hand in his own, suggesting, "Let's sit on the patio, and you can tell me about your family and life in Daquiri. We have a whole year to catch up on. Are you still nursing poor soldiers?"

* * * * *

The well-spoken conversation in English at the supper table was pleasant enough but three-sided, Pilar picking at her paella after complimenting Consuela on her cooking. Her eschewal of any eye contact with Scott, even to his polite questions, made him realize her reserved attitude was directed solely at him. It became pronounced, actually irritable in manner, when the subject of the Spanish-American War came up.

Doctor Chavez asked about Scott's quest to discover the fate of Jack-Jack Sixes, and the name of Jose Guevera was mentioned in the resulting conversation. Pilar reacted with a hiss of scorn, and finally looking at Scott, she muttered a hateful, "He's a peon and a rebel!"

Her glance reflected intense hostility as she faced him, announcing with pride, "My husband was the captain of infantry who was shot by the peons of El Caney before the Americans attacked. One of his fellow officers told me Jose Guevera and Alberto Salazar led the rebels."

Juan interrupted in conciliatory tones, "The war is over Pilar, forget the sadness of death. We cannot change anything."

Tears appeared in the corners of Pilar's eyes as she agreed, "I know, I know, but Ricardo was so full of life and in his prime. War is terrible."

Scott spoke up, "You're right, ma'am. My cousin Albert died in my arms up there and was only twenty years of age. He would have been a lawyer in Oregon if he'd lived. The boy who is missing was only seventeen when I saw him last."

Maria added, "Scott was wounded in that same battle, Pilar, and he is our good friend now."

"I'm still around because of Maria's nursing and Juan's doctoring," Scott inserted.

The doctor waved off the credit as negligible, and he reciprocated, "Scott's friends talked to the rebels on my behalf or I might not have my home. We are just people when the war talk is gone."

Pilar's eyes appeared to Scott to be less hostile and her manner less agitated as she apologized, "I'm sorry my feelings are spoiling supper for everyone. Juan and Maria have told me your story, and I bear no spite toward you personally. But I will always hate those peasants of El Caney, and so-called liberators of Cuba, who killed my Ricardo – los bastardos."

Juan threw up his hands and said to his daughter, "See why we talk of living in Spain after we marry, my dear. Pilar will never be comfortable here."

* * * * *

The following morning Scott accompanied Maria down the hill to the hospital where Doctor Chavez worked. She had explained that she volunteered as a nurse there in the "enfermeria," and sometimes in the "clinicos" of the peasants. Today she would arrange for him to check the records of patients in the hospital during the summer of 1898. Maria attested, "You will not find Jack-Jack Sixes listed as you are,

Scott. However, many names are incomplete or misspelled, and you might find a clue which Father and I missed."

Inside the hospital lobby, she led him to a small alcove similar to a church confessional box. As he sat on the narrow bench and rested his forearm on the wall table while waiting for her to bring the records, he glanced about and spotted a sliding panel on the back wall. Chuckling quietly to himself, he decided the closet doubled for that purpose as well.

"Scott McClure, do you need to confess?" Maria teased as she slid the panel aside and lifted the shadowy screen, adding quickly, "Here are all the records for July, August, and September of last year."

As she handed him the box full of papers, he rose and leaned forward, bypassing the records mischievously to kiss Maria. Startled but accepting she raised her lips expectantly, and as awkward as their embrace turned out to be, each was reluctant to break their moment of tempestuous ardor. Maria felt the box slipping and moaned for help, Scott adroitly catching the box but losing the kiss.

Flushing prettily Maria's laughter tinkled in admonishing him playfully, "I think you need to confess after that kiss, dear Scott. Ha! Ha! Me, too! I could have carried the records down the hall to you."

"I will confess that I love and cherish you with all my heart," Scott murmured in adulatory tones.

"That doesn't sound solemn enough for an oath, my sweet. Here I've waited for an eternity for you to return, wondering if my feelings were to be unrequited. I love you...," Maria avowed before silenced by another kiss.

"Hmph! Perdone! Maria..." a grinning nun interrupted their tryst, Scott quick to recognize his other nurse and greet her warmly in poor but acceptable Spanish. Maria disappeared with a tinge of guilt and closed the panels while Scott and the sister talked of last summer, she in Spanish and he in English.

* * * * *

In the ensuing days Scott visited churches and government officers from Guantanamo Bay to Santiago's eastern villages, sleeping in the great outdoors or a kind farmer's shed, staying with Jose Guevera on two occasions. As with the hospital in town there was no hint of his missing friend in any of the records he reviewed.

Maria was his companion one day in the outskirts of Daquiri, meeting an old priest in an arrangement set up by their nun friend. Discovering nothing new from the senile old man, they took their picnic lunch to the beach and shirked any further work. They had not repeated romantic kissing like the interlude in the hospital alcove, Scott being sensitive to Maria's conservative upbringing. After all, he was a guest in the Chavez house.

Sitting atop a derelict sun-bleached log on the sandy beach east of the harbor, the breeze was brisk and cool coming off the sea, causing Maria to shiver. It seemed natural that she nestled into the shelter of Scott's arm as they watched an old island steamer leave Daquiri, passing a small fishing ketch returning home with the day's catch. Their peaceful idyll lasted through the siesta hours with little talk, but neither of them napped in the mutual awareness of their emotions.

Maria shivered again and Scott stirred, planting a platonic kiss on her forehead as he rose to his feet. Smiling he made a tongue-in-cheek comment, "My dear, how can a little sea breeze bother you with a hot sun overhead? Come on, it's time to go home. Tomorrow's a busy day."

Laughing gaily in consonance with their happiness, she didn't reply as she packed her basket and walked with him towards town. Tomorrow Maria would work with her father in a clinico visit to El Caney, while Scott visited with Jose and his friends, including the itinerant Catholic priest who served several mountain villages to the north. He thought, *at least I don't have to walk this time; Juan will drive his buggy to the village.*

* * * * *

After supper Maria and Consuela retired, Juan pouring brandy into two snifters, Scott remarking in appreciation, "Theses goblets are works of art, Juan. I'm almost afraid to drink from them."

"Ha! Ha! Salud! You are right my young friend, they are heirlooms from my mother's side of the family, antique as well as the work of an artisan. However, the real treasure is this brandy from Jerez – my last bottle. Pilar's family has vineyards in the hills above the Guadalquivir Valley near Arcos de la Frontera. If we move there after we get married, my supply of brandy will be assured. What are your plans, Scott?" Assuming that Juan's question was rather pointed in regards to Scott's intentions toward his daughter, Scott chose to be direct and speak his mind. Nervously picking his words, he stammered, "Uh, right, I uh...sir, I respectfully ask for your daughter's hand in marriage. I mean, I love Maria and want her to be my wife, but I must talk to her about marriage."

"Do you think my daughter would be kissing you through a confessional box window if she didn't return your love. Ha! Ha! Yes, I heard all about that incident – it's no secret in the hospital," Juan replied. Enjoying the young man's discomfiture for a moment before confiding, "I shouldn't tell you this story, but why do you think Pilar and I haven't married already? Because Maria wanted us to wait until you returned to Daquiri. I believe you stole your nurse's heart last summer. I'd be sadly disappointed if you two young lovers didn't get married."

"Thank you, Juan. I'll talk to Maria tomorrow when we have a moment alone. I understand we're driving to the clinico in El Caney in your buggy. Do you visit there often?"

"No, only once since the fighting last summer. I sewed up a mangled foot caused by a woodcutter's own carelessness. However, my services have been requested by Jose Guevera, who reports several peasants from the interior have come down with fever. It's probably yellow fever like your comrades suffered in the war. We don't see much of it around here – near the sea, but in the swamps and forests it's common enough. Well, it'll be a long day tomorrow so I'm off to bed. Goodnight, Scott."

Chapter Thirteen

Wiping sweat from his brow he watched Doctor Chavez's buggy bounce along the faint trail in the heavily wooded creek bottom, Scott slapped his straw hat against his knees and declared, "It's hot in Cuba even in December, Jose. How far is it to Salazar's village?"

"Just over this hill ahead. It's small and well hidden. The Spanish army knew it was out here but never suspected it was Alberto's hideout. Don't tell the good doctor, but this spot is where we shot the señora's husband. His patrol was following a trail of blood left by three wounded comrades of ours, and the village was in danger of discovery," Jose concluded.

"You say your wounded were taken to this village for care? Why do you think Jack-Jack Sixes might have been here?"

Jose shrugged enigmatically, replying with practical logic, "Your search in America and Cuba has found no sign of your comrade, and my friends tell me that no American is living in our villages. I don't believe your friend is alive, and bodies were not left lying about after the battles. A mystery, no?"

Bobbing his head in thought, he explained further, "The rebels fought near El Caney that week, mostly salvaging Spanish weapons...er...and a few American rifles, too. I heard from Salazar's son that the wounded were brought into this village for treatment. The old midwife who tended the wounded men is still living here. She and Alberto will answer your questions honestly."

"Good! I thank you my friend for helping me. Are there any other such rebel bases in these hills?"

Jose laughed as he teased, "Not since our rebels became the government! To your serious question, no. Salazar's people took care of all our wounded men."

Guevera paused in a hillside clearing, pointing to a jungled forest in the canyon's bottom and speaking, "See the smoke in the treetops. Salazar's people are cooking their noon meal. We'll be in the village in twenty minutes. Let's hurry, young Salazar invited us to eat with them."

* * * * *

Alberto Salazar was an unimposing man of medium stature and appearance, his high voice offsetting the shaggy look created by a full beard and wild hair flecked with gray. His peasant hands were gnarled from hard work and confirmed his age as close to that of his friend Jose, and when he talked they came alive with the conversation. Alberto had welcomed Scott to his casa in effusive Spanish, Jose's friend receiving the smile of the Salazar family. No one spoke English in the house – probably not even in the village. Jose would have to translate for him when the village midwife arrived.

A peasant he certainly is, Scott mused to himself, *but his gaze commands respect and his words demand attention. I can see where Alberto was the rebel commander in the area while Jose was the intellectual side of their partnership. And I suppose that old Springfield on the wall was one of the weapons Salazar "found" in the battle for San Juan Heights.* An unconscious chuckle rumbled in his throat, ending his reverie.

Their host turned to him and asked several questions, Jose grinning as he translated, "Alberto sees you are admiring his trophies. He wants to know about that rifle given to him by an American friend, and he asked about your fighting…experience, I guess is the right word."

Scott told his story in a short version, answering questions to the best of his ability, and finally posed a question of his own about the sword displayed beside the Springfield. No answer was forthcoming as Alberto changed the subject and food was served. Later Jose would identify the Toledo blade as belonging to the late Captain shot on the trail nearby – Chavez's friend.

An old crone Scott hadn't seen before served some fruit as Señora Salazar cleared the dishes from the table. The woman was quite old and wrinkled, her twisted form and toothless grin in contrast with cheerful eyes and graceful hands. Jose introduced them as the woman squatted on the mat against the wall, "Tia Rosa is the village midwife and loves to talk about her children. She says she has delivered over two hundred babies."

"Why don't you ask her about Jack-Jack Sixes now? Does she remember the battle of El Caney?"

Jose spoke for several minutes with Tia Rosa, who responded in monosyllabic utterances, usually a no, accompanied by a negative shake of her head. He finally looked at Scott to report, "Tia Rosa remembers the wounded men being carried in from the fighting at El Caney, but she doesn't remember any American soldier ever coming to this village. Can you describe your friend?"

Nodding thoughtfully Scott replied, "Jack-Jack was Tututni Indian from the coast of Oregon. He was seventeen years old, dark-skinned, black hair and eyes, and smaller in build than I am. His Tututni name was Hi-to-mah."

"Tomas! Tomas! Si! Si!" Tia Rosa cried excitedly, breaking into rapid-fire Spanish monologue.

When she paused for lack of breath and new information, Jose interrupted quickly, "Tia Rosa remembers a dying boy who she thought was a Carib. Now that she recalls him, she thinks he spoke English and called himself "Estoma," which she took to mean Tomas. He came to the village clad only in bandages and shorts."

Tia Rosa interrupted as she recalled another fact, Jose continuing after a moment, "She remembers he had the fever as well as a chest wound. Either injury could have been fatal. He died the second morning and was buried in a common grave down by the river. Tia Rosa says six men died that week, and only one man had a family to care for him."

"Where is this grave?" Scott asked.

After a brief exchange, Jose told him, "The river changed channels last winter in a flash flood, and graves were swept away. We may have discovered the fate of your friend, Scott. Do you have any other questions?"

An hour and countless questions later, the old woman abruptly rose to her feet and left the Salazar home with a grinning adios. Scott thanked her profusely as she walked away, Jose finally saying, "She said she doesn't know any more answers, and it's time for her siesta. Come along, my friend, Alberto will show us where the graves used to be."

* * * * *

Trudging along the path between wheel ruts left by Doctor Chavez's buggy, Scott divided his attention in wiping sweat from his brow and swatting persistent mosquitoes. His mind was at ease with Jack-Jack's fate – all-but-determined in Salazar's village. Surely his friend had been the "Carib Indian" described by Tia Rosa and buried in the washed-out gravesite.

He drifted into a melancholy mood as he marched inland, *I wonder how Maria is doing in the unnamed village clinico, or old shack which Doctor Chavez described. Juan had to return to Daquiri to tend his patients, and Maria had volunteered to remain and to nurse the fever victims. Maybe I can help her, and maybe find an opportunity to talk about marriage. Juan and Pilar want to marry and move to Spain after Christmas.*

Scott slapped himself out of his daydreaming, inspecting the remains of a large mosquito in his palm, "Damned pests," he muttered loudly enough to turn the heads of a half-dozen peasants sitting on a decaying log before the clinico–Maria waving from within.

Kissing her unabashedly on her upraised lips, his spoken words were terse, "Show me what to do, Sweetheart!" A playful grin warmed her tired face, and she pointed fleetingly to a half-dozen bedpans and a chamberpot scattered below a dozen cots in the room.

Disregarding the stupefying odor, he carried each to the latrine trench behind the old shack, dumping its contents into the hole and kicking dirt into it. He washed the vessels and stacked them near the doorway, sweeping the floor and then mopping it. An elderly woman arrived to watch the patients while Maria checked the peasants waiting on the log bench.

An hour passed before Maria signaled her helper that she was taking a break, leading Scott down to the stagnant pool in the creek. She washed her hands and face with vigor, remarking, "Daddy says cleanliness is half the battle in fighting fever and infection. Some people think yellow fever is contagious, but Daddy read somewhere it's carried by mosquitoes. We should all have yellow fever in that case; this water is a breeding area for the pests."

"Are you all right, Maria? You're awfully pale, and your hands are shaking," Scott asked with concern as he observed her tired countenance.

"I'm fine, a little rest is all I need. What did you find in Salazar's village?"

Scott related his discovery and subsequent conclusion as Maria laid her head on his shoulder and fell asleep, stirring briefly every time he stopped talking. So he kept the one-sided conversation going, speaking of anything that came to mind, keeping his voice low and soothing to ensure Maria would rest.

"...and so much for San Francisco. We'll visit that city one day and explore its mysteries. How about going there for a second honeymoon? We could get married next week, take the first ship to the United States, and honeymoon in our cabin. Of course, I have to find the right moment and enough courage to propose. You know I love you, Sweetheart, but do you love me, too..."

"I do, dearest Scott. With all my heart, and I accept you proposal," Maria stated in emotional tones.

Maria's eyes were wide open and adoring, confirming her soundness of mind and lucidity. She continued, "But you'll have to ask Father for my hand – he's very proper you know."

"I do know, he asked my intentions night before last after you had retired. He gave his blessing, claiming he knew your answer already. I wasn't as confident as he was. Can you give up all of this for a rancher's life in Oregon? I think I'm getting the best of everything, a beautiful wife to love and my life on the Sixes River – and lots of children."

"Mm! But I get everything you do, dear Scott, including a handsome husband to love the rest of my days."

They discussed their feelings in wonderment and their plans in expectation, punctuating talk with emotional embraces and gay laughter. Eventually their tryst was interrupted by a call from the old nurse, "Señorita Maria! Pronto per favor."

Maria sprang to her feet, a peculiar expression crossing her face as her knees buckled, laughing nervously at herself as Scott held her erect, muttering, "I guess I'm wearier than I thought. Can you find a little soup for us next door? I'll check my patients."

* * * * *

Scott responded to the old nurse's soft call, awakening in his chair to find the sick room illuminated by a single candle. He rushed to the bedside of a heavyset patient in need of a

bedpan. The man breathed a sigh of relief as the nurse perfunc-
torily performed her duty, Scott loathing the odious chore.
However, Maria was able to get her rest so he just gritted his
teeth and did as told.

Daylight blossomed throughout the village, and Scott repeated his janitorial task of emptying the night's bedpans and
cleaning up the room. He was afraid his swabbing the floor
would awaken Maria, but she slept peacefully while all the patients woke up, their fever demanding attention.

"Señor! Señor!" the old nurse called urgently as she
hunched over Marie. Feeling her forehead, the woman cried,
"Señorita esta un fevril- enfermo?"

Maria's forehead felt hot and dry, her cheeks were flushed,
and she was groggy as he shook her awake. However, she recognized the symptoms and whispered her own diagnosis, "I've
got yellow fever. I'm so weak, Scott! How can I help my patients?"

"Just stay where you are, Maria, and drink lots of water. I'll
bathe your face in a minute. It'll cool you a little."

As soon as Scott found a healthy lad to deliver a message to
Jose Guevera, he resumed his "nursing" rounds, always finding
a few minutes to spend with his sweetheart. During the siesta
heat, one of the women patients died and was quickly carried to
her grave, but an old man took her place before nightfall.
Illness seemed to feed on its own flame, and Scott began to
worry in earnest.

That evening cooler air prevailed, and Maria ate soup and
talked normally, her remission short-lived after an hour of conversation about her wedding and Scott's family, deteriorated
with a spat of vomiting and a rambling diatribe on caring for
her patients. The only bright spot during his night vigil was
one woman leaving her sickbed to return home – and no fever
victim claimed her cot.

* * * * *

A cooling breeze blew out the night candle, Scott feeling
welcome relief from the humid and hot air which had prevailed
for several days. None of his patients reacted to the darkness,
so after bathing Maria's brow he settled back in his chair and
dozed.

His nursing partner awakened him at first light, and they set about their morning chores. Gruel for breakfast was unappetizing to Scott, and he could empathize with his sick charges, but he still made sure they ate the meal. Within the hour two villagers left their cots and staggered home at the same time a small boy was carried into the clinico by his distraught mother. While cleaning bedpans Scott found the heavyset old man had died quietly after eating breakfast.

He had been sitting at Maria's bedside for a few moments when he heard a horse and buggy clattering into the village. Hurrying forward to meet the doctor, he found Pilar and the old man priest from the beach at Daquiri had accompanied him to the village. Several families gathered about the priest, eager for him to pray for their sick and dead.

"I'm glad to see you, Juan – and you, too, Pilar. Maria is very sick, and I don't know what to do for her," Scott bemoaned before adding, "Come with me, I'll take care of your horse in a moment."

The old nurse was busy with the newly arrived boy, who was retching and crying at the same time, and on cue from her, he hurried to the bed of the old man who had fallen to the floor. The partners worked in unison to tend their patients and clean the room. It was several minutes before he could join Pilar and a very pale but lucid Maria. The doctor was making a round of the other sick ones.

Maria's small smile brightened her fever-gaunted face as she spoke in faint tones, "Scott dear, I told Daddy and Pilar that we want to marry. They gave us their blessing."

Pilar nodded in encouragement, seeming to feel that the girl's condition was improving with conversation. Scott was dubious about keeping Maria awake, but he enjoyed her company with its hint of optimism. But he soon found himself talking to Pilar, with his fiancée dozing beside them.

* * * * *

Scott awoke from his siesta feeling refreshed, a rarity during his stay in the clinico.

"The cool breeze is a lifesaver in more ways than one Scott. I sent the boy home with his mother, and one of the women just walked out on her own two feet. Are you rested enough for a little exercise? We need to talk," Juan uttered in somber tones.

The two men quietly exited the shack, walking down to the creek pool before Scott asked tentatively in a strained voice, "Maria isn't getting any better, is she?"

"No! Dios, dime por que! Why can't I help the one I love, when everyone else is getting better? Forgive my blasphemy, son, but my day has been terrible. Dear Maria is ill with the fever, Pilar cursed Jose Guevera when he was helping us, and I had a shouting match with the hospital director when I left. I either was fired or resigned, I'm not sure which," Juan confided.

Scott placed a sympathetic hand on his friend's shoulder and tried to cheer him up, "You were leaving your position at Christmas anyway, and Pilar no doubt feels much better after venting her feelings at Jose. But I worry about Maria's condition. Yellow fever is so unpredictable. What can we do?"

Juan studied the young man for a moment, suggesting hopefully, "Sometimes a spiritual boost will help a sick person. Your marriage to Maria might have such an effect on her. Pilar thought we could have a double ceremony before the priest leaves this evening. Does that make sense to you?"

"Yes, it's kind of what Maria and I talked about earlier – marrying simply and soon. I'll round up the priest, and we'll do it," Scott concluded with anticipation.

* * * * *

Maria was awake with a touch of delirium clouding her voice and her thoughts when the ceremony began, her bright acceptance of the rite overcoming the priest's concern. The impromptu wedding party was a mixed collection of people, Jose Guevera and the old nurse serving as witnesses, even though the rebel leader's presence brought a scowl from Pilar. One of the patients arose from her cot to stand nearby, while a second woman observed sitting up in bed, and a dozen villagers stood outside the clinico.

Hands embracing his beloved's inert fingers, Scott said "I do!" on cue, followed by Maria's gasping assent, smiling happily as her eyelids drooped. The priest blessed the two marriages, and while Juan and Pilar chatted with their guests, Scott continued to sit beside his wife and talk to her sleeping countenance. Pilar thanked Jose, albeit grudgingly and without any smile, the old man patting Scott's shoulder before he returned to El Caney with the priest.

After an hour or so Pilar brought two cups of broth and a handful of small biscuits to them. Doctor Chavez started his rounds and chewed on biscuits during the interim. When Juan frowned, the newly married husband worried, and when the doctor smiled he was relieved.

Pilar pillowed Maria's head so Scott could spoon hot broth between her still lips. Still only half conscious, the patient swallowed dutifully until the cup was empty, and Scott breathed a big sigh of relief.

Smiling wanly, the bride puckered her lips to receive Scott's gentle kiss. He held her hand as he carried on a one-sided conversation until her eyelids fluttered and she drifted back to sleep again. His own eyes felt grainy and his vision was blurry, so he dropped onto the next cot over for a snooze – it being empty like most of the others.

* * * * *

Awakening in the flickering candlelight of the familiar shack, Scott lay quietly on his back, wide-awake without knowing why. He flattened the mosquito feasting on his bare shoulder and wondered at the stillness of the night. A glance around the room showed a woman sleeping in the far corner, Maria's tranquil form next to him, and no one else in the clinico. *What woke me up*, he thought to himself, *everything is as silent as can be.*

A sudden dread shadowed his spirit as he realized he could not hear Maria's labored breathing any longer. Rolling off the cot and reaching out for his wife, his fingers caressed her thin face and felt her throat unsuccessfully for a pulse. In an uncontrolled and eerie tone, he wailed, "Maria! No God, not Maria!"

Like pictures of still life flashing by in a frozen moment of time, his mind remembered his beautiful wife and their dreams of a life together, and too suddenly came the realization that their hopes had died with her. His head fell on her bosom as another wail escaped his tortured mind, his spirit battered into unconsciousness by the tragedy.

* * * * *

Observing the red-tiled rooftops of Santiago and its blue harbor from a buggy seat atop the heights did not produce any enthusiasm for his journey home. The city's panoramic beauty left Scott untouched, a warped normalcy for his lethargic state over the past three days. Juan worried about his mourning Maria, even wondering if the young man had a touch of fever.

Scott's shrug at his own thoughts went unnoticed by his companions as the neared their destination. *I hope Juan and Pilar find happiness in Spain. With Maria buried in Daquiri and the Chavez casa sold, they can look forward to being near Anita's family and leaving their troubled memories behind. Only Consuela appeared a bit lost when we left their old house, not quite sure if she would be happy serving the new owners.*

I can't believe my sweetheart is gone. Oh I guess I know it's a fact, but I don't want to think about it. We were married but a few hours and my prayers went unanswered. But I agree with my father-in-law, time is the best healer and there is nothing for me here.

"Scott, are you awake? Maybe you have a touch of fever," Juan asked with a doctor's concern.

"I'm all right, folks. And don't say fever around the waterfront, or I'll never get aboard a ship going to Florida. Let's try that steamer at the pier ahead, maybe it's going to America."

Juan reined his horse to a halt beside a gang of sailors working new hawsers near the ship's stern, emboldened letters revealing her to be the *Zeeland of Rotterdam*. The men responded to Juan's Spanish inquiry with puzzled smiles, Scott's English remarks lost on the seamen as well. One lad had the intelligence to guess the purpose of their questions and state "Rotterdam" in a clearly enunciated but foreign voice. He pointed to a sailing ship at the next wharf and shouted "American" before returning to work.

Juan flicked his reins over the horse's rump, driving the beast forward to a gangplank leading up to the deck of an old sailing ship, quite similar to the lumber schooners of the Oregon coast.

Scott jumped to the wharf, landing lightly on the balls of his feet and calling out to the officer at its head, "Pardon me, sir. Are you bound for Florida?"

"No sir, but we are sailing on the tide for Biloxi. We delivered pine timbers and Long Beach radishes and are loaded with sugar and tobacco," the officer replied in friendly tones. "Have you room for a passenger?" Scott asked. "Well, we don't have passenger accommodations, but I guess I could share my cabin with you – Third Mate Jason Canby at your service." "Scott McClure of Port Orford, Oregon here. Mate Canby, what's the price of a fare?" Scott queried as he fingered the gold coins in his pocket.

A gray-haired older man emerged from the galley, Canby's attitude alerting Scott that he was the ship's captain. A brief murmur of conversation from the skipper, "You're welcome aboard if you can pay the forty dollars fare, lad – and five dollars to Mate Canby."

Scott nodded affirmatively, accepting a gold coin from Juan as he embraced the Chavez couple. With a wan smile and grimace of true regret, he bid them goodbye and fair sailing. Grasping his single bag of personal goods, he climbed the gangplank to step on the ship's deck and turned to wave farewell one last time – Juan and Scott both aware they'd never see each other again. He followed the two officers into the galley and consummated their deal, a hidden five-dollar gold piece and a few Cuban coins his only cash.

* * * * *

The "Creole Trader" moved gracefully through the Caribbean under full sail, the hills of Cuba well to her starboard. Tomorrow they would be in the Gulf of Mexico, and Scott hoped the fair weather would hold. He was not comfortable with his shipmates, the sailors ignored him and the captain and first mate were coolly courteous. Passengers were confined to midships he was informed the first day, and there he paced the deck alone. Jason Canby was friendly and talkative in their cabin but respectfully quiet around the skipper.

Scott felt hot despite the cool breeze and realizing he was feverish, sought his bunk for a rest. His brow was fairly burning up when Jason came off duty and quickly recognized his roommate had yellow fever. The mate moved into the spare bunk in the first mate's cabin, and the galley boy – cook's helper became Scott's occasional nurse.   Three days later the patient was feeling well enough to eat in the galley, but Jason told him the captain has confined him to his bunk until further notice.

Asserting his independence within the order, Scott dressed and sat before the open door, several minutes passing before he realized his handful of coins was missing.   He checked his leather belt for his hidden gold coin, and finding it in place he decided to forget his silver.   The boy probably needed the money, and reporting the theft to the captain would cause trouble for both of them.   He went back to bed with that thought.

The next morning Jason came to see him, asking after his health before hesitantly informing him that he wasn't welcome aboard ship any longer.   The friendly officer explained, "We've sighted land and are sailing to Gulfport, which is west of Biloxi.   I'm to take you ashore in the captain's gig so you won't be aboard when the pilot boat meets us off Biloxi.   He doesn't want to report a yellow fever victim to port authorities."

The mate paused to judge the patient's reaction, and Scott concluded correctly that his agreement was desired, so he said, "That's fine, Jason.   I don't want to cause trouble for your ship.   Can I find work on shore?"

With a visible sigh of relief, the mate suggested, "Yes, the lumber mill can always use a hand, but with the fever I think you'd be better off working the radish fields along Long Beach.   There's a town called Rosalie west of Gulfport where work and rooms are available."

"Ha! Ha! And where no one will ask if I'm from the *Creole Trader*. Thanks Jason, let's go sailing together. I'm feeling strong today. Can I help?" Scott volunteered, thinking to himself that getting off this schooner would be a blessing. He wondered how picking radishes would suit his weakened condition.

Chapter Fourteen

Fortune smiled on Scott as he waded ashore near Gulfport, Jason and his two seamen beating a hasty retreat to the *Creole Trader*. He grinned in silent amusement as he plodded through fine white sand, knowing full well he had been beached west of the fledgling town for a reason. The ship would be out of sight before anyone knew a fever victim had landed.

Coming upon a horse-drawn wagon mired in deep sand beside the coastal road, Scott helped a vociferous bandy-legged man pull free of his entrapment. The bushy-haired, round-faced teamster offered him a ride to Long Beach and a spate of local lore. Barney Jones was a good-natured if homely fellow who claimed to be a cousin of Captain Joseph T. Jones, founder of Gulfport. By his newfound friend's logic, he was, therefore, a leading citizen of the new town himself.

Scott's guided tour of the gulf coastline included a non-stop visit to Mississippi City, Harrison County Seat, and ended in Long Beach, or Rosalie as Barney called it. The newcomer spotted a sign by the railroad tracks in town which read Scott's Landing, another name which Barney used without explanation. His benefactor claimed to be acquainted with Nathan Brown and D. L. Hayes, a fact substantiated when he introduced Scott to the businessmen, resulting in employment in the radish fields and room and board at the Brown Hotel at half price – for doing Brown's chores every morning.

Mrs. Brown's fine cooking quickly succored Scott's gaunt physical condition, and his strength returned without anyone's guessing he was recovering from yellow fever. Or so he believed until his landlady remarked on his improvement, "You're a healthy young man, not many people beat yellow fever so easily."

Scott's surprise at her correct diagnosis was reflected in his expression, Nathan chuckling as he teased his boarder, "Not many women are as good a nurse as my wife. We've seen plenty of cases of yellow fever along this coast although it's usually during a hot summer. I expect it's warmer in Cuba this time of year."

* * * * *

As the days of January passed busily for the young adventurer, the changes within himself were visible to Scott with considerable clarity. Christmas had been a null memory of fevered days at sea, and New Year's Day had been but a day of rest among strangers although he enjoyed Mrs. Brown's special dinner for hotel guests.

Outwardly his strength and physical health rebounded in abundance, Scott finding that he'd grown an inch and gained twenty pounds since arriving in Rosalie. Being hale and hearty had allowed him to do odd jobs in the evenings, his accumulated savings growing daily.

Finally his grief had abated although he still dreamed of Maria often. His sorrow was changing as happier memories dominated his thoughts – both conscious and unconscious. Scott finally composed a long letter to his family explaining his lack of correspondence for these many weeks. A Christmas card in early December and a perfunctory note to Jack Sixes confirming his son's burial in Cuba had been his only contact with Oregon.

Walking west toward the bayou where Breezydale stood grandly before the coastal beach, Scott pondered his job working for the Boggs family. He thought, *I hope Archie and William repaired the veranda railing. I'd like to prime the new wood this evening and paint tomorrow. Eliza said Robert would pay me Monday if all the work is done. I wonder if I should talk to the Quarles about clearing the land behind their place. I could use a few more dollars before I move on.*

* * * * *

Barney Jones stood forlorn on the Scott's Station platform, having changed his mind about going to New Orleans for a holiday. His expression brightened momentarily as the engineer blew his whistle and the cars jerked forward, his farewell to Scott a gentle jibe, "Remember the town isn't named after you, my friend, but the Scott family. We'll always call it Rosalie anyway. Come back and visit Long Beach some day."

Scott laughed at the little joke and waved enthusiastically at Barney, a bit more nostalgic about leaving the Mississippi beaches than he had expected.

After the depot disappeared behind a screen of coastal pines, Scott entered the car and settled into a seat, watching the countryside roll by his window. Memories of the troop train ride from San Antonio to Tampa were triggered by the bays, bayous, and marshes along the route, and as the train neared New Orleans, he fancied that he recognized several landmarks.

His glance passed over a familiar roughneck several times before he noticed the man was studying him, yet would not look him in the eye directly. He'd seen the fellow hanging around the store yesterday when Mister Hayes paid him his weekly wages and decided he didn't appreciate the man's interest. His money belt was full enough to attract a sneak thief or two, so he'd have to watch his back in New Orleans.

Debarking his car at their destination, Scott hastened inside to buy a ticket to Saint Louis. He planned to spend a couple of days exploring Grandpa's old stomping grounds in Saint Charles before moving on to Denver. He'd have to work for railfare before he managed to reach Salem.

When he saw the same roughneck loitering in the station lobby, Scott walked directly toward the man. He noted the yahoo's eyes still wouldn't meet his own, just focused on a point behind his head as a nasty sneer creased his lips. The man began walking toward him about the time Scott heard the whisper of steps to his rear. He acted quickly and with decisive force, throwing his knapsack at the now-charging roughneck's legs while diving sideways. His slashing right foot caught the stumbling ruffian in the chest, and Scott rolled clear of any entanglement with the three men attacking him.

From the floor he kicked the feet out from under a second hoodlum and scurried to his feet to face the third. As rapidly as they had appeared, the two disappeared into the crowd of travelers. When the ticket agent asked if he was all right, he nodded and strolled toward his waiting train's platform before realizing that his bag had vanished with the thieves.

* * * * *

Having watched a baseball game, eaten supper on a riverboat moored alongside the levee, and drunk a beer in the old courthouse tavern, Scott wandered back to his rooming house in good spirits. His thoughts, however, were more conservative, *I've been in Saint Louis for three days, and my money belt is thinner. I'll have to find a job if I'm going to explore Saint Charles as well. Maybe I'll pack my new belongings and move over there to find work.*

Turning that idea into reality the next morning, Scott walked all the way to Saint Charles under gray drizzling skies. Slogging along the muddy streets of town, he stopped to help an old farmer load his wagon with a dozen feed bags, a barrel of flour, and a gunnysack of groceries. Then a younger man needed a hand in lashing two kegs of nails to his mule's jack saddle, followed by a well-dressed lady with clean boots. For her Scott threw a plank over the mud and held her hand as she took mincing steps to her waiting carriage.

"Looking for a job, mister? As you can see, I'm swamped since my clerk quit yesterday," a middle-aged but pleasant merchant offered hopefully.

"Yes, sir! You've got yourself a new clerk. My name is Scott McClure – out of Oregon."

"Welcome to Saint Charles, Scott, I'm Frank Berry. Just keep helping my customers with their purchases for now. We'll visit some when the trade quiets down."

An hour later Scott was stocking shelves with canned goods from the storeroom when he felt a hesitant touch on his arm. Turning with a smile, he faced a weather-beaten and wrinkled old man grinning toothlessly at him.

"Say, Sonny, did I hear your name is Scott McClure? Same moniker as my boyhood friend who left here in 1850. Any relation of his? You kind of look like him, as I remembered him anyway."

"He's my grandfather, old-timer. Who shall I say remembers him?" Scott asked.

"Red Offkins! Course my red hair is gone – like my teeth, but my memory is still good. Scott and I got the three R's together in '33, or was it '34? Did a little hunting together, too, when his momma was well. Went off looking for his daddy. He ever find him?"

* * * * *

The days passed comfortably for Scott, saving his wages while enjoying his work. Frank Berry was a good boss, and most of the customers were friendly people. Occasionally he bought the old-timer a beer, his stories well worth the purchase even though his professed memory was not as sound as claimed. Comparing his grandpa to Red made him wonder – were they really age mates? Grandpa Scott seemed much younger and more vital.

One day Frank asked him to supper, off-handedly describing his offering as simple roast beef – nothing fancy. Scott was happy to eat a home-cooked meal and readily accepted. As he thought – despite Frank's modesty – the Berry women were superb cooks. His wife Abigail, his mother Alice, and his daughter Katherine all conspired to impress Scott with their culinary artistry – and succeeded markedly.

Katie was a pretty girl a little younger than Scott, with a quiet demeanor and friendly disposition. As the evening progressed it became clear that her family was looking for a husband for Katie – and a partner for Frank perhaps. Her embarrassment at her parent's intentions was accompanied by a sparkle of interest in Scott. He was attracted to the girl but still too inhibited by Maria's loss to think of loving another.

In fact, Scott's response became defensive, thinking of how to extricate himself from the Berry home and perhaps from his job as well. *Maybe it's time to leave for Denver and visit the McCarty's*, he thought, *summer will be here before long*.

"Young man," Alice Berry said in clear tones, "Red Offkins tells me you are the grandson of Scott McClure. Is he alive and well in Oregon?"

"Yes, ma'am! Grandpa Scott's just dandy. Did you know him in the old days?"

Alice smiled wistfully, remarking with fondness, "Oh yes, my dear boy, Scott and I were sweethearts before I met Frank's father. I might have been your grandmother if Sarah McClure hadn't been so ill – and irascible. Has Scott ever mentioned Alice Tidwell?"

"Yes, Ma'am, Tidwell is familiar but not Berry. Grandpa talks of his past often enough, but not so much about Missouri," Scott affirmed.

"Well, tell me about Scott and his...your family in Oregon. Where does he live and what does he do?" Alice queried in piqued curiosity.

* * * * *

Scott received two letters on the same day, his mother's neat handwriting filling three pages with family news and a postscript of sympathy signed by both his parents. It seemed his twin sisters each had a boyfriend, Donald Gerbrunn squiring Melissa when he accompanied Billy Tucker home from the Klondike. No further mention was made of Anne's beau, which raised Scott's eyebrow in curiosity. Billy was courting his cousin Mary Anne and had been working on the Myrtlewood Grove with haying while his father was laid up with lumbago.

Tucked into Grandpa's scrawled half-page note was a five-dollar bill. Scott read where it came from a wager with Uncle Johnny that Scott and Maria would marry. Grandpa wrote he was sorry for the girl's death and trusted his namesake was carrying his grief with reverence but tending to his own health, too.

Scott grinned to himself as he pictured Grandpa and Johnny betting and warmed to the sentiments about Maria, sparse as they were. The two Scotts were truly kindred spirits, and the young man felt another homing urge, both letters an encouragement to move on.

Visiting the Berry home that evening to give Frank a week's notice, he loaned his grandfather's letter to Alice. Her quiet chuckles were accompanied by an explanation to her family, "This note is so like Scott, short and newsy with both his humor and his compassion showing through."

Turning to face Scott, she added, "I must write my dear friend greetings and tell him what a fine grandson he has. Thank you for sharing his words with me. I didn't realize you are a widower, and you have my heartfelt sympathy."

The family murmured appropriate condolences, Katie placing her hand over Scott's as she asked, "Can you tell me about your wife, Maria? Was she Cuban?"

* * * * *

Scott waved goodbye to his friends through the open window beside his train seat, finally settling back to watch the Missouri landscape pass by. He paid little heed to his fellow passengers as he daydreamed the afternoon away. When the quiet and somber teenage boy seated next to him spoke to his sister across the aisle, their resemblance making that conclusion inevitable, Scott's attention was drawn to the lad's use of biblical pronouns and a Germanic accent.

Glancing at the unusual appearance of the pair, Scott eventually concluded they were Pennsylvania Dutch and wondered what they were doing so far from home. With a smile of self-humor, he acknowledged his own distance from home before returning to his view of Kansas City and the Missouri River.

He awoke to the nagging voice of a bellicose man berating someone behind him, "...not good enough to talk to your daughter. I'm of a notion to punch you in the nose, you foreigner you!"

"I am not a foreigner, sir. We are an Amish family who mind our own..." the father began to explain.

"You ain't got no right to talk down to me. Stand up and fight!" the roughneck shouted furiously.

"Sir, we do not believe in violence. We are peaceful people as thou can plainly see," the Amish patriarch explained in gentle tones.

"Well then sit there old man, and I'll talk to your pretty girl," came a challenging rejoinder. As the truculent cowhand laid a roughened and dirty hand on the girl's shoulder, she mewed in alarm and her brother stood up.

With a jeering laugh came a slapping blow knocking the boy back into his seat, a murmur of protests coming from the other passengers. The glowering bully stared down a dozen older men and women in the car, his hand possessively caressing the distraught girl's hair. When his eyes met Scott's flat stare, he postured, "You got something to say, boy, just step over here and speak up!"

Scott lifted an eyebrow feigning uncertainty as he rose to his feet, stalling for time and stance as he replied, "Why I believe like this gentleman does, violence is not necessary in a civilized society..."

"Huh, yellow as the old man," the crude cowboy interrupted as Scott finished, "...but in your case I'll make an exception."

He promptly slapped the yahoo's face with his open palm, smashing the man's nose.

With a roar of pain and outrage mixed together, the culprit released the girl's hair to retaliate, allowing Scott freedom to attack with driving force, his shoulder digging into the cowboy's midriff and taking his breath away. Seizing an out-thrust fist in a clamping grip, Scott twisted aside as they hit the aisle floor, rolling away from the roughneck's kicking boots. Pinning the would-be fighter's arm behind his back as both men struggled to their feet, Scott pressured his foe's hand into his shoulder blades and drove forward.

An elderly lady with spirit showing in her bright eyes caught his intent, and with a conniving grin unlatched the car door. Scott pushed the yahoo through the opening, the unlucky miscreant striking his head against a vestibule post before a swift kick in the pants sent him flying into the next car. The hapless offender scurried away, shaking his fist malevolently at the cheering passengers from a safe distance. Scott caught the Amish father clapping his hand in approval while his wife and seven children smiled gleefully.

* * * * *

Scott strolled along Brighton Avenue, following the friendly conductor's directions toward Denver's stockyards and McCarty's slaughterhouse. *As if I couldn't find it by following my nose alone*, he thought, *I smelled the livestock before I ever saw them.*

I hope that Amish family has luck in finding their cousins – Denver's a big city. Well at least they won't have that crude cowboy bothering them. I saw him get off the train right after we crossed the Republican River. Not much in that country out there but big ranches and small cowtowns. It certainly doesn't compare to my Oregon.

Ah, there's McCarty's office across the street, and I believe that's Aunt Ann and Louise in the window. I'll see if the McCarty's have time for a guest or not. Maybe Mr. McCarty has work for me.

Scott hustled through wagon traffic to the boardwalk before the office, rapping on the glass door before entering. He grinned at the surprised but welcoming faces and quipped, "The bad penny returns, ladies. Is your offer of room and board still good?"

Ann laughed lightly as she stepped forward to kiss Scott on the cheek and proclaimed, "Scott McClure! What are you doing in Denver? Of course you're welcome in our home. Isn't he Lou?"

Louise Simms suddenly threw her arms around the young man and emulated her aunt with a welcoming kiss on the cheek. She stepped back with flushed cheeks and a happy grin, bemoaning, "Darn, I'm going home tomorrow and won't be able to show you the sights. Yes, Scott, school's out and Dad needs help with a roundup."

Before Scott could say a word, McCarty came up behind him with a congenial slap on the back and seconded his wife's offer, "Please stay with us while you're in Denver. June's a slow month for my business so I'll have time to visit, and Louise actually leaves Monday."

"Oh, Uncle Tim, did you get a ticket for Aunt Ann, too?"

When he nodded, Lou entreated, "Can you get another ticket? Maybe Scott will escort the two of us back to Auburn. Will you, Scott? Daddy will hire you for the summer. He's short on hands."

Scott quickly agreed, "You bet, Lou. I'll enjoy seeing Art again even if there's only a little work to pay my fare back to Salem."

* * * * *

Feeling like a true cowhand after a month of days in the saddle, Scott nudged his cowpony forward, joining Art Simms in herding the last of his cattle into the railroad pens. Lou swung the gate closed, and everyone gave a sigh of relief, sweat and dust covering the trio under the hot July sun.

Art swept his Stetson from his head with a flourish, wiping his brow with an exaggerated sweep of his sleeved arm, well aware that his efforts did nothing to remove the grime from his skin. He remarked to his daughter, "Well, sweetheart, let's go find your brother and see how good a deal he's made with the buyer."

He included Scott in the conversation with an offhand explanation as they rode down the street, "Les has never handled cattle sales before, but I figure his college degree might help him get a better deal than his old man. Anyway, he's a working partner as of last month and needs to manage ranch operations."

"My brother's smart enough for both of us, Dad, but he needs the experience of trying some of those husbandry theories his professors have been pushing. Practice makes perfect, while college is the icing on the cake."

"Ha! Ha! Now who's full of Les' learning clichés? But I agree that his education is a wonderful experience for the Simms ranch. However he's a good boss with the crew because he takes after his father – practice at work," Scott observed with sincerity singing true in his voice.

"Hey Scott, I heard that – thanks. You can work for the Simms family anytime. In fact, I need a partner to check on the ranch's summer graze next week. Want to come along? I know a lake or two where the trout are huge," Les Simms said from the bank's doorway, handing a deposit slip over to his father with a pleased grin.

"Come along Scott," Louise ordered demurely as the cattle buyer engaged father and son in conversation at the bank's entrance, "You promised to treat me to a lemonade or a sarsaparilla after work. Is this like a date?"

"You bet 'little sister.' How about an ice cream sundae, too? Do you think the general store will serve a couple of trail-dusty cowhands in their cool soda fountain?" Lou gracefully accepted his filial comment, aware that whenever he had a pang of homesickness she substituted for his three sisters in his thoughts.

* * * * *

A week later Scott rode one of the Gerbrunn mares into the ranch yard ahead of the flagging cowpony Les Simms was riding. He called over his shoulder, "You owe me a night on the town, Boss. I told you the Gerbrunn horses have real bottom, but you had to wager against a 'sure' thing. Old Kurt knew how to breed his horses and so does Uwe."

"Fair enough, old buddy, but I'm cleaning up before we ride into Auburn. There's a shindig at the Grange, and Betty promised to save a dance for me," Les declared.

"You mean we left that idyllic fishing hole for a party? This Betty must be a real charmer," Scott gibed.

Les' only reply was a sly grin, and when his sister appeared on the porch he changed the subject adroitly, "Hey Sis! Is that letter in your hand for me or for Scott?"

Louise responded, "Scott! It's from Salem by way of Saint Charles and Denver. I recognize Aunt Ann's handwriting as the last forwarding address, but not the other two women."

Scott dismounted and led his horse to the veranda railing, accepting the letter in good-natured appreciation, "Thanks, Lou, Alice Tidwell must have sent it to Denver. Now that we know its history, who wrote it and what does it say?"

"Hee! Hee! My curiosity was great, but Daddy forbade my opening it. Doesn't your sister Jane live in Salem?"

Scott grinned as he extracted two pages of paper from the battered envelope and began reading, soon muttering, "You're clairvoyant, Louise Simms. Hmm, Jane writes that she's expecting a child in late fall."

His face sobered as he perused the second page, relating his family news to his friends, "Daddy's very ill and Grandpa sold most of the steers. My baby sister Anne – she's the younger twin – has a boyfriend my father doesn't approve of. Jane thinks I'm needed at home. Says Momma won't ask. Thinks I need time on my own to get over Maria. Hmph! Jane was never bashful in speaking her mind to me – and vice versa. She's right, of course. My family needs me on the Myrtlewood Grove."

* * * * *

As the speeding train bounced and swayed along steel tracks laid over the middle Willamette prairie land, Scott stood spraddle-legged on the open vestibule of its last car. His distant thoughts were busy with plans for his Sixes ranch now that he was committed to heading home. He glanced over his shoulder, alerted by the sound of the car door opening.

"The engineer always pours the coal to his boiler on this stretch of valley because of the grade ahead. We'll be in Salem in twenty minutes or so, but I'll say goodbye now and wish you the best of luck on your coastal farm. I'm glad we had a chance to visit and hope we'll meet again someday," the conductor from the Shasta gunfight stated with an amicable smile.

Scott returned the pleasantry in like manner, saying, "Thanks, John, this trip was interesting if not as adventurous as my horse-handling ride last year. Look me up if you ever get out to Port Orford."

With a mutual nod of casual friendship, the two men parted, Scott watching the Oregon countryside pass by as his mind reviewed his plans to return to the Myrtlewood Grove.

What seemed but moments later, the monotonous chug and clank of the train were shattered by a shrill whistle from the engine, repeated again and again. Scott felt the change in momentum of the train as the engineer slowed down, and hurried back to his seat. By the time he gathered his gear, the station was beside his car. With a final wave to his conductor friend he swung down to the platform and headed toward the Gerbrunn freight yard.

* * * * *

Striding around the corner of the station, Scott spotted a Gerbrunn wagon leaving the freight dock. Recognizing horses and driver simultaneously, he ran down the street and tossed his knapsack into the half-filled bed. His brother-in-law heard the thud and turned to investigate as Scott sprang onto the seat beside him, throwing an arm around Kurt's shoulder in a miniature bearhug.

"Scott, where...did...you come in on the northbound just now? Say, Jane's letter must have found you. We were sorry to hear of Maria's death. Are you all right?" Kurt rattled on as he belatedly returned the hug.

"Watch where you're going, brother-in-law of mine. How's the baby coming along? Am I to be an uncle soon? Tell me about everyone," Scott replied, ready to listen to all the news. He did notice in Kurt's chatter that his items were limited to Salem and the Gerbrunn family, and no mention was made of his father.

When their wagon entered the freight yard, Uwe's voice sounded from the office door, "Scott McClure, welcome home! Angela, Jane, come outside and greet our world traveler."

Scott jumped from the moving wagon running to meet the women as they stepped onto the porch, hugs and kisses abounding in his welcome home – his second home was his thought. Uwe's heavy hand gripping his shoulder, and Don's wave from the barn completed the Gerbrunn family greeting.

Chapter Fifteen

Don related many tales of the Klondike as the family gathered for supper, Uncle Johann's arrival heralding a lengthy political discussion. Gerbrunn family news crept into the conversation during the meal, with Scott telling the story of his yearlong odyssey traveling across America to Cuba and back. The conclusion of his tale featured his friendship with the Simms family and the birthday party they celebrated with him before he caught the train to Salem.

"Jane, it's your turn to talk. Tell me why you're worried about the folks. Is Dad really unable to work?" Scott asked questioningly, her earlier report being sparse of detail.

Jane nodded expectantly, "Of course, Big Brother. Let's see, it was weeks after Christmas when Mom finally told us that Daddy was very ill. He had a cold, and then pneumonia got him in bed for a long time. That bullet wound which almost killed him when we were babies left his lung vulnerable to infection – that's what the doctor said. I'm not sure Daddy can ever work much again."

Scott inserted, "And Grandpa isn't getting any younger."

"That's right, he and the twins tended the livestock while Mother nursed Daddy. Jack Sixes isn't well either, so Uncle Johnny helped out – Billy Tucker, too. He's courting cousin Mary Anne so he's around the Larsons a lot of the time."

Don blurted eagerly, "I helped some, too!"

Smiling knowingly, Jane continued, "Yes, Don, when you were visiting Melissa," and added to Scott, "Don went down to help Billy and Grandpa with haying in late spring. Besides telling me how beautiful my sisters are, he's given the only firsthand report on Dad."

"Rick looks almost as old as Scott, and he was still pretty weak when I visited your ranch," Don volunteered.

"Anyway, Grandpa found a buyer in the Coquille Valley and sold all the steers, keeping a bull and six cows. He bought that piece of land north of our hay field and paid ranch bills with the sales money. Then Momma sent me a hundred dollars for our baby, even though she needs the money more than we do. I kept it because the folks would be hurt if I sent it back. Any ideas, Big Brother?" Jane queried.

"Yes I do, Little Sister! If Grandpa has paid all the ranch's bills as you say, I can afford to buy a couple of young cows with my reserve," Scott declared as he pulled his money belt from beneath his shirt.

Uwe nodded approvingly, remembering their deal of last summer, "Right my young friend, your horse is browsing in the east pasture."

Kurt interrupted hastily, "Jane found four cows for sale last Sunday in Keiser where we were visiting friends. She had absolute faith that her letter would fetch you home. Of course, this 'find' is her third this month."

Following chuckles over Kurt's rare attempt at humor, Don volunteered, "I'll ride to the Sixes with you, Scott. Two hands will make your drive easier."

"In that case, maybe we can find a pair of steers to trail with our cows. Six cattle are no more difficult than four. Let's check my finances to see if we can do it," Scott suggested as he emptied the contents of his money belt on the table.

* * * * *

Well, I've always known Oregon is God's country, Scott thought to himself, *but I wish I could relax and enjoy the scenery. I've been itching something fierce to see my family ever since dinner last week in Salem, I hope Jane's worries are for naught. Somehow I can't picture my father as anything less than fit as a fiddle.*

Don is good company for this drive and a much better trail cook than me, but he's sure a worrywart. Hmm! Keeps seeing rustlers behind every tree this side of Cottage Grove. I reckon he's been listening to Grandpa's stories of the old days. Well, maybe I ought to swap places with him and watch our back trail for awhile. Makes me wish I had my rifle with me.

Putting the notion into reality, Scott pulled his three tethered cattle to the side and motioned his partner with his string forward.

"What's up, Scott?" Don queried with raised brow.

"You lead the way while I check on those fellows riding behind us. I swear, you've got me spooked, too."

Scott led his charges up a nearby rise to afford him a bird's-eye view of his back trail. His mare seemed to sense his purpose and climbed a small knoll, tossing her head as she faced northerly. Sure enough, there was a party of four riders following their trail, ignoring the rail right-of-way but a hundred yards away.

"Come on, Daquiri! Let's catch up with Don," Scott muttered softly to his mount, smiling as he remembered the Gerbrunn's reaction to his renaming the horse. Anne had disapproved of calling his mare Maria but acquiesced quickly when the name of a small Cuban town was used. Besides, Scott figured that Doc was a nickname handier for horse and rider.

Out of sight of the other riders, Scott kneed Doc forward at a trot. The two cows and a steer matched the horse's pace by necessity, tethered ropes all taut with reluctance. The gentle slope was easy-going, and when the string passed a surprised Don, he quickly followed suit.

Riding a creek trail under the cover of the forest canopy, Scott slowed his animals to a walk but wouldn't let the cattle rest nor graze until he spotted Drain in the distance.

Don called out, "Can the cattle drink now?"

Scott explained to his partner, "Sure, I saw your four riders on our trail. Don't know why they aren't following the railroad, but maybe I'll ask them if they get too close. Take both strings into Drain, and I'll follow at a distance."

"You want my rifle?" Don asked.

Smile a bit strained, Scott shook his head and replied, "No, I don't expect trouble. Besides Doc and I can run plenty fast."

Daquiri pranced back along the trail, spirited in manner now that he was free of the cattle. Scott mirrored the young mare's frolicking with riant chatter into her twitching ears. Momentarily without a care in the world, horse and rider cantered through the forest right up to the approaching riders.

"Whoa! Easy girl!" Scott soothed his mount as he faced the four riders, obviously as surprised as he was.

One of the strangers roared loudly, and raising a fist into the air spurred his horse directly toward Scott, who reared back in his saddle with alarm until he recognized the whooping figure of Bernie Heisel. He met his old friend in a fierce bear hug – horses standing shoulder to shoulder.

"Whoop! Gave you a scare, didn't I, old friend? Why were you cowboys so cautious about our following you from Cottage Grove? Would have caught up with you sooner but figured you might take a shot at us. How have you been? Haven't seen you in over a year," Bernie rambled on.

Scott finally broke in his friend's chatter to answer, "I'm fine Bernie, but we can visit tonight if you'll offer Don Gerbrunn and me a piece of your bearskin rug for a bed. I'd better get back to my partner before he gets nervous – he has the rifle."

Bernie laughed playfully, slapping Scott on the back as he introduced him to his traveling companions. He invited everyone to his cabin after supper, indicating Scott was a great storyteller and would treat everyone to a beer, his broad wink assuring his friend that the host would buy the spirits.

* * * * *

Four days later the familiar landmarks took on new meaning for the homeward-bound world traveler, the hamlet of Denmark showing little change in his year of absence. Scott returned a friendly wave from one of the Langlois clan sitting on the porch of the general store, but eschewing any delay in reaching home he continued riding along the coastal road. When Denmark was out of view, his impatience became evident as he urged Daquiri forward with constant pressure from his knees. The tether line stretched taut as his charges trotted behind the laboring horse, obedient to Scott's voice and Doc's rope although bawling out their unhappiness.

Don called out, "If you're in such a dadburned hurry, give me your string and ride on home. I know my way to the Myrtlewood Grove. The Sixes River can't be more than a couple of miles ahead."

Grinning guiltily as he circled back to Don, he untied the tether from his cattle and handed it to his partner. Reining Doc around, Scott spurred him along the road yelling an afterthought over his shoulder, "Thanks, Don. See you at the ranch."

Minutes later he sighted the Sixes River, and before he reached the crossing he swung the mare up the river trail into the gap. Horse and rider continued their rapid pace along the gravelly Slide Ridge trail and over the Cascade Creek bridge, Scott pulling back on Doc's reins before proceeding down the knoll into the yard.

* * * * *

"Hello the house! Where is everyone?" Scott bellowed at his deserted home – not a soul in sight.

"Scott, is that you? Oh my, it's good to see you, Big Brother," one of the twins cried as she emerged from the chicken coop with a basket of eggs.

With his uncanny ability to identify each identical twin by their expression and personality, Scott greeted his sister with a hug and kiss, suggesting tongue-in-cheek, "Give me your basket Melissa and climb up on Daquiri here. Don needs help bringing our cows across the Slide Ridge trail."

"Oh Scott…" Melissa gasped in surprise with a tear and a smile, planting another kiss on his cheek as she exclaimed, "Is Don really here?" Without further questioning the girl swung gracefully into the saddle, and with feet dangling short of the stirrups she rode away eagerly.

Setting the eggs gingerly on the stoop, Scott looked about the ranch, spotting color before form as his sister Anne stepped out of the apple orchard, waving as she ran toward him. He sprinted past Grandpa's cabin to meet her halfway, another warm embrace resulting. He remembered that his sisters' seventeenth birthdays had fallen earlier in the summer and could see why men were calling on them.

"Anne, you and Melissa are as pretty as can be. You've grown up since I went away."

"And you're a handsome brother, Scott. Are you as healthy as you seem? We're all sorry about Maria's death. Are you up to talking about her?"

Scott smiled, and with a nod replied, "Yes, but let's wait until the family is gathered. Melissa went downriver to meet Don – another surprise. What's this I hear about your having a boyfriend?"

"Oh yes, Scott, but our parents disapprove of Robert because he's twenty-six years old. Father had an argument with him one day he visited me and ordered him off the ranch. I go to town as often as possible to see Robert. Daddy can't stop my feelings for him. He's so handsome and a real gentleman – good to me. Oops, there's Father. Can we talk later?"

Giving Anne a quick hug of assent, Scott hurried toward the barn, where his father stood squinting at his long-absent son, finally recognizing him with certainty as he drew closer. Scott was shocked at his father's appearance, gray hair, wrinkled face quite pale, and shoulders stooped from his illness. Rick's eyes bespoke his aged condition, being more like Grandpa than the vital and energetic Daddy he remembered fondly.

Both men had tears in their eyes as they came together in a filial bear hug, neither deigning to voice their affection nor happiness in greeting one another.

When they separated both wore wide grins, and Scott found his father's sense of humor intact as Rick remarked, "About time you got home, Son. I wondered if I'd still be around when you showed up. Damned lungs almost gave out last winter, but I feel better now that you're home."

"We need to get some color into your cheeks, Dad. Maybe a little hunting?" Scott suggested, adding another idea, "Or sit on the riverbank and catch a few fish."

"You bet, Son. Although your grandfather is fetching in a load of venison from up on Cougar Hill across the Sixes. I suppose Jane told you that we'd sold our steers," his father replied.

"Yes, but I brought replacements. Here come Don and Melissa with our new cattle. How do you like the looks of my new Gerbrunn mare, Daquiri?"

"Hmm! Mighty fine animal, Son. I bet Uwe hated to part with her, and I see you brought some breeding stock along. Caesar will be happy to have company again. That old bull has been lonely with only a couple of playmates on the ranch," Rick joshed cheerfully as he hurried forward to greet Don – obviously an approved suitor for Melissa.

"Dad, can you and the girls take care of these cattle. Don and I will help Grandpa with the venison he's carrying in," Scott suggested as he took Daiquiri's reins from Melissa and swung into the saddle.

Almost an afterthought, Scott queried with puzzled brow, "Where's Mom? Is she visiting Uncle Fred?"

"Julie went to town to barter eggs for flour and salt, and she'll stop by her brother's ranch on the way home," Rick replied.

Scott thought for a moment, eager to see his mother but aware that Grandpa needed help first, finally saying indecisively, "I guess I'll take Don and say hello to the old-timer. I can ride into Port Orford afterwards and meet Momma. Might as well let everyone know that I'm home."

* * * * *

A dry chuckle echoed through the forest as the two riders climbed out of the shallow Sixes River, a teasing voice revealing their quarry seated on a weatherworn stump. Grandpa declared, "Scott boy, I saw you come into the ranch yard from up on the ridge – my old eyes are working just fine, thank you. Whew! Just beat you here with my last quarter of meat. Welcome home, Grandson!"

"Grandpa, you're still a true frontiersman," Scott praised the old-timer, leaping from his horse to rush into a bear hug with his grandfather. Stepping back, the two men conducted a silent inspection which confirmed they had both aged in the past year.

Old Scott looked his seventy-six years, lines of toil and worry etched into his face. His eyes were lively, however, and belied any notion that he was nearing his dotage, his sharp mind displaying perception and sensitivity as he ordered in a soft tone, "I'm glad you're home, Scott, only sorry Maria isn't with you. Now hurry into town and give your mother a kiss. Don and I will handle this venison."

Scott nodded, and with a grin of anticipation, he mounted the mare and rode away down the valley, a casual wave the only attention given to the wranglers in the corral. As he crossed the old wooden bridge, he nudged Doc into a trot and raced for town.

* * * * *

Scott nodded at several acquaintances along the wind-blown street, riding his mare directly to Johnny's store. As he dismounted his glance scanned the area and tying the reins to the hitchrail, he entered the store to say hello to his uncle and ask about his mother's whereabouts. He had no more than passed through the front door when Johnny erupted from his lawyer's desk in the corner and rushed forward to greet him.

"Scott, you've grown some this past year and looking mighty fit. Are you home to stay? Your folks need you, I know."

Reciprocating the warm reception, Scott declared, "That's why I'm here, Uncle Johnny. Is Momma visiting Aunt Anne? Hey! It's good to see you, too."

"Yes, Julie's at my home while my clerk fills her supply order. Robert Wilkes was in the store when she arrived, so she wouldn't stick around. He tried to strike up a conversation, but all he got was a polite good morning. She doesn't like him any more than Rick does," Johnny concluded with an uncertain look in his eyes.

"Huh! I know my sister's boyfriend is *persona non grata* at the Myrtlewood Grove. Jane and Anne told me quite differing opinions of that fellow. Oh, by the way, Don Gerbrunn is at the ranch spooning Melissa – with everyone's approval naturally. What do you think of the situation? Is Wilkes that bad?"

Shrugging his shoulders with an elegant expression of fence straddling, Johnny replied, "He's charming to the ladies and 'one of the boys' with the men. Most people like him – including your aunt. She can't understand why Rick dislikes him so, but I lean toward your Dad's feelings. Wilkes is a bit too much of a smooth-talking salesman although he makes more money gambling than selling liquor. He seems too sophisticated for little Anne."

A young store clerk emerged from the back room with a sack of flour over his right shoulder and a half-filled gunnysack grasped in his left hand, nodding amicably to Scott as he asked,

"Should I load your mother's purchases on your horse, Mr. McClure?"

"Thanks, Zeke. Let me give you a hand. How are your folks doing on their Humbug ranch?" Scott replied as he hurried to open the front door for the youngster, calling over his shoulder, "I'll see you Sunday for supper, Johnny. Grandpa brought in fresh venison today."

Quickly stepping up to his nervous mare, he stroked her neck as Zeke flopped the flour sack across the saddle and hung the gunnysack from its horn. Scott helped Zeke lash the bundles firmly in place as he heard footsteps approaching.

A friendly voice offered, "Can I be of any assistance, gentlemen? You have a fine horse, sir, a McClure mare I'd say. Are you by any chance Anne's long-absent brother?"

Scott turned to survey the stranger standing beside him, seeing a strongly built and well-dressed man in his late twenties with handsome features, a quizzical smile creasing lips beneath a dark, trimmed mustache. *An impressive fellow* was Scott's fleeting thought, *but his eyes are hard, or more fairly they show no emotion. With those uncalloused hands of his, he looks his role of a gambler or a salesman.*

Offering his hand in greeting, Scott returned the smile and declared, "That's right, I'm Scott McClure. You must be Robert Wilkes. Anne's spoken of you."

Shaking hands firmly, Robert quipped, "As have other members of your family, no doubt, but I'm really not such a bad fellow. I'm very fond of your sister."

Hesitating a moment, he continued, "I'd like to ask a favor of you, Scott. Jane expects to meet me in town tomorrow, but I have to ride down to Gold Beach on business. Will you tell her for me?"

"Yes, of course. I wouldn't like to see Anne disappointed, now or ever, Robert," Scott said with double meaning, Wilkes nodding in understanding as well as agreement.

* * * * *

Scott looped Daquiri's reins over the porch railing and entered the Larson's back door without knocking. He surprised Julie and Anne in the parlor, both women jumping up to hug him. His aunt seemed unchanged, but his mother's face was a bit haggard under her jubilant expression. It wasn't necessary for the returning son to utter a sentence during the ensuing hour, a mere yes or no usually holding up his end of the conversation.

Finally interrupting the chattering women with a good-bye peck on Aunt Anne's cheek, Scott told her, "Let's talk more when you come to supper Sunday. Would Mary Ann like to bring Billy along?"

Both women answered in unison, "Ha! Ha! Of course!"

Scott laughed in turn as he fetched Salem from the barn and rode home with his mother, Julie still chattering about the latest gossip and news. She was pleased when he told her Don had come courting but failed to comment on Anne's beau.

"Come on, Mom! Stop dodging the issue of Robert Wilkes. I've talked to Anne, and Wilkes introduced himself to me in front of the store. Fill me in before we get home."

* * * * *

Supper was a happy and lengthy affair, Scott relating his travel to Cuba, his marriage to Maria for a day, and Jack-Jack Sixes' fate. Billy and Don enthralled everyone with tales of the Klondike, an original story only to Scott. Finally Rick reported on the status of the ranch, his halting and sometimes embarrassed voice a sad moment for those listening.

He concluded his speech with a plaintive moan, "Oh! Damn that Burton bullet. It's caught up with me after twenty years. Can't do a full day's chores anymore."

"Relax, Dad. I'm home to stay, and I actually look forward to good honest labor. We'll make out just fine," Scott replied encouragingly.

Grandpa and Rick exchanged glances, a silent message passing between father and son before the old-timer declared in a quietly serious voice, "Then take over, Scott. Your Daddy and I will help as usual, but you're the boss now."

"Ho! Until I pull a darn-fool stunt you don't like, and then you'll both set me straight."

"No Son, Dad and I are still your partners, but your decisions are final. We may second-guess you, but we'll never reverse any deal you make," his father averred with a determined expression on his tired face.

* * * * *

After chores were completed the next morning, Scott rode over to the Sixes ranch, spotting the stooped figure of Jack mending the corral fence. He called out across the freshly cut hay field, "Hello, Cha-qua-mi! How are you and your family?"

Jack straightened with a grimace turning into a grin as he recognized Scott, jibing in return, "Welcome home, good friend of my son Hi-to-mah. Is your wandering over? Are you ready to take care of us old men?"

"I'm home for good, but what old men? You all seem capable enough to me," Scott rejoined as he dismounted to exchange a hug with his friend before inviting the Sixes family to Sunday dinner.

Jack nodded quickly and accepted, "Of course, we'll come. All of us Sixes love Julie's cooking – it's a treat."

Hesitating briefly, a pair of false starts ensued, Jack finally blurting out, "Tell me about my son. I've read your letter many times, but written words aren't very satisfying."

Scott talked for over an hour, interrupting his rambling discourse to answer questions or to allow Jack to wipe away a tear. He concluded abruptly, both men silent as they leaned back against the corral fence.

Nodding in both acceptance and finality, Jack spoke in clear and untroubled tones, "Thank you, Scott. Jack-Jack died being a man, and I'm proud of my son – but he is gone. Now I must train his brother to handle our ranch. Will you help me again my friend?"

"Of course, young Jack is a fine lad and a quick learner. What about his sisters? Shouldn't they learn about ranching, too?"

Jack shook his head sadly, bemoaning, "Susan went to visit her sister on the Umatilla Reservation and married a friend of Henry's – Julie's husband. Then Mary had an accident in the river and almost drowned. She's a cripple in both body and mind. But Sandra is bright and should learn the ranching business with her younger brother. Did I tell you that we're grandparents? Julie and Henry have a baby they named Sandy after her grandma. Speaking of my wife, there she is in the doorway squinting to see who came visiting. Her eyesight isn't so good, but she's healthier than I am. Come on, you'll have to say hello."

* * * * *

Scott awakened in the middle of the night to the muffled sound of a horse being led up the knoll above Grandpa's cabin where he and Don had been sleeping the past week. He quickly dressed with his money belt under his clothing, and toting Grandpa's Sharps he crept across the starlit yard to the barn. Lighting a warm kerosene lantern he confirmed that Salem's stall was empty.

Guessing that Anne was rendezvousing with her beau, he saddled Daquiri and duplicated her stealthy departure, mounting his mare after crossing the noisy wooden bridge over Cascade Creek. Scott let Doc pick a comfortable pace along the dark lane, urging her forward when they were on the coast trail.

A foggy dawn was in the offing as Scott searched for Salem at the town stable, Larson's shed, and finally the Knapp Hotel – all without success. The blowing mist coming in from the harbor carried voices of a crew preparing to sail, and he drove Daquiri down the bluff to the sandy beach. There stood Salem, ground hitched to a driftwood log.

Cradling the Sharps in the crook of his arm he strode to the water's edge, finding a small gig beached and waiting for someone. To the pair of idling sailors he waved his rifle barrel in their direction and ordered, "Take me to your captain!"

The nervous seamen complied readily, Scott's glowering demeanor eliciting a cautious query, "Are you kin to that young lady who came aboard earlier?"

"Yes. Is she with Robert Wilkes?"

The second sailor bobbed his head and replied hurriedly, "Don't know his name, but he's that fancy gambling man who calls himself a salesman."

Scott's adrenaline was flowing as the gig bumped into the side of the lumber schooner, and he swung over the ship's railing in one smooth motion, his Sharps swinging freely and somehow threateningly. A brief scream from Anne greeted his intimidating arrival.

To Wilkes' credit, the salesman-gambler stepped in front of the girl and faced Scott with a pale but determined visage, denying any wrongdoing, "Scott, your sister and I are getting married as soon as we're at sea."

Anne piped between sobs, "Please, Scott, we love each other."

"Scott McClure, what are you doing aboard my ship with your Grandpa's blunderbuss in hand?" queried the captain in firm yet humorous tones.

"Good morning, Captain Holmes. Sorry about the Sharps, but I wanted to make sure any wedding was consummated posthaste," Scott replied and turned to Anne with a question, "Sis, are you sure you want to elope with Robert?"

"I love Robert, please...," Anne pleaded as Wilkes interrupted.

"And I love your sister."

Captain Holmes nodded in good humor as he suggested, "Then why don't I marry you two lovers right now. That is, if Scott will give the bride away."

Scott wagged his head in both wonder and a trace of confusion, but agreed forthwith, "Very well, Captain Holmes, if Anne insists."

The schooner captain ordered the anchor weighed, commenting to all on deck, "We're now 'at sea' so I'll make the rites short before we end up on Battle Rock." Whereupon he performed the wedding ceremony and congratulated the bride and groom, quickly dropping the ship's anchor. Scott laughed at the show of propriety as he shook the skipper's hand.

Turning to Anne, he kissed his sister tenderly and wrestling his money belt free of his shirt, he handed it to Anne with his blessings, "Have a happy life, Sis, from all the family. This money is the only dowry we can manage on such short notice. Write us from San Francisco."

"Thank you, Big Brother. I promise to write you," she replied amid tears of joy.

Scott accepted Robert's extended hand as the groom volunteered, "We'll be in Los Angeles, Scott. I'll see my wife writes home once in awhile."

"Goodbye, Robert, take care of my sister," and with a gentle pat to Anne's shoulder he slid over the rail into the gig, waving farewell as the boat headed to the beach. Two crewmembers took his place in the gig, and it quickly returned to the schooner.

Ten minutes later the ship disappeared into the misty air hugging the Orford Heads, headed for open sea and Los Angeles. Scott stood rooted in place beside Daquiri and Salem for some time, finally mounting up to return home with the news of a wedding in the family.

Chapter Sixteen

Much to Scott's surprise, his father and family gave silent approval to his handling of Anne's elopement – wedding, although only Grandpa voiced his approbation for his action. While the two fisherman angled for trout that evening, the elder Scott grew loquacious.

Grasping his grandson's shoulder in a warm gesture of support, Grandpa rattled on, "You looked flabbergasted when no one found fault with your decision this morning. Actually your father seemed relieved at the outcome. I think he regretted his ultimatum to Anne but was too proud to take it back. Besides, none of us particularly like Robert Wilkes as an in-law or not. I remember Buzz Smith's advice when I was courting my Missy, 'Don't say anything you can't live with the next day!' His saying was an unexplained message from his past, which I always figured was why the girl married the other guy."

Grandpa hesitated but a short moment before changing the subject, "Now comes another challenge for you – Melissa and Don. Young Gerbrunn is staying for a long visit, isn't he?"

"Ah Grandpa, the folks approve of Don, and Melissa is old enough to know her own mind. What's the problem anyway?"

"None, I reckon, but I bet Don talks to you right soon. He'll hem and haw until you agree to have him as a brother-in-law, and then the youngster will talk to Rick and Julie. You see Scott, you're boss around here nowadays, whether you think so or not."

Scott shook his head in disagreement, asserting, "Dad's the father and head of our family."

A tear trickled along Grandpa's wrinkled but straight nose, his downcast expression momentarily at odds with his optimistic persona as he moaned, "Scott my boy, Richard's lung almost killed him last winter. The doctor suggested he move to

Arizona Territory for the dry heat – the only treatment he could offer. Your father would have none of it, refusing to leave his home – the Myrtlewood Grove."

"And you don't think he'll live through another bout with pneumonia, is that it, Grandpa?"

The old-timer wagged his head with ambivalent disclaimer, nodding and shaking simultaneously in agreement – disagreement, finally admitting his fear, "I think I'll outlive my son and so does he. We talked about family at length last spring. We didn't know if you were coming home or not. You eased his mind considerably when you came home and then agreed to be boss. So you see, you can't avoid making decisions, nor can you back away from responsibility. And I'm proud of you, Scott my boy, for growing into the man you are."

"Thank you, Grandpa. I still feel too young to be boss, but I'm a McClure and we do our duty."

* * * * *

Scott lay awake in his blankets listening to the nocturnal sounds outside Grandpa's cabin overlain with an occasional snort from the old-timer. After several minutes of mulling over their evening conversation, Scott experienced a rare flashback, a dreamlike vision of his beloved Maria's wan smile from their final moments together. His empathy for Melissa and Don eschewed any further thoughts of teasing, deciding his impish notion might be more irascible than jocular. The young lovers deserved his support in their serious affair of heart.

Don turned over in his bunk, blankets swishing as he tossed about, his breathing indicating that he wasn't asleep either. Scott extended his hand with a brotherly pat on his shoulder and announced in whispered tones, "I think you should marry my sister. Mom and Dad are sure to approve of your marriage."

His friend sighed volubly in relief as he replied less quietly, "Thanks, Scott. Will you help me with your folks? Rick is kind of grumpy these days."

Smiling in the darkness Scott responded, "Sure, how about during breakfast? Grandpa and I will be there to congratulate you two. Now go to sleep."

* * * * *

Don spoke to the McClures with respect but determination at their morning meal, the low gray clouds enveloping the Sixes Valley not dimming his declaration of love and hopes of marriage. As Scott anticipated, his parents embraced their future son-in-law, plans for a wedding quickly dominating the day. In fact, Don became an errand boy for Julie and Melissa, riding to Reedsport to telegraph his parents of the news, escorting the women into Port Orford for shopping and visiting, and hiking the Sixes hills with Grandpa seeking game for the wedding feast.

In the meantime Rick and his son hunted the Elk River, bagging three bucks for Johnny's store – payment for the coming party. Don's complaints about never seeing his sweetheart fell on deaf ears as the women claimed Melissa's attention. The betrothed decided to be wed under the myrtlewoods, rainy season no deterrent to their romantic notions.

* * * * *

Concomitant to a light drizzle on the Sixth of November was a whistling breeze out of the west, surely the harbinger of another rainstorm. The men tied a tarpaulin between two stout old myrtlewoods to shield the wedding party and its makeshift altar in what turned out to be abbreviated and somewhat terse nuptials. As soon as Don kissed Melissa to conclude the ceremony, Kurt and Jane led their families and friends in congratulations to the newlyweds.

Julie and Aunt Anne were practiced in rearranging their supper party, gathering the women and children in their house, while the older men followed Grandpa to his cabin. Kurt, Billy, and a couple of the Hughes brothers stayed with Scott at the barbeque pit, tasting the venison and fish beside the open fire. Soon young Jack Sixes ran from the house with a simple question, "Aunt Julie says she's ready. When will the meat be done?"

Scott threw his arm around the lad's shoulder, declaring, "You're my helper now. Our friends will take this meat to the party while you and I clean up the grove."

With an admonishment to Kurt to save some food for them, Scott and Jack scattered the ashes, then untied the ropes holding the old tarpaulin and let it drop to the ground. After folding the canvas sheet in a bundle, he carried it to the barn while his young friend toted the "altar" table to Grandpa's cabin. Rick was pouring wine for a toast when Scott entered the house to congratulate the newlyweds.

From that point on, guests roamed the ranch, eating and visiting, the young men finding the barn a comfortable spot and several of the women wandering over to inspect Grandpa's cabin. When a gentle dusk descended upon the Sixes Valley, guests began departing, the Knapp family leaving with the newlyweds. Louie had offered his best hotel room to Don and Melissa for their honeymoon night. Tomorrow morning they were due aboard a steamer for a voyage to Portland, compliments of Grandpas Hermann and McClure.

The two old-timers were feeling good as they rode away, Julie claiming they were both potted as she laughingly threw up her hands in mock bewilderment. Rick signaled to Scott and Billy Tucker to saddle their horses and escort their guests to Port Orford, and make sure the two old-timers navigated the Sixes Crossing safely. River waters were bound to be rising with rain along the coast.

* * * * *

During the first weeks of winter, little socializing was possible, stormy weather and ranch work occupying the McClure family. Holiday greetings from Jane and Melissa were reassuring, and an overdue letter from Anne brightened the holiday season. Aunt Anne hosted a sumptuous Christmas Day feast, George toasting a timely celebration of Christ's birthday, a premature quaff to the new year, followed by a sentimental tribute and more brandy, to Mary Anne and Billy Tucker as they announced their engagement to be married. George's frail body was no deterrent to his partying mood and happiness as his last grandchild was to be wed.

Riding home under darkening overcast, the McClure's felt the first snowflakes of winter, melting as they touched the ground. With an exuberant shout of "Merry Christmas!" Rick spurred his horse towards home with Scott urging Daquiri to match his stride. Grandpa's warning yell as father and son raced down the slope fell on deaf ears, both horses charging into the Sixes River, pace abruptly slowed on hitting the deep water. The Gerbrunn gelding Don gave Rick was a stranger to the flooding Sixes. The horse swerved violently, throwing Rick over his head, but fortunately the veteran rider had a firm grasp on the reins. Doc handled the plunge with experience, allowing Scott to reach out and grab his father's coat collar. With his helping hand, Rick regained the saddle before they reached the north bank of the river.

Rick was soaked to the skin and shivering in the cold air, but with his resilient spirit surfacing anew, he laughed and made fun of himself despite Julie's nervous frown. Grandpa and Scott aped her worried look when Rick began coughing as they rode up the Sixes Valley trail.

"Damned lungs! Can't have any fun," Rick complained as they dismounted before their front door, Julie fussing over her husband as he continued to cough. By the time Scott had cared for the four horses, his father was in a warm bed and Grandpa was saying goodnight to Julie. Mother and son enjoyed each other's company while subconsciously keeping a vigil over Rick, his coughless sleep encouraging them to retire early as well.

* * * * *

Rick was up at dawn milking cows side by side with his son and then both tossed hay into the corral as the bleak wintry sun rose over the valley. He coughed once but grinned as he said, "No heat in that sun up there, but at least it's a cheerful relief from the rain. Thanks for pulling me out of the Sixes yesterday. I should be more careful, I guess. Your mother worries when I kick up my heels."

"Glad you're feeling better this morning, Dad. That's the first cough I've heard today. How are your lungs?"

"Fine, Son," Rick hesitated as the hollow sound of hoof beats came from the wooden bridge over Cascade Creek, concluding, "Hmm! Wonder who's coming?"

Johnny Larson galloped down the knoll and across the yard, reining his horse around the house as he spotted Rick's wave from behind the corral. He shouted loudly enough to be heard by Julie in the doorway and Grandpa walking in from the orchard, "George died in his sleep last night, peacefully it seemed to me when I found him in bed this morning. His funeral will be tomorrow afternoon at one o'clock with a short graveside service. I'm riding up to Reedsport to telegraph Angela."

"Oh Johnny, I'm so sorry. Your father seemed so alive with energy yesterday. We'll all miss him," Julie uttered in sorrowful tones.

Grandpa reached the corral and offered, "Can we help, Johnny? Maybe tell our neighbors?"

"Thanks, Uncle Scott. Billy and Jacob are riding south of town, and Louie Knapp is walking around town with the news. I figured Rick could notify Jack Sixes, and you could ride over to tell the Hughes clan. If Scott would visit the Elk River ranches, I'll stop at the Langlois place on my way to the telegraph office."

"Of course, Johnny. But tomorrow afternoon? Angie won't be able to attend," Grandpa Scott replied.

"I know, but the trains aren't running this week. There's a bridge repair crew in Drain at work. It'll take her family a week to get here, and I decided the funeral couldn't wait," Johnny explained with a questioning tone, apparently wondering if he was right.

"I'm sure you did right, Johnny. Angie's family will remember a happy George at the wedding party."

Nodding at the old-timer's agreement, Johnny added, "Would you deliver the eulogy, Uncle Scott? You were his best friend for so many years."

* * * * *

Spring came slowly to the Oregon coast, the McClures working diligently to keep their livestock healthy, Scott selling their last steer to Johnny in March as their hay supply ran out. He bought supplies, including feed and seed from his uncle's store with the cash, and waited out the wintry weather. George's funeral with a short visit by Angie and Uwe the following week seemed ages ago, as did Rick's worrisome bout with influenza in February.

Grandpa had inherited George's supply of brandy, the sextant a sea captain had left behind in 1854, and fifty dollars cash, with the latter going to his mother-to-be granddaughter in San Diego. Scott rode north every day for two weeks to work with a black sand goldmining operation, his wages also sent to Anne. Both received thank you votes with a rosy picture of marriage and impending motherhood in July.

One sunny day in late May Scott trudged up to the corral after a sweaty day's toil in the east pasture stacking hay. He heard voices in the yard, and then Uncle Fred rode up the knoll, evidently heading home. He hurried to the doorway to find his mother in tears, her woebegone expression a sign of bad news.

"Oh Scott, Fred told me Angela has a lung disease, 'tubercolist' or something like that. Delores is taking her to Arizona day after tomorrow. They're going to sell their ranch and move down there. The doctor says a dry climate is her best medicine. I'll miss them so," Julie bemoaned.

"I'm sorry, Mother...poor Angela. Are Fred and Delores all right? I heard that disease is contagious," Scott queried.

"I hope Angela will heal with sunshine and plenty of rest. Her parents have begun taking precautions against infection, but it's a little late when they lived in the same house all along," Julie answered thoughtfully, her tears held at bay as she added, "Fred asked if you would escort his family to Arizona – he'll pay you. But maybe you'd rather not travel with them under the circumstances."

"Of course I'll go with Aunt Delores and Cousin Angela to Arizona Territory. They need a man with them for such a long trip. Are they going to Phoenix or Tucson?"

"Neither! It's a town near Phoenix called Mesa. Fred wants to open a store, and that town seems a likely choice because it's growing fast. What will you charge Fred?"

"Oh, I can't take any money beyond expenses. Hmm, maybe I'll go to San Diego before coming home," Scott mused, casting a questioning eye at his mother.

Nodding in agreement, Julie offered, "Take my egg money along and give Anne what you don't use, and our love."

* * * * *

With Fred in Port Orford wooing a prospective buyer for his Elk River ranch, Grandpa volunteered to ride along to

Reedsport and bring the horses back. The foursome left the Madsen house before noon, Grandpa scouting the way while Scott led Fred's old nag laden with two trunks strapped to his saddle. The trip north was speedy and therefore tiring to the women, but the Reedsport Hotel was comfortable for an overnight stay.

Grandpa knew an old horse trader in town and sold the two saddle horses without any problem. Aunt Delores looked relieved as she accepted the gold coins, giving half to Scott as she parroted her husband's advice, "We'll keep the eggs in two baskets Scott. You can buy our tickets in the morning and pay the hotel bill. The old gelding is yours, Uncle Scott. Take him home and put him out to pasture if you can't sell him."

The trio boarded the train at the Reedsport station and were soon rumbling easterly through the coastal hills to Drain and then south to Los Angeles with nary an incident to mar their trip. Three days later they reached Mesa and a comfortable rooming house. Scott left the weary women in their room to rest while he walked the town looking for a suitable house for the Madsen family.

Aunt Delores joined him the next day and found a two-story house on a pleasant street behind the business district, Scott negotiating with the owner over its price for a couple of days. When Fred's telegram arrived telling Delores that he had sold the ranch, she bought 'her house' with a hundred dollars downpayment, the rest of the money due within thirty days.

Scott helped Delores and Angela move into their new home and set up housekeeping, the former owner selling them a few pieces of furniture. When Fred's second telegram was delivered announcing his arrival next week, Scott caught the next westbound train to Los Angeles. He hitched a ride to San Diego on a night freight train, paying Jake, the conductor, for a seat in the caboose and a share of the enterprising man's lunch.

His garrulous companion leading the way, Scott plodded through the railroad yard in the pre-dawn hours, shortly entering an alley near the freight depot. Following Jake through all but invisible door in the side of a ramshackle building, Scott found himself in a lamplit dining room, cooking aromas tempting his palate as his stomach juices began to flow.

Jake chortled aside, "Ha! Ha! See I told you so! Best food in San Diego. A Chinaman owns this eatery, and his wife is a fine cook. Sit down here with me, and I'll buy breakfast."

* * * * *

Scott plodded along the waterfront street in search of the elusive address given to him by Anne's former landlady. The old biddy had clucked in sympathy when asked about his sister, changing her tone at the mention of Robert's name. She derisively called him a "deadbeat," more damning epithets muttered under her breath. He learned the Wilkes had left their rooms several weeks ago, owing almost three months' rent. Anne returned now and again to pay a dollar on that bill and collect her mail.

Spotting a police officer walking his beat at the next intersection, Scott accosted the smiling patrolman and inquired about his sister's address.

The officer pointed behind Scott towards an arched entry and suggested, "Try the courtyard behind that open gate, sir. I believe your number is in there." After a brief hesitation, he flashed a smile and volunteered, "This is a rough neighborhood for strangers, young man. Let me walk over there with you. We'll find your sister."

The two men chatted companionably on the short route back up the street, the visitor learning a little about San Diego and the policeman hearing a bit of the lore of Oregon. Waving a casual but friendly farewell, the men parted as Scott entered an old warehouse-type structure, former offices now serving as rooms to let. After stopping a half-dozen shifty-eyed denizens of the building to ask about the Wilkes couple, one wary old codger pointed to a door at the end of the hallway, scurrying away without saying a word.

Scott shivered involuntarily, thinking that fellow reminded him of a rat and began worrying about his sister amidst such weird people. He knocked on the door with trepidation, repeating his action more loudly as no answer came to either knock. Shrugging with impatience he tried the doorknob and found it unlocked, the door swinging open at his touch.

Before the room's sole window stood a small table covered with three or four dirty dishes and a half-filled bottle of curdled milk, an orange crate along the wall serving as a depository for a handful of clothes. The dilapidated bed occupied most of the small room, crumpled covers exposing a sagging and torn mattress.

What a pigsty, was Scott's thought as he stepped forward. *Anne's always been a good housekeeper – Momma's best helper. I wonder where...?*

A bare foot extending from a tangled blanket on the floor beyond the bed caused him to gasp in surprise and dread. He reacted by first stumbling backward, aghast at the sight, and then rushing forward to kneel beside the form of his sister. Wrapped in a blood-soaked tatter of wool, her pale face showed but little life as his fingers gently touched her throat. He felt a languid heartbeat, its faint and erratic pulse fighting vainly to sustain life.

Scott shouted urgently to footsteps in the hallway, "Help! Get a doctor! Help me! My sister is dying!"

Turning his gaze to Anne's face, he saw her eyes were open and she was talking in a barely audible voice, "...alone. Where is Robert? I love him so, Scott. Will you find him...don't fight with him...don't hurt him, Scott, I love him. He means well. Tell Papa...and Momma...I love them...and take care of my baby. You're a...," she coughed once and her breath grew still, eyes open in a lifeless stare.

Tears amid sorrow obscured the following moments as a kind neighbor brought his policeman-guide into the room. The two cared for Anne's body and comforted him, a pair of strangers arriving to carry Anne's remains from the room. The officer beckoned Scott to follow as he accompanied them.

"What about dear Anne's things, sir?" the neighbor lady queried in plaintive tones.

"You keep them, ma'am. I appreciate your act of kindness. Thank you," he replied as his eyes surveyed Anne's pitiful and valueless collection of belongings. As he walked away he muttered through gritted teeth, "I want nothing to do with this place, but I do need to find Robert Wilkes, Anne's plea or not."

* * * * *

Staring sleepily at the orange groves passing his train window, Scott mused over the past day and his quest to seek out Robert Wilkes. He had remained at the police station until the coroner showed up to sign a proper death certificate and then learned that Anne's baby girl had been stillborn. The doctor had complied readily with Scott's request for a second certificate.

It was dark before the undertaker had arrived in a hooded coach pulled by two handsome white horses, a simple wooden casket within the vehicle. Scott spent the night at the mortuary, insisting on two coffins and a double burial the next morning, an eccentric notion to honor Anne's request in his mind.

At the gravesite only five people were present for the funeral, the undertaker and his gravedigger, a priest, Scott and the police officer. Following the short service, Scott paid the undertaker with his last gold coins and walked out of the city cemetery with the officer.

"Mr. McClure, it's a sad day for you, and you have my sympathy," the policeman said as they stopped on the street.

"Thank you, Officer, for your kindness as well as doing your duty. Did you find out where Robert Wilkes went?"

"Aye, one of his neighbors told me that Wilkes went to Long Beach to play poker with a couple of cronies last week. My young friend, let me give you a piece of advice, don't seek him out with murder in your heart. He isn't worth your going to prison, McClure," the officer concluded, laying a fatherly hand on Scott's shoulder before turning away.

As the rail car clickety-clacked through the Los Angeles railyards, Scott grimaced ruefully at his empty money belt, contents fulfilling a need to honor one of his sister's last wishes – to care for her baby. While at the funeral he began worrying about the denial of her other request not to hurt her darling Robert. Any final decision on that wish could wait until he found his scoundrelly brother-in-law.

* * * * *

During the following days, Scott worked on the Long Beach waterfront to pay for his board and room at a local hotel and buy a beer or two for patrons of the local bars as he sought

Robert Wilkes. His search for information was partly successful when he found the location of a "floating" poker game. His seven dollars in change crossed the felt table to the "house" gambler's pile slowly enough for him to learn that Robert had been shot to death in this very room for cheating at cards.

Scott considered the allegation might be true, even as the dealer palmed a card ineptly. *It seems everyone in the game is cheating except me*, he thought silently, conceding the pot as his three deuces lost to the dealer's three aces.

His last coins gone, Scott left that den of inequity, thankful for getting out of the game in one piece and sorry that Robert hadn't. His life for a few dollars had been such a waste – not only Robert but his wife and unborn baby as well. Scott confirmed his information with a quick trip to the cemetery and a pauper's gravesite.

His mind at ease, Scott set out to save his wages for a train ticket home. Even so, he reckoned it would be spring before he reached his myrtlewood grove.

Chapter Seventeen

Scott stood flat-footed on the starboard bridge wing with his right fist grasping the rail firmly – his favorite spot when sailing. Amidst the swirling fog surrounding the Alameda Ferry, visibility was less than a hundred feet in any direction until the rocky shape of Yerba Buena Island thrust itself into view off the port bow. Within moments a partial vision of the east bay shoreline emerged from the dissipating fog, Oakland shimmering under the morning sun. He chuckled aloud, bemused at the vagrancies of San Francisco weather where within a few hundred feet dampening mist could turn into bright sunshine.

"San Francisco will be as clear as Alameda on my return trip, but I'm always a little surprised at Mother Nature's changes when I sail this bay," the skipper spoke with a companionable smile creasing his lips.

Scott chuckled anew, remarking, "I've been in this area often enough to understand its weather. I told my mother she should come on deck with me, but she was chilled from waiting at the ferry landing. Says she's an East Bay girl, or Sacramento anyway."

"Then she'll enjoy the rest of the day. It'll be warm in Oakland, a good afternoon for a picnic lunch on Lake Merritt. Will you be returning today?"

Shaking his head, Scott replied, "No, we've enjoyed our visit to San Francisco, but we're going up to Auburn to visit friends. What's the easiest way to get to the train depot?"

Before his question was out of his mouth, the westbound ferry signaled with her horn, and the ferryboat captain replied in kind as he hastened across the bridge for the port-to-port passing. Scott shrugged his shoulders casually and fell back to his woolgathering, recalling his rail trip of three years ago.

Here it is April and California feels like summer, Scott pondered silently. *It's probably raining at home. I hope the ranch isn't too much for Grandpa. Nah, most of our livestock have gone to pay for Momma's trip. Daquiri, old Salem, five steers and a dozen laying hens are all that's left on the ranch after our big sale. Momma got to visit Fred and his family in Mesa, and we'll poke around Sacramento for her folk's store and home.*

He smiled at his next thought, drawing a comment from the deckhand coming to the open wheelhouse window, "Yes sir, it certainly is a fine day. Captain Alvarez asked me to give you directions to the train depot."

* * * * *

Thanking the young deckhand for his courtesy, Scott reminisced as he gazed at the hills behind the Alameda landing. He had returned home in May of 1901 flat broke, carrying the sad news of the deaths of Anne, Robert, and their stillborn daughter. His family was desolate with grief, particularly his father who seemed to harbor a hidden guilt. Rick never did voice his feelings concerning Anne's elopement and flight to San Diego, nor her subsequent travail in marriage.

His father remained the hard-working rancher and loving husband during the ensuing months, but something was missing in his demeanor. Family and friends noticed little of the change, but one autumn day at the fishing hole Grandpa confessed with teary eyes, "Scott, I'm worried about your father. He seems to have lost his zest for life. Somehow he's not the same man since you brought us the news of Anne's death."

Shortly after Christmas had passed and the new year of 1902 was ushered in, Rick took to bed with congested lungs, pneumonia ravaging his wounded lungs until his breathing ceased. Dead before his forty-third birthday, Richard Erastus McClure was buried in the family plot beside the Sixes river amid the blessings of his loved ones.

Jane, Melissa, and their husbands came home for the funeral, Uwe the only other Gerbrunn able to make the tedious train and horseback trip to Port Orford. The next day the

McClure heirs gathered in Momma's home for dinner, Johnny Larson speaking as the family lawyer. Rick had left no will, but Grandpa and Julie upheld his wish that Scott become sole owner of the Myrtlewood Grove. The McClure men had reached a clear understanding long before Rick's death that Scott should own and manage the ranch. Each daughter was to receive cash payments as their inheritance, due within the next two years, with Momma and Grandpa drawing whatever they needed from the ranch income.

Rick's death came two years after George Hermann's and over six months following Patrick Hughes' death after a horse rolled over him. Jane Hughes lived in her new house and assumed management of the ranch with the help of her grown children.

The Sixes family history paralleled their neighbors' the following year when Jack Sixes passed away quietly in his sleep at fifty years of age, an ailing Sandy holding the ranch for her youngest children. Julie and Susan had families of their own in Umatilla and seldom wrote, never visiting the Oregon coast again. Eleven-year old Jack became the man of the house, inevitably following Scott's example in caring for the family ranch. Mary's accident years before had left her crippled and feeble-minded although she was cheerful in tending the chickens and cooking meals. Sandra was a bright young woman at fourteen years and was attending an academy in Portland. Her mother had already paid for another year, and young Jack took it for granted his sister would continue her education.

With Billy Tucker's father killed in a logging accident down in Eureka, Grandpa concluded that only he and Louie Knapp were really "old-timers," and Louie's sons were still young lads. He took to visiting Johnny and Anne more regularly and then dropping by the hotel to see the Knapp family. Occasionally he would rent the hotel's grand bathtub, the only real one in Port Orford, and sip brandy while bending Louie's ear about the good old days.

"Things sure have changed since the 'Four Musketeers' went to Cuba," Scott muttered aloud, glancing around at his mother's playful chuckle.

"You had to grow up in a hurry, Son, and I'm proud of you. I know your father was greatly pleased when you took over the family ranch. Of course, Grandpa means it when he swears you're a 'true McClure' – no higher compliment is possible. But seeing so much death these past few years had sobered you too much. What happened to that musketeer who enjoyed playing?" Julie asked thoughtfully. Laughing gently again she concluded in half-jest, "and when are you going to marry again. We need a McClure heir to run the Myrtlewood Grove."

* * * * *

Scott followed his mother along the plank walkway traversing the Alameda Ferry dock, Julie carrying her purse and a hatbox while her son toted their two leather bags. The sunlit terminal was a busy place with cross-bay travelers scurrying aboard the ferry as the McClures wended their way onto the open and fast-emptying waiting platform. His attention was held by two of those new-fangled gasoline carriages chugging noisily down the dock past him, seemingly chasing a milk wagon pulled by a skittish old mare.

"Scott!" had barely registered in his ears when Scott was struck by a flying body, arms encircling his neck as a beautiful young woman's lips sought his. He dropped his bags and embraced a grown-up Lou Simms, enjoying both the kiss and the closeness of her full body snuggling in his arms. As she tilted her head back in grinning delight, she murmured for his ears alone, "Isn't this romantic, Scott dear?"

"Whew! You have grown up some, Louise Ann Simms, but still as sassy as ever, I see. Why hasn't one of those Auburn cowboys married you? Or do you have one pursuing your hand?"

Lou laughed gaily as she gave a pert answer, "Several beaus are pursuing, but I promised a certain Oregon rancher that I'd marry him one day. Don't you remember, Scott McClure?"

Releasing his grasp, he bowed slightly as he jibed, "Yes, ma'am, and you were furious with me when I ignored that fourteen-year old girl. Now stop flirting with me. You're too darn distracting, and I want to introduce you to my mother Julie."

Lou's eyes flashed a hint of pleasure that remembered her tomboyish declaration while her face reflected a host of con-

fidence – an attractive woman's self-assurance. It was quickly
replaced by open apprehension as she turned to Scott's mother.

"I'm pleased to meet you, Mrs. McClure. Forgive my exuberant display of affection in greeting your son, but we're old
friends," Lou flushed pinkly in meeting the older woman's
steady gaze.

Her rather formal greeting made Scott a bit anxious until he
read his mother's look as being conspiratorial. He chuckled
quietly as Julie reached out her arms, and Lou moved forward
reciprocating, a welcoming hug and women's chatter ensuing.

Art Simms appeared at Scott's side, the two men laughing
ruefully as they greeted one another with a backslapping clasp
of arms on shoulders, the older man exclaiming in mock anger,
"What were you two doing? I'll have to dig out my shotgun."

Scott replied in kind, "You don't own a shotgun, Art.
Besides you can no more control your daughter than I can, so
don't blame me for her forward ways."

A small fist punched his shoulder as Lou reacted, declaring,
"Wait and see when you'll get another such kiss from me,
buster. Now mind your manners and introduce our parents to
each other."

"Yes, ma'am! Art, meet my mother, Julie Madsen McClure
of Sacramento before coming to Oregon. Mom, this gentleman
is my old friend, Art Simms of Auburn," Scott elucidated dutifully.

Art doffed his Stetson, displaying a pate of clipped gray
hair, and bowed slightly as he added his welcome, "And your
host for a couple of weeks, if you'll accept the hospitality of
our ranch. Hmm, Madsen was your maiden name, I take it.
Any relation to the folks who owned a general store up our
way, Mrs. McClure?"

"Please call me Julie, and since Louise and I are on a first
name basis, we certainly will accept your offer with thanks.
Scott has spoken of the Simms family often enough that I feel I
know all of you. Is Lester minding the ranch?"

Lou quipped in light voice, "Yes, and he's wooing Sylvia
Brinkley around the clock. When we decided to come down to
Oakland to meet you, he was buying a diamond ring. So I
expect they'll be engaged when we get home."

"Isn't Sylvia that pretty blonde who's your best friend?"
Scott asked in quizzical tones.

Art jibed, "She was her best friend until Sylvia started spending all her time with Les."

"Oh, Dad, she still is, but I'm a little envious of those two lovebirds. They are blind to the rest of the world. I seldom chat with Sylvia anymore. By the way, Scott, that 'pretty blonde' is a beautiful woman these days."

* * * * *

As the passengers debarked the platform car onto the station platform at Auburn, Lester and Sylvia were waiting with beaming faces, the engagement news a foregone conclusion. Scott murmured for Lou's ears only, "By golly, Sylvia is a beauty, isn't she, Lou? Your brother is a lucky fellow."

Despite a pleasant nod from his sober-faced friend, he felt an elbow dig into his ribs. Deciding a little diplomacy, even flattery, was in order, he offered, "But you're every bit as attractive a woman as your friend, Louise."

Lou grinned despite herself, accepting his compliment with flashing eyes if in silence, and greeted her girl friend with a hug and an exclamation of joy at the sight of the diamond ring on her finger.

Scott observed the family to-do with equanimity, congratulating the affianced couple when the excitement abated. Weddings were not a cause of jubilance in his experience although he understood the women's feelings on matrimonial trappings.

Louise introduced his mother as they walked across the wooden platform toward the ranch's cleanest coach, a two-seated wagon in reality. Julie joined the youngsters in talk of a wedding as they mounted the vehicle.

"Dad, we'll have to buy one of those horseless carriages this year," Les averred with a wishful tone of voice.

Art surprised his son with an acquiescent nod in reply, "I reckon so, Son, if we're going to escort womenfolk to town and back. You'll have to figure out how to fix our wagon trail into a road for an automobile. Why don't you and Scott start working on that problem, and Mrs. McClure and I will look for a proper ranch carriage."

* * * * *

The following two weeks passed quickly, western hospitality exemplary on the Simms ranch. Julie and Lou conspired with Sylvia to produce Auburn's finest wedding even though a June date was nixed by Sylvia's bedridden mother. The afternoon of July 21, 1904 was finally set, and Scott was startled when Julie announced she intended to stay and assist with the wedding plans.

His darting glance caught his mother's distraught expression, a tinge of guilt mixed with pleading showing in her eyes. Suddenly a light dawned in his mind as he realized the close relationship between his mother and Art must be something more than mere friendship. Scott smiled and nodded approvingly, bemused by his thought that two old people could be in love. Smiling anew as he reminded himself that Art was not quite fifty years and his lovely mother's forty-third birthday party was celebrated yesterday – at Art's insistence. Mentally kicking himself for being insensitive to an obvious situation, he made quick amends as he suggested, "I have to go home and help Grandpa, but I will return for the wedding."

Promptly receiving warm smiles and kisses on both cheeks from Lou and Julie, Scott understood intuitively that the girl was aware of their parents' feelings for each other. Lou clasped his arm securely against her body, Scott enjoying her closeness as she steered him on to the sunlit veranda.

Once out of earshot, her silence ended in exasperated chatter, "I wondered if you'd ever open your eyes, Scott McClure. Your mother is still a beautiful woman, and Dad absolutely dotes on her. Did you see his face when she volunteered to remain our guest? Hee! Hee! I've never viewed my good old Daddy as a suitor. Mother died when Les and I were young, and he's never showed interest in any woman while we were growing up. It took me a while to get used to the idea of my father as a lover, but you should have seen yourself. You really…"

Scott stilled her jocular rambling with a sound buss on her lips, the first kiss since they'd met on the ferry dock, and Lou stood wide-eyed as he admitted, "I know I've been guilty of paying too much attention to a certain young lady and not enough to my mother, but I finally understand the situation. I agreed with Momma's decision, didn't I?"

When Lou nodded meekly, quieted by his show of affection, Scott mused, "I'm worried about Grandpa and the ranch. Maybe I'd better catch the morning train home. Will you ride into Auburn with me?"

* * * * *

Scott was daydreaming about Lou's goodbye kiss on the Auburn platform when his melancholy was disturbed by the distant toot of the Reedsport train in the western hills. He was pacing the cinders beside the tracks in Drain, stiff from the day and a half trip from Auburn. Stretching his legs felt a luxury, but sleep would have to wait until he reached Reedsport this evening.

His musing was shattered by another shrill whistle of the oncoming locomotive nearing Drain's station. A flash of color and movement caught Scott's eye as a figure ran toward the tracks from behind the water tower.

A raucous "Whoopee!" sounded from the platform as a tall man stepped forward and lashed a nasty looking bullwhip about the runner's ankles, tripping him as he crossed the tracks. Before anyone could move, the teamster unwound his whip and slashed the scrambling figure across his back, red shirt and white skin lacerated by the blow.

Scott was moving as the whip hand drew back for another stroke, grasping the extended rawhide and jerking it unceremoniously from the brute's grip. Another waiting passenger helped the injured boy to his feet, leading him to the platform. *A boy*, Scott noted briefly in his thought, *young but rangy in build and maybe fourteen years old.*

"Give me my bullwhip and stand aside, mister! I'll show this petty thief a thing or two. Give it to…"

"No! There'll be no more whipping. Have you lost your mind, fellow? You're ten years older and forty pounds heavier that this boy," Scott admonished the bully.

Pulling a knife from his belt and sneering his disdain, the yahoo faced Scott and declared, "I'll have my whip or your ear…"

Scott reacted with dispatch, reversing the solid handle and swinging the butt across the culprit's arm, his blade flying askew. Throwing the bullwhip aside, he moved a step forward and half a step to his left, his right fist crashing straight into the man's nose. A surprised expression was followed by an incredulous look of shocked pain as the yahoo's nose dripped blood and he stumbled over the steel tracks onto his pratt. Scott advanced a step to meet any counterattack, but the bully squealed and ran away.

A murmur of disapproval from a woman in the crowd reached his ears, "That Connor boy is in trouble again."

When Scott's glance fell on a well-dressed, middle-aged couple, the husband offered, "No offense, young man, but the town's fed up with the boy's begging and stealing, although that Hanks fellow isn't any angel."

Nodding respectfully to the speaker and his wife, Scott turned to the boy and asked, "What do you have to say for yourself, lad?"

"I didn't do nothing, mister. He just…"

"No! Think before you answer, boy. I can't abide a liar. Just tell us the truth," Scott commanded with an intense stare, concluding, "I'm Scott McClure, tell me your name and what's going on here."

Gulping visibly as the boy's downcast eyes finally lifted to meet Scott's, he replied in a low-keyed voice loud enough for everyone to hear, "I'm Irving Connor, and I thank you for saving me from a whipping. Mrs. Bauer is right – I'm trouble. But I never stole anything from these folks. I…well I…guess I stole food from that fellow's camp."

Scott nodded calmly, asking, "You got any folks hereabouts, Irving?"

"No sir, my mom died last year over in Cottage Grove, and I never knew my father. We worked for an innkeeper, but I ran away when he wouldn't pay me my wages. Claimed I was lucky to have board and room. I heard there were mill jobs in Drain, but no one will hire me – they say I'm too young, but I'm almost fifteen years…well, I've passed my fourteenth birthday anyway."

"What do you owe that follow Hanks? He seemed mighty steamed up."

"Ah, he's always picking on me. I ate some of his biscuits and stew while he went to the outhouse. I reckon he had a right to be sore," Irving finished, flinching as he remembered his pained back.

"Come along, Irving. We'll have the doctor look after that wound."

* * * * *

Scott dug deep into his trouser pocket, extracting a silver dollar for the nurse, and a few silver and copper coins for Irving, suggesting quietly, "Buy yourself a good meal."

Leading the lad onto the plank sidewalk fronting the doctor's office, Scott was surprised when Irving bolted to his rear. Turning as thud and a moan sounded, he found the bully Hanks strike the boy a second time. His reflexive action was a fist to the culprit's swollen and discolored nose, eliciting a roar of sheer rage as he staggered backwards.

"Watch out, Scott!" Irving yelled as he dove from scrambling knees to butt a second man's knees.

Scott was driven against the building's wall by two men trying to wrestle him to the ground, a sneering Hanks charging toward them. Gathering his strength as he slipped aside, he twisted the man holding his right arm into the bully whose stinging blow struck his shoulder. A punch to the nape of his neck stunned him, but he kept moving, throwing his body sideways and toppling the fellow on his back into the dust. Dancing away from his attackers, yet did he catch a fist behind his ear as the yahoo charged by.

The familiar bull voice of Bernie Heisel roared a challenge, "Take care of Hanks, old buddy. The lad and I will keep his friends busy."

Scott glanced aside briefly, seeing his powerful bunkmate clobber one bruiser while Irving tackled the legs of another. He skipped about, brushing Hanks' long arm aside to slam a fist in his muscular midriff.

A backhand slap knocked Scott down, and he lashed out with both feet to fetch Hanks a painful lick in the shins. Rolling away from a return kick missing his ribs, Scott grabbed the bully's boot and dove under the body of his antagonist, "Whoof" blew out of Scott's lips as the other boot knocked the wind out of him. Hanks went sprawling in the dust, with Scott staggering to his feet, gasping for air and shaking his aching head to clear his befuddled thoughts. He backed away from the flying body which Bernie tossed aside in joyful glee, a good fight just his cup of tea. Irving punched and chased one of the attackers who kept running until out of sight, and Bernie calmly encouraged his old friend, "This lad is quite a scrapper, Scott. Hanks' cronies are gone, let's see if you can do as well."

"Thanks Bernie, I owe you a beer for sure," Scott gasped as he evaded Hanks' awkward charge, tripping his enemy with a swinging leg, and smashing his right fist into the exposed ribs of the bully as he reached out to catch his balance. Scott's left caught him above the kidney, scurrying away as Hanks' massive fist swung backward in defense. Scott slipped and fell away from his foe, scrambling to his feet behind a hitchrack.

The infuriated bully charged forward, breaking through the pole with a snap which threw him off-balance, Scott quick to pound his beleaguered nose with both fists. His face a bloody mess, Hanks fell onto the boardwalk and roared his frustration in a string of epithets questioning Scott's ancestry and his manliness.

He lumbered to his feet as the marshal called out, "That's enough! Hanks! McClure! Back off!"

Scott stumbled compliantly to the officer's side, but Hanks ignored the order until the marshal fired a bullet into the dust at his feet.

"Hanks, go back to your camp and stay there until you cool off. I don't want to lock you up."

Arguing in petulant fury, Hanks pointed an accusing finger at Irving and charged, "Then arrest that vagrant, Marshal. He stole from me, and McClure is protecting him."

Scott declared impetuously, "Irving Connor is not a vagrant. He works for me. What do you say he stole from you, Hanks?"

"Why...ah...he snuck into my camp and stole food. He's a sneak thief!" the man asserted.

Bernie chuckled as he flipped a silver coin to Hanks, who caught it in surprise, and related, "He caught you with your pants down, Hanks. Helping himself to your dinner was no cause to use a bullwhip on him. That four-bits will cover the food."

"This matter is closed, gentlemen. Go your separate ways. Any more fighting in my town will land you both in jail," the marshal concluded decisively, ordering, "And you get out of town, Connor."

* * * * *

Scott and Irving drove their jaded livery stable horses down the knoll into the ranch yard; a full day's ride from Reedsport tiring as well as famishing. The boy ogled the ranch in wide-eyed wonder while Scott called out loudly, "Grandpa, are you home?"

The old-timer rushed out of the barn to greet the two riders, surprised when he saw a stranger beside his grandson. In worried tones he asked, "Where's your mother, Scott? Is she all right?"

Scott slid from the saddle and greeted his grandfather with a bear hug, assuring him, "Momma's just fine. She's still visiting the Simms. I'll tell you all the news at supper. Now meet Irving Connor, our new ranch hand. He's about to dismount and tend these tired old nags."

"Howdy, Mister McClure," the boy said as he complied hastily, shaking hands with the elder Scott and leading the horses into the barn.

Four McClure eyes followed the lad's progress, both men wondering if he knew anything about horse grooming. Grandpa sighed and entered the barn, saying over his shoulder, "You get settled in, Scott. I'll teach Irving about horses."

Chapter Eighteen

Scott rode Daquiri up the Sixes River trail, having spent the day in Port Orford. He mused at Aunt Anne's reaction to his mother's being courted. She was as happy for Julie as Uncle Johnny was shocked. His exclamation of "Why, Richard's hardly in his grave" drew smiles from both Anne and Scott. She delivered a teasing reminder that her brother had been gone for over two years, but her remark did little to soften Johnny's disapproval.

When Cousin Mary Ann stopped by her folk's home for one of her mother's recipes, her concurrence with Anne's felicity drew her father's reaction. He threw up his hands and headed back to the store.

Scott had visited briefly with Louie Knapp at the post office, their conversation cut short by the mayor. Both men excused themselves as they hurried over the town's plans for the annual Battle Rock celebration. Scott and young Orris Knapp were left to chat, Louie's number-two son full of family news. Paying the lad a penny to deliver Larson's mail to the store, Scott wandered over to the tavern to have a beer and listen to Grandpa's old cronies tell of the good old days in Oregon Territory.

"Well, it's good to be home, Doc," Scott muttered to his trusted steed, quickly slipping into silence so his chuckling echoed only in his mind. Drifting through the tall firs came the sound of distant laughter, lost amidst his daydreams until he neared the knoll. *Hmm!* he thought, *Grandpa and Irving seem to be getting along just fine.*

As Scott dismounted at the corral, the two "hands" continued their hay fight inside, Old Salem disdaining to make their raillery form his course. It was clear that Grandpa approved of the youngster.

* * * * *

During supper Grandpa complimented Scott's judgment, announcing, "Irv is a welcome addition to our family, Grandson. He's going to bunk with me, and I'll teach him to be a rancher."

"Fine Grandpa. What are we going to pay this young 'troublemaker' from Cottage Grove? Have you figured that out, too?"

"Yep, five dollars a month, plus room and board in the deal. Oh, and I promised you'd buy him a set of new clothes. Does that seem reasonable to you?

Scott nodded agreeably, adding one condition that was on his mind, "Yes, as long as Irv attends school regularly. I won't brook any truancy, Irving Connor."

The lad was quick to complain, "Ah, Scott, I don't need no more 'learning'. School's not for me."

"Oh yes it is, Irv! You've been skipping school for over three years by your own confession. Everyone needs to know their three R's," Scott rejoined.

Grandpa concurred, actually interrupting his grandson, "He's right, boy. Your rithmatic seems good enough, but reading and writing need considerable polishing. Consider school as part of our deal."

"Gee whiz, Grandpa, everybody treats me like a child," Irv moaned, his attitude showing that the old-timer's words were law, even if Scott was the boss.

* * * * *

Jack Sixes appeared at their door two mornings later, his young face anxious as he looked over his shoulder at the ominous clouds to the west. He explained that his hay field was ready, and he'd cut a couple of acres yesterday. Without further explanation Scott and Irv hastened to their neighbor's ranch to help harvest all they could before the summer storm hit the valley.

Grandpa arrived before noon with McClure biscuits and Hughes cheese to sustain the crew. By mid-afternoon when the rain began to fall, ninety percent of the field hay was stacked, if not tedded properly.

Jack invited everyone to an early supper of venison stew, Grandpa and Irving following the boy into the house while

Scott stored the tools in the barn. He slipped through the half-open door with a wide grin on his dripping face, strands of rain-soaked hair plastered to his skull. Sandy rewarded him with a warm hug and a happy thank you.

"You're welcome, San-a-chi. I think we saved most of your hay. Your son is a good worker," Scott replied, greeting the girls as well, "Hello, Mary Ann, your stew smells wonderful. And Sandra, I see you're home for the summer."

A silent Mary Ann nodded hello, a pleased expression at the compliment, while her sister spoke cheerfully, "Yes, Scott, and I'm going to school in Port Orford this fall. Irving says he will escort Jack and me to school every day. Isn't that nice of him?"

Scott's raised eyebrow was directed at the school-hating Irving, bringing his straight-faced comment, "Sandy and I'll be in the same grade, boss, so we can study together, too."

With a touch of levity in his tone, Scott agreed, "Of course, Irving. I know you will enjoy school this year."

Grandpa and Sandy echoed Scott's low chuckle, the youngsters too busy making plans to catch the irony. Scott thought quietly as he watched the children during the meal, *Sandra has become an attractive young lady since I saw her last fall. No wonder Irv's not complaining about school. Well, maybe I shouldn't knock a good thing. Both boys will attend school all winter, and Irv will no doubt volunteer to help Sandra and her brother with chores over here.*

His contemplation shifted to their mother, *Sandy looks as old as Grandpa, yet he's twice her age. I wonder if she's ailing, she isn't her peppy self since her husband died last year. I guess I should talk to Sandra about her mother seeing the doctor.*

Well, I reckon I'd better see if Johnny found a market for our steers. He only needs one animal, but he heard that butcher in Gold Beach was buying beef. Grandpa caught his eye, and his thoughts returned to the supper table, nodding as the old-timer declared, "Rain's down to a drizzle, and darkness is coming on. Time to go home, Scott, Irving. Thanks for the delicious stew, ladies."

* * * * *

The three steers followed Daquiri docilely enough, Scott mused, separate lead ropes tied to his saddle. *I hope I can sell them in Bandon, nobody in Denmark or Langlois wanted any beef.*

Scott spurred Doc ahead with a trace of impatience, the steer reluctantly lumbering along the coast road behind the horse. Slowing the pace as soon as he saw the houses of town, he took a deep breath and waved to a familiar passerby, wending his way between two delivery wagons toward a butcher shop. He haggled with a friend of Grandpa's for some time before accepting a fair offer for his largest steer.

On his way again, his progress was easier on Daquiri with only the two more compliant steers to lead. Within the hour he halted before the old tavern south of Coos Bay and negotiated a complicated deal for his smallest steer. Over a free counter lunch and a nickel beer he bartered playfully, finally accepting the cash-poor owner's available coins, a rusty old Derringer pistol, a bag of cartridges, and a twenty-five pound gunnysack of navy beans.

In the town itself he took only a few moments to sell the third animal, deciding to return home immediately. He and his young horse were tired but still frisky, and he figured to stop at the Langlois store for a meal. Some bread and cheese for him, and a bag of oats for a hungry horse should suffice.

* * * * *

Scott woke Grandpa and Irving after he'd taken care of his horse, offering the lad a bottle of sarsaparilla he'd bought in Langlois. Grandpa poured a pair of brandies from his near-empty bottle while Irv reported on his Port Orford trip.

"I delivered that steer to the store and walked Old Salem home with a load of supplies. Johnny said you're all square with him. He gave me five dollars to boot, and Grandpa said I should keep it as my July pay. I can wait if you need the money, boss."

"No, keep it and any cash you get from selling eggs while I'm gone. I've enough cash for Momma and me. I reckon I'll leave next week and help Les finish his road project before the wedding. We should be home by the middle of August," Scott declared.

Turning to Grandpa he added, "I bartered one steer at your favorite old Coos Bay tavern. Got a little cash, bag of beans, and this rusty old gun. Can you fix it up for me, Grandpa?" Taking the pistol in hand, the old-timer checked the empty chamber before working the trigger mechanism. He stripped the weapon and inspected each part carefully, his jibe softened by an amused smile, "Going to carry this Derringer in Drain, Scott? Yes, I can clean it up and test fire it for you. Give me a day or two, I'm going back to my blankets now."

* * * * *

Scott's eyelids were drooping by the time moonlight shone upon the magnificent forest of evergreens. He struggled erect, not quite ready to doze off until he'd stretched his legs. He left his seat with a slight push, and walked to the rear platform. Opening the door he sniffed the aromatic Siskiyous air mixed with the taint of coal smoke from the laboring locomotive.

Closing the door behind him, he leaned his shoulder against its steel frame and chuckled aloud at his parsimonious nature. Quietly he pondered, *I can't see spending good money for a Pullman bed nor a dining car meal. Not when I have a perfectly good seat and a sack of jerky available. Besides I ate a good meal with Bernie in the Drain tavern between trains.*

And I behaved myself when Hanks came in – offered him a beer. He ignored me to sit at the far end of the bar, but I noticed he drank a beer and the barkeep collected a nickel from me. Glad there was no trouble, the marshal probably would have thrown us both in jail.

It seems funny to travel night and day to reach the Rogue River valley. Gold Beach is just fifty miles west but I've covered a couple of hundred miles to get here. Well, I should be in Auburn sometime tomorrow afternoon, I expect. Maybe I'd better get some shut-eye while I can. He slipped inside and returned to his seat, pushing a young cowboy's boots aside before settling into their joint space.

* * * * *

He was conscious of the train's stops in Medford and again in Yreka, but was drowsing peacefully when all hell broke loose. A cacophonous shriek of grinding and clashing steel pierced the night air as Scott was thrown askew, he and his seat partner entwined as they bounced off both ceiling and floor before the car came to a stop right side up but crossways to the track.

"What...?" the cowboy muttered in confusion, Scott answering more coherently, "I guess the train is wrecked, fellow. Are you hurt?"

"No, I don't think so."

"Well, you're bleeding from a cut or two – so am I. But everything in my body seems to be in working order. Let's see if our fellow passengers need help," Scott suggested.

His companion nodded readily, accepting Scott's lead as they escorted a dazed but stumbling lady out the rear door onto the dark tracks. Her mumbled objection quickly registered as she called for her children. The two rescuers carried four crying young children to the distraught mother, finding one boy did not belong to her. A man and woman struggled down from the twisted platform to claim the lad, and the three men reentered the car to assist other passengers.

Scott silently noted two men with lanterns approaching the wreck from a small building beside a siding, reckoning that it was likely that their car had hit its open switch. *But how did the rest of the train avoid destruction?*

Deferring such thoughts, he and his sidekick reentered the wreckage to continue their rescue effort. A middle-aged gentleman wearing a suit met them in the aisle with a plea, "My wife's trapped under our seat. Can you help me pull her out?"

Scott nodded in the dim light, quickly assuring the man, "Of course, mister. Pard, do you have a match?"

The resulting flare of sulfur showed a well-dressed lady struggling vainly to extricate herself from the twisted frame of a passenger seat. The three men grasped the steel support and heaved upward, the spunky woman squirming free with nary a word of complaint. His cowboy ally escorted the couple onto the right-of-way while Scott ascertained the coach was now empty.

In dismounting from the tilted platform, Scott observed their train was backing up to the two signal lamps. After the conductor called for the passengers to board the undamaged cars, he talked to people, stopping before Scott and the cowboy,

"Thanks, gents. I understand you've been very helpful. Would you be willing to stay and work with Fred here?"

"Be glad to help. I'm Scott McClure."

"Me too, mister. I'm Ralph Taylor."

The conductor put his hand on the shoulder of the lantern carrier and ordered, "Fred, these men are staying to work. Tell the freight train conductor to pay them ten dollars each and carry them south."

The foreman handed Scott block and tackle and Ralph two coils of heavy rope, explaining his plan, "See if you can pull that wrecked car off the tracks while my partner heads up the tracks to signal the southbound freight. I'll get a sledge and crowbar to knock that useless steel track out of the way. There's a spare track at the shed."

The two partners located a solid stump to moor Scott's block and tackle, Ralph running a spliced rope to the undercarriage. With surprising ease the heavy coach rolled free of the tracks and landed on its side in the ditch. Ralph set about freeing their rope and gear while Scott checked the wreckage's clearance from the tracks.

Satisfied with their job, Scott headed for the lantern and sledge sounds, helping Fred clear the mangled steel from the railbed. The three men drug the replacement segment from the siding shed, standing aside to let the railroad worker set spikes into place. By the time the freight train chugged slowly to stop a rail length away, the foreman announced the job was complete.

A familiar face appeared before the locomotive's headlamps, mutual recognition by Scott and his conductor friend evident in their affable grins. A warm handshake supplanted any conversation or railroad business being conducted.

Seated in the caboose as the train headed southeast beneath the dawning skies, the three men shared the conductor's lunch as he relayed the foreman's words, "Scott, you and your friend were a big help up at Shasta, earning this railroad's thanks and wages which I can vouch for in Sacramento. Are you both all right?"

"I'm fine, and this meal is ample pay. You know, I heard the engineer say he was headed for Reno. Can I stay aboard as far as Auburn?" Scott replied.

Grinning conspiratorially, the conductor jibed, "Wasn't there a girl in Auburn? Is this trip business or personal?"

"Purely social and yes to the girl! Her father is the rancher I delivered those horses to him back when."

Ralph's interest was sparked, and he inserted, "Can your friend use a hand?" and at Scott's nod, he told the conductor, "I'm fine, too, I'd like to tag along with Scott to Auburn."

* * * * *

And so it was that the two sidekicks dropped off the slowly moving freight in the Auburn yards, their farewell waves lost in the midnight darkness. Eschewing rest and livery horses, the 'pardners' set out on foot for the Simms ranch. Thoroughly weary and questioning the sagacity of their night-long walk, they passed through the outer gate as first light brought the ranch alive.

Catching a glimpse of Art, Lester, and their two hands entering the kitchen door for breakfast, Scott made a beeline across the yard in their direction, walking through the open door on their heels, and exclaiming, "Got a meal for a couple of grubline riders, er, walkers?"

Surprise produced a hubbub of greetings, backslapping in a western welcome, and capped by the cook's squeal of delight as Lou launched herself into Scott's arms, her warm embrace punctuated by a woman's kiss. Her men's dress of Levi's, plaid shirt, and moccasins did not deter her thoroughly feminine appearance.

Scott ignored the men's teasing looks and remarks and told her so, "You're beautiful, Louise Simms. Do I rate another kiss?" and promptly repeated their greeting.

Disentangling their hugging arms, Scott nonetheless held Lou cradled in one arm as he introduced his companion as the new Simms hand, "Meet Ralph Taylor, an addition to your crew. I figure since Lester is getting married, and Art and I are too busy to work, the ranch could use another hand."

Lester was perplexed momentarily by Scott's words, "What are you and Dad going to be doing...oh...well, all right." He grinned lop-sidedly, a leer almost, at his sister and asked, "And I suppose you're 'too busy' as well?"

Laughing gaily, Lou merely replied, "If Scott says I am, yes."

* * * * *

Ralph trailed Les and the hands to the bunkhouse, satchel in hand as he sought his bunk. Scott chatted with Art at the comfortable table, leaning back in his chair until he heard women's voices coming from the bedroom wing. He was across the kitchen by the time his mother rushed into his arms. Kissing her forehead and looking into her smiling eyes, he chided, "Well, Mom, loafing suits you just fine. You look wonderful."

Art joined the crew in the yard, and Lou dropped out of sight in the house while mother and son caught up on family news and his "adoption" of Irving Connor. He served her Lou's leftover breakfast while talking, working the conversation around to their host.

Julie smiled wistfully as she reported, "Arthur started to talk marriage, but I told him to wait until you returned for the wedding. You're the man of our family. What about you and Louise?"

Scott chuckled in response, ignoring his mother's query artfully, "I'll have a heart-to-heart talk with your beau after the wedding. In the meantime I'd better earn my keep. Les wants to finish his road project before that horseless carriage arrives in Auburn."

Lou appeared in the doorway with work gloves in hand, volunteering, "I'll help you and my brother. Julie said she'd clean up the kitchen."

Julie nodded agreeably, smiling as the two youngsters playfully set off to work, fully aware that Louise had been within earshot of their conversation. She thought

I hope my son has the good sense to grab that lovely girl. No, woman is what she's become. I worried about my favorite child when he wooed every girl in the country, and after meeting Maria Chavez, I worried when he ignored girls entirely. Next time I'll not let him brush my question aside as she watched the "road crew" ride out the gate.

* * * * *

The Simms-Brinkley wedding in Auburn was a pretentious affair in Scott's mind, his opinion unvoiced as he escaped Sylvia's milieu of family and friends. Slipping out the garden door when no one was looking, he wandered out to the front gate for a little peace and quiet. Hearing other footsteps cross the tiled patio, he turned to find Art close behind.

"I need a moment away from those yakking women. Mind if I join you?" Art asked tentatively.

Scott opened the gate, waving his friend through as he replied, "Let's take a walk."

Both men started to speak as they strolled up the street in the afternoon sunlight, neither managing to utter more than a "harrumph" until Scott blurted out, "I've been meaning to talk to you since I returned, Art."

Equally blunt now that the ice was broken, the older man asserted, "Yes, I know. Julie told me she'd talked to you. I love your mother, Scott, and want to marry her, but she won't discuss it with me without your approval."

"Oh...of course I approve, Art. She loves you I know. Ha! Ha! But that wasn't what I wanted to talk to you about. I'm here to ask for your daughter's hand in marriage. Lou's my best friend and I love her, but does she love me or is her interest a childhood infatuation?" Scott responded.

"Whew! Here we are both nervous and talking about two different women. I'll make you a deal, son. We'll both propose and see what they say."

Grinning unabashedly, both men nodded in unison and did an about face, Art adding jovially, "Want to try for a double wedding?"

Julie was standing anxiously at the street gate of the Brinkley home, and Scott managed a knowing wink and nod as he hurried past her.

Reentering the house through his exit door, he caught Lou's waiting gaze and nodded. Her smile brightened in understanding as Sylvia drug her away by the arm. He followed them into the large kitchen – dining area where all the women seemed to have gathered in a noisy hubbub. Unable to catch her eye again, he shouldered his way between women politely but firmly, reaching between two bridesmaids to seize her fingers in a tight clasp.

Drawing her aside, he winced as one of the girls squealed in his ear. He whispered, "I love you," just as another girl stepped between them, Lou obviously unable to hear him. A frown crossed his face as his frustration grew. Here he was struggling to propose, and his sweetheart was swamped by the din of girl talk.

Lou solved the problem by shouting, "What did you say, Scott?"

He raised his voice, nervously blurting out, "I love you! Will you marry me?" amidst the sudden quiet engendered by Sylvia's signal. He was stunned by everyone's sudden attention, his face flushing and flustered by their burst of laughter, good-natured but embarrassing nevertheless. Lou was wide-eyed by his declaration, but seeing his red face and confusion, she could not hold back her gay laughter. However she compensated for his discomfort immediately, nestling in his arms as she spat out a string of yeses between guffaws.

Across the room Art called out, "Well, is it a double wedding or not, Daughter?" When she kissed Scott thoroughly, he added, "It'll be hard waiting for Les and Sylvia to come home from their honeymoon."

* * * * *

Driving the team and ranch wagon along Lester's refurbished road, Art announced that his son would be a full partner when the newlyweds returned from their honeymoon in San Francisco. He was obviously pleased by Lou's reaction when she approved, "Oh Daddy, he'll be so pleased and proud! This land means everything to him."

"What about you, Louise? The same thing can be said for you," her father asked deferentially.

"Daddy, don't worry about me. I've been learning everything I could about the Myrtlewood Grove since the day Scott came into my life years ago. You understand, don't you, Julie? I'll be an Oregonian next month and share my husband's dreams."

Julie chuckled and agreed, "I guess we'll trade homes, Louise. I'll miss Grandpa and family and friends, but we can visit now and again."

"You'll have to leave Les in charge and come see us in the fall because I'm going to be busy helping Scott run our ranch. Oh, I hope Grandpa will like me, that's my only worry," Lou ended uneasily.

Julie assured the impulsive bride-to-be, "Scott takes after his grandfather and vice versa. When my son marries you, Grandpa will adopt you as a McClure. I'm sure you'll be able to twist both Scotts around your pinkie with just a lovely smile, dear."

Art teased, "Like you've done to me ever since your mother died. I'm going to miss you more than I can tell you, Daughter. We'll be sure to come and see you after roundup, right Julie?"

Julie nodded as she joined the girl in a freshet of tears, Art and Scott shrugging their shoulders at such an emotional display even as their eyes moistened.

Art pulled gently on the reins, calling out to his team in a gentle voice, "Whoa! Easy does it!" resting his foot high on the wooden brake handle.

Lou sat up with interest, tears forgotten as she pointed to the east pasture, "Why is the high mountain herd down here so early, Daddy? There's still a lot of feed in the upper meadows."

Art smiled secretively relishing his bit of news until Julie admonished him, "Quit teasing our children, Arthur. Tell them what Louise's dowry is."

"Dowry?" Scott quipped in jest, "You mean Lou is more than a pretty face."

Giving her fiancé an elbow in his ribs, Lou disclaimed any needs, "Aside from my personal riding horses, we don't need anything but each other."

Art laughed in approval, but contradicted her intent, "Julie and I insist on helping. We will pay off your sisters, Scott, so that your ranch will be free and clear of debt. Louise, you are to cull that herd as you see fit. Take what you want, and I'll throw in Butch, your favorite bull. If I'm giving Les half the ranch, I can sure as hell afford to help you two. And don't say no to your father!"

"Yes sir," Lou agreed eagerly, standing up to kiss her generous parent.

"We can have the cattle shipped from San Francisco whenever you're settled in Oregon," Art concluded.

"Oh, no! We're taking the stock with us to Reedsport and driving them down the coast. I'm perfectly capable of siding my husband," Lou averred positively, Scott's frown eliciting a persuasive smile and further comment, "Wouldn't you love to honeymoon with me on the trail, dear?"

* * * * *

Before Lester and Sylvia returned from their Golden Gate honeymoon, Art and his carpenter-cowboy remodeled the office and storeroom off the north corner of the house's great room into a spacious bedroom. The paint had barely dried when Art and Julie's furniture and personal belongings were moved in. The master bedroom was filled in turn by Brinkley family heirlooms and the youngsters' personal things.

During the same week, Lou and Scott culled the herd for twenty young cows, breeding and/or milking stock, plus ten steers to sell during the winter. Ralph drove the remainder of the herd back into the Alpine meadows above the ranch house. Butch, the bull, was in the small corral, and Lou's two California-bred cowhorses, a calm old gelding and a lively young mare, were kept in their stalls after the workout.

Scott rode a spirited brown stallion cross-bred between a Simms stud and a Gerbrunn mare. Their relationship seemed a love-hate partnership, the horse following his master around the yard for a well-deserved carrot or behaving fractious enough to earn a few McClure curses.

As they waited on the veranda for Art and Julie to drive the Simms couple home in their new gasoline-engine Ford horseless carriage, Scott explained his thinking, "Cicero is a stud with good blood lines for your Quicio and my Daquiri. He's a good cow horse so I'll take him on our Oregon cattle drive, but if he acts up around children, we may have to sell him."

"Look, dear, here comes the automobile. It doesn't move very fast, does it?" Lou opined.

"Faster than the team and wagon, I reckon. Let's meet them in the yard and hear all about their honeymoon."

As it turned out Sylvia was the talker, Les smiling admiringly as she rattled on. Even when she heard about the partnership and saw "their" master bedroom, she didn't seem to slow down, Lou whispering to Scott that she was nervous.

Smothering a chuckle at such an assertion, he teased the bride openly, "Sylvia, tell me about how Lester liked Fisherman's Wharf and Chinatown."

"Oh, Scott, you're probably poking fun at my gossiping, my husband can tell you himself," Sylvia rejoined good-naturedly, raising Scott's admiration for his beautiful sister-in-law-to-be several notches. He even complimented her the next evening for her prodigious efforts in preparing the house for a double wedding.

* * * * *

Guests arrived throughout the midday, a padre from the local mission performing the ceremonies on the veranda. Scott was dazed by the bright sunlight as well as the momentous occasion, but recovered his poise when he kissed his bride. She returned his buss with considerable ardor, much to the delight of their family and friends.

His mother was a lovely bride as well, looking radiant and youthful on the arm of her new husband.

Conspirators all, Art and Julie slipped away immediately after cutting their cake, hurrying to catch the afternoon train to San Francisco. Scott and Lou were attraction enough to entertain guests until shadows covered the Simms foothills. Retiring to their parents' remodeled bedroom, they endured a pair of shivarees, first from the departing guests at dusk and then an hour later from Les and the crew.

So began their marriage and wedding night in Louise McClure's former home. Tomorrow they would begin their long journey home to the Myrtlewood Grove.

Chapter
Nineteen

A whispered voice repeated his name through the heavy green drape, Scott answering in kind with a "Thanks!" He pulled on his pants, and with the rest of his clothes in hand, slid out of his Pullman berth to stand beside his conductor friend.

"Good morning! That last stop was Roseburg, and first light is showing over the Cascades. I figured your wife could sleep for a bit while you feed your stock – no rustlers in the Siskiyous this trip. We'll be in Drain for breakfast."

"Thanks again, I can find my way to the stock car now that I'm awake," Scott replied as he staggered down the aisle, matching the rolling gait of the speeding train. He passed through the dining car, two-day coaches, and a general freight car before reaching his destination.

Entering the stock car he began talking in low tones to his animals, raiding his cache of carrots to treat the three horses in the nearest stall. He threw one carrot to Butch who disdained to notice the treat in his fit of snorting and stamping. Scott divided his remaining oats between the four beasts before throwing a few handfuls of hay in the stalls.

Still crooning his greeting of nonsense, he scattered a half-dozen hay bales around the four corners of the car for the rest of his charges, inspecting his herd while carefully avoiding their mindless quest for food and water. All seemed well, so he dumped water into their troughs and left them to find a restroom. He'd clean up and take his bride to breakfast.

The sun was high in the sky amidst a scattering of fleecy white clouds when the McClures watched the northbound disappear up the tracks. Their car was parked on a siding waiting for the train from Reedsport. Scott carried his last carrot over to Cicero, shoving it between the slots to the restive stallion. Lou strolled around the car to check the locks and look over the town. Hearing the sound of voices, Scott followed in her footsteps, all but bumping into his nemesis Hanks.

Startled to meet him so abruptly, he was slow to return Hanks' smile and nod. Laughing at his own reaction as he gestured toward Lou, he remarked, "I see you've met my wife Louise. Dear, this Drain logger is Mr. Hanks."

Hanks doffed his cap and politely said, "Howdy, ma'am," before turning to Scott and offering, "I'll watch your cows if you and your lady want to stretch your legs."

"Oh, can we, Scott? We could buy some oats for the horses and fruit for ourselves. Mr. Hanks says the train isn't due for an hour or two," Lou implored.

"Sure, can I bring you a beer, Hanks? We'll be right back," Scott said as his wife took his elbow and urged him to follow her.

"Sure, but no hurry, McClure," the logger said with a suddenly gleeful expression, which didn't dawn on the happy groom until they were in the street. Hanks' volunteering was out of character entirely, and Scott remembered the flash of the bully's hateful eyes. When a crack sounded from the siding area, Scott cursed angrily and raced back to the tracks in time to see the yahoo slide the car door open a notch. A single steer squeezed through the opening, brushing Hanks aside as it tumbled askew onto the railroad.

"Hanks, get out of there!" Scott howled in frustration, pulling his Derringer from his pocket and firing into the air. The culprit scrambled to his feet and ran into the forest, laughing insanely in his escape. Scott saw the steer's foreleg was shattered as the bleating beast flailed it in the air. His second bullet was fired into the animal's head before Scott climbed over the carcass, waving his arms to drive an old bossy away from the gap. He managed to slide the door closed and then tied the hasp closed with a short length of rope Lou produced.

"So much for the saying, 'forgive and forget'. That Hanks is as crazy as a loon," Scott gasped out between gulps of fresh air.

The marshal ran up to the car, agreeing, "He's a vicious brute and due for a bit of time in jail – if I ever catch him. I'm glad you didn't shoot him, Mr. McClure. My jail is a terrible place to spend your nights."

Lou asked meekly, "What do we do with this carcass?"

The law officer replied in humorous tones, "Sell it! Look at our butcher friend hurrying over here to buy some cheap beef. If we ignore him, ma'am, the price will go up."

Scott took the hint and changed the conversation, agreeing with his earlier remark, "Yes sir! Let's stay out of your jail, I'm on my honeymoon. Marshal, meet my wife Louise. We're bringing her stock in from Auburn, California. I guess Hanks isn't worth a bullet if Bernie Heisel will buy this beef."

The butcher quickly said hello and offered to buy the beef as is, haggling for several minutes until Louise took his money. The man's brother-in-law appeared with a team and tackle to drag the carcass clear of the tracks, just as the whistle of the eastbound's locomotive sounded through the hills. Lou was already inside the car gentling her stock as her dead steer was taken away.

* * * * *

Scott and Lou swung onto the station platform as the train rolled to an abrupt stop. A railroad crew was already moving a ramp up to their stock car, Grandpa's coaxing voice instructing the men in their everyday job.

The newlyweds hastened to join the old-timer in making sure the ramp was positioned correctly, Scott calling out, "You tell 'em, Grandpa. What's all this special service going to cost me?"

"I promised the saloonkeeper a steer for my weekend stay, and these fellows a round of beer when the herd is unloaded," Grandpa explained laconically, eyeing Lou all the while.

She blushed at his attention but smiled as she greeted him, "Hello, Grandpa Scott," and then impetuously strode over and hugged him.

As she took a step backward, he continued his study of the young bride, nodding with a welcoming grin on his lips, "Bless you, girl, but you do remind me of my Missy when I was courting her years ago. I hope you like our ranch as much as she did."

"Oh I do already, Grandpa. I've been studying it from afar since I first met Scott."

The patriarch nodded gleefully, directing his approval at his grandson, "By golly! You've married a real woman, Scott. Just like your Grandma, too good for a pair of roughnecks like ourselves, but mighty welcome in my mind. Boy, you take Daquiri here while my new granddaughter and I saddle up a couple of mounts. You got an extra horse to haul our supplies?"

* * * * *

Scott rode point as their small herd headed south out of Reedsport. He was leading the gelding, a crate of chickens on one side of the packsaddle and a case of brandy on the other. Mixed between Grandpa's "deal" with the bartender were two gunnysacks of trail vittles for the drovers and their horses – beans and oats.

Lou brought up the drag, her close leash on the temperamental Butch demonstrating her skill in handling the bull. Grandpa caught up with her at Winchester Bay, chatting amiably before spurring Cicero to the point.

With a touch of pride as well as approval, he remarked, "Your wife's quite a cowhand. I doubt she even needs our help on this drive, but I'm glad she enjoys our gentlemanly company. Ha! Ha! You showed mighty good sense in marrying that gal, Scott. Did Julie do as well in picking her daddy?"

"Yes, Grandpa, Momma's very happy. But you'll see for yourself when they visit us this fall. Art's a great guy and my good friend, and my brother-in-law Lester is just like his dad. In fact we're one big happy family now."

Grandpa nodded at the expected reply, suggesting with a gleeful leer, "Well go on back and keep your wife company. I plan to camp near the dunes this evening. And take that pack horse along, this stallion's fractious enough without another horse around."

* * * * *

Busy choosing a stubborn steer out of the sand dunes, Scott didn't see the lake ahead until Lou called out, "Grandpa is signaling a stop. Is that water fresh up ahead?"

"Yes dear, that's Ten Mile Lake, although I'd say we've come about fifteen miles or so. These critters are weary – me, too. You'd better join Grandpa, Butch will demand the best piece of grass and water in camp. And, of course, the cows will stay near him."

By the time Scott reached the campfire to hand Lou the packhorse's lead rope, dusk was settling along the coast. He rode Doc around the herd one more time, talking all the time to soothe the cattle. Counting heads as he moved about, he arrived at the right number of twenty-nine.

Doc's ears twitched, and Scott being alert to his mount's nuances, scanned the backtrail and nearby forest until he spotted the object of the horse's attention. A farmer riding an ancient nag was headed toward camp along a faint path on the south lakeshore.

Grandpa sat on a cedar stump in the deepening shadows with the Sharps cradled in his left arm while Scott rubbed his horse down. Taking a steaming cup of coffee from his wife, he turned to answer the rider's hallooing call as he approached their camp, "Come ahead and have a cup of coffee, stranger."

A lanky, not-so-young man slid off the bareback of his weary dun mare, his frame covered by nondescript bib overalls and a homemade cotton shirt sewed from a flour sack. A dark stocking cap crowned a heavy head of scraggly brown hair, no doubt streaked with gray like his matching beard. Powerful and bony hands accepted Lou's cup of coffee as he belatedly doffed his cap. The stranger's homely appearance was in contrast to curiosity-filled eyes and a melodic voice as he uttered, "Thank you, missee. My wife ran out of coffee last week, so this drink is a real treat."

Shifting his glance to Scott, he introduced himself, "Good evening, mister. I'm Zeke Russo, and this here land is mine. My house is just back there a ways."

"Mr. Russo, I'm Scott McClure from the Sixes valley. This lady's my wife Louise, and the old-timer on the stump is my grandpa, Scott McClure. No offense intended, but I thought this area was state land. I've camped here before," Scott replied with a mildly perplexed frown on his face.

"Used to be, until I bought it along with the old homestead back there. Actually that stump your grandpa is occupying is my boundary marker. You're only half on my land and welcome to stay for the night. I came over to ask a boon of your family. My wife's milker died last week, and I hoped you'd sell me a milk cow from your herd. Sarah's a mighty happy cook when there's milk in the cooler."

"Of course, Mr. Russo," Lou answered spontaneously for the McClures, offering generously, "And I'll take your wife a couple of chickens as well. Can you meet us in the morning as we pass your place?"

The farmer rode away on his broken-down old nag as happy as a lark, the two Scotts exchanging perplexed looks which expressed a concern for Lou's business acumen. Then they nodded in silent agreement that Louise McClure had a mind of her own, and this deal was hers to handle. At least they'd be friendly neighbors to the Ten Mile Lake farmers.

* * * * *

The herd ambled past the familiar saloon south of Coos Bay in mid-afternoon, Grandpa falling out of the formation, Cicero dutifully pushing a steer toward the grinning proprietor. Scott waved Lou to ride drag and spurred Daquiri south with the packhorse in tow, cows docilely plodding behind them. He figured on camping in a Coquille River meadow north of Bandon where the old-timer could join them after his toast with the gang back there. Tomorrow it was his turn to sell a steer at the butcher shop in town.

For two days the herd moved steadily south, all three drovers enjoying the travail ensuing, but for different reasons. Lou was exploring new territory and married life, and Scott was discovering how bright and cheerful his new wife could be under diverse circumstances. For Grandpa the time was reminiscent of the old days when he and his Melissa had challenged the frontier of Oregon Territory. He was pleased that Lou was a lovely and wholesome partner in the McClure family and just the kind of wife that his grandson needed on the Myrtlewood Grove.

The afternoon sun was shining warmly on the Sixes River valley as Scott and Lou coaxed the cows forward, a solitary rider breaking out of the forest near the gap before Slide Ridge. Irving's whoopee could be heard across the distance as Old

Salem reflected the boy's enthusiasm with a seemingly youthful gait up the trail.

The lad was happy to greet Scott, his big grin vanishing as he remembered Grandpa's lesson in manners, doffing his hat before shaking Lou's extended hand. His look was awed and apprehensive under the new Mrs. McClure's gaze, perhaps her good looks and position of authority hard for him to handle at one moment.

In turn, Lou's expression was noncommittal, her smile a bit friendly but a shade challenging. Just because she was taking Irving on her husband's say-so, didn't mean she couldn't make a studied judgment of her own.

Scott shrugged at the hint of coolness and ordered Irv, "Go say hello to Grandpa. The two of you can drive the herd up the Sixes trail while I show Lou the Myrtlewood Grove."

* * * * *

Scott was loquacious in describing landmarks along the Sixes River to his wife, telling stories of the valley as well. Passing Slide Ridge he related a story his father had often told of his own boyhood and his hideout on the ridge's skyline. He and his brother had kept watch so Indians and bad men couldn't sneak up on the McClure ranch, irritating his mother by missing dinner all too often.

Clattering across the Cascade Creek bridge, he described how Grandpa had built it years ago, and before they crossed the knoll he pointed south to the twisted ravine where the Great Fire of 1868 had trapped Buzz and Uncle George. Their dog Cougar had led Grandpa to the dying old-timer and the injured boy he had saved.

He recounted the history of the ranch as they rode down the knoll and across the yard, dating its development structure by structure, tree by tree until Louise commented, "I see why it's called the Myrtlewood Grove, those trees are lovely."

Sensing Lou's lack of enthusiasm and her sober expression, Scott smiled dryly and commented, "Not quite the Simms Ranch, is it, dear? I guess I sort of take our frontier image for granted, but maybe it'll take a little getting used to."

She answered his grin with a sigh, and said, "I see why Grandpa Scott has put his soul into this spot. I'm glad we came ahead, I wouldn't want him to see my disappointment, er, I mean it's all new to me. Am I being a spoiled brat, Scott?"

"No, sweetheart, but I hope you come to love our home as I do. Do you want to ride around our land?"

"In a little while. Can I look in the house now?"

Scott nodded, and grinning to cheer his recent bride, he dismounted and walked to her stirrups offering, "Come on, Louise, slide into my arms and I'll carry you over the threshold of your new home before I take care of the animals." He was sensitive enough to realize his wife needed to be alone for awhile and quickly went about the business of tending the livestock.

* * * * *

By the time Butch and the gelding were munching oats and the new chickens were exploring the McClure coop and its old inhabitants, Grandpa and Irving were driving the herd into the east pasture. The dinner triangle soon dangled, and the cook's call could be heard over the ranch, "Come and get it!"

Lou's normal smiling self greeted them at the kitchen table. She'd managed to fire up the kitchen range and prepare coffee, pan-fried biscuits, and a pot of potato soup. Scott was proud of his wife, no hang-dog expression on her face nor "it's your house" tone in her voice as she chatted with the men.

He told her so during their ride over to visit the Sixes family. Sandy had asked to buy a cow, and Irving was well ahead of the couple, leading a good milker to their neighbors. Pointing to his energetic young friend, Scott surmised, "I bet Irv is talking to young Sandra when we reach the Sixes place."

Smiling his approval he added, "They're two nice youngsters, but maybe a little young for romance."

Lou laughed aloud, "No, my husband, they are just the right age for romance. Now comes the need for responsibility and a little good judgment. I think Irving has the right heroes to learn from – you and Grandpa. You know he looks up to both of you."

"I'm glad to hear your gay laugh again. I was afraid your new home was too much of a shock for you. However, you're flexible as well as efficient and adjusting well. But you're welcome to change things that don't suit you."

"Well, I think we'd better reduce the herd or get more winter feed. Maybe we could make the pasture larger by cutting those trees along the north side, "Lou contemplated thoughtfully, her manner serious until Scott caught a teasing light in her eye.

He grinned as he acceded, "All right, I give up. You tell me when you're ready to talk about our log cabin house."

"Ha! Ha! I have real plans for our home, but I'd better meet everyone before I spout off. Who killed the cougar hanging on our wall?"

* * * * *

The next morning Scott and Lou led two milkers down the Sixes valley to the Hughes place. Grandpa accompanied them over the Sixes crossing before taking his steer into Port Orford. As the couple came into sight of the beautiful house Patrick had built before his unfortunate death, Louise sighed deeply in appreciation of the seeming mansion set in the wilderness. Jane's Irish hospitality included a walk-through of her home, a cup of morning coffee, and a lot of questions for Louise.

Her son Edward soon took Scott aside for a look at his young bull, both ranchers quickly agreeing to an exchange of stud services by their bulls. As the newlyweds waved goodbye, Lou remarked, "My, the Hughes clan is busy, how big is this ranch?"

As they topped the rise near the Cape Blanco Lighthouse, Scott made a sweeping gesture with his right arm toward their rear, answering, "Look back now. Most of the land you can see is part of the ranch. On a clear day you can see smoke from Denmark or Langlois, or make out Port Orford Jakie's lodge over there. He's the 'tyee' of the Sixes 'Qua-to-mahs' and probably will be their last chief. Jack Sixes' family is descended from old Chief Sixes, Grandpa's friend who died long ago, so technically Jakie is their tyee."

"Look, Scott. Is that ship coming into Port Orford? This lighthouse is in a good place."

"Yes, it's a lumber schooner headed for the mill. It'll have no problem reaching the harbor with fair skies, but a lot of ships have gone aground in foul weather. Why, it was less than a year ago that the *South Portland* wrecked on this very cape.

Grandpa can tell you a few tall tales when the only guiding light was in Knapp's Hotel window, and shipwrecks were common events."

Scott paused for a moment before continuing with a nostalgic thought, "The lighthouse is one of my favorite places – Grandpa's, too. We can meditate while we watch for a ship or sometimes just a storm cloud coming toward us. It's very peaceful here."

Lou nodded, following her husband as he rode along the ridge, finally asking, "What's next? Is that the Elk River over there?"

"Yes, Mom's family owned a ranch upriver from the crossing. The Elk valley is a bit larger than the Sixes, but we have about the same number of people in each area. Come on, I'll race you to Port Orford."

* * * * *

Cantering through the outskirts of town, the two riders reined their horses to a gentle walk, a few moments passing before Lou whispered, "Everyone is looking at us, Husband."

"So I see. You're the main attraction, Lou – a newcomer to Port Orford. Are you ready to meet these people?"

Without waiting for an answer, Scott stopped before the post office and dismounted, his wife following suit as young Louis Knapp stepped forward to hold their reins. His shy hello earned him the first introduction to Mrs. McClure. Not to be outdone, his eight-year old brother Orris piped up, "Hello, Mrs. McClure, I'm Orris and my birthday is next week."

A smaller Lloyd only nodded as Scott introduced the third Knapp boy, continuing with their father and several local residents. Louie waited patiently with his sons until the small crowd dispersed and then invited the newlyweds to the hotel, "Ella will want to meet you, Mrs. McClure. She's staying close to home these days," and at Scott's raised eyebrow Louie added, "Ella's in a family way. We're hoping for a girl this time. Please come by for a visit after you've seen Anne and John."

Thanking the Knapps, Scott led the horses across the way toward Johnny's store, Lou commenting, "I'll never remember all those people. Didn't I meet a Tichenor?"

"Yes, dear, a member of the first family of Port Orford – a grandson of the Captain. And the Lindbergs are pioneers as well, P. J. built most the buildings in the area. Mrs. Marsh lives on the Elk River not too far from the Madsen place. Young James Crew comes from another old family of the town – good folks. The Curtis couple are newcomers. Who else did you meet?"

From the storefront Johnny's young clerk called out, "Your grandpa and the boss went home for dinner. You folks are supposed to join them."

Scott and Lou crossed town on foot, wending their way along back alleys and empty lots as he pointed out landmarks in town. Lou finally interrupted to ask, "I can see the Knapp Hotel and Battle Rock, but where's old Fort Orford?"

"It's been gone for some time. The grade school over there sits on the old parade grounds. By the way, Irving and Sandra will be going to classes there next week. I hear that one teacher will have about a dozen older children in her room. Anyway, here's the Larson's barn," Scott announced as Grandpa appeared at its open door.

"You two go visit while I put up the horses," he ordered as he grasped the reins in his hand.

Scott nodded while setting off across the yard, opening the kitchen door with a flourish to usher Lou inside. His aunt embraced the younger woman in welcome as Johnny chortled, "See Anne, I told you Scott would come in the back door. Welcome, you newlyweds!"

* * * * *

The weeks passed effortlessly, or so it seemed to Scott, even the autumn rains forestalled by an Indian summer. Lou was spoiled by the good weather, and Scott managed to clear two acres of timber adjacent to his east pasture. He helped an Elk River sawyer drag a dozen big spruce logs from his property to the mill, and even though both men agreed that spruce had little value as lumber, Scott brought home two loads of boards for Lou anyway.

She hired one of Lindberg's carpenters, and he closed in the children's bedrooms, and then the craftsman extended the stoop into a real porch with a roof wide enough to counter the southwest winds. After new curtains were hung in the clean house, Lou tackled Grandpa's cabin, the old-timer docilely accepting her efforts by taking Irving up Cougar Ridge to hunt game.

When Art and Julie rode into the ranch yard in late October, the Myrtlewood Grove looked great even though fall rains pummeled the valley. Their horses were a pair of Simms' best stock and a gift to the newlyweds.

Grandpa took to Art and vice versa, the two men hunting, fishing, and visiting McClure friends from Humbug to Langlois. Scott escorted his mother and his wife to neighbors' homes and into Port Orford, visiting the old Madsen ranch for a nostalgic moment.

They were sipping tea with Ella Knapp when a steamship sounded her horn and soon dropped anchor in the harbor. Louie stepped into the parlor to announce the ship was unloading freight and leaving for San Francisco on the morning tide. Julie turned to Scott and asked, "Will you find Art and tell him to pack our things and come to the hotel. I'm going to book a cabin on that ship. No riding to Reedsport in this weather!"

Louie volunteered, "Allow me to talk to the captain, Julie, I'm sure I can arrange passage."

Scott stood momentarily in mild shock, his mother laughing at his expression, "A week is a long visit, Son. Besides Lou has agreed to come to Auburn for a visit next summer."

"Yes, Momma, but I was just getting used to having you around again. It's been fun for all of us. Grandpa's going to miss your company, too."

"Well, try to talk him into coming along. Art would love to take him through the old gold fields in the Sierras. Maybe all of us could spend this evening together in the hotel. Do you have room for us, Ella?"

Chapter Twenty

Winter arrived with a vengeance during Christmas week, the Sixes flooding with the rains, and then a spatter of wet snow fell on the Myrtlewood Grove. With the inclement weather at hand, Lou's party plans were dashed since crossing the coastal rivers was a prohibitive danger. On Christmas morning she sent Irving to the Sixes Ranch to help Sandy's family over to the McClures for dinner. At least her roast chicken wouldn't be wasted.

When Scott came inside to wash up, Lou fretted, "I wonder if something is wrong with the Sixes. Irv's been gone over three hours."

"I'll wash up there and lend a hand. I hope Sandy's well enough to ride down here," Scott muttered as he redressed for the wintry weather. He went back to the barn and saddled Daquiri again, the horse not enthusiastic about going back outside.

Scott was nearing the Sixes house and blinking snowflakes from his eyes when he spotted Irving's gelding by the riverbank. Spurring Doc across the yard to the river, he watched in horror as the beast fought for footing on the collapsing bank, only to be pulled backward by a taut rope attached to its saddle.

Searching the length of the rope to its far end, he espied Irving swimming toward a deadfall hung up in mid-channel, Sandra and Jack clinging to its gnarled roots and a bundle of cloth in the water. The gelding lost its tenuous footing in the muddy soil and slid exonerably into the swollen river, finding a bit of purchase on its graveled bottom.

Scott had removed his rope from the cantle and spun a noose overhead experimentally, wishing his talented wife could make this cast. She had taught him well on the Simms Ranch, but he was still an amateur. However, his lariat settled over the gelding's head and tightened nicely just before the horse tumbled into the current. Ordering Doc to hold steady was a superfluous command, as his mare knew well enough not to move as Scott slid along the taut rope. He could see the gelding's neck was broken as the carcass twisted and turned in the swirling waters.

Irv had reached Sandra and Jack with his rope, the three lashed themselves together as they pulled Mary Anne's lifeless body onto the deadfall. Scott ran down the bank, waving to the three castaways until Jack saw him and waved back. Stopping below the now-shifting old mass of roots, he signaled Irv to get off the mammoth old tree trunk and drift free toward him on the bank. He was worried the rope might break.

The young man waved, spoke to his companions, and led a synchronized leap into the river, the dead girl's body in his arms as they separated from the deadfall. The rushing waters carried them away with great force, yet it seemed to Scott their approach was very slow.

He grabbed a hefty spruce limb and leaned over the swirling currents to grasp Mary Anne's dress in his fingers, pulling her body onto the grassy rim atop the bank. Next he took Sandra's extended hand and lifted her and Jack onto solid ground, the rope now hindering his efforts. A shot resounded upriver, a moment passing before Scott realized its significance. The rope beyond Irv sagged loose, the gelding tumbling in the river waters as he passed them.

Scott drew his knife and sliced the still taut rope between Sandra and Jack, his blade in place against the rope between Irving and the bay as it snapped taut. Scott sliced the rope cleanly while Sandra grabbed her brother's hand, Irving disappearing from sight beneath the roiling surface.

Sandra emitted a single sob as Scott laid a comforting hand on her shoulder, everyone breathing a sigh of relief when Irv popped up just a few feet from shore. By the time the trio reached him, he was sitting on a grassy knoll clutching an alder bole and spewing muddy water from his mouth. Scott slapped his back sharply to expel any remaining water and shouted, "Let's go to the house and dry out. We're apt to catch pneumonia if we aren't careful. Good work, Irving!"

The commendation brought a tired grin to the lad's lips, but Sandra's vibrant kiss brought full life back into the sixteen-year old young man.

Scott cradled Mary Anne's inert form in his arms, and Irv led Doc up to the house, a very sallow and pained Sandy out of bed to meet them with tears of grief and relief. One daughter had died, but three would-be rescuers were alive and well.

Realizing everyone was motionless and at a loss for words for what to do next, Scott took charge, ordering, "Irv, take my horse and ride home for Grandpa and Lou. Sandra, Jack, go to your rooms and put on dry clothes. Sandy, you get back in bed. Sandra can dress her sister in her Sunday dress while Jack and I dig a grave next to Jack's."

Sandra reappeared, pulling a dress over her head as she agreed, "Yes Mother, I'll help you into bed. Jack and Scott will take care of the grave."

Jack came out of his room buttoning his rain jacket and then tugging a hat on his head. He led Scott to the barn and a pair of shovels, announcing in his firmest about-to-be-a-man voice, "We'll find some canvas and make a coffin later. Let's dig Sis' grave first."

* * * * *

Christmas 1904 was a sad day, but one that none of them would ever forget. The simple and crippled girl who has wandered too close to the flooding river was buried in an equally simple grave beside her beloved father, dressed in her Sunday best, wrapped in a tarpaulin, and buried in a hastily built spruce coffin. A prayer was said for her at graveside by her mother, and later another by his sister as the two families sat at the dining table.

Lou had carried dinner from her stove to Sandy's, and she insisted everyone eat as they remembered Mary Anne. Sandy even smiled approvingly as Irv and Sandra looked moon-eyed at each other, a second smile for her son Jack, suddenly the young man of the family and behaving like it.

As they finished their brief repast and silence reigned over the gathering, Irv decided, "I'd better stay here tonight. I can sleep in Jack's room."

Sandy said in a tired and frail voice, "Scott, would you stay with us tonight?"

The younger Scott almost answered when it dawned on him that Sandy was talking to his grandpa and not him. As the old-timer nodded in agreement, Sandra and Lou helped Sandy to bed. Scott suggested, "Grandpa, I'll try to salvage Irv's saddle, and I'll inform the town marshal of Mary Anne's death. Lou can do the chores. You two come home when you're ready."

* * * * *

I feel like the Grandpa I am, Scott mused silently, *not too different, I suppose, from Buzz in the old days when I was the young Scott McClure. What's depressing is that only a handful of old-timers are left, like Knapp, Hughes, Tichenor, Sixes, and McClure. Sandy qualifies as much as Port Orford Jake, but she's only forty years old.*

Young folks are taking over the county it seems. Why, Scott's commander, Teddy Roosevelt, is president and the Tichenor and Hughes children are running their property just like my Scott. Just as well I reckon, land's getting settled and not much time left for old-timers. I bet..."

"Scott! Scott, we need to talk," Sandy whispered harshly.

The old man crossed the room to enter Sandy's bedroom, settling on the edge of her blanket like a bird on its perch, studying his ailing friend's expression while quietly awaiting her words.

"I'm worried, my old and true friend. My family is gone except for Sandra and little Jack, and I feel the breath of death nearing my bedside. Heh! Heh! No laugh Scott, I remember some words from the shaman of all the Shas-te-koos-tees people. Think words foolish but shaman dead very soon."

"Ah, San-a-chi, you are only depressed because of poor Mary Anne's death. You're not an old woman, and I hope you'll see your children grow up right here," Scott fumbled with consoling words trying to comfort his friend.

Sandy smile tolerantly as she reminisced, "You are the only person to honor my tribal name. Even my children forget Tututni ways. I worry that Sandra and Jack will lose land, too. They are young and don't think like Tututnis, but they are.

Many people hate the Tututnis. No, don't shake your head. It is true. What happens to Sandra and Jack when I die?"
Scott wrestled with words again, finally eschewing any attempt to soften his answer, "I can help, but I'm an old man. Scott will honor my wishes, and Louise will support him, I'm sure. San-a-chi, I respect your Tututni vision of death. When will you die?"
Sandy's eyes flashed of old in the candlelight before clouding in sorrow, "No see apple blossom or bright sun of spring. Protect my children! You see Irving and Sandra eye each other. Is marriage to a white man protection? Am I a foolish old woman to think so?"
"They are very young, San-a-chi, although I agree they are smitten with each other. Perhaps I could serve as their guardian until Irving is of age. I'll ask Johnny," Scott contemplated in a conciliatory tone.
Sandy chuckled, "Sandra is older than when Jack married me – and prettier and smarter, too. Sixes land is for Sandra and Jack. I follow you, Scott, and give it to my children before I die. You see Johnny for white man's paper?"
"Yes, I'll ride into Port Orford tomorrow and talk to Johnny. Now get some rest, old friend. You must save your strength."

* * * * *

So now I'm an official guardian for those children, the elder Scott reflected soberly as he spurred Cicero up the Sixes River road with snow continuing to fall. *That judge in Gold Beach talked right over my head, but Johnny knew what to do in court. Lawyers! Good thing Saul Langlois came up to visit the Sixes family and be a witness. His word as a deputy sheriff made a big impression on the judge. Imagine! Five weeks to satisfy San-a-chi's request. Well, I reckon I'll ride up to her place when the weather lightens up.*
By the time he rode up to the barn, the myrtlewoods and the pastures were covered with snow. *Hmm! Third time we've had snow this month. Kind of unusual*, he concluded as he stepped into the house.
He was relating the court goings-on to Scott and Louise, savoring the warmth of a hot cup of coffee, when a cougar's

unmistakable scream came from the east pasture. All three donned hats and coats before grabbing their rifles and running outdoors.

Another cat screech mingled with a horse's trumpet filled the wintry air, Grandpa calling out to the younger racers in a puffing voice, "Is that Old Salem with the steers?"

Scott replied easily without slowing his pace, "Yes, there they are over by the bend in the river."

Grandpa ordered without hesitation, "Hold it right there. Shoot that damned cat before it sees us."

He ran forward and dropped to one knee beside his grandson, his Sharps firing as soon as it came to bear on the cougar. Scott's rifle sounded a fraction of a second later, the horse going down and the cougar streaking away. When Lou's rifle blast echoed in the wake of the two others, the cat cartwheeled in the air, striking the earth in a brush patch which he was seeking for cover.

"Damn, girl, that was a fine shot. I think I hit Old Salem instead of my prey. Come on, let's make sure that cougar is dead. His hide belongs to Louise," Grandpa rattled on excitedly. His thoughts drifted back to a day over fifty years ago when he and Buzz had chased a cougar in this very spot. He was almost reliving the experience when a chuckle sounded in his throat and he chided himself silently. *Yes, but Lou is a better shot than any of us men.*

Lou proved to be the fleetest afoot as well, her husband calling out a warning, "Be careful, dear! Grandpa will check that cougar for any sign of life. Cats are tough to kill with one shot."

Grandpa soon verified that the beast was dead, but of two gunshot wounds. He declared, "Well, Louise, your husband's bullet creased his chest, but yours hit dead-center in his heart. Scott, how is Old Salem?"

"Dead as well! That cougar ripped her throat open. She was dying when your bullet broke her neck. Golly, I'll miss Old Salem, she's been around since I was a boy. Shall we dress out the carcass?"

Lou paled at the notion but kept her silence as a pragmatic Grandpa replied, "Yup, some folks like horse meat. Louise, why don't you go back to the house and finish supper. Scott and I will butcher the meat – cat tastes good, too."

* * * * *

Grandpa wasn't surprised at the end of the month when Irving asked for Sandra's hand in marriage. After dinner they had worked in the barn together, the lad nervous and uncommunicative, absent-minded it seemed to the old-timer.

As they entered their cabin and removed their coats, Irv blurted out, "I want to marry Sandra, Grandpa. We love each other, and her mother says it's all right as long as you approve. You're the guardian. I know we're young, but we're mature, too, seventeen and sixteen years are of an adult age, don't you think?"

"You youngsters are very responsible people, Irv, even if you are a few months shy of seventeen and sixteen. Yes, San-a-chi and I will give the bride away, and Scott and Lou will be your witnesses. Jane told me that her son, Father John, will visit home next month or send another priest to Mary, Star of the Sea Mission for Catholic mass. You could be married at Cape Blanco in that case, or the padre could come to the Sixes Ranch if Sandra's mother can't ride over there."

Irving breathed a sigh of relief and declared, "I'll have to give Scott my notice. Can I stay here with you in the meantime?"

"Of course, my grandson will pay you for February. We need your help even if most of your time is spent at the Sixes," Grandpa said with tongue in cheek.

Scott knocked on the door, called out, and let himself inside, announcing, "I forgot to tell you that Louie and Ella are proud parents of a fourth son, Marion. Besides, I want you both to ride up to Langlois and buy those oats I heard about. Can you do it tomorrow?"

Grandpa nodded, teasingly vouching for Irving as well, "Yes, if I can tear this lad away from his fiancée for a whole day. We're losing a hired hand, but gaining a new neighbor when the youngsters get married."

"Congratulations, Irv! If the McClures can do anything to help, just let us know. Maybe Sandra would like to come over for supper and visit with my wife. Women-talk, you know," Scott slapped the young man on the shoulder as he left the cabin as quickly as he had arrived.

* * * * *

By mid-February Irv and Sandra had finished school, Jack being the only remaining student riding to Port Orford every weekday. The young lovers were constant company for Grandpa until he took them to Gold Beach to obtain a marriage license. With Sandy bed-ridden and failing in health, it was obvious the wedding would be at the Sixes Ranch.

Father Paul arrived from Portland to hold mass in the chapel at the Hughes home and the next day walked all the way up the valley to meet Irving and Sandra. The young priest immediately questioned the marriage of two "children."

It took womanly advice from Lou, an ailing plea from Sana-chi, and a proper marriage license from the county court before Father Paul agreed, performing the brief ceremony that very day and leaving the valley for Portland soon after.

Two cows had fallen into the river the previous week, and Grandpa led one crippled milker up to their neighbor's ranch when he did their chores. Irving had insisted on nursing the cow back to health after the newlyweds honeymooned at Knapp's Hotel, so he bought the animal with his January and February wages.

Scott had put the other beast out of its misery when his best efforts to keep it on its feet failed. He hauled meat and hide from its carcass to Johnny for sale while escorting the couple to Knapps'. He got a look at baby Marion who looked a mite peaked to him, but then all babies were strange to him.

Riding home he mused over the family's fortunes, *we have cash, credit, and no bills. Plus we have a passel of cows, too many actually. Fifteen cows, six steers and a bull eat an awful lot of hay. Even if I clear a few more acres, buying feed will be an added expense to keeping them. And most of those cows are carrying calves I bet. Hmm! Edward Hughes said he wanted to buy any extra milkers when we traded bulls last month. Grandpa, Lou and I need to sit down and discuss ranch affairs.*

Besides we'll need more horses with the two mares carrying as well, and Irving needs a horse of his own. We certainly do need to talk soon.

The thought was barely out of Scott's mind when he spotted Edward pulling one of his cows out of a muddy slough. He swung Doc off the trail to lend a hand to his neighbor, their friendly conversation afterward confirming Hughes' need for two or three cows.

* * * * *

Wintry storms continuing into March inhibited the advent of spring and the growth of grass in their pasture, the oats gone and hay down to a couple of days' feed. Scott decided his steers would have to forage in the forest along their hillsides, but he soon found it took all of his time and much of Grandpa's to keep six animals on the move.

Irv was sent north to find hay, a Coquille farmer supplying two wagons of hay at an exorbitant price and three days' labor in delivering it to the two ranches. But sunlight did finally shine on the Sixes Valley, and the grass began to grow.

The Knapp baby died in early March, and an old prospector-hermit living up Hubbard Creek was found dead on the trail to his cabin. Just when it seemed San-a-chi the Tututni had survived another winter, she was strong enough to get up and walk around her house, her prophecy came true. She died in her sleep a scant day or two before the apple blossoms answered the sun's call for new life. The Sixes and McClures accepted her vision at last, wondering about the mystique of the Tututni shaman, but figuring the old days were gone with their friend's passing.

* * * * *

Grandpa's cheerless demeanor during the funeral soon abated, his resolute spirit reemerging one evening as he announced, "I'm going to Salem in the morning. There's a ship in the harbor bound for Portland tomorrow, and I plan to sail on her. Irv needs a horse and we could use another since our two mares are in foal. Kinda be nice to see your sisters and their families, and of course, the Gerbrunn boys."

Scott chuckled as he asked, "You need company in finding these sixty-year old 'boys', Grandpa?"

"No Scott, I'm going to Salem on my own for a little business and a lot of pleasure. You know, just one last time before I feel too old for such shenanigans. I'll ride home with my two horses over the old trail about the first of May. You could ride into Port Orford with me in the morning. Aren't you supposed to deliver a steer to Johnny this week?"

"Yes, Grandpa, and Lou can go along, too. She wants to see the doctors about having a baby – we hope toward the end of the summer," Scott announced with a Cheshire cat grin on his face.

"Well, well! Louise, I hope you're right, I'd welcome another McClure in the house. All the more reason for me to kick up my heels now; great-grandchildren make me feel my age."

Chapter
Twenty One

Hoof beats echoed over Cascade Creek as a pair of horses crossed the timbered bridge, Scott striding purposefully to the front yard expecting to greet Grandpa. It was the first week of May, and his only letter from Salem had reconfirmed his schedule to be home in early May.

The rancher was surprised by the sight of a strange young woman riding an old gray mare down the knoll trail, the indistinct shape of a big man astride a large brown gelding following her.

Scott called through the open door to Lou, "Honey, strangers have come to visit."

No more were the words out of his mouth than the fellow emerged from the shadows, lifted his broad-rimmed hat, and shouted a greeting, "Hey, Scott! Put the coffee on. The Heisels are coming to say hello. Meet my wife Sarah!"

Bernie rode past his wife and slid off his horse, grabbing Scott in a bear hug and announcing, "Sarah and I are moving to Port Orford. Billy Tucker and I are going partners on a wildcat logging job up Hubbard Creek."

With a flamboyant gesture, Bernie spun around and lifted his wife from her saddle, setting her carefully on her feet. Scott watched his deed with a friendly grin, studying Sarah's reaction.

The woman was not as young as Scott had first believed, nor was she a dainty type. Sarah was sturdy of figure in a pretty gingham dress, mostly covered by a blanket-like cape. Her features were plain, almost homely but with strong character lines. She looked perfectly capable of taking care of herself, but she obviously adored the burly and rough-hewn logger she'd married as her face softened at his gentle directness.

246   The Myrtlewood Grove Final Episode

Lou spoke quietly from the doorway, "Welcome to our home, friends. Sarah, you must want to freshen up after your trip. Our husbands can take care of the horses while we get acquainted. I hope you can stay for a nice visit."

* * * * *

Lou remarked softly as the Heisels rode away in the early morning sunshine, "Sarah is very nice, and not an old maid at all. She confided that's how she thought of herself until Bernie came along. The first time he told her she was pretty, her confidence bloomed and so did her love for him."

Scott nodded agreeably, adding Bernie's story, "He thinks she's too good for him, being a real lady and all. They make a nice couple. I'm sure Billy and Mary Anne will agree."

"I told her about my baby coming in four months. Hee! Hee! But she seemed to know. Do I show already, Scott?"

"Well, maybe a little, dear," Scott answered too quickly, softening his answer with a compliment, "But you're the best looking mom-to-be in Port Orford."

He considered it fortunate when interrupted by hoof beats on the bridge, wondering aloud, "What did Bernie forget?"

Lou was more attuned to the sounds and guessed correctly, "I bet that's Grandpa. He's riding like he's familiar with the road."

Sure enough, the old-timer rode down the knoll with a hoot and a holler, astride one Gerbrunn mare and leading another. All smiles he shouted, "It's fun to travel, but I love coming home. How's things on the ranch, Children?"

"We're fine, Grandpa, and so is your next grandchild. How was the ride from Salem?"

"Good for an eighty-year old pioneer, Louise. Say, was that Langlois youngster right about Johnny? Is he really a county commissioner?"

Scott shook his head and jibed, "Wrong in both counts, Grandpa. You're eighty-one years young, and Johnny's only on the county road committee. Takes after George, I reckon."

* * * * *

Art and Grandpa perched atop the corral bar, watching Scott work with the older of his two colts. The hot summer sun beat down on the glistening red-brown shoulders of the stallion-to-be, his handler finally offering a half carrot and a rubdown to the sweaty beast.

"What do you think, Art? Do you want the dun or this chestnut?" Scott asked deferentially, ready to follow up on Lou's promise to her father.

The rancher nodded thoughtfully as he studied the colt, smiling wistfully as he chose, "The dun will have to do, Scott. I saw my girl's eyes as she looked over the pair last evening. She's already attached to this young fellow."

Scott agreed, "That's true, he's a fine-looking colt, but I think your dun will make a better stud horse. He inherited a little streak of meanness from his sire that makes a difference."

"Ha! Ha! Is that a character trait which you're looking for in my grandchild, too? Mean and tough rather than handsome and lovable. The baby had better be a boy then," Art teased playfully.

"Lou's going to name him Arthur, so he can take after you."

Grandpa joined the jocular banter, interjecting, "I hope the baby's a boy then. Being a mean child named Art would be a curse on a granddaughter."

Scott climbed to sit beside the two men, all of them quietly surveying the idyllic scene of green pasture, lowing cattle, frisky horses, forested hills, and stately myrtlewoods. The McClure ranch looked its best on this late August summer day.

"It's worth looking at, isn't it? And so peaceful. Sitting around our kitchen and waiting for Art is boring. I wish I could join you up there," Lou declared, grimacing briefly as she held her round belly with both hands. Her time was very near.

* * * * *

Julie and Anne served supper in the kitchen while Lou complained about the baby's kicks as she lay in the bedroom. The men adjourned to Grandpa's cabin for an after-dinner brandy to escape the tumultuous setting.

Scott was the first to awaken to a baby's cry during the dark night, rushing into his home to be greeted by Aunt Anne with a congratulatory smile, "Your son will be out to say hello in a moment, Scott. Grandmother is taking care of him."

Julie emerged with the blanketed form of a tiny baby, carrying her grandson to his father as she crooned nonsense into its reddish and wrinkled little face. Scott accepted the baby, holding him at a distance like a fragile basket of eggs, not quite sure if he was breakable.

"No! No! Here Scott, tuck him against your warm chest. He needs a lot of loving as well as your body heat. Why don't you take him to Momma," Julie advised.

Scott minced steps carefully across the room and up to Lou's bed, perching beside his wife and showing off their son. He bent over to kiss Lou, suggesting, "Well dear, go ahead and name the baby while Aunt Anne writes in the family bible."

"Isn't he just perfect, Scott? Can we use my favorite family names? Arthur after father and George after your little brother? And he was born on August 31, 1905," Louise prattled, happy and a mite weary as well.

Anne did as instructed, correcting Lou on the date, "Arthur was born on the first day of September, dear – after midnight. Now suppose we let the new mother sleep. Everybody out! Scott, you sit on the rocker and keep your son amused. I hear a couple of grandpas coming to help."

Grandpa and Art hovered about the rocker admiring their newest family member. Another generation of the McClure clan was introduced that dark night, ensuring the pioneer dreams of the Myrtlewood Grove Ranch on the Sixes River as envisioned by Scott Addis McClure in 1851.